THE
SERIAL
KILLER'S
DAUGHTER

THE
SERIAL KILLER'S DAUGHTER

LESLEY WELSH

Bookouture

Published by Bookouture
An imprint of StoryFire Ltd.
23 Sussex Road, Ickenham, UB10 8PN
United Kingdom
www.bookouture.com

ISBN: 978-1-78681-193-6
eBook ISBN: 978-1-78681-192-9

To Ian

PROLOGUE

Blues-and-twos, speeding through the dutifully dividing traffic as each driver yields to the ambulance with one hive mind. That poor sod inside could be one of them some day, hooked up to life-support equipment, fighting for survival. So they get out of the way and breathe a sigh of relief because right now it is someone else.

Tonight it is my turn.

I suck in the oxygen and turn my head to the rain-splattered window. The streetlights swirl and glitter like lurid fairground illuminations, transporting me to another place, another time. I can almost hear the music of the carousel, the grinding huff and puff of the steam-run calliope, the screams of laughter from the girls being spun on the waltzers by randy faux gypos, all knotted bandanas and muscular bronzed arms. Lords of the travelling fair, unwashed vagabonds to a man: a shag with a slag in every town.

Woozy on cheap cider and mesmerised by perceived exoticism, at least one of those shrieking girls would stand and deliver behind the caravans, skirt pulled up around her waist, hoisted upon my thrusting petard, the back of her head banging rhythmically against the side of the grimy tin can I called home.

I despised those slappers but they never realised until too late. The fair moved on and the tawdry dance began again in another muddy field.

The *nee-naa* song of the siren jolts me back to the present. The streetlights swoosh by, each beam merging with the next to become one continuous stream. The paramedic is speaking but her words are indistinct and I don't care to hear them. The ambulance stops, doors open and the bitter November night air hits my face. The gurney glides down the hospital corridor, with staff and medical kit in attendance.

'Stay with us,' I hear a soft female voice say.

I don't know what's going on here, but I don't like it. I want to get up, to run away, but there is a weight pressing on my chest and I can't move: it has me paralysed. I try to open my eyes to see what is holding me down, but I already know its nature, with its long teeth and its demon claws tearing into my body, then ripping out my beating heart, triumphantly holding aloft the pulsing flesh in gnarled hands. I recognise its contorted face, I hear its twisted words; it comes to me in the night and spills forth its filthy bile. In daylight hours, it lurks in gloomy corners, just out of sight, laughing at me, calling me a fool. I'm safe from it until I weaken and it waits for those moments to strike.

I struggle to surface but my eyelids are too heavy and there is a sharp sensation in my arm. 'Relax,' the voice says. 'This will help.'

I'm going under. It's cold and I have lost my sense of self. I hear someone ask, 'Can you tell me your name?'

'I don't know who the fuck I am, love,' I slur.

It's on my chest again, pressing all its weight on me, pushing its ugly snout so close that I can smell its stinking breath. It grins, saliva dripping off its fangs as it runs razor-sharp claws down my face.

'We're losing him.' The voices retreat into a hollow, echoing distance.

A surge of current engulfs my body, almost shattering my bones and I am falling, being flushed down the drain, around and around.

The world is swirling, flickering and dying. The universe being switched off like so many skyscraper lights in the midnight hour.

But the pressure is off my chest and I've escaped from it for the first time in my life.

This is the end, my friend, my demon sneers as it tumbles down ahead of me into the void. *This is death.*

CHAPTER ONE

Ask most people about the day their life changed forever and they might tell you it was the time they met their partner, the moment their child was born, or the like. But for Suzanne, it was the day she encountered Rose Anderson.

The light from the overhead window was fading fast, the dark clouds bunching up menacingly, plotting to let loose a deluge. Suzanne heard the kitchen door slam and presumed that Mark's team had lost a game and he was taking his frustration out on the innocent wood. She was no longer a bored spectator at his cricket matches and had stopped feigning interest in his tennis triumphs and woes a while back. She had her art and he had his sport. That was fine by Suzanne. *Marriage is compromise*, she'd told him but Mark remained peeved. His obvious dismay when she informed him that she was painting once more had maddened her. 'Oh, back to the art again,' he'd said as though she had revived a penchant for shoplifting. 'Don't you get enough art teaching those kids?' The fact that her own father's cruel dismissal of her paintings earlier in her life had cut her so deeply only strengthened her resolve. Nothing was going to stop her now, not even the husband who had once declared his undying love for her. Okay, she thought, that starry-eyed honeymoon period is long gone, lost somewhere in the mire of mortgage payments and the daily grind, but wasn't marriage also about showing support for the other person's needs and ambitions?

So she had called Mark a philistine. Whenever he mentioned 'art' there were invisible air bunnies around the word. It crossed her mind that her husband was the type who'd have looked up at the bare ceiling of the Sistine Chapel, handed Michelangelo a tin of Dulux and said, 'We just want it painted, mate. How's about a nice beige?'

Despite Mark's protests, Suzanne had chucked out all of his rubbish from the attic and converted it into a studio that he was forbidden to set foot in. That had been twelve months ago and he was gradually adapting to the idea.

Eight years back, teaching the subject that she had once been so passionate about had been a compromise with herself. Though these days, unlike her neighbour, Mrs Jones, who always adored the job and was sad when she was forced to retire, for the past year Suzanne had found herself yearning for the school holidays. When the bell rang signalling this Easter break, she had imagined hearing prison doors being thrown open, allowing her the freedom to return to her one true love.

'You'll be banged up in your studio again, I suppose,' Mark had sniped.

Well, he was just going to have to lump it. She had the fire back in her belly and nothing was going to stop her this time. When her star pupil, Jason, had burst into her classroom to breathlessly announce that he'd got a place at Goldsmiths, she had heard echoes of her long-abandoned hopes in his voice and seen her own youthful ambition reflected in his intelligent young face. He had so much ahead of him – and what had she achieved? The once promising artist was now a full-time teacher and a part-time painter. Slave to the mortgage. She mouthed the words to the tune of Grace Jones extolling the siren song of the rhythm.

She was passing most of this too-brief respite in her studio, although right now the picture she was working on was simply not happening for her. Every brushstroke seemed to make matters worse; something about it was just not right. What had started out as an imagined and hopefully commercial landscape had gradually transformed into a brooding dreamscape with the blue sky murkier than she originally intended. Today Suzanne had added two tiny figures to the tableau, a woman guiding a small child by the hand across sands that appeared to be shifting beneath them. She stood back and surveyed the image she had created and realised that it disturbed her in ways she could not quite fathom.

She looked across the room at the portrait drying in the corner. It was of her mother and Suzanne intended it as a gift for her sixtieth birthday. Although portraiture was not Suzanne's forte, she thought it a fair yet flattering depiction, with the buttery sun cascading through the window behind her subject, emphasising the pale skin and strawberry-blonde hair, the green eyes alive with merriment and intelligence. That would be sure to please her mother. A glance back at the new painting confirmed Suzanne's suspicions that the figures in the dreamscape, a mother and child, represented the only family she had ever known.

When Suzanne was a child her father was rarely mentioned, apart from the few times he had visited her with his arms laden with expensive presents. It was as though he hadn't really existed; a spectre to be ignored until he reappeared from out of the mists of her memory like a one-man *Marie Celeste*, full of smiles and jokes, laughter, games and teasing. Only to be gone again within a couple of hours after hugs and kisses and promises to come back soon. But his meaning of 'soon' never tallied with Suzanne's childish understanding. She could recall crying after one visit as her mother held her gently in her arms and reassured her that her father would be back one day but she didn't know quite when. He was busy; he worked abroad, she told her. Suzanne could still remember the hurt, but had learned neither to ask questions about the past nor to expect to see photographs as her mother had told her emphatically that they were 'all gone'. Her mother, Joan, always clammed up when questioned and although she had tried not to show any signs of personal distress, even as a small child Suzanne could sense these things. So Suzanne's father had remained an almost mythical creature in her mind. Until that time ten years ago when he had turned up out of the blue. Though how he presented to her adult self was very different from the person of her childhood recollection…

She crammed the memory of that last visit back inside the 'don't think about it' compartment in her mind and surveyed her painting once more. Those two small figures had a poignancy that took her by surprise, expressing as they did a feeling of loneliness and regret.

Suzanne's grandparents had died long before she was born and as the only child of an only child there had been no aunts or cousins in her life either. She gazed at the two figures she had instinctively added to her painting. Her young life had been exactly like this image with always just the two of them. Until her mother met Harry. Suzanne recalled the initial resentment of this stranger sharing her mother's affection: an older man who had never been married, so she hadn't even had the consolation of step-brothers or sisters. Was this picture an expression of an inner longing for the distant past? Enough, she decided, if this is the way my work is to proceed then I'll have to give it some more consideration. So she put down her brushes and was running her hands under the cold tap when Mark called up from the hallway.

'Suze!' Mark's deep baritone carried up the stairs. 'There's a woman on the line for you. Says her name's Rose. She says you don't know her but it is quite urgent.'

'I'll take it in the bedroom.' Suzanne dried her hands, walked down the stairs and sat at the desk by the window as the rain began bucketing down outside. A typical English Easter.

The telephone pinged and she picked up the receiver.

'Am I speaking to Suzanne Tyler?' The voice at the other end was softly spoken and tentatively refined, though with just a hint of an estuary accent.

'My name *used* to be Tyler.'

'Your father's name is Donald Tyler?'

'Yes.' Suzanne hoped this wasn't one of those genealogy freaks trying to trace their roots. The internet was choc-a-bloc with those websites – trace the Tyler family back to the Stone Age and bollocks like that.

'Yes, my father's name is Donald Tyler. What is this about?' The last thing she needed was for him to come elbowing his way back into her life. It had been ten years since she'd last seen him and the very thought of him still made her feel sick with disgust.

'I'm sorry to disturb you,' the woman said, 'but I found some things among his papers; photographs, diaries and other strange bits and pieces. And I really think you should see them as soon as possible.'

'Found them?'

'They were left in my house.' The woman paused as though she had forgotten her words and had got so caught up with the detail that she had skipped the main event. 'I'm sorry to tell you,' she finally added, 'but Don died five months ago. It's taken me all this time to track you down.'

The news of her father's death, though a jolt, didn't cause Suzanne too much anguish. After all, she hardly knew him. Since her mother had divorced Donald Tyler when Suzanne was only four, she barely remembered him being around during her early childhood. Over the following eight years, Don had made the occasional fleeting visit with arms full of toys, but the two were never left alone together; her mother, Joan, was always present. Suzanne recalled that her father had made her laugh a lot, told tall stories, and sent her birthday cards with a fifty-pound note taped inside. She had been thirteen when her mother remarried and Don's visits ceased abruptly, as did the birthday cards. And that had been that, until that one distasteful meeting after which he disappeared once more. So, although Don Tyler was no longer a part of Suzanne's life, she agreed to meet Rose Anderson out of politeness and, if she was being candid, more than just a little curiosity.

*

He had shadowed Rose Anderson to the Piazza Café in Covent Garden. As usual she carried her grey shopper. Even though the April sun was shining, there was a chill in the air and he watched as she pulled her black coat around her thin body, sat down at one of the tables under the tented umbrellas outside and placed the shopper at her feet. She looked at her watch. He sensed that she was waiting for someone. And, as this was the first time she had ventured this far into central London since he'd been tailing her, he assumed this to be an important meeting. If it turned out to be his prime target then he could put the next part of the plan into action.

It was well before lunchtime and there were only two couples braving the cool breeze and drinking coffee. One couple, speaking Spanish loudly and at breakneck speed, were arguing but he couldn't make out what it was about. The other two were poring over a map they'd set out on their table. Tourists. How he envied them. It was his first trip to London and he wouldn't have minded seeing the sights.

He had chosen a table that gave him a clear view of Rose but was far enough away for her not to notice him as he pretended to read the free newspaper handed to him at the tube station. The Eastern European waitress took his order of black coffee and a croissant, though the waffles with maple syrup had tempted him. Rose spoke to the waitress, who nodded and went off to another customer. Rose was definitely expecting company.

His order arrived and Rose was still alone. She seemed anxious, constantly checking the time and looking around. He took a bite of the croissant. When he looked up again, another woman was approaching Rose. Damn it all, he thought, she's just meeting with a friend. Though there was something about the formal way they greeted each other, shaking hands as though they had never met before, that caught his attention. But mainly it was Rose's facial expression on sighting the slim woman with the shoulder-length dark-brown hair that lit up his radar. So he took out his phone. To anyone idly watching it would look as though he'd just received a text message. He stared at the screen intently, and then photographed the two women.

*

The woman waiting for Suzanne at the Piazza Café was in her fifties with short brown hair. Rose Anderson had a kindly face with just a hint of make-up. She could easily be mistaken for a social worker.

'Don lived with me for two years,' Rose began after they had ordered coffee. 'Though, looking back, I don't think I ever really knew him. He was very secretive in his way.'

'I wasn't aware that he knew my address,' Suzanne said. 'So I'm curious as to how you found me.'

'It was while I was spring cleaning,' Rose said. 'There was a piece of paper with three phone numbers tucked down the side of the cushion on the chair he used to sit on.' She paused as though recalling a painful memory and swallowed hard before returning to her story. 'One was unavailable, the other was his doctor's office and the third one was yours. Perhaps he intended to call you to say he was ill but…' Her voice trailed away as she visibly suppressed rising emotion. Once Rose regained her composure she glanced at Suzanne shyly and gave a wan smile. 'You look like him, you know. You've got his eyes.'

Suzanne felt uncomfortable about so personal an observation. 'I didn't really know him, either. Maybe it's my mother you should be speaking to.'

The smile flickered and died. 'Oh, Joanie?'

'She doesn't allow anyone to call her that.'

Rose looked surprised. 'That's how he refers to her in his diaries. Joanie this and Joanie that.' She sighed. 'I think he really loved her.'

Now it was Suzanne who was taken aback. Was Rose jealous? How could she be envious of the woman who divorced my father over thirty years ago, she wondered.

'Did he talk about my mother?'

'No.' Rose shook her head. 'He never mentioned anyone. This is all new to me. And there are all these pictures.' She reached under the table for her grey leather shopping bag and pulled out a manila envelope, which she opened. Then she took out eight photographs and placed them on the table.

Rose laid them face down as each had a name written on the back. On one it read 'Joanie' in the ragged scrawl Suzanne recognised from the birthday card greetings from her father. She picked up the picture, turned it over to see her mother, so young, so very much the hippie, her head thrown back in a joyous laugh, her red hair wild and flowing. She was standing in the middle of a field, her long skirt fluttering in the summer breeze while a shadow cast by whoever was taking the photo crept along the ground close to her feet. Suzanne smiled at the image. She had never seen a photo of her mother from those times.

'Yes, that's my mother.'

'How about Betty?' Rose turned over another photo.

This one was black and white. Thin-faced and very pregnant, the dark-eyed young woman with the ponytail looked equally as happy as Suzanne's mother did in her photograph. But there was no idyllic field here, just a drab terraced house behind her.

Suzanne shook her head. 'Never seen her before.'

So it continued with different names: Sheila, Naomi, Annabelle, Gloria and Moira, each photographed in a radically different setting. Sheila had been snapped in a fairground, in front of the waltzers, with her hair backcombed and dressed in an early sixties flared skirt, a frilly blouse and a cardigan, one of her stiletto heels firmly embedded in the muddy ground. Despite the high-heel mishap, she looked very pleased with herself. She could not have been more than sixteen.

Naomi, on the other hand, looked considerably older and more sophisticated, with immaculately styled dark hair that framed her face. She posed half-naked on a chaise longue, her elegant silver mules emphasising her long tanned legs. She was smiling and smoking what appeared to be a joint. Suzanne shook her head again. She didn't recognise this woman either.

The photo of Annabelle had been taken at dusk with an evidently tropical sun sinking below the horizon. She was a striking blonde with sky-blue eyes, like a typical California surfer babe or a model in an upmarket shampoo advert. Suzanne didn't know her at all.

Shot in close-up, Gloria was black with natural Afro hair, wearing a silver ankh on a chain around her neck. She was in the driver's seat of a car. By contrast Moira was a fair-haired, freckle-faced country girl in a heavy jacket and green wellies, standing on a heather-covered hillside.

'I think there is something decidedly odd about these photographs, don't you?' Suzanne said to Rose. 'It's almost as though they have been plucked from several different lives. There is no continuity, no common factor.'

'I agree. Perhaps you should have his diaries,' Rose remarked enigmatically. 'I started to read one but it was too painful for me to continue. So I can't bring myself to look at the rest. I'd rather remember him as I knew him.'

With the eighth and last photo of the batch, the sense of recognition shook Suzanne to the core. Sophie was the name on the back and Suzanne had expected she would react in the way she had to the others, to not know the woman pictured at all. But with Sophie it was different. The face burned itself onto Suzanne's retina, her hand began to tremble and she started to shiver. It was all there, the hair dyed to the brightest of electric reds, the elfin face and the almond-shaped soulful eyes. The girl was photographed standing in front of a sculpture Suzanne had watched her create. This one she certainly did know: it was Sophie Chen.

CHAPTER TWO

The last time Suzanne had seen her father was the first year of the new millennium, back when she was a full-time artist. She had been working in the studio in Dalston, northeast London, which she shared with her close friend, Sophie Chen. They were both twenty, just a few months out of art school, though it was Suzanne who was already making a name for herself. To date she had sold four paintings to private collectors and was about to have her first gallery exhibition. She could recall being full of herself at that point in her life, convinced that the future promised nothing but success. Twenty paintings of abstract landscapes, the final one almost completed. She had stepped back from this last one, satisfied, convinced it was the best so far.

The bell buzzed and there he was on the doorstep, in black leather jacket, jeans and white shirt. He was all smiles, with one hand behind his back.

'Ta-dah!' He laughed as he presented the bunch of freesias to her with a flourish, like a magician hauling a rabbit out of a hat.

'Dad!' He was chunkier than she remembered, though that was to be expected of a man in his fifties. Apart from a few laughter lines, the face didn't seem to have aged, though she suspected that he dyed his hair. 'How did you know where my studio is?'

'Anyone can be found,' he said as he sauntered past her. 'Even if they don't want to be.'

'I haven't been hiding from anyone,' she said, puzzled by the insinuation and a little indignant.

'Yeah, I know that.' He prowled around the studio, peered at each painting in turn and frowned. 'But your mother has,' he said. 'She really should know better than that.'

'You haven't come to see me for years.' She ignored his remark, not sure how to respond. 'So this is a surprise, to say the least.'

'I've been away,' was his flat response. He glanced about the airy studio with its hanging ceiling lamps and white walls adorned with wooden shelves that Suzanne had constructed to hold all of her brushes, paints and arty bits and pieces she had picked up for inspiration. 'You don't live here, then?'

'I have a house share not far from here.' She tidied away her brushes as she watched him fiddle with the joints of the articulated wooden hand she used for character study. He bent the pale fingers until only the middle digit remained erect.

'Sorry,' he said, 'couldn't resist.' He smiled, cheerily. 'So tell me about your friends.'

'I share the house with a couple and another guy.'

'Boyfriend? I do hope you're not living in sin, my girl.' He stood with his arms folded, his face set with disapproval.

Suzanne stared at her father in disbelief. *Great*, she thought, *he barges back in from wherever the hell he's been and thinks he can tell me how I should live my bloody life.*

He glared back at her for a moment before a slow grin emerged. 'You should see your face.' He chuckled. 'I'm joking. Lighten up.'

He pulled up a paint-spattered plastic chair while she made him a cup of instant black coffee. That was the one trait she did remember about him, revulsion for milk – probably the only thing they had in common.

'Anyway, I bet the other bloke is gay,' he said. 'A right screamer, I reckon, mincing along.' He placed one hand on his hip, flopped the other hand at the wrist and wiggled his shoulders.

'There's no need for that,' Suzanne scolded as she handed him the cup. Don's guess had been so accurate that she felt the need to leap to her housemate's defence.

'Fuck me, aren't you the serious one?' he chuckled. 'Joke!' He sipped his coffee. 'That hits the spot,' he said, his dark eyes full of merriment. 'Bet the couple are dead straight, though. Not in your line of work. Accountants, solicitors, or something like that, I suppose.'

Spot on again, and it dawned on Suzanne that Don's observations were not mere stabs in the dark. He had actually seen her friends. 'You've been to my house?'

'Just happened to wander by,' he said as though it was of no consequence.

'How did you know where I live?'

Don shrugged. 'I told you. I know everything.'

A feeling of unease crept over Suzanne. 'Well, I don't appreciate being spied on.'

Don put the coffee cup on the floor between his feet and leaned forward, his facial expression denoting concern writ large. 'You've got nothing to hide, have you Suzy-Q?' He waited a beat until he raised his eyebrows as the cheesy grin returned. 'Oh, you are just too easy to wind up, girl.' He sat back in the chair and snorted a laugh. 'Calm down, it's nothing sinister. I just thought it would be better for us to be able to talk alone, rather than in front of a house full of strangers, that's all.' He retrieved his coffee and glugged it all in one go. 'How long has it been since we last saw each other? What, seven or eight years?'

'About that.' Despite his breezy explanation, she felt a knot in her stomach, but tried to retain a casual tone. 'Where have you been?'

'All over the States, the Caribbean, Thailand…' He laughed. 'You know what I'm like.'

'Do I?' *You're a bloody stranger* is what she wanted to say.

'Don't you remember all those toys I used to bring you from all around the world?' He looked puzzled, if not a little wounded.

'Sorry, but I don't recall.' She straddled the chair opposite him. 'In fact, I don't even know what you do for a living these days.'

He winked and chuckled once more. 'If I told you, I would have to kill you.'

'Groan. Old joke.'

'But,' he said, straight-faced, 'in my case only too true.'

He looked around the room, appearing to take in all of the paintings at a glance, though he made no comment. Suzanne held back a childlike urge for approval that echoed from their previous fleeting shared moments. *Look at my paintings, Daddy. Do you like them?* But both time and her father's mercurial behaviour had erected a barrier too daunting to tackle. They fell into an awkward silence, and then his expression suddenly brightened.

'How is your mother? How is my Joanie?'

Suzanne was relieved by both the change of subject and his swift mood swing. 'Doing fine, she's happy. She's managing a sales team and loving it.'

'Magnus and Co.' His eyes shifted from side to side as though there was some internal dialogue going on inside his head.

'Yes. But if you knew already, why ask?'

He gave a wolfish grin. 'Just checking.'

She didn't like this one iota; it was as though he was testing her, first with his pretence of not knowing where she lived and now this. Becoming increasingly frustrated but not sure how to deal with the situation, she made an attempt to take control. 'And I'm an artist, thanks for noticing.'

He gave a snort edged with contempt but otherwise ignored her remark. 'Is she still playing guitar, my Joanie?'

'Guitar?' Suzanne had never seen her mother so much as hold a guitar, let alone play one.

'Yeah,' he said. 'Back in her old hippie days she played guitar and sang like a dream.'

'That's news to me.'

'She was a real goer way back then.' He grinned and looked straight at Suzanne, taunting her. 'I shagged the arse off her on the first day we met. Glastonbury it was, 1979, in a field. I was a roadie and she was one hot little hippie chick with a slippery snatch. No panties.' He stared her down, challenging. 'Man, I was shocked.'

'I don't think we should be having this conversation. You're talking about my mother here.'

'Respectable now, of course, married to what's-his-face.' He looked down at the floor, shifted in his seat, sucked his teeth noisily and gave a sidelong glance up at her breasts.

'Harry.' She tried to ignore Don's increasingly antagonistic manner. 'His name's Harry.'

'Fucking wimp,' Don sneered. He idly scanned the room once more while he searched in his pockets to retrieve a pack of cigarettes.

'Please don't smoke in here. Paints.'

'Yeah.' He held the packet and lighter in his hand for a moment and then reluctantly tucked them back into his jacket. 'Anyway.' He focused on her paintings. 'Anyway, what is all this shit?'

'This shit is my art.' Suzanne felt a mixture of anger and humiliation. 'You don't have to like it, but quite a few people do.'

'These all your leftover ones, then?' He gave a humourless laugh that hung in the air between them. 'The art that nobody wants.'

'These paintings are for an exhibition. I'm just finishing up.' She climbed out of the chair.

'Best not sit like that.' Don stood too and moved towards her, too close for comfort. 'Quite a provocative pose that. You might get yourself taken advantage of.'

'Like my mother was, you mean.' They were face-to-face right then. Suzanne was itching to slap that vile provocative smirk off his supercilious mug. What she felt must have shown in her expression because suddenly his demeanour hardened, his jaw tightened, eyes narrowed. It had the intended effect because, under his intense scrutiny, Suzanne felt as though she was slowly unravelling.

At that moment she heard Sophie's key in the lock and with it came a surge of relief. Sophie carried a large heavy bag into the room.

'This is my friend, Sophie. She's a sculptor. We share this space.'

He put on a dazzling smile. 'Call me Don,' he told the ruby-haired girl as he took her bag from her in chivalrous fashion and meekly followed her into the studio space beyond.

Suzanne could soon hear Sophie's laughter from the other room and was astonished by how Don could switch on the charm, change mood with such ease, like an actor stepping out into the spotlight. She tried to resume her painting but her hands shook and she was seething. She just wanted him gone, to make him disappear back to wherever he had materialised from, yet the laughter from the other studio continued, making her more incensed by the minute. Who did he think he was, appearing out of nowhere after all these years and dismissing her art as though it was of no importance? What sort of father behaves like that? *One that pisses off and leaves your mother to raise you alone, that's who*, she thought. *Why do you care whether you have his approval or not? He's nobody. He's nothing to you.* But she knew deep down that wasn't true. Even her most confident self would have been delighted for him to have seen her work and been proud of her. Tears pricked at her eyes but she blinked them back. *Other people believe in you*, she advised herself, *and so must you.*

At last Don returned, walking back towards Suzanne while Sophie leaned on the doorway between the two studios. 'I'll leave you two to talk,' Sophie said, flashing Don a conspiratorial smile. 'Nice to meet you, Don.' She closed the door after her.

'Have you seen her work in there?' Don asked. 'Those sculptures!'

'Of course I have.'

'Now,' he said, looking straight at Suzanne, his smile erased and the intimidating hard-man posture back once more. '*She* is what I call a *real* artist.'

They stood in silence for what seemed to Suzanne like forever. She met his glare head on, her mind screaming, *Who are you to criticise my work? Why have you come here to tell me dirty stories about my mother? Get The Fuck Out Of My Life!*

'Well,' she said calmly instead, 'nice to catch up with you, Don. But I really must get on.'

'You're like me.' He turned to leave.

'Shit,' she said, half under her breath. 'I hope not.'

'Yeah,' he smirked, 'all my kids are like me.' Another jibe under the cover of insinuation, a sideswipe revelation left floating.

'What did you say? What other kids?'

'Oops!' He threw back his head and chortled as he kept walking. 'Let the cat out of the bag there.'

He stopped by the front door and turned on the spot, very agile on his feet for a man of his size. His eyes were icy, hard and unforgiving. 'There's not one ounce of your mother in you,' he said evenly. Then he was transformed once more, the grin in place, the eyes merry. 'Shame that, because she was the greatest fuck I ever had.'

Suzanne followed him to the door, relieved to see him leave.

'See you around, Suzy-Q,' he shouted over his shoulder as he walked away.

Suzanne slammed the door behind him.

Sophie had popped her head in when she heard the door bang so loudly, though she had clearly heard nothing of what had passed between them.

'Wow,' she said. 'He's a proper charmer, your dad. He raved about my work. I wish my folks were like that. All they do is send me money and bitch about how I should have become a pharmacist.' She smiled brightly and put her MP3 earplugs back in as she always worked to music.

'Yeah, lucky me!' He had made Suzanne feel unclean and tainted. All she wanted was to forget the whole incident. Sophie closed the door and they never spoke of Don again.

*

The fire at the Dalston studio happened late at night, ten days after Don's visit. It destroyed the space and every one of Suzanne's paintings in it. In the adjoining studio Sophie had been working on her current sculpture. The fire raged so fiercely and spread so quickly that the roof fell in and crushed her. She did not survive.

Sophie's parents lived in Hong Kong. They had made arrangements to fly to London when they got the terrible news but their plane was delayed due to fog at Heathrow. Consequently, Suzanne was asked to make the initial identification of the burned and broken body to aid the police investigation.

Suzanne had watched episodes of forensic crime dramas on television and thought she'd become inured to blood, gore and mangled remains. But this nightmare vision was barely recognisable: scorched and twisted. This was a horrific end to a young life. Nothing could have prepared Suzanne to confront such reality close at hand.

A mortuary attendant in a white coat pulled back the sheet to reveal the victim's face. To Suzanne's shocked and tear-filled eyes it was only the nose ring Sophie wore to scandalise her conservative Chinese parents that made her identifiable. At the sight of her friend and fellow artist, Suzanne swayed on her feet. The young policeman, who had accompanied her, caught her in his arms before she fell.

And with him supporting her, Suzanne confirmed the identity of the corpse. 'Yes.' She tried to steady her voice, to hold back the tsunami of emotion. 'That is Sophie Chen.'

CHAPTER THREE

It was two days after her initial meeting with Suzanne and Rose Anderson was tidying her fastidiously neat north London home before she went to work, making a vain attempt to get on with her life. She stopped for a moment and looked around the sitting room, aware that everything she touched reminded her of Don. It was as though his dominant spirit had taken over every corner of the house, slowly dissipating her childhood memories of being raised there.

Even the recollection of the brief and painful marriage that had resulted in her scurrying back home, heartbroken and penniless, seemed like a play she had watched on TV, so unreal had her life before Don become. Rose looked across at the faded photo of her mother that she had recently returned to the mantelpiece. Don said it gave him the creeps so she had tucked it away out of sight in a drawer. But now it was back where it belonged and Rose smiled at the image as she recalled her mother's stoicism. Gladys Anderson had been a warrior of the old school. 'Cancer,' she scoffed when diagnosed. 'You have to fight these things, Rose, not surrender like your father did.' Tears sprung to Rose's eyes as the pain of eight years of suffering, with her mother reduced to an almost bloodless husk, came back to her. Cancer had raised its triumphant banner above the battlefield to leave Rose alone once more. The hollow loneliness of those times still saddened her.

Then, like a dream come true, Donald Albert Tyler entered her life and made her laugh again, made her feel special. He'd sung to her, changing the title of 'Layla' to the name Rosie. The sound of his voice echoed in her mind and her eyes filled with tears in memory of their secret life together and the recollection of the joy she had felt in the early days of their relationship.

In Rose's eyes, Don was gentle and kind, loving and sexually undemanding. Plus, he'd shared all his exciting secrets with her and that made her feel special. That was something she had craved, to feel a close tie with another person.

A sense of bitterness engulfed Rose as she recalled that when she first met Don he'd claimed to have no family. She'd had no reason to doubt him. He had insisted that he never talked about the past and when asked he would joke, 'If I tell you, I'll have to kill you.' But early on in their relationship he had hinted darkly at having been in the Special Forces. Perhaps, she mused, that was why he had become estranged from Suzanne – for the girl's protection. Of course, she decided, that would be the reason. Feeling newly reassured, Rose sat down in Don's chair and allowed her memories in once more.

When Don had moved in with her, he'd recounted various tales of adventures abroad, though not in too much detail – for her own safety, he said. He swore her to secrecy for, he told her, only she knew his real name to be Donald Tyler, as he also had several professional aliases.

'See how much I trust you,' he'd confided. 'If they got to know my whereabouts, I'd be a dead man.'

His last few months had been grim. Hooked up to a portable oxygen tank, he had not been able to leave the house. Not that she had ever known where he went even when he had been able. He appeared not to have any friends, at least no one who seemed to have known him for any longer than she had.

During his time confined to the house, Don had taken to writing in his atrocious longhand scrawl. She was sent out to buy his lined notebooks on a regular basis, though she was neither told what he was writing in them, nor allowed to read them.

He scribbled on, night and day, insisting that she stay quiet, complaining if she wanted to watch television. He took food breaks then swiftly cleared a space at the dining table and went straight back to writing.

'Isn't this becoming a wee bit obsessive?' Rose had once dared to ask him.

'This is my life in these books,' he'd said, in a tone that brooked no argument. 'I'm the only person able to tell this story.'

'But the Official Secrets Act?' she wondered. 'I thought you had to sign that.'

'Fuck 'em!'

The books had filled up and though she hadn't counted them she reckoned there must be at least fifty. He'd lock them away in the wooden chest he kept in the hallway, the only piece of furniture he'd brought with him when he moved in. All his secrets in one place, the key kept she knew not where. It would simply appear as if from thin air when he opened or locked the chest.

At one point the doctor had upped his medication, which made him drowsy for a few days. She arrived home from work one evening to find him fast asleep, face down across his latest notebook. She shook him. 'Don!' Momentarily panicked, she checked to ensure that he was breathing. He grunted but remained asleep.

Tempted beyond endurance, she took a peek at the last line he had written.

June 1980. Suzanne was born. When I saw her for the first time I knew she would change my life forever.

Rose reacted like she'd experienced an electric shock. She backed away from him. She stared at him as though for the first time, noted his cropped white hair, his meaty hands and the sensuous mouth she had kissed so rarely in the past six months. *Liar*, she screamed silently, *liar!* She glared at him. *You said you didn't have a family. You said you'd told me everything it was safe for me to know. Now this: there's a daughter, maybe a wife, perhaps more children, more wives.* Her body quivered with shock and anger. Or was it fear? The way his hazel eyes could be filled with gentle emotion one second then switch to terrifying anger the next disturbed her. But the most alarming of his mood swings was the coldness he displayed if she should displease him in any way. And she shuddered at the thought. Who was he, this man her friends had warned her not to have anything to do with? Those friends he had driven out of her life with his ill temper, his jealousy and his mistrust.

'You have to be careful of people,' he'd say. 'You are very naïve, Rose. There are so many people out there just itching to take you for a ride.'

He had prohibited anyone visiting the house, *her* house, so she would meet her friends in bars. Gradually, once he could no longer get about under his own steam, he'd make her feel guilty every time she left him alone. Until, in the final months, it had been just the two of them, together all of the time, except for when she went to work, out food shopping or on errands for him. Even then, he would time her to the minute and interrogate her if she ever strayed from his internal schedule.

'That stranger you talk to in the street, or the shop, or the bar, you don't know who they really are. They could be trying to get to me through you.'

There were times when she thought this was total madness, that he was living some kind of fantasy life. But where did all his money come from? Once he fell ill, he allowed her to collect money for him from Western Union. It was always in cash.

'They can't trace cash,' he said, as though confiding in her.

'The government pays in cash?' This came as quite a surprise.

He gave her one of his dead-eyed stares. 'Only to people like me.'

Each month she had collected over four thousand pounds. It was sent at the rate of nine hundred and fifty pounds a week and she picked it up from seven different collection offices across London.

'Nobody would be suspicious of paying out a nine-fifty from time to time. Anyway, that's the maximum Western Union allow without all sorts of checks being made. And in my game that's a no-no.' Don opened the envelope and laid the money out on the table. It upset Rose to see him count it out so carefully. Did he think she might pocket a twenty?

'The chap in Western Union counted it out in front of me,' she reminded him.

He looked at her pityingly and shook his head slowly. 'You are such an innocent,' he snorted. 'They count it out and palm a fifty. I've seen it done a hundred times. But not to this mug.'

'Has it ever been short when I've collected it?'

There was that look again, the frozen stare. 'Don't question my judgement, Rose. Don't you *ever* question my judgement.'

Step by step, Rose had been subjected to the insidious creep of control, isolated from her friends, trapped inside Don's suspicions and made an active participant in his intrigues. And under those circumstances she discovered that paranoia was a very infectious disease. She often found herself scrutinising cars that were parked in the street for any length of time, becoming jittery when anyone rang the doorbell, turning up the volume of the radio when Don was in the mood to recount any of his adventures. She took different routes to work and the shops and was reluctant to speak to strangers on the telephone, even if they were from BT attempting to sell her additional phone services. Don paid no tax, and did not appear on the census or electoral roll. She was living with an invisible man. Until he became ill. That was when he had to surface.

'I don't trust the NHS. They'll need too much information on me,' he told her. 'I'll find a private doctor. I'll tell him I'm your cousin visiting from Poland and that I'll be paying in cash.'

The news that his days were numbered devastated Rose but conversely hardened Don. Not for him the vulnerability of the dying, the voicing of regrets, or why-me anger. He closed her out, only issuing orders and wishes into a Dictaphone that he purchased. She was allowed to listen only after the recording was completed. No arguments, no questions: just follow the instructions. And what chillingly calculated instructions they had been.

Direct cremation. Body to be collected from hospital and taken for burning. No service. No death notices. Ashes to be scattered in the crematorium grounds. Clothes and any other possessions to be disposed of into several different dustbins on the day of the death. No keepsakes. The chest to be taken into the yard and set on fire with a gallon of petrol. Do not try to break the chest open.

'But what about your papers?' she asked. 'All that stuff you've been writing?'

'It won't matter any longer. That was just insurance, but I won't be around to collect on it.' He reached across and held her hand, the first sign of affection he had shown her in months. 'For your own sake, Rose, please do as I say. I don't want anything bad to happen to you. They can disappear you, just like that.' He clicked his fingers. 'Nobody would ever discover what had happened to you.'

She stared at him wide-eyed. He believed all this. Should she do the same?

'Burn the chest and stay safe.' He took off his oxygen mask and kissed her hand. 'I know I haven't shown it much lately,' he said, 'but you are the love of my life and I hate to think that I might have put you in harm's way.' He smiled and his eyes were gentle and loving once more. 'So, please, promise me you'll destroy the chest. For your own safety's sake, promise now.'

'I promise.'

*

On their final night together, a loud thud had woken Rose and she sat bolt upright, her anxiety-filled dreams still resounding in her head. When she heard him calling her name, she leapt out of bed and stumbled down the stairs.

Don was propped up in his chair fighting for his life. His torn pyjama top flapped open and she could see his bulky chest rising and falling laboriously. The panic on his face sent chills coursing through Rose's body. She saw in his eyes the raw fear of the void, the terror of the nothingness that came after.

He held out his arms to her. For a moment he seemed so childlike and helpless, his former steely resolve to confront his fate with dignity having dissipated in the struggle to survive, so that Rose felt stricken and close to tears.

But change came swiftly to this man and his expression darkened. 'You dozy cow, help me stand up. I'll be okay as long as I'm walking.'

She rushed to his side and tried to pull him to his feet but he was too heavy for her. 'Get out of my way!' He pushed her and she fell against the solid wooden table. His oxygen tank had rolled away beneath it.

'I'll call an ambulance,' she said.

'No, I need to walk.' He levered himself to his feet, using the arms of the chair. But he couldn't walk; he couldn't even stand and he swayed, eyes closing with the strain, sweat pouring down his face.

'Sit down, Don. You need your oxygen. You need a doctor.'

Instead of collapsing back into his chair, he took three steps forward to the window. His knees buckled beneath him as he desperately reached for something to hold on to, and he tore the curtains down with him as he fell. The glare of the streetlights flooded the room. Rose dialled 999. 'Ambulance,' she told the operator. 'I think he's having a heart attack.'

Don lay on the floor, his hands plucking at his heaving chest. 'Get it off me!' he kept shouting until the ambulance arrived. 'Get it off me!'

In under five minutes they were at the door: a male and a female paramedic, calm, efficient, professional. 'Where is he?'

Don fought them with all his remaining strength. A glass vase smashed on the carpet, the flowers trampled by the paramedics as they struggled to get him onto the stretcher. They had to strap him down and wouldn't allow Rose to ride along. 'We're taking him to St Francis',' they said. 'You follow on.'

She rang the local cab company. 'They're all out on calls,' the dispatcher told her in a hybrid Indian-cockney accent. 'Friday night, you know. It'll be at least half an hour.'

'Don't bother.' She pulled on a pair of sweatpants and a jumper over her nightdress, snatched a tenner off the table and ran out into the street to find a taxi. It was a cold November night and the moment she stepped across her threshold, it started to rain. The area was deserted. As she locked her front door, she realised she was still wearing her slippers but there was no time to go back in and change them. She had to get to Don, to be with him. He needed her.

There was a taxi rank outside the local tube station but that was a five-minute walk away and the last train would have gone by now so the taxis would be out searching for other fares. All the commuters were safely at home, watching TV, having sex, whatever normal people do. But that wasn't Rose's life, not any more. She ran up the street towards the main road. A few cars whizzed by, one vibrating rhythmically to the deep bass of rap music. A lone passenger gazed morosely out at her as a night bus passed by, headed in the wrong direction. She wished then that she'd waited for the mini cab.

Suddenly a black cab appeared and, though its taxi sign was unlit, Rose could see no passenger in the back. She rushed into the road in front of the vehicle and waved him down.

'I've ended my shift now,' the driver shouted out of his wound-down window. 'I'm going home.'

'Please help me.' She waved the ten-pound note at him. 'I need to get to St Francis' hospital.'

He relented grudgingly. 'Okay, hop in. It's on my way.'

When she got to the hospital A&E was teeming with people. She had to push past a drunk who was shouting blue murder at the reception desk. All around the room, seated in moulded plastic chairs, were minor casualties of one form or another. A woman in a full-face veil held a screaming infant close while her gaudy-shirted husband nonchalantly read a newspaper. A young black girl, all hair extensions and plastic nails, held a bloodied scarf to a deep gash on her knee while her two still-tipsy friends fussed around her. An elderly couple – the woman pale-faced and trembling – huddled together like desperate refugees in an alien world. They were all walk-ins, destined to wait until overstretched doctors could get around to them. They muttered and murmured in unison whenever a more critical emergency was wheeled past them, aware that their place in the queue had slipped down yet another notch.

'Donald Tyler,' Rose said to the weary-faced woman behind the reception desk. 'They've just brought him in by ambulance.'

'Oi!' the drunk slurred. 'I was here first.'

'You can just sit down and wait.' The receptionist dismissed him with a finger pointed firmly at the seating area and turned back to Rose. 'What name did you say?'

An ambulance crew wheeling a man on a gurney trundled by. A small boy with a thuggish crop, his arm in a dirty sling and the start of a huge shiner on his left eye, held his nose. 'Pooh! He stinks.'

'We treat everyone here, young man,' the receptionist told him. 'Even you,' she said under her breath.

'Homeless man. Found collapsed in the street,' the paramedic announced.

'Cubicle three.'

'Donald Tyler,' Rose insisted. 'Where is he? I want to see him.'

The receptionist checked her computer screen. 'The doctors will be treating him right now. You can't go through, you'd just be in the way.' She glanced up at Rose's stricken face. 'Sorry,' she added but she didn't mean it. She pointed towards a door along the corridor. 'Wait in there. Someone will come to inform you of his progress.'

Five hours later, someone did.

*

Rose remembered the agonising wait in the hospital's family room with painful clarity. She had been alone in there and the place reeked of sickly disinfectant, sweat and fear. She stared at the blurry posters on the walls for minutes before realising that, in all the frantic rush, she had forgotten to bring her specs with her. She looked down to see she was wearing one navy-blue slipper and one black. She wanted a coffee from the machine in the corner but she'd given the taxi driver all the money she'd had. She had her house keys in her pocket and that was the lot. There was no mirror in the room but she knew that her face was a mess. She licked her finger and patted below her eyes, unsurprised to find splodges of mascara on her fingertip. What a time to rediscover the pride in her appearance she felt she had lost such a long time back.

She dragged herself to her feet and crossed the room, wearily pushed open the door marked 'Visitors' Toilet' and stared at her reflection in the grubby mirror. She moistened her hands under the tap and ran her fingers through her light-brown hair. With a dab of powder and lipstick she could look younger than her fifty-two years but tonight, this morning, she reckoned she looked sixty. The lipstick had disappeared hours ago and tears had smeared the mascara she had been too exhausted to remove before she went to bed. Panda eyes, he called them and they would laugh together as he kissed the pain away and begged her forgiveness. She had always accepted his grovelling apologies because it meant that he still loved her, despite the tears he had forced her to shed. Life would be so empty again without him. She reached for a paper towel, ran it under the cold water and began to scrub away the remnants of make-up.

'Mrs Tyler?'

Cold dread gripped her as she turned off the tap and hurried back into the waiting room to find a doctor there, with a tired young face, professionally grave. And she knew before he spoke what he was about to tell her.

'My name is Anderson,' she said. 'Rose Anderson.'

He frowned. 'Are you Mr Tyler's next of kin?'

'Yes.' Then she corrected herself. 'No.'

She wasn't sure what Don might have put on his admission form. 'I don't know really,' she said. 'He's been living with me for two years. He's been ill for a lot of that time. I called the ambulance.'

The doctor nodded.

'He has a daughter somewhere, I think,' Rose added.

Simultaneously they both looked up at the digital clock on the wall. Five o'clock – as good a time as any to leave this world.

She didn't go to see his body because she just couldn't cope with it. Her mother's death-shrunken face had haunted Rose for years. The person she knew had departed, there was nothing left now but an empty husk, like the death masks she had seen in museums, the ones that had frightened her so badly as a child. Now that Don was gone, Rose was fearful of viewing his corpse. The very memory would give her nightmares and he would have hated that.

*

A taxi had dropped Rose off at six and the driver eyed her suspiciously when she asked him to wait.

'My purse is in the house.' She had briefly considered telling him why she was coming from the hospital at this unearthly hour in such a dishevelled state and with no money on her but he didn't look the type you could confide in.

All the lights were still on downstairs. She opened up. The detritus of chaos from eight hours ago surrounded her and she could only gaze at it all in stunned silence. A loud rap on the open front door brought her back to her senses. The taxi driver stood there; he appeared to be pissed off.

'I'm looking for my purse,' she told him.

'Jesus, darlin',' he said as he peered into the house. 'Must have been one hell of a party.'

She gave him a tenner, the flat fare with no tip. 'My partner has just died,' she shouted, venting her anger on him. 'Take your bloody money and fuck off!'

*

Once Don's body had been taken from the hospital to be cremated and her house was silent, Rose sank into a seemingly bottomless mire of depression and despair. There was so little of the past two years for her to hang on to. It was as though Don had never even existed, apart from her memories of their time together and that wooden chest in the hallway. Rose sat and turned the key over in her fingers. She had found it taped to the underside of the dining table. She considered her options. She could take the chest into the yard, douse it in petrol and burn it to ashes as Don had instructed. Then she might be able to draw a line under this bizarre episode in her life and move on. But what if she did open up the chest? How would 'they' ever know – whoever the mysterious 'they' might be? There was so much about Don she couldn't comprehend. There was his daughter for a start. Surely she had the right to know that her father had died. All Don's stories flooded back and, without his potent presence, they appeared to be increasingly far-fetched.

What a fool she would feel if she read his notebooks only to discover the ramblings of a fantasist. No, maybe she should just burn the chest as he had instructed and hang on to her illusions. But the moment that thought passed through her mind, she knew what she had to do. So, like a modern-day Pandora, she held the key firmly in her hand and opened the chest.

Rose had immediately regretted her actions. The photographs of all those other women distressed her and the one notebook she had read was filled with Don's obsession with Joanie. That experience had been too hurtful for her to want to read any more.

Rose put down her duster and started to get ready for her evening shift at the pub. Now she had finally found Don's daughter, all she wanted was to hand over to Suzanne everything that had belonged to him. Perhaps then Don's ghost would leave her in peace.

*

He had observed her movements for three weeks from the rented terraced house across the street. His vantage point wasn't ideal from five doors down on the opposite side but it was all that was available on a short rental and they'd had to wait months for even this to become vacant. It came fully furnished and was comfortable enough but nothing like he was used to. From this angle, there was no way to see directly into the windows of her house, so he had walked past on many occasions but had seen no sign of the man he was looking for. The dowdy woman appeared to be the only person living there. The local pub where she worked was just around the corner and he had been in there every day since his arrival. He sat alone at a table across from the bar, drinking beer and reading the newspaper.

'American?' The barman had asked, when he ordered his first drink there.

'Canadian,' he had lied, and made it obvious that this was as far as any conversation was going to go. After that, the barman had simply acknowledged him each time he entered the pub.

He watched her as she worked. She was the quiet kind. He'd heard her called Rose and thought the name apt, as there was something fragile about her. Unlike the other barmaid who was sassy and hot, flirting and joking with all the men, Rose seemed to be of a nervous disposition. He sat there until her shift ended and followed her home at a safe distance. But working and grocery shopping was all she seemed to do, apart from that one trip to Covent Garden. He'd emailed the photographs of Rose and the younger woman on, but the response had been in the negative. *Not known. But keep an eye on Anderson.*

He had a rental car parked outside the house and had been compelled to purchase a six-month permit to keep it there. But so far he hadn't needed to use the car because Rose shopped locally and spent the rest of the time watching TV with the volume turned way up high. He had heard it as he passed her place at night, but had never been able to see in as she always had the drapes closed.

After four days he'd decided to verify the information he had been given.

'You sure this is correct?'

'He was traced there,' she told him. 'The guy from the agency saw him eleven months ago. He was collecting the money every week then visiting some safe-deposit place in Kensington.'

'I guess he might have moved on by now,' he suggested.

'The cell phone he uses is registered to that address,' she said. 'Wait for the next message and follow her because she may now be the one collecting. Also, see who visits the house.'

'And if someone does visit?'

'You follow whoever it is. Work it out, will you.' She wheezed and he could hear her impatience. 'If there's no sign of him, then it is possible that he may have skipped recently.' She paused as she led him through her thought process. 'But as this woman is still alive and kicking, then he obviously needs her for something. So any visitor to her home may lead you to him.'

CHAPTER FOUR

Suzanne was proud of her mother's achievements. Joan had worked her way from heading up the sales team to becoming the first female board member of her company, rising through the glass ceiling with ease and grace. Over the years, Suzanne had also come to love her step-dad, Harry, and was relaxed in his company. He had been a stabilising force and gentle influence on the sometimes cool relationship she had with her mother. Even so, Suzanne was still rather apprehensive the day she arrived on the doorstep of the couple's Essex home with a manila envelope full of photographs.

Her mother opened the door to her and Suzanne felt the usual rush of affection. *How lovely she is*, she thought. The sunlight emphasised the traces of white in Joan's auburn hair, yet Suzanne thought that her mother wore her fifty-nine years lightly. Joan's daily workouts ensured she remained slim, and as usual she was casually well dressed, hands manicured, fingernails painted to match her lipstick, her face never seen without artfully applied make-up. *Lucky genes*, Suzanne thought and hoped that, even though they were not alike in looks, at least some of that luck had rubbed off on her. Harry, older than Joan by ten years, waved hello and went out to potter around in their huge garden, his normal pastime for most of the spring and summer. Then come December, the couple were planning to head off together on a cruise to exotic places, as usual. They were a content and happy pair, ideally suited to each other it seemed.

Suzanne tried to assure herself that nothing she would say today could possibly upset her mother's equilibrium, but as perceptive as ever, Joan sensed her daughter's tension.

'Something's wrong,' she said once they settled down opposite each other in the light and airy sitting room.

'I've just heard that my father died five months ago.'

'He's dead?' Suzanne found the expression in her mother's green eyes impossible to read. Joan looked away, down at her hands and picked at one of her vermilion-coloured nails. 'Are you sure?'

Suzanne fished out the copy of the death certificate that Rose had given her and placed it on the coffee table between then. 'It's all there,' she said.

Joan picked it up and stared at it, absorbing the information. 'Thank God,' she said, after a few moments.

'I'm not sure I expected that response.' Though Suzanne hadn't been sure quite what her mother's reaction would be.

'He was a wicked man,' said Joan. 'Thank goodness you never got to know him.'

'Why didn't you ever tell me that before? Why was even the mention of his name always out of bounds?'

'Because you were just a child, and once you were older I saw no point in burdening you.' Joan chipped at her nail. 'And because,' she said as she looked up once more, 'I was ashamed.'

'Ashamed of what?'

'Of not having been strong enough to leave him sooner, of consenting to his seeing you and allowing him to upset you with his visits.' She took a deep breath and composed herself. 'I wanted you to have a father in your life but he let you down so many times. He would ring to say he'd be there and you'd get all dressed up for him, watching the door, fizzing with excitement. Then he'd not show up and you would be devastated. So I stopped telling you of his intended visits until he was actually on the doorstep. I hated him for that in the end and was so relieved when he stopped seeing you altogether.'

'Didn't he turn up that night when I was about thirteen?'

'Yes, that was just before we moved house.'

Suzanne could remember a dreadful row in the middle of the night, when she'd heard shouting and doors slamming then come downstairs the next morning to find her mother picking fragments of glass out of the sitting room carpet. Someone had hurled a heavy garden statue through the bay window, and in the driveway Joan's car tyres had been slashed.

'Calling the police in will just make matters worse,' Joan had told Harry. 'We're going to move house anyway, so let's just get on with it and make sure he doesn't find out where we go.'

'Hasn't he got away with enough in his time?' Harry questioned in frustration.

'It's involvement he wants. A court case would take a while, and we would have moved by then but he would be entitled to see all the legal papers. That way he could keep tabs on us. Anyway, how can we prove he did this?'

'Who else?' Harry examined the broken window frames and shook his head.

'Who did this?' Suzanne butted in, her head still fuzzy from one of those delicious teenage lie-ins.

'Your bloody father, that's who,' Harry snapped.

'You can't prove that.' Joan sucked the finger she had nicked on a stray glass splinter.

'Oh, come on, Joan.' Harry made an attempt to look fierce. 'After all you went through with him, are you telling me that you don't think he's capable of this?'

Joan stood up and looked her husband in the eye. 'Harry, dear, you have absolutely no concept of what he is capable of.' She smiled at him and kissed him on the cheek. 'And that is why I love you.'

'Was that Dad at the door last night?' Suzanne asked. The voice she had heard from her room had been distorted yet belligerent, not something she would have then immediately associated with the father who had turned up out of the blue from time to time.

'Yes. At three in the bloody morning,' Harry snorted. 'He was drunk and abusive, demanding to see you. I told him to sober up and come back at a decent hour. And ten minutes later…' He gestured towards the broken windows. 'This.'

'That,' Joan had said firmly, 'does not constitute proof.'

'That was the last time I saw him.' Joan said now. 'Though over the years I've thought I'd glimpsed him in the street quite a few times. But I could have been mistaken.'

'He came to my studio once.' Suzanne realised as she said it that she had never mentioned his visit before. Joan and Harry had been on holiday at the time and when they got back, Suzanne had been so traumatised by Sophie's death that she had put Don's visit out of her mind. After the fire, anyone who asked was reassured that Suzanne was doing fine and coping well, but from her current perspective she could see that she had been numbed by the experience. After the first few months when she had felt she was walking through treacle, she had blocked out everything that had led up to the fire and its aftermath. But her encounter with Rose had unlocked many of the memories she had sought to suppress.

'When did he visit you?' Joan suddenly looked older, and a little distraught.

'Ten years ago, just before the fire at my studio.'

'Oh my God!' Joan wrapped her arms around her body protectively. 'How did he behave?'

'He was fine at first,' Suzanne reassured her. 'He even brought flowers.'

'Freesias?' Joan's eyes were full of a pain her daughter had never seen there before.

'Yes, I think so.' Suzanne did remember very clearly, because she had later torn the delicate blooms to shreds and tossed them in the dustbin.

Joan nodded. 'That was his usual peace offering.'

'After a few minutes he became agitated, pacing around, criticising my paintings,' Suzanne told her.

'Did he try to hurt you?'

'Only my pride.' The look of loathing on his face, his aggressive, overt sexual innuendo and the smutty tales of conquest had chilled Suzanne to the bone. She felt repulsed by the memory she had sought to expunge.

'There's something else, isn't there, Suzanne?' Joan's green eyes scanned her daughter's face.

Suzanne knew that her mother sensed she was being evasive so decided to tell all. 'He said things about you, about how you met at Glastonbury in '79. How you made love that first day in a field.'

A faint smile flickered across Joan's mouth. 'We were all young once, dear,' she rebuked her daughter. 'It was no different from how it is today. Don't look so dismayed.'

'But he was much more vulgar about it, Mum.'

The shadow of her smile retreated: 'He was trying to intimidate you. Men like him will use your sexuality as a weapon against you, in the same way that they use their own.' She sighed. 'It's just a pity I didn't know that way back then.'

'He told me that you used to play the guitar.' Suzanne recalled her father's sly sideways glance as he said it. He had challenged her, watched for her response and manipulated her.

Joan held her left hand out for inspection. The little finger had an odd bend in it that Suzanne had asked her about several times in the past only to be told, 'I was born like this.'

'Yes, Suzanne, I did play. Until he broke my little finger.'

'Is that why you left him?' Suzanne couldn't imagine her smart, feisty mother as anyone's victim. This revelation gave even more of a lie to Suzanne's memory of Don referring to her mother as 'my Joanie'.

'No, that was before you were born.' She stopped for a moment and looked Suzanne in the eye, seemingly embarrassed. 'Don't ask me why I stayed with him, because I don't know. He had been raised in an orphanage, brutalised by a lack of care and affection. I was young and idealistic. I thought I could change him with love.'

Suzanne heard a catch in her mother's voice and she wanted to hold her, to comfort her. But physical contact was not Joan's accustomed way of dealing with emotions. Self-contained and always in control was how Suzanne would have previously described her mother. Though now she was not so sure.

'I was wrong, though,' Joan admitted. 'I had no idea just how wrong. After you were born, he became deeply jealous and increasingly violent. There were times when he really lost it, when it seemed as though he was lashing out at someone else entirely, trying to punish them and not me.' She shuddered. 'In the end, for your sake as much as for my own, I summoned up the courage to divorce him. But for a long time afterwards I continued to blame myself for his violence, thinking I must have provoked him. So when he wanted to see you, I consented. Although I made sure that he was never alone with you.' She looked out of the window at Harry enthusiastically digging up weeds, his elbows poking through his threadbare gardening cardigan. 'It was only after I met Harry that I fully appreciated that grown-up relationships are based on equality and that all rows do not end with being smacked around.'

'Oh, Mum, I had no idea what a bastard he really was all along.'

Joan composed herself. 'No reason you should have, sweetheart. But it's all over now, thank goodness, and he can't do any more damage.' She sighed. 'I really loved that guitar, you know. My parents chipped in to buy an Epiphone with a solid-spruce top and a lovely sunburst finish for my eighteenth birthday. I knew every

Joni Mitchell song, note for note. Your father always called me Joanie. And what a sick joke *that* turned out to be.' Joan looked up and waved to Harry through the window. 'Harry bought me all of Joni Mitchell's CDs for my last birthday. He's such a dear.'

Joan noticed the manila envelope for the first time. 'So what have you got there?'

'I have some photographs.' Suzanne opened it. 'There's one of you from those days.'

Suzanne handed her mother the photograph depicting her younger hippie self, laughing in a field, thirty miles and thirty years away.

Joan looked at it, and the recollection of a long-gone past caused her pale features to flush. 'Where did you get this?'

'Rose Anderson, the woman Don was living with, contacted me. She has these and some journals of his. She wanted me to have them.'

Joan shook her head. 'Don't get involved, Suzanne. You should leave the past alone. It's over. Now it's time to move on with your life.'

'I know, Mum, but when Don came to see me that time he told me he had other children,' Suzanne insisted. 'I'd almost forgotten about that until now, but I have siblings, Mum. So I'm asking you to please help me out here.'

Joan hesitated before speaking. 'I was an only child too, you know. And I never felt it to be a hardship. It would have been good to share the burden when my parents died, but…'

'I would never suggest anything as strong as hardship,' Suzanne soothed, not wishing to upset her mother. 'But if there had been brothers or sisters you didn't know, wouldn't you have been at least curious?'

'Ah, curiosity.' Joan sounded sceptical. 'Okay, I'll tell you what I know. Don was married at seventeen, before we met. But I don't know about his having any children.'

There was something in her mother's tone of voice that made Suzanne uneasy. Joan had always been evasive when it came to talking about Don Tyler but this denial of having no knowledge of his other children just didn't ring true somehow. Still, to keep the peace and get her mother's cooperation, Suzanne decided not to put pressure on Joan to come clean. She could deal with that another time. 'All I'm asking is for you to take a look at these photos.'

Joan sighed her compliance. 'Fine, but I don't think this is a good idea.'

Suzanne then placed on the table the picture of Betty, with her happy smile and her protruding belly.

'I've never seen her before.' Joan examined the picture closely, clearly intrigued despite her misgivings. 'Looks like quite an old photo. Maybe that was his first wife. So perhaps there was a child. With your father you never knew what was real as all his lies had some element of the truth. It was like unravelling knotted string.'

Then Suzanne placed the six other photos face-up before her mother. Joan picked one up and examined it for some time. She turned it over, and looked at the name for some time. 'Sheila,' she said out loud before taking a deep breath and blowing it upwards onto her face.

'Do you know her?' Suzanne asked.

'No, but I have a vague memory of something…' She shook her head. 'It will come to me.' Joan pointed at the picture of Sheila standing in front of the fairground ride. 'This looks like it was taken in the early sixties from the fashion she's wearing. Don worked the travelling fairgrounds before he became a roadie. Maybe she's a girlfriend from those days.'

But she drew a blank with the other five photographs and it was obvious to Suzanne that her mother knew no more than she herself did.

'What about this?' Suzanne laid down the image of Sophie, and her heart raced as it did each time she looked at it.

'Isn't that…?' Joan stared at the picture and then at her daughter. 'This is one of the pictures he had?' Her voice took on a sharp edge. 'When did he meet her?'

'The day he came to my studio, about two weeks before the fire.'

Joan frowned but did not respond.

'I find it odd that he kept these photographs,' Suzanne said, just as the thought struck her. 'Yet there are none of us as a family, or of me as a baby.'

Joan hooked her hair behind her ears, a gesture Suzanne knew so well, which her mother did when she felt uneasy. She sat back, her face pensive. 'That bastard destroyed them all,' she said vehemently. 'He came to our house in a rage and demanded to see you. We had been divorced for only a few months at the time. As soon as he was through the door his manner changed. He became all bright and cheery and you were delighted to see him. He asked to see the family albums, including ones I had from my own childhood, with pictures of my parents and family. I disappeared for a few minutes to make some tea and by the time I returned, you were both in the garden. He'd scooped up all the albums and placed them on the lawn. Then he set fire to them. You were four at the time and he led you by the hand and encouraged you to laugh at the "lovely bonfire". Yet he looked at me with such venom that I didn't dare…'

'What possessed him to do something as awful as that?' Suzanne could hardly imagine why anyone would be so vindictive. 'What did you do?'

'What *could* I do? I didn't want you to be upset. He had turned the theft of my life – the obliteration of our past few years together – into a game to amuse you.'

'That's plain nasty and unforgivable.'

'Fire,' Joan said. 'Absolute annihilation.' That look again, that anxious expression etched on her face. 'Don't do this, Suzanne,' she warned. 'Get rid of these photographs and don't speak to this

Rose woman again. Tell her to destroy all his stuff. Forget him, he's dead. Don't delve, for your own peace of mind. Please, I beg you.' She reached across the table, gripped her daughter's hand in hers and Suzanne noticed once more the bend in her mother's little finger. 'Don't take this any further,' she said. 'You never know what you might uncover.'

'Mark is pressing me to have children, and I've been resisting. I never realised why before but I now know that I have always felt that there was something missing from my life. And before I go any further, I have to know what it is.' There, that was the first time Suzanne had voiced it. Whatever lay beneath – about Sophie, about these unknown women, about any siblings – she had to unearth the truth.

CHAPTER FIVE

Joan lay in bed that night with the image of Sheila playing in her head. The bell that name rang echoed in her memory and dragged her unwillingly into a past she had tried to forget. Everything she wanted to keep at bay, everything she had dreaded, was coming back to haunt her. She had evaded all of Suzanne's questions for so many years, telling herself that one day she would reveal all, but had never done so. How, she wondered, do I tell my daughter that she is a permanent reminder of her father? Not just because of her dark hair and eyes, but the way she tilts her chin when angry; some of her hand gestures; the way she throws back her head and screws up her eyes when she laughs. All inherited traits from Don because Suzanne was far too young when we divorced to have copied them from him. How do I tell her about the phone calls to my office when my 'hello' was greeted by silence, yet I was convinced it was Don on the other end of the line? How do I explain the sightings of him in a car driving by, walking behind me in the street or reflected in a shop window, without sounding like a mad woman? And how do I tell her about the postcards that Don sent to me and I kept secret even from Harry? How do I explain stashing them away when I'm not even sure of my motives myself?

But, despite her unease, Joan knew the time had come to face her ghosts. *Don's dead*, she reasoned, *he can do no more harm.* So she allowed her mind to venture back to a simpler place and time; to turning twenty-eight and thinking that her youth was slip sliding away; to seeing her friends pairing up and wondering if there was such a thing as a 'Mr Right' for her. She wanted to reach back into her past, shake her unworldly self and say, 'You don't know how lucky you are to be this young and this free'. So she visualised that fine morning in the June of 1979, when she yanked the bedcover off her sleeping boyfriend.

'Come on, Robin.'

He was curled up in his usual position on his side, lying on his left arm with his hand close to his lips as though he was about to suck his thumb. She playfully smacked his naked bottom. 'Get up, dressed and packed. Alice and Geoff will be here in half an hour.'

He warily opened one blue eye. 'Let me sleep, will you?'

'No more sleep for you, sunshine.' Joan opened the bathroom door, reached in and got the shower running. 'Glastonbury today. Come on, quick shower. Get a move on!'

He turned on his back, his half-erect penis lolling arrogantly against his thigh. 'Not going,' he said.

Joan threw a towel at him. 'Of course we're going. Alice bought four tickets for a fiver each. We're travelling in their camper van and borrowing their tent to sleep in.'

'Not going.'

'Come on, Robin, this has been arranged for weeks. Peter Gabriel's playing, so are Alex Harvey *and* John Martyn. He's my hero and you've been looking forward to this too.'

When Robin didn't budge, it dawned on Joan that he was not messing about.

'I'm not stopping you from going,' he said, 'but I'm staying in London.'

'Oh great! I'm supposed to sleep in a tent all on my own, am I?'

'Sleep in the van with Alice and Geoff. Have yourselves a little threesome.' He turned on his side and closed his eyes as he muttered. 'It might do you some good.'

'What's *that* supposed to mean?'

Robin sighed, sat up and pulled the bedcover up around his lower half. 'Things between us have been getting a little stale of late.'

'I don't see that.'

'Well, you wouldn't, would you? You might live in the heart of the King's Road, play your folk songs and dress like a hippie but you're still a nice Sussex girl at heart. You're out of time, my baby.'

'Robin, why are you being so horrible? What's brought this on?'

He stretched lazily, as though to impart the fact that her concern was no concern of his. 'I've decided that I want to spend some time with Shelley, okay? You go to your Glastonbury bloody hippie Fayre, have a "fab" time and I'll talk to you when you get back.'

Joan stood and stared at him, trying to take in what he was saying. She watched him casually flick his sleep-scrunched blond hair away from his face. Seemingly unable to meet her gaze, his blue eyes remained fixed on the Stones' *Some Girls* poster tacked on the wall.

'Shelley? From work?' Robin had briefly mentioned that this girl had recently started at the record company he worked for, but no more than that. 'You want to spend three days with *her*?'

'That's about it.' He was staring straight back at Joan now, his jaw set, a look of determination on his face.

'You want to fuck her, you mean.'

He let out a snort, as though she had just said the dumbest thing he had ever heard. 'Already done that, Jo. Now I need more time with her, okay?'

'No, it's not bloody okay.'

Another sigh, with much shaking of his blond head. 'What are you getting so upset about? I could have invented some work-related problem but I'm being honest here.' He sat back on the pillow and folded his arms across his hairless chest. 'Since when are we joined at the hip? No commitment, we agreed. Free spirits, we said.'

A sinking feeling overcame her. That had been the deal when he'd moved in with her and, when their relationship had been a more casual affair, she'd been happy to agree to it. But three years along the line, now she had convinced herself that she loved him and, more importantly for Joan, that he loved her…

'What has she got that I haven't?' The words slipped out before she had a chance to grapple them to the ground.

Astonishment filled his eyes. 'I can't believe you just uttered such a bourgeois statement.' He waved his hand at her dismissively. 'Get back to the 1950s suburbs, Jo. That's where you belong.'

Stomach clenched with anxiety, she took a deep breath and tried another angle. 'You know you're letting everyone down by not coming.'

He let forth a sneering laugh. 'My god, it gets worse. What a naughty boy I am for letting everyone down. Don't say another word, Jo, or you'll morph into my mother.'

*

'What a shit!' Alice narrowed her eyes and patted Joan's hand. Alice was a bountiful seven months' pregnant and already adopting the motherly mantle. 'Don't you think he's a bastard, Geoff?'

The VW camper van was just passing through Woking in Surrey with Geoff driving and Alice making an attempt to comfort Joan.

'He even had the nerve to quote *The Female Eunuch* at me. The bit about lovers who are free to go when they are restless always come back.'

'Well,' Geoff offered, 'if an open relationship was the deal…'

'What utter crap! I could strangle that bloody Germaine Greer,' Alice spluttered. 'These men have had it all their own way for far too long and she writes that bloody feminist book and makes matters even worse. Love is *not* free, sex has consequences for both parties.'

'You can say that again,' Geoff muttered half under his breath.

'What did you say?' Alice snarled at him.

'Nothing.'

Joan felt too sorry for herself to feel any sympathy for pussy-whipped Geoff. 'Robin told me that this Shelley is magic for him. She's half-Indian, apparently. He said she's exotic. She's beautiful.' She sniffed back her pain.

Alice handed her friend another tissue and reached up to brush a stray strand of long auburn hair from her wet cheek. 'There's more beauty in you than anyone.'

'He never told *me* I was beautiful.' Another tear slid down Joan's cheek.

*

Following a hiatus of several years after David Bowie headlined way back in '71, this was to be the first commercially organised festival at Glastonbury. Though the chaos of tents, camper vans and cars that littered the campsite did not even hint at the word 'organised' to Joan. With Alice playing the role of pregnant matriarch to the hilt and staying firmly put in the van, Geoff helped Joan to assemble the two-man tent. Joan pinned up her long red hair, pulled the back hem of her ankle-length skirt through her legs and tucked it into her belt at the front, so it looked as though she was wearing harem pants. She crouched down and started knocking the tent pegs into the ground.

'You can't park that van here, pal. The caravan site is across the road.'

Joan looked up to see the source of the Liverpool-accented voice. He was medium height with broad shoulders, curly dark-brown hair, an air of insouciance and a cigarette dangling from his lips. She thought he looked like a gypsy, a bit like David Essex, but with darker eyes and a deep cleft in his chin.

'He's helping my friend to put the tent up,' Alice called from within the van with obvious irritation. 'Come on, Geoff, get on with it.'

The guy gave a cheeky grin. 'His master's voice, eh?' He glanced at Joan and winked. 'Look, mate, I'll help this beautiful lady put her tent up so you can get your missus a choice spot on the caravan site before they're all gone.' The grin widened. 'Don't want you getting into any more trouble, do we?'

'We're expecting around twelve thousand people to turf up, so best get a place now before the queues start.' He waved his arm to indicate somewhere 'over there'. 'Go back up through the entrance, turn left and the signpost for the caravans is on your right.' He handed Geoff a scruffy piece of paper that passed for a pass. 'Give that to the guys on the gate when you come back in.'

Geoff climbed into the van, started the engine and set off with Alice craning her neck to get a better look at Joan's helper.

'You working here, then?' Joan asked him while they assembled the tent together.

'Yeah,' he said, 'I'm between roadie jobs.' He pointed in the general direction of somewhere else. 'I helped erect the Pyramid Stage, set up the food stalls, dug the holes of the bogs... You know, general dogsbody work. Hoping to pick up another band gig here. If not, I'll go to a mate's place and crash on his floor till I get something sorted.'

'No regular place to live?'

'Footloose, fancy-free and rootless. Just like a rolling stone.'

'Even Jagger's got a house in Chelsea.'

'Yeah, well. There's more to life than money.' He laughed. 'You? Where do you stay?'

'I've got a flat on King's Road.'

'Nice.'

'Used to be. It's packed with punk-types right now.'

'My last job was with a punk band. A bunch of university tossers dropping their aitches, changing their names from Quentin to Bert, and making out they grew up on a council estate.'

'You sound as though you don't like music.'

'Oh no, don't get me wrong.' His eyes flitted across to her guitar case placed next to a sleeping bag on the groundsheet at the back of the tent. 'I love it. But punk isn't music, is it? It's crap. I give it two years max. Then all those pretenders can go back to being an "artist" or to work in Daddy's firm or get a job in the City.'

He indicated towards the guitar. 'That yours or your boy-friend's?'

'He's not coming. The guitar is mine and I play folk.'

He smiled wistfully. 'Joni Mitchell, Sandy Denny, now that's music.'

'What happened?'

'Sorry?'

'To the job with the band.'

'Oh, *them*,' he laughed. 'They were just about to break into the big time when they split up. Artistic differences, they claimed, which translates as couldn't stand the sight of each other any more. Been mates since they were nippers and suddenly they're tearing each other's throats out. Life on the road can do that to some people.'

Joan opened the cool box she'd brought with her and took out a couple of beers. 'Want one?'

'I never take beer from strangers,' he said, holding out his hand for her to shake. 'Don Tyler.'

'Joan Bell.'

'Joan Bell, my belle,' he sang to the tune of 'Michelle' as he raised the cold bottle in salute. He fished a joint from the top pocket of his jean jacket. 'Do you partake?'

They sat in the tent, got quietly stoned, and Joan found herself telling Don about the light plane, piloted by a racing-driver friend of her father, that had crashed ten years before, killing the pilot and both passengers, who happened to be her parents. She'd been just eighteen and, as their only child, had had to deal with the practicalities and the grief.

Don's eyes were moist and there was a catch in his voice when he finally spoke. 'I can't even imagine how hard that must have been for you.'

'I sold the house in Sussex,' she said. 'I couldn't bear to live there any more. So I bought the flat on King's Road with the money. It was at the height of Swinging London, a great place to live.'

'At least you had that,' he said. 'I grew up in an orphanage. They take good enough care of you until you're sixteen, then they boot you out the door to fend for yourself.'

She took out her guitar and played him her version of 'The Circle Game'. Don lay back with his eyes closed, listening. 'I shall call you Joanie,' he said. Moments later, he was on his feet. 'Can I buy the lovely Joanie a plate of hot and spicy salmonella?'

Don left to trudge all the way to the food stalls and Joan lay back, strumming her guitar. Sod Robin and his exotic tartlet, she wasn't doing too badly herself.

The tent flap opened and Alice crawled in. 'We have been *so* worried about you. Are you okay? That gypsy type sent us in totally the wrong direction. I swear he did it on purpose. And the piece of paper he gave us was absolutely worthless. Thank goodness I'd held on to the ticket stubs or we would never have got back in again. There are some really rough-looking people around. I think you should sleep in the van with me and Geoff can have the tent. He won't mind.'

'No thanks, I like it here,' Joan said. She could hear Don apologising to Geoff outside, something about not knowing his left from his right. She reached across Alice, opened the tent flap and looked up at a beaming Don Tyler holding two paper plates filled with something or other that was possibly toxic but she didn't care. 'So I'll stay here, if you don't mind, Alice.'

Three days and nights of dodgy food, even dodgier sanitation, loud music, potent weed and gloriously gentle lovemaking left Joan floating on air. Don touched her as though she was precious, told her that he worshipped every inch of her, said she was the most beautiful woman he had ever seen and how he would remember these days until he drew his final breath. Joan told herself that this was just a line, that these were merely pretty lies but, deep down, she longed to believe him.

The day they were packing up to leave there was no sign of Don. Joan kept looking out for him in the vicinity but couldn't spot him anywhere. *Oh well,* she thought sadly, *it was nice while it lasted.*

Alice appeared smug. 'What happens in Glastonbury, stays in Glastonbury, it seems. Though it's for the best. I mean, nothing wrong with a bit of rough but nobody wants that Spanish waiter from Barcelona turning up on their doorstep, do they?'

Joan felt an almost irresistible desire to hit her.

Then, just as the tent was finally tucked back into the van and Geoff was about to start the engine, Don appeared as if from nowhere. 'Any chance of a lift?'

'Don't they need you to dismantle stuff?' Geoff asked.

'Oh that? I quit. Got a chance of a roadie job with a London band. I have to see the guy tomorrow. I'll crash with a mate tonight. So…?'

*

'I'll get out with you,' Don said, as the VW camper drew up outside Joan's place. 'My friend lives in Fulham, I can walk from here.'

'I thought you said Putney,' Alice sniped.

'No,' Don said cheerfully, 'that was someone else.'

'Hmm,' Alice said, 'you've got a lot of friends.'

'As I'm sure you have, Alice,' Don said. 'Seeing as you are so charming and friendly.'

Geoff laughed.

'Ah,' Alice suddenly sounded triumphant. 'I see the prodigal has returned.'

Joan looked out of the van window to see Robin standing in the doorway of the punk clothes emporium that glowered beneath her first-floor flat.

'Maybe you should stay where you are, Don,' Alice sneered. 'We'll drop you in Fulham, or Putney… or wherever.'

'No, ta!' Don said. 'I'll be fine here.'

Joan got out of the van first and Robin approached to embrace her. 'I'm sorry,' he whispered in her ear.

She pushed him away. 'Throw you out, did she? So you come crawling back to stupid Joan.'

'I never left you. It was just one of those things.'

Don was standing by the van, watching them. He grinned broadly as he began swaying from side to side and singing Cole Porter's 'Just One of Those Things'. Joan rushed to his side and they sang together in a raucous imitation of Ethel Merman.

Robin's face blushed red with anger and humiliation. 'Who is this clown?'

Joan, now in paroxysms of laughter, linked her arm into Don's. 'He may be a clown,' she said. 'But he's *my* clown.'

Don kissed her.

*

Next morning he was singing in her shower. It was a rather more baritone version of Roy Orbison's 'Running Scared'. Joan lay on the bed and listened to him. When he got to the line about the girl choosing him, there was a catch in his voice. And, at that precise moment, Joan Bell fell in love with Don Tyler.

*

Six months later, just before Christmas, Don was working on a tour of France with some 1960s once-weres desperate to stay a safe distance from being booked for nostalgia gigs at Butlins in Pwllheli. That was when Joan discovered she was pregnant. Alice, now the world's fussiest mother of a son aged just four months, came to visit.

'You can't be serious about this?' Alice was breastfeeding baby Joshua in Joan's sitting room and, in between complaining about the loud music coming from the punk shop below, she made it clear that she was horrified by her childhood friend's news.

'I'm sure Don will be a good father,' Joan said. Not that she had told him yet.

'He's not even capable of looking after himself, let alone you and a baby.'

'You've never liked him.'

'Damn right! He may have you fooled, but not me. I wouldn't believe it if he said the sky was blue – I'd always want to check for myself. He's an absolute phoney. He can refine his accent till the cows come home but he's still a character straight out of an Alan Bleasdale play.'

'Don is attempting to better himself.'

'He's a roadie, Joan. You deserve better than having a baby with an itinerant. There's no future there for you.'

Joan, with early pregnancy hormones kicking in, was close to tears. 'What is wrong with you, Alice? Robin was too posh and Don is too common. You're supposed to be my friend, but it's as though you don't want me to be happy.'

'Robin was a manipulative, self-regarding bastard who couldn't keep his dick in his pants and Don…' She stopped while she tucked her breast back in her blouse. 'Last time I saw you, you had a horrible bruise on your face.'

'I told you, it was an accident.' Don had lashed out at her and caught her cheek with his hand. He had later lain sobbing in her arms, full of contrition.

Alice was not convinced. 'Have it your way. But if Geoff ever hit me—'

'Let that drop, Alice. It was nothing. A one-time thing.'

'That's not the only reason I have a dreadfully bad feeling about this.' Alice was patting Joshua on the back and he let out a loud burp.

Joan watched and tried to imagine doing the same thing with her own child. But her friend's animosity spoilt the moment and she resented that. 'Come on, don't hold back to spare my feelings.'

Alice sighed, heavily. 'If you want the unvarnished truth, Joan, then here it is… Don gives me the creeps. He laughs and cracks jokes but there's always something cold and calculating lurking behind his eyes.'

Don hadn't liked Alice from day one and was always taking the piss out of Geoff for being a wimp. But because Joan insisted they all got together, Don put his best face on and was charm personified, and she had thought that the other couple were not aware of the deception. But at that moment the ever-perceptive Alice was making Joan feel foolish, and her words felt like a slap in the face.

'You don't know the real him.' And nobody ever would, as Joan firmly believed that Don's loveless childhood in the orphanage had forced him to adopt a protective carapace that would never enable him to show his vulnerable side to anyone but her.

Alice was unmoved. 'I don't need to know the "real" him, because I can already see right through him. I'll tell you straight. I don't want him anywhere near my baby.' She cuddled her snoozy child. 'And you shouldn't let him near yours either, if you decide to have it.' Then Alice delivered the killer blow: 'If you really want my advice, Joan, you should drop this loser, have an abortion and move on.'

Joan stood and strode to the front door. 'Get out, Alice. *Now!*'

Without another word, Alice packed baby Joshua into his papoose sling and left. And with that, a friendship that had started in junior school and lasted for twenty years ended forever.

*

'Donny!' an unmistakably scouse voice yelled from across Sloane Square.

'Hey, look at this,' Don turned Joan in the direction of the Peter Jones shop window.

Expecting to see an array of cots or something baby related, she stared confusedly at the display of hi-tech stereo equipment, and instinctively rubbed her hand protectively across her eighth-month bump.

A stranger panted up to them. 'Donny. It's me, Tommy McCarthy. I lived in Dryden Street in Liverpool when we were kids. Don't you remember me?'

'You've made a mistake, pal, I don't know you.' Don took Joan firmly by the arm and began to walk away.

The man followed them. 'Come on, Donny. Don't mess about. I'm Sheila's brother. You *must* remember Sheila.'

Don eased Joan to one side, turned to the man and hissed. 'Fuck off. I don't know you. You got that?'

Don's face bore an expression Joan had never seen before and it scared her. Then he turned on his heel and guided her through the doors of the department store in search of a cot.

'I saw your Vera the other day,' the man called after them. 'Your mam's not well, Donny. You should go and see her. Before it's too late.'

*

That night, as Don took a shower, Joan was leaning on the bathroom door. 'That man today, I was wondering—'

'I told you I don't know him. Let it drop, will you.'

'It's just that he called you Donny.'

'Coincidence. Nobody has ever called me that.'

'And this Vera he talked about, and Sheila…'

Don stepped out of the shower, his eyes blazing, and she backed away. The baby began kicking furiously. Joan, thrown off balance by the sudden movement inside her, had to support herself by holding on to the doorjamb.

'Who the fuck do you want to believe, Joanie? Some nut job or me?' he raged.

Joan was overcome by dizziness. 'It's just that—'

Don backed into the bathroom and slammed the door. It banged closed and mashed the little finger of Joan's left hand. She never picked up her guitar again.

Three weeks later, Suzanne Tyler was born.

*

Joan looked at the bedside clock. 4.30. Harry shifted his position beside her. She reached out and touched his arm, the familiar warmth of his skin soothing her a little. She closed her eyes and made an attempt to conjure sleep but her mind was racing. Even in the few years she had been married to Don, he had always had so many secrets, been so cagey and evasive about his past. Who was the Sheila he had vehemently denied knowing, and all of those other women in the photos now in Suzanne's possession? Perhaps some of them had been girlfriends or wives? But the worst shock of all had been the picture of Sophie Chen. Joan remembered the emotional pain Suzanne had suffered for all those months after the fire. It had taken her such a long time to get over Sophie's horrific death that the loss of her paintings had appeared to mean little to her. Joan recalled watching her clever and talented daughter lose that spark, retreat into herself and settle for the security of a dull teaching job and an over-swift marriage to Mark. But today had been different. A bright flame flickered where previously there had been none; the old Suzanne was emerging from her self-imposed chrysalis.

Joan had seen the set of Suzanne's jaw, heard the determination in her voice and was half-pleased she had found a goal at last. But even though Don Tyler was dead, she felt a chill, as though someone was watching her from the dark recesses of her bedroom, and she couldn't cast off the feeling of being afraid for her daughter.

CHAPTER SIX

Mark was uncomfortable talking about Suzanne's mother. Joan had always made him feel unworthy, as though she believed her daughter had married beneath her. Okay, so he was an insurance salesman, not 'something-in-the-City' like her precious Harry. When he and Suze had first got together Joan herself had been in sales but Mark always suspected that she'd have been happier if Suze had tied the knot with a fellow artist. She'd even tut when he called her daughter 'Suze', tossing him a disgruntled look with her green cat-like eyes. Inevitably, once Joan was promoted to company director it made the situation even worse – not that she ever said anything specific. It was just a tone he detected in her manner. She was always polite but Mark often felt that she judged him and found him wanting. Everything had to be perfect in her world and she had a certain theatricality about her that got on his tits.

'Your mother's a very nice woman, Suze,' Mark said as they discussed Suzanne's visit, 'but she does have a tendency to be dramatic.'

'You never met my father,' Suzanne said. 'He was a very strange character.'

'Okay,' said Mark, 'but if you believe he torched your studio, then describing him as "strange" is putting it a little mildly, isn't it?'

'Mum didn't exactly say that, but Don did set fire to all the family albums and she looked alarmed when I told her he had met Sophie. Then she begged me not to take it any further.'

Mark looked at his watch, 'Let's talk about it later, because right now I have to go.' Evening calls were part of his routine. This was one of those times when he wondered why he hadn't joined the Metropolitan Police like his brother Luke. 'But before you jump to conclusions, just think on this. Luke wasn't involved in the investigation into the fire but he did see the report. The portable gas heater Sophie used in her studio malfunctioned. She was overcome by the fumes and collapsed. Then the heater exploded, something to do with the gas fumes mixing with certain flammable chemicals she'd been using, and that was it. The fire brigade investigators are the experts and they determined that it was an accident. Therefore…?'

'It was an accident,' she echoed, though doubt still tapped her on the shoulder.

Luke had been a young police constable back then and had accompanied Suzanne when she identified the body of Sophie Chen. Once off duty, and breaking every rule in the book, he had taken her for a coffee afterwards. He'd been sympathetic and kind. He was new to the job, and unlike the other brusque cops she had encountered. He had even taken her phone number and called her a week afterwards to check if she was okay. A few weeks later he had introduced her to his older, more attractive brother Mark.

'But why did Don have Sophie's photo?'

'I don't know. Maybe he returned to apologise to you for his behaviour. You were elsewhere and he took a photo of Sophie instead of you. Didn't she tell you he'd raved about her sculpture?'

'But don't you think that's odd?'

'Of course it's odd. People are. But who takes a picture of some stranger and then sets a fire to kill them? That, my darling, would be far more than odd. And maybe he was having a thing with her. Ever think of that one?'

'My dad and Sophie? That's ridiculous.'

'Well, you said he charmed her,' Mark reminded her. 'Maybe he went back when you were out and had his wicked way with her.'

'He made her laugh, sure. He was good at that. And she was flattered by how effusively he praised her work. But Sophie would never have had anything to do with an older man like him.'

'How can you be so sure?' Mark was more serious now, though glancing at his watch as he was late already. 'The thing is, Suze, there is nobody left to ask. And there's no evidence to suggest it was anything other than an accidental fire.'

He kissed her on the top of her head. 'So if you want to find out about any half-brothers or sisters you might have, then you should go ahead.'

*

Suzanne sat on the floor in Rose's terraced two-up, two-down house in north London, with dozens of lined notebooks set out in neat piles on the carpet beside her. Rose was in the kitchen, which opened straight onto the sitting room. She was making the umpteenth cup of tea. Although she had invited Suzanne over, Rose appeared nervous and had been chain-smoking for the last hour.

'Don would hate to see me doing this.' Rose lit another fag as she emerged. 'He wouldn't let me smoke in the house, said he hated the smell.'

'Had he given up?' Suzanne remembered her father smoking heavily – he'd been a total addict. Even when he had visited her in her studio, he had been most put out when she had asked him not to light up. Maybe he'd quit once he became ill.

'Oh no,' Rose countered, 'he'd never smoked in his life. He was really strict about it. I had to brush my teeth every time I had a cigarette.'

'Maybe I'm mistaken, then.' He'd been controlling this woman, taking the high moral ground when in reality... The more Suzanne discovered about her father, the more she wanted to distance herself from him. *Perhaps Mum's right*, she thought, *I should put all this behind me.*

Rose told her that she worked in the pub on the local high street and that was where she had met Don. Though she didn't strike Suzanne as the typical barmaid type.

'Have you always done that kind of work?'

'Oh no,' Rose replied. 'I used to be a legal secretary but...' A pause as she lit another cigarette. 'Things happen. Life gets in the way. After my mother died, I had a bit of a breakdown. The bar job was supposed to be a stopgap until I got back on my feet. But I guess I'm just lazy.' She shrugged. 'I've been there five years. Don't suppose I'll ever leave now.'

'You said you met my father there.' If any of the women in the photographs had been Don's previous lovers then, apart from the two young women in the black-and-white photographs, Rose was unlike any of the others. There was nothing exotic or unconventional about her, just a perfectly ordinary individual, it seemed, apart from the current emotional state she was in. But that was to be expected, given the circumstances.

'Yes, in the pub.' Rose brightened. 'He came in one Friday night and he was a right charmer. And funny too, so full of jokes and quick-witted with it. There's another barmaid at the pub, she's very pretty; all the men like her. But Don ignored her and started chatting me up. Then the next thing I know, he's moved in with me.'

'A whirlwind romance,' Suzanne suggested. Although she secretly wondered if Don had been down on his luck and wanted to find some lonely, vulnerable woman with a house he could doss in.

'Must have been,' Rose replied wistfully.

'Was there anything else in here?' Suzanne asked as she reached the bottom of the wooden chest. Then she wondered if that might appear to be a rude question, as though she doubted Rose's honesty. 'Just to give us any clues,' she added.

'Only the notebooks and photos,' Rose called from the kitchen.

'No passport, bank books, statements?' Suzanne persisted. 'That sort of thing?'

'No.' Rose hesitated for just a moment too long and Suzanne wondered whether she was keeping something from her. 'Nothing.'

'What did he live on?'

'Don't know, really.' Rose fussed around, straightened the tablecloth in a deliberate and unnecessary way. 'But he always paid his way. He always had money.'

'Any keys anywhere? Maybe he had a safe deposit box.'

'No.' Rose's voice took on the tone of a sulky teen. That flat note of denial, which, in Suzanne's teaching experience, generally meant the complete opposite.

She tried to sound more casual. 'Nothing hidden in any nooks and crannies in the house or the garden?'

'I haven't found anything like that.' Was it annoyance or something else in her manner, Suzanne wondered.

'I see you have a landline.' She could see the old-fashioned cream-coloured British Telecom phone on the sideboard. 'Did Don have a mobile at all?'

'You sound like a policeman,' Rose rebuked Suzanne as she sat by the table, cup in hand, drinking her tea yet looking a little agitated.

'Sorry, I didn't mean it to sound like an interrogation.' Suzanne idly considered that her brother-in-law's interview techniques had rubbed off on her by some kind of osmosis. 'Though, as it happens, we do have a detective in the family.'

Rose's china teacup hit the floor. It smashed to pieces and the hot tea soaked into the carpet.

'Are you okay?' Suzanne could see that the colour had drained from Rose's face. She rushed over to her to pick up the broken crockery and to check if the tea had scalded her.

'Leave it!' Rose yelled. 'Take the books and go.' She stood up and backed away from Suzanne. 'Don said they'd find me,' she blabbered to herself. 'Fool.' She scratched compulsively at her face. 'Bloody fool! Should have burned the lot, the box, the money.'

Rose collapsed onto the sofa and started to sob hysterically. Suzanne sat beside her and attempted to hold her hand but Rose pulled away.

'He said they'd track me down.'

'Rose,' Suzanne made an effort to soothe her. '*You* found *me*, remember. I didn't even know Don had died until you told me.'

Rose stared with frightened eyes. 'He was in Special Forces, you know. He did dangerous work and they paid him in cash. He told me all the stories about his work overseas. He shouldn't have done that but he trusted me, you see.' The words all rushed out in a fast gabble and she suddenly jumped to her feet, peering this way and that out of the window as she smoothed the curtain with her hand. 'He collapsed right here.' She turned towards Suzanne and pointed to the carpet beneath her feet, tears rolling down her cheeks. 'He trusted me.'

'You've been through a lot, Rose.' Suzanne speculated that she was witnessing the first stages of a nervous breakdown at this point. 'This has been harder on you than on anyone. But, please believe me, I want to be your friend. I want to help you.'

Rose shuddered, seemingly unsure of what to do next.

'Just take the books.' Her eyes glazed over. 'He wanted me to burn them, but I thought you should have them.' Then, almost in slow motion, she reached beneath one of the sofa cushions and extracted a white folder. 'This was in the chest, too.' She thrust the folder at Suzanne. 'Now, please take this and the books and go.'

'I came on the train,' Suzanne said. 'There are too many notebooks for me to carry. I could get a courier to pick them up tomorrow.'

Rose rushed to the front door and yanked it open. 'I want no strangers in my home.' There was a newly measured control to her voice as she tipped her head to one side as though listening to a voice that only she could hear. 'Come in a car or a taxi – alone – and collect them when I tell you to. I'll ring you when I feel ready to see you again.'

Suzanne picked up the white folder, headed towards the door and extended her hand to Rose but she had already turned her face away.

'I'll phone you.'

Rose banged the door closed behind Suzanne.

CHAPTER SEVEN

He recognised the woman he had photographed in Covent Garden entering and then leaving Rose Anderson's house. She had a white folder tucked under her arm. He thought that she appeared flustered but it was hard to tell from across the street. Convinced that Anderson would stay put for the night, he decided to follow her. He grabbed his jacket, wallet and house keys and headed out. He caught sight of her just as she turned the corner headed for the tube station. He used the Oyster card he'd bought for twenty pounds' worth of travel on the underground and buses – thinking all the time it might come in handy. She had one, too. He kept tabs on her as she travelled down the escalator, and headed towards the platform for the south-bound line. When the train arrived, he hopped on after her. The carriage wasn't very busy, so he stood by the doors with his back to where she was sitting. He glanced at her as each station was announced but she remained seated. For nine stops he was braced to move but for nine stops she just sat, apparently lost in her thoughts, idly fiddling with the white folder on her lap yet without opening it. At Victoria she got off and he was right behind her. Once outside the tube station they were absorbed in the multicultural chaos of the London streets. Every colour and creed on the planet rushed towards him, pushing and jostling, seemingly determined to get in his way. She dashed across the road towards Victoria mainline railway station just as a red bus chugged across his sightline. He dodged behind it only to be hooted and yelled at by the driver of a black taxi. 'Trying to get yourself killed, mate?'

By the time he made it to the bustling station, he'd lost her. Dark hair, navy jacket, navy pants – that described half the people swarming onto the concourse from multiple entrances. He looked up at the departure boards. Where the hell was Selhurst? He'd never heard of it. Orpington, East Grinstead, Rochester – the names might have been in Greek for all the sense they made to him. Where the hell was she?

Then he spotted her, running towards the train that was about to leave platform twelve and he hared across the congested concourse after her. The train was already pulling out by the time he got to the gate. He cursed and walked back to the tube station to resume his vigil on Rose Anderson.

*

On the train back home from Victoria station, Suzanne opened the white folder. It contained a credit card-type driver's licence with Rose's address on it, along with a black-and-white ID photo of Don. He looked old, his hair white and cropped short, and his face was considerably thinner than the last time she had seen him. But it was the coldness in his eyes that took her aback. Being required not to smile in these photos transformed even the most benign expression into that of a prison mug-shot glare, but here soulless eyes looked out at her. The light had deserted this man long before he died.

The only other item in the folder was a birth certificate. Donald Albert Tyler, born Liverpool, 1 January 1946. Mother: Julia Jane Tyler. Father: Alfred Herbert Tyler. These were the names of the grandparents she had never met and she pondered what misfortune or twist of fate might have prompted them to place Don in an orphanage.

She logged on the internet as soon as she got home and searched on Google street maps for the address on the birth certificate. What she discovered was a road of terraced houses, each eerily similar to Rose's home in Tottenham. She trawled along the Liverpool street to find the number she sought: fifty-seven. Then a bell rang in her head and she fished out the image of Betty taken so long ago. The house in the picture was almost identical to the one she could see on the computer screen. And due to the angle the picture had been taken from, the number on the door was clearly visible above Betty's pregnant belly: fifty-seven.

The image on the screen showed the house where Don's parents had lived when he was born. Joan had confirmed that he had been married at a young age. So was Betty the first Mrs Tyler? And if she was, then Suzanne wondered why he would choose to photograph his pregnant wife in front of the home that must have held such painful memories for him. She remembered her mother telling her that discerning the truth in Don's lies was like unravelling knotted string. She looked closely at the photo of smiling Betty and noticed for the first time that the door to number fifty-seven was slightly ajar and she could see the outline of a face peering out from the shadow of the doorway. There was only one way to find out.

Suzanne checked the train timetables to Liverpool and, without consulting Mark, she booked a ticket for the next morning.

CHAPTER EIGHT

Rose sat in front of the television. It was a new flat-screen number and, other than her meagre living expenses, this was the only extravagance she had allowed herself from the money she continued to collect every week on Don's behalf. The news of his death clearly hadn't filtered through to whoever was sending the cash and although basically an honest person, Rose thought she might as well make the most of it for as long as she could. Anyway, she needed it now. She had given up her job at the pub. New faces she saw in there made her nervous, as they watched her from behind newspapers, or looked at her for far too long over their beers. They didn't speak, were never served by her, but they were always spying. She had seen one of them behind her in the street and he'd followed her most of the way home. She had become clumsy due to this daily torment, breaking glasses to the extent that her boss had started to take notice. He had claimed she was behaving 'weirdly', then asked if she needed to take some more time off to get over Don's death. 'It often takes a few months for reality to hit home,' he had offered kindly. She had laughed in his face and told him to shove his rotten job up his fucking arse.

'I've never heard you use language like that before,' he said, taken aback by her outburst. 'You're not yourself, Rose. You've always been one of my best workers. Come back and see me when you feel well again.'

Well again? What a laugh. It was Monday, seven o'clock, and although it wasn't yet dusk, she had the heavy curtains drawn tight, with all the lights blazing in every room of the house. Not one dark spot in the whole place. She slept with the lights on too, often not going to bed at night. She'd fall asleep in Don's chair only to be woken up to the early-morning TV twitterings of two fools on a couch.

When she did make the effort to take herself to bed she heard the echo of human activity coming up from below: the creak of the front door, the urgent whispers in the hallway, the soft footfall on the stairs. Every groan of the building gave her the jitters and she'd lie awake with the bright lights searing her eyeballs no matter how exhausted she was. So her preference lately was to eat, sit and sleep each day and night in front of the telly. But even here, with barely recognisable colour images flashing before her eyes and the volume turned up, her senses were attuned to every noise from without, no matter how far away. Shadows of pedestrians on the pavement outside her sitting-room window caused her to hold her breath until they were gone. *One, two*, she counted as they passed, *three, four, five, six…*

If the footsteps halted at her door on an odd number, she imagined hearing a scrabbling knife picking at the lock. Her heart would thud, anticipating a kick that would tear the door off its hinges, sending a rush of air into the room, followed by her murderous assailant. If, however, the footsteps passed the door on an even number, *six, seven, eight*, she breathed a sigh of relief and returned to her own personal kaleidoscope of dancing hues and garbled noise. Police helicopters circling above her patch of the city sent her scrambling beneath her big old-fashioned dining table. She would remain there for hours, long after the sounds had receded, eventually driven out from hiding by the need to pee or the magnetic pull of the signature tune to her favourite programme on the box.

She was aware that this was a bizarre way to live. She'd some-times catch herself about to act on these obsessive compulsions and make an effort to hold back. A trick of the imagination, that's what this is, she'd think. But, try as she might, she couldn't shake the fear. It stalked her, a silent invisible predator, ready to pounce without warning.

She genuinely believed that the pills helped. After glancing across to the row of bottles lined up in precise timeline order on her table, she looked at her watch. She had to take the pink and green one in ten minutes' time. Three of the bottles were from her GP, a kindly man on the brink of retirement, whose glittering golfing trophies took pride of place in his ramshackle surgery. The rest were courtesy of Don's private doctor, a sombre man with a foreign accent, who would dish out anything to anyone – for a price. He was expensive, that one, but hell, she had the money. Don would want her to be well; he told her as much. He appeared to her just out of vision. She'd spot him out of the corner of her eye but no matter how quickly or slowly she turned to face him, he was always gone by the time she got there. Yet his words reverberated and when she sat in his chair, she felt close to him. She stroked the worn plush arm gently, as though to ease him through his final pain. It was a tenderness she had felt but rarely been permitted to show. But she understood and believed he had his reasons. He loved her, she was sure of that.

On Monday at five o'clock – bang on time – the mobile phone on the arm of her chair vibrated. There was a text message with the collection code she had been waiting for. Tomorrow morning she would leave the house with Don's passport in her grey shopping bag and the letter of authorisation written in his own scrawl many months before. She would get on the Tube, or catch a bus, take a taxi or even walk – because she diligently changed her route every time. That was what Don had taught her to do. She'd duck into alleyways, enter a department store through one door and quickly exit by another, pretend to look at goods in a covered market while she surveyed the people walking behind her, convinced that this ensured she had not been followed. Then she would hurry to her true destination and collect the nine hundred and fifty quid from one of the seven Western Union offices she regularly visited in strict rotational order. She would then make her way back by any circuitous route that took her fancy.

'Never be predictable,' Don had told her. 'If they can second-guess you, then you are dead meat, baby.'

So she wouldn't even think about the return journey until she was about to set off for home. Even if she had decided to catch the number 46, she might get on the first bus that came along, no matter how far out of her way it took her. Tube trains offered the best opportunities for losing a tail, by waiting until the doors were closing before nipping off, going to the opposite end of the line, then doubling back. All the tricks of the trade, Don had said. And Don was always right.

*

The morning after the text message had been sent, he saw Rose leave her house, grey shopping bag in hand. Bypassing her usual stop-off at Sainsbury's supermarket, she had hurried off towards Tottenham Hale station and he followed as closely as he dared. She was a very jumpy one. He had noticed that when he had observed her working in the pub, but since she quit that job her behaviour had become even more watchful and skittish. She constantly looked over her shoulder, stopping in doorways every few minutes to survey the street behind her. So he had taken to strolling as nonchalantly as he could manage on the opposite side of the road and that had seemed effective, as she never bothered to glance across the street.

It was rush hour and the train was packed with commuters on their way to their shitty office jobs, sports shoes on their feet, day shoes crammed into backpacks the size of small children. *No wonder these fucking trains are full*, he fumed after being thumped in the chest by yet another bag. These passengers toted more stuff to work than your average US Marine took into combat.

He could just see the top of Rose's head through the troublesome throng. She had somehow managed to get a seat and, unlike all the other passengers who behaved as though they were the only person on the train – reading bestsellers, listening to some shit on headphones and so forth – she looked carefully and deliberately at the faces of her fellow seated travelling companions.

One or two commuters twitched from her scrutiny while others met her gaze momentarily and then looked away. When a woman smiled at Rose, she leapt to her feet and pushed her way to the opening door as 'Next stop Liverpool Street' was cooed by the actressy voice of the on-board auto voiceover. He managed to shoulder the man next to him out of the way and get off at the same station as Rose just as the tannoy announced, 'Stand clear of the closing doors!' He headed for the exit but then spotted Rose standing stock-still on the platform, waiting for the next train to the same destination. He hung around for more work drones to arrive, walked back in with a group of them and stood right behind her as the next train approached.

After that he had found her relatively easy to read. Anything that made her apprehensive caused her to react immediately: to run for the exit, change direction or cross over the road. But she was too nervy and agitated to play this game with much success; this sophisticated form of dodgeball demanded a cool head.

After much train changing she made her way to a large Indian newsagent near Brick Lane. The Western Union sign hung on the wall like an open invitation for muggers but Rose didn't appear to be fazed by that. He thought that perhaps she deposited the cash in her grey old-lady shopping bag so as not to look a likely target. To the casual dimwit bag snatcher her shopper was more likely to contain cabbages than cash. He was looking in the newsagent's window at the postcard-sized ads for local hookers when Rose walked straight out of the shop and hopped on a bus that just happened to stop outside at that precise moment. He had to be quick off the mark to follow that unexpected move.

The bus chugged off and he noticed it was taking them on a route that even he, a stranger to these here parts, knew to be in the opposite direction to her home. He supposed that she might be taking the money to Don Tyler so he stuck with her and, by changing buses and direction every few stops, she led him on a diverting tour around the city, by riding one bus that passed close by the Tower of London. But, other than seeing sights he had not been able to visit since he had been given this lousy job, there was no stop-off for any handover. After a total of five exhausting hours travelling back and forth across London, she was at the door of her little house, her grey shopper clasped tightly to her skinny bosom.

*

Rose gathered up the money she had collected and stashed it in a suitcase on top of the wardrobe. She had made it safely home once more. But the fact remained that if they found out where she lived, they would eventually come for her, as Don had threatened. She glanced across the room to the pile of Don's notebooks neatly stacked in the corner. Ring Suzanne and get her to come and collect them – that was the thing to do. Pass them on and then she'd no longer be in harm's way. Then it could be just the two of them once more.

CHAPTER NINE

Liverpool: European City of Culture 2008, hometown of the legendary Beatles and origin of that often parodied, nasal-cum-guttural accent. Plus the Tate Liverpool and Walker art galleries, slave trading, two cathedrals and 'Ferry Cross The Mersey' – a song Joan loved to loathe. Though less than a three-hour train journey from London, that just about summed up Suzanne's entire knowledge of the city. Which, now she had learned, was also the birthplace of her father. This fact had not been mentioned to her, not that she could recall, and she had never detected even the slightest trace of a northern accent in Don's voice, never mind one so distinctive as Scouse. Maybe he had made a conscious effort to lose it and gone to elocution lessons to cast off the accent along with his past, along with his children.

She looked at the printout from the latest census that she had downloaded from a government website. The only name on the electoral roll for 57 Dryden Street was that of Vera E. Tyler. Maybe the E stood for Elizabeth, hence Betty, or maybe not.

Lime Street station was noisy and bustling, the whole structure topped off with a vast iron and glass roof, presumably dating back to the city's Victorian glory days. The hiss of ghostly steam trains and images of misty-eyed departures in grainy black and white flooded her brain. Once outside the station, she was confronted with a huge neoclassical building on the opposite side of the road that did nothing to dispel her feeling of having stepped into the past. A black cab hove into view and she hailed it.

'First time in the city?' The cabbie weighed her up with that extrasensory ability that his profession instilled.

'What is that building?' she asked as he made a screeching right turn.

'That's St George's Hall. Finest neo-Grecian building in the world.' An air of impatience crept into his voice. 'Thought everyone would have heard of it, even in London.'

The conversation ended there with the cabbie's nose decidedly out of joint.

Dryden Street could have been straight off the set of *Coronation Street*. It was a dreary row of terraced houses with no front gardens but doors that take you off the pavement and directly into the house. Almost a double for Rose's Tottenham home, an irony of Don's life and death that Suzanne didn't wish to dwell on at that moment.

She stood outside and had just grasped the cast-iron lion-head knocker in her hand when the door next to number 57 opened. A woman with greying hair pulled back in a tight ponytail, a cigarette firmly attached to her bottom lip, and togged out in a pink leisure suit, leaned against the doorframe and stared at her.

'Vera's gone to the shops,' she said in a broad Liverpool accent, with a manner that managed to be friendly, nosy and belligerent all in one.

'I'm looking for Betty Tyler,' Suzanne said.

'Are you now?' The woman's face lit up as though she had just been handed a choice morsel of tasty gossip on a platter. 'Best see Vera about that.' She indicated a white-haired woman walking down the street towards them. The woman wore a shapeless beige coat that had seen better days and she carried two bags of shopping.

'That's her now.' The neighbour hurried back indoors. Suzanne could hear her on the phone, breathless with impatience to pass on this titbit. ''Ere, Debbi, you'll never guess…'

The woman in the beige coat halted at the doorstep. 'You looking for me?'

'Mrs Tyler?'

'*Miss* Tyler.' She eyed Suzanne suspiciously. 'If you want my mother then you're twenty years too late.'

'Betty Tyler,' Suzanne said. 'I'm looking for Betty Tyler.'

The woman put down her shopping bags on the doorstep. 'Are you some kind of newspaper reporter?' She took on that slam-the-door-in-your-face expression. 'Because if you are, then you're trawling through ancient history.'

'No,' Suzanne told her. 'My father's name was Donald Tyler and I'm looking for his first wife, Betty.'

'Is that so?' The woman eyed her suspiciously. 'I think you're mistaken, love. I'm his sister and I don't know anything about him having a daughter.' She reached into her pocket and took out a door key. 'I don't know where you got your information from but our Donny lives in America with his second wife and son. He's been there for twenty-odd years.' She opened the door and picked up her shopping bags. 'End of story.'

'Please, Miss Tyler,' Suzanne persisted, unwilling to relate details of Don's demise while standing outside on the doorstep. 'I've come all the way from London. If I have the wrong information then perhaps you can set me straight. I won't take up much of your time.'

'Time?' she said. 'Time is all I've got.'

Suzanne stood for a moment while the woman looked directly at her as though trying to make up her mind. And she may well have told Suzanne to clear off had the nosy neighbour not reappeared.

'Got a visitor, Vera?'

'Okay.' Vera hurried indoors. 'Come in, then.'

Suzanne stepped inside a neat and tidy two-bedroom house, one of those Victorian dwellings originally built to house the poor of the parish. She moved directly into what would have once been termed a parlour, where every stick of heavy dark furniture was polished to a high shine. Vera led her through to another room that contained a sofa, a dining table and a TV, where she took off her coat and hung it up on a hook behind the door, then went out into the small tacked-on kitchen just beyond. Outside was a walled yard where, no doubt, the lavatory was situated.

The room was spotless, though the wallpaper was faded, and it had probably been last decorated in the early 1960s. The floor was covered in ancient lino and a worn rug. On the sideboard under the stairs was a faded black-and-white photograph in a fake silver frame of a young man wearing jeans, a plaid shirt and what used to be referred to as desert wellies. His dark hair was slicked back from his high forehead into a rock'n'roller DA. He smiled back at the camera. Young and slim, this was her father as a teenager.

'I hope you like your tea black,' Vera called from the kitchen. 'I don't have many visitors and I don't drink milk myself. It makes me feel sick.'

'Me too,' Suzanne shouted back to her.

'It runs in our family,' Vera said. 'Our Donny is just the same.'

Suzanne had the photograph in her hand when Vera came back into the room.

'That's our Donny.' Vera set down the teapot, cups and saucers on the big wooden table. 'He never did like having his picture taken, so that's the only one I've got.'

'This is my father,' Suzanne said. 'Younger and thinner than the last time I saw him, but it's definitely him.'

'How old are you?' Vera poured the tea.

'Thirty.'

'Well, I suppose it is possible.' Vera stared at her long and hard. 'And you do have a look of him.' She shook her head as though dismissing the thought. 'But I'm sure he'd have told me if he had a daughter,' she added. 'I mean, why keep that a secret from your sister?' She handed over a cup of black tea. 'No, there must be some mistake.'

Suzanne opened her handbag, took out the manila envelope and placed the picture of Betty on the table.

'Oh.' Vera reached to pick it up. 'I've never seen this before.'

'Is that Don's first wife?'

'Yes,' she said, 'that's her, alright.'

'And the baby?'

'That would be Raymond.'

'Does he still live around here?'

'No.' Vera dropped the photo as if it had caught fire. 'No, he's staying down south somewhere.'

'And Betty?'

'Dead. A long time ago. Where did you get this picture, anyway?'

'It was found in a wooden chest with other belongings.'

'I don't understand.' Vera looked as though someone had just slapped her. 'Our Donny lives in America with his wife Cynthia and his son Jared. They came here for Mam's funeral. His wife was a lovely lady, very dark hair, sounded like that woman out of *Gone With The Wind*.'

'Scarlett O'Hara?'

'That's the one. And Jared was a fine-looking lad, too, about five then, looked just like our Donny.'

'Don told me that all his kids are just like him.'

'When did you last see *your* dad?' Vera asked, clearly still doubtful that he and her brother could possibly be the same person.

'Ten years ago. He came to my studio in London. I was an artist back then.'

'No, you've got your wires crossed.' Vera countered emphatically. 'He hasn't been back to England since Mam's funeral. If he'd been in the country, he would have come to see me.'

'I really can't say.' Suzanne's recollection of her childhood and her father's empty promises came back to her. She had trusted him at the time, just as vehemently as Vera was now asserting her own beliefs in the man. She decided not to pursue that subject any further and return to her own task. 'Do you know *this* person?'

Suzanne put the photo of Sheila in front of Vera.

'Sheila Johnson,' Vera said without hesitation. 'Donny's first girlfriend.' She stopped, apprehensive. 'Was this in that chest as well?'

Suzanne nodded.

'She killed herself, poor thing. Jumped in front of an express train. Our Donny was devastated.'

Suzanne placed the photo of her hippie mother down before Vera.

'No.' Vera shook her head. 'Never seen her before.'

'That's my mother.'

Vera sat down heavily. 'Why don't you ask the owner of the chest about all these pictures?'

'Because he's dead. Donald Tyler died in St Francis' hospital six months ago.'

The harshness of her own blunt statement took Suzanne by surprise. What a cruel way to learn of the death of your only brother. She half-wished that she had never come here, allowing Vera to continue to live with the fantasy of Don's perfect American life.

Vera visibly steeled herself. 'There has to be some mistake. Someone would have let me know.'

Suzanne handed her a copy of the death certificate. Vera stared at it. 'There's got to be hundreds of Donald Tylers in this country.'

Suzanne passed over the birth certificate and driving licence. The colour drained from Vera's face as she scrutinised one document after the other and then back again.

'He's really dead?' No tears though, just a gradual realisation.

'I'm sorry you had to find out this way.'

Vera picked up the photo of Joan. 'She looks like our mam,' she said, half-smiling. 'What with the red hair and all! I remember Mam looking young and happy like that. But that was back when

I was little, during the war. Dad came back from the Navy when I was ten but then he left for good just after Donny was born in '46. Everything changed after that. Mam took to the drink and I had to look after the baby.'

'Did she work?'

'Off and on, but not much. Mainly sat around all day doing her drawings.' Then Vera smiled at the memory. 'Put anything in front of Mam and she could draw it. She did lovely ones of Donny and me as kids. Beautiful they were.' She gazed at Suzanne. 'Did you say you are an artist?'

'I teach art now.'

'You must take after Mam then. I can't even draw a straight line. And Donny – well, did you ever see his handwriting?' She gave a little laugh and then appeared overcome with sadness. 'I did my best for him, you know, but I was only a little girl myself.'

'Tell me about your mother. I'd love to hear about her.'

'She was always a lovely-looking woman. She had lots of boyfriends when we were kids. All those flashy types with loads of money – Uncle Jim, Uncle Jack, Uncle Charlie and the rest. She always made us call them "Uncle". We shared a room, Donny and me, and she used to put us to bed and then go out on the town with these "uncles" and come home roaring drunk. We used to listen to the bed creaking in the next room and giggle about it. Not so she could hear us, mind you. She had a fierce temper, did Mam – especially when she'd had a few. She used to beat poor Donny with a leather strap if he so much as looked sideways at her.'

Suzanne imagined some little boy quaking in a corner while his boozed-up, red-haired mother took out her anger and frustration on him.

Vera caught her concerned expression. 'I wanted to help him, but what can a ten-year-old do?'

'Of course.' Suzanne could almost see Vera, crying at the top of the stairs while their mother laid into her little brother, and wondered how she could still manage to speak of this woman with such obvious affection.

'When we were old enough to realise what was going on in her bedroom, we'd put cotton wool in our ears and try to sleep through it.'

'Did she never remarry, then?'

'You're joking!' Vera responded scornfully. 'Mam had the reputation of being the town bike, anybody's for a couple of drinks and a few bob in her purse. No decent man's ever going to marry someone like that. Not round here, anyway.'

*

Even the most lecherous of men, enchanted by Julia Tyler's titian-haired good looks and reputation for being easy, had her down as trouble. Just one drink too many and she switched from party girl to belligerent harpy. It could happen in the blink of an eye. Laughing one minute then screaming like a banshee, fighting and cursing the next. On such occasions her escort might make sure she got home safely, although he knew there was no chance of a leg-over that night. Other times a gentleman friend would just dump her at the end of her street and hop it pretty sharpish. And Julia would weave her way down Dryden Street, shouting, swearing and singing at the top of her voice.

The only reason the local cops never locked her up for the night was because they knew she had two kids and no husband. Though, with hindsight, it was a shame that the police didn't chuck her in a cell to sleep it off, because the children, Donny in particular, often caught the brunt of her intoxicated wrath when she finally made it back home.

Mercurial as she was, the longer the walk home, the more time allowed mawkish sentimentality to sneak up on her. Few of the neighbours dared to stick their heads out of their windows to admonish Julia on her tipsy stagger back home, only to be told, 'Get the fuck back in, you nosy old cow!' But if that night's beau had been reasonably polite to her (Look, love, I'm on earlies tomorrow. Catch you next time, eh?), or if it wasn't raining, or snowing, or if she didn't catch sight of her inebriated self in a shop window, or one thousand other triggers to her self-loathing violence, then Julia would crawl up the stairs to her children's room, wake them up and tell them how much she loved them.

'You're my world,' she would slur and both kids knew it would be okay, this time.

*

'The drink took its toll,' Vera said. 'She started seeing things in the dark shadows in corners of rooms, and she'd get all panicky. If she dropped off to sleep on the couch, she'd wake up shouting about demons sitting on her. Screaming her head off, "Get it off me, get it off me!" It frightened the life out of Donny. He was often too scared to come down to go to the toilet at night and he started to wet the bed. That made her mad at him and so she beat him even more. I put a bucket under his bed at night so he could go in that and I'd sneak it down in the morning and empty it.'

'I wondered, but did she ever put you in an orphanage?' Suzanne asked. This had been the Don's story to both Joan and to Rose.

'Orphanage?' Vera sounded outraged. 'Mam would never do that to us. For all her faults we were *always* together.'

Lie number one then, no orphanage.

Suzanne was flummoxed by the way Vera clung tenaciously to her mother's one virtue, and decided to change the subject. 'What can you tell me about Sheila?'

'Oh, Mam hated Sheila and called her a little tart. She used to come round looking for Donny when he got the temporary job with that travelling fair. Don't know what happened after that except that the girl killed herself and our Donny stayed on with the fair. He never lived here again.'

'What do you remember of Betty?'

'Donny brought Betty here in '63. He'd met her in Northampton, got her pregnant and they'd been living in his caravan. But she couldn't stay there with a baby, so he brought her here to have the baby until he could find a place for them. Mam was on the wagon then. They got married in the registry office up the road and he went straight back to the fair. I gave Betty my bed and everything was fine until Raymond was born about three months later. He was the spit of our Donny. Mam took one look at him and started drinking again. Betty – she was a really nice girl, was Betty – she got scared for little Raymond's safety and moved back to her own family.'

'What did Don do after she left with Raymond?'

'I was working at Crawford's biscuit factory then and when I got back one day Donny was here. Mam was in a drunken stupor and Betty had been gone for about a month. He wasn't angry or anything. He was silent and – I don't know how to describe it – cold.'

That look on Don's face, the last time Suzanne had seen him: icy and impenetrable.

'He didn't shout or anything. He just went up to Mam's room, gathered up all of her drawings and brought them down here. He looked at them one at a time and then he threw them on the fire.' Vera motioned towards the grate, which now housed a gas fire. 'We had coal in them days,' she said. 'Donny sat down in front of the fire and burned all of the drawings, slowly, deliberately, one by one.'

A shiver ran through Suzanne. More fire… The utter contempt Don had for her own paintings.

'Them drawings were the only things Mam had ever really cared about,' Vera said reflectively. 'And Donny knew that was the only way he could ever get his own back on her. I'll never forget the look on his face as he was doing it.' She grew silent, and every instinct told Suzanne that Vera was recalling how frightened she had felt of her younger brother's disturbing behaviour.

'Did Don look for Betty, try to find her?'

'I don't know. He said that day he wouldn't come back here while Mam was alive. So I never saw him again until Mam's funeral.'

'Can you tell me a little about Raymond, maybe?'

'Well, you see Betty was murdered in 1990,' said Vera. 'You might have read about it? It was in all the papers at the time. They said it was a frenzied attack.'

'What, Betty was murdered? God, I knew nothing about it.'

'Yes. Raymond beat his mother to death.'

CHAPTER TEN

Mark gazed at his wife across the restaurant table, concern in his grey eyes. 'You don't really believe this, do you?'

'I don't know what to believe,' Suzanne said. 'Of the eight women in those photographs, there has been one suicide, one murder and one accidental death. That is what I know so far.'

'None of which had anything to do with your father.' Mark tucked into his lasagne. 'Jilted teenagers often take their own lives, Betty's son is in prison for killing her and Sophie's death was a tragic accident.' He tipped her a knowing smirk. 'Your engaging mother is still alive and well, I notice.'

'Vera reckons that my mother bears a close resemblance to my grandmother, who abused Don. And my father repeatedly beat my mother.'

Mark raised his eyebrows. 'How very Freudian. Although domestic violence is horrible, it doesn't always lead to murder, you know,' he told her. 'Or we'd be up to our necks in corpses.'

'There is more to this.' Suzanne shook her head. 'I know it. I feel it, I am certain of it.'

'Are you sure you're not demonising your father because of his appalling treatment of your mother?' Mark tried to calm her down, doing his best salesman routine. 'Or for his bad behaviour towards you, even?'

'He told my mother he'd been raised in an orphanage.'

'Would you want to introduce your wife to your mad drunk of a mother? Because I wouldn't, not after she maybe drove one girl to suicide and another wife and child away. I'm almost beginning to feel sorry for the sick bastard.' He signalled to the waiter for another bottle of wine.

'Don told Rose he had been in the Special Forces.'

'Delusional,' Mark said. 'No wonder your mother told you to keep out of this. Let it drop, Suze. I blame *Who Do You Think You Are?*' He grimaced. 'I wonder how many of those celebs ripped up their contracts when they found out great-granddad ended his days on the funny farm. Or was hanged for sheep stealing.' He pulled his tie to one side, stuck out his tongue, crossed his eyes and mimed.

'I wish you would take this more seriously.' She pushed her fork aside, her appetite having suddenly deserted her.

'I'm trying to be supportive about this.' Mark poured more wine. 'But I think your visiting this half-brother of yours in the nick is a very bad idea.'

*

To reach Camp Hill prison on the Isle of Wight, Suzanne chose a short hop on a plane from Gatwick and a cab ride from the airport. Originally built in 1912 by convict labour, the prison had been opened by Winston Churchill. It had a chequered history and had been renamed HMP Isle of Wight just two years earlier in 2008. From London the place was not easy – or cheap – to get to by any route but Suzanne had been informed that the majority of the long-term C-category inmates had few relatives or visitors anyway.

The cab pulled into the prison car park and she wondered what it must be like to be incarcerated in this nether world. How different an environment for the men in there to that of the hordes of holidaymakers arriving on this island every summer, or that of the young urban fans and ageing hippies nostalgic for the old days, who made the pilgrimage to the annual live-music festival. How much better to be banged up in a prison on a dark moor somewhere, where normality does not parade past you every day, as a constant painful reminder of what might have been, what should have been. The main gate was reminiscent of a portcullis, the forbidding sight of it conjuring up sounds of clanging doors, rattling chains and heavy footsteps marching along institutional corridors – *Porridge* without the laughs.

Raymond had agreed to see her. Except for the occasional lawyer, Suzanne was the first person to visit him in all of his time behind bars. Despite his greying hair, his face held up a mirror to the Don she knew as a child. He had Don's voice too, deep and resonant, though with a slight northern cadence. Raymond's hand was icy cold when she shook it. They sat in the visitors' room, at a table with four chairs, all firmly bolted to the floor. The whole place smelled of cabbage, of sweat, of grubby laundry and testosterone, and of the perfume wafting off the other females who had come to see their other halves, their sons, their lovers, their brothers, their fathers.

Raymond had been in prison for twenty years of his life sentence. The judge had recommended he serve a minimum of fifteen. However, he had no automatic entitlement to freedom after the set tariff. Release was only possible after the time had been served and when the Parole Board was satisfied that the prisoner posed no further danger to the general public. Raymond had been a model prisoner. He'd taken education courses, become a keen gardener and had never been in any kind of trouble in any of the prisons he'd been held in. But he had never even been considered for parole, for one reason alone: he had always maintained his innocence.

'Confess and say that you're sorry and you get out,' he said bitterly. 'The Home Office has categorised me as IDOM.'

'What does that mean?'

'In denial of murder.' Raymond's tone was matter of fact. 'In the view of the Parole Board, IDOMs are the worst kind of scum, worse than the ones who really did kill someone, so there's no chance for me. I've had prison governors telling me to confess 'cos they know I'll never get out unless I admit it.' His eyes were melancholic but determined. 'But I'd rather rot in here than say I did those things to her.'

*

Raymond had lived with his mother, Betty, and been courting a girl called Margaret, who worked as a shelf-stacker at the local Tesco. He may not have been the sharpest tool in the box but he did have a steady job in a petrol station. At school he had been classified ESN, an acronym for educationally subnormal, which would these days be described in more euphemistic terms such as 'having learning difficulties' but would mean essentially the same. He could read and write but bus and train timetables often had him foxed until they were explained to him. But he was happy enough until he came home to find his mother with her brains beaten in. There was blood everywhere and broken glass all over the floor. Raymond had rushed to his mother's side and held her in his arms. He howled, oblivious to the fact that the broken glass surrounding her body was shredding his knees. Betty's next-door neighbour, who had just arrived home from work, heard the commotion and, seeing the front door wide open, she rushed in, screamed, and dashed back into the street wailing, 'Murder, murder!'

'Call an ambulance!' Raymond yelled to her in a traumatised daze. 'My mum's hurt.'

The ambulance and police arrived simultaneously. The police dragged Raymond away from his dead mother, handcuffed him and pushed him into the back of a patrol car.

'The accused appeared deranged,' a policeman later told the court. 'It took three of us to carry him out of the house.'

Raymond was subsequently charged with murder.

Neighbours interviewed said that, although they hadn't known them for long, Raymond seemed to be a good son to Betty. But one woman told police that she had heard Raymond and his mother arguing on the day of the murder. 'I recognised his voice,' she confirmed, though she was unsure about the time.

Raymond said that he had walked back home across the park at dusk, listening to the birds settling down for the night, watching the moon rising in the gradually darkening sky. He had been looking at his favourite plants, taking his time as he always did in this haven of nature. Customers at the petrol station treated him with disdain, while his boss called him stupid. And his mother was itching to move house again and kept nagging him to stop seeing Margaret. Yet birds never gave him any grief, while plants and flowers made him feel calm with their silent beauty. So he strolled along quietly, taking the air and enjoying the solitude. As the dog walkers had all gone home for their tea, he had the place to himself. Nobody saw him in the park that evening. And no one had caught sight of him walking along the street, or entering the house. His clothes were heavily stained with Betty's blood. The murder weapon, with his fingerprints on it, was his hammer from the garden shed. A long handle used so sadistically in the attack on his mother belonged to the broom Raymond was seen with every Sunday when he swept the pathway at the front of their home.

A neighbour claimed she saw him cast the broom down in temper on the Sunday before the murder, when his mother refused to let Margaret into the house. He had then stormed off with Margaret and shouted to his mother that she would be sorry one of these days.

At the trial, Raymond testified that he had fought with his mum about Margaret, but he had no recollection of the incident with the broom. He said that he loved his mother dearly and denied killing her.

Betty Tyler had been throttled until she lost consciousness. Her attacker then removed her underwear and taped her knickers into her mouth to muffle her screams once she came to. He sexually violated her with a glass bottle, beat her with the heavy broom and then proceeded to bugger her with the handle. Not content with abusing and torturing the terrified woman, her assailant then battered Betty to death with a hammer. 'Frenzied' was the word the newspapers used to describe it.

Son with IQ of 80 Slays Mother in Frenzied Attack!

Raymond sat in the court, heard the evidence, and was shown the photographs of his mother's broken body. He sobbed helplessly. On hearing the distressing details of her violent assault and death read out in the cold grey morning light of a Crown Court, Raymond sat with his knees tucked under this chin, his handcuffed hands gripping his ankles as he rocked back and forth, repeatedly chanting, 'I'm sorry, I'm sorry.'

It took the jury a little over three hours to convict Raymond of his mother's murder.

*

Although the information Suzanne had gleaned from her research on the internet had given the basic facts of the case, to hear Raymond's side of the story was far more revealing than the sensationalist newspaper reports she had seen. But one detail perturbed her. 'Why did you say you were sorry?'

'Mum was always telling me to hurry home from work, but I didn't that evening. I dawdled in the park. If I'd hurried up, I might have been back in time to save her.'

Suzanne was sure that this was the Derek Bentley case all over again – 'Let him have it'. The final verdict of the jury had hinged on what that remark had signified. Was he urging his younger accomplice to hand over the gun to the policeman? Or was he telling the other youth to shoot the cop? Bentley was hanged. Likewise Raymond's heartfelt cries of 'I'm sorry' were wide open to misinterpretation when taken out of context. Plus, the evidence against him appeared to be largely circumstantial and uncorroborated, from Suzanne's point of view.

'Did you ever meet our father?' she asked him.

'Never,' he said. 'Mum was scared of him. That's why we moved house so many times. I lost count in the end. She'd get a job in a factory and rent a house close by. I'd go to the local school for a year or so and then we'd move on again.' He sighed. 'I never had time to make friends, and any I did make she wouldn't allow to come in the house. I was always bottom of the bottom class, the teachers all thought I was daft, and had me down as one of the thick ones.'

Unsure of what to say and deeply touched by his story, Suzanne reached across the table to his cool hand, which he withdrew swiftly.

'They don't allow touching.' He motioned towards the uniformed prison officer sitting in the corner of the room, whose watchful eyes scanned inmates and visitors alike.

'Sorry,' she said. 'I'm new to this.'

'I don't know why you've come here.' He sat back in his chair, appraising her, bemused and suspicious. And she couldn't blame him. She couldn't begin to imagine the horror of what it must be like to lose the sole parent you knew, only to be wrongly accused of her murder and then be incarcerated indefinitely for all these years. She looked across at the man before her and wondered just how he had retained his sanity.

'When I was first inside,' Raymond said, as though he had tuned into her thoughts, 'I went over that day in my head, again and again until I thought I was going to go mad. But when I was still A-category, one prison doc said I had to let it go and get on with whatever life I could have, read books, do lessons, get an education. "Use the time to improve yourself," he said. So that's what I did.' His sad, flickering smile almost broke her heart but then his frown was returned. 'But he's still out there.' He paused and looked Suzanne in the eye for the first time. He had Don's eyes – Don's eyes but without the malevolence. 'The person who murdered my mum is still walking free.'

Looking dejected and pensive, he continued. 'And you still haven't told me why you've come here.'

'I wanted to meet you,' she said, looking at him, hearing him, believing him. Now she knew why, now she understood what had drawn her here. 'And after what you've told me, I'd like to try to help you in any way I can.'

'Why? Why now?'

'Because you're my brother.' The words came out before she even considered their implication. But that was the bond that she felt: *This man is my brother.* Suzanne was aware that this was the response of a formerly self-contained only child of a busy working mother; that of a little girl who had always envied her friends' unselfconscious closeness to their siblings. And she had to admit her underlying jealousy of Mark's relationship with his brother Luke, which emphasised her sense of something missing in her own story.

Raymond's bottom lip quivered and he bit it, cleared his throat, leaned forward and shook his head. 'There's no new evidence,' he said. 'And without new evidence, I am in here forever.'

'Did you tell your lawyer that Betty was intimidated by Don and that she took all those measures in the hope that he wouldn't find her?'

'Yeah.' He grimaced. 'But my brief discovered that our dad was living in America with some rich woman, together with her kid. That was confirmed by the lawyers in the States, so after that, nobody listened to me. The police were convinced I did that to Mum. They had me and they weren't interested in looking for anyone else. They kept hitting me to force me to confess, but I refused. They called me a pervert, a spaz, a mong.' He clenched his fists. 'Which to them meant subhuman.' He smiled briefly at this point, obviously not an expression his face was accustomed to. 'But I showed them. I've got O-levels and now A-levels.' The smile faded as quickly as it had appeared. 'Not so stupid, after all.'

*

Mark wasn't very sympathetic. 'The jails are packed with "innocent" men.'

'Even if that claim of innocence denies Raymond ever being granted release on parole? That he'll remain in prison for the rest of his life?'

'Maybe some of Granny's genes are kicking in there. There is clearly some kind of mental problem in that family. You're on a hiding to nothing here, Suze. You should just let this drop.'

'Well, I believe him and he is my brother.'

'Genetically speaking, he's your half-brother and you've only met him the once. So you owe him zilch. I know I supported you when you wanted to investigate but this is a step too far. Do you really need a convicted murderer in your life? You must be crazy. I suggest you get out of this while you can.' He reached out and touched her hand. 'I'm your husband, Suzanne, and I don't want you hurt in any way.'

'Or is that just the policeman's brother talking?' she snapped at him and withdrew her hand from his. The only time he ever used her full name was when he was doing his paternal act and it pissed her off no end. 'Sergeant Woods' precious little boys sticking together because, as we all know, cops are never culpable of nabbing the wrong person.'

'It takes a jury to get a conviction,' he retorted.

'Depending on the evidence presented to them.'

'He'd have had a lawyer.'

'Yeah, right. Some overworked solicitor appointed by the court on a no-win case against a traumatised simpleton who sexually abused and killed his own mother. Not much mileage there, is there?'

'That's the sort of case they defend, isn't it?'

'With the media breathing down their necks, sensationalising the case. And the neighbours, who didn't know either of them very well, sticking in their two-penn'orth just to see their own names in the paper.'

'Well, at least you can't try to pin this one on your father,' said Mark. 'He was well out of it in the USA.'

'There are such things as planes, you know. Vera told me she thought Don was in America when he was actually at my studio in London. Who the hell knows where he was at most of the time.'

'Jesus Christ, Suzanne! You're becoming obsessed.' Mark could not conceal his frustration. 'So he was violent towards your mother. That's not good at all, but it doesn't make him a murderer.' He banged his fist on the table. 'Your father's dead and you're trying to portray him as some monstrous kind of psycho killer. It's not healthy. It really isn't.'

CHAPTER ELEVEN

'You've got to come now.' Rose's voice sounded otherworldly and far away. 'The doctors want me to go into hospital. They say I'm clinically depressed. But I know they're lying to me. They want to get me out of the house so they can come in and search it. You've got to take all of Don's things before they get here.'

It took Suzanne an hour and a half to get across London by which time an ambulance and a police car were parked outside Rose's place. She could hear Rose shouting blue murder from within the house. Her frantic voice echoed down the street. The neighbours were out of their houses milling around, rubbernecking, gossiping and laughing about the 'loony'.

Two paramedics leaned against the side of the ambulance, chatting to each other amiably, all casual, as though deranged women were part and parcel of their everyday routine. You think this is freaky, their stance seemed to say, you should have seen the one this morning. A young uniformed police officer and a stocky bald man in a brown suit stood at Rose's door and both turned to Suzanne as she approached.

'Where is Rose?' she asked the policeman.

'Are you a relative, miss?' the constable asked.

'Yes,' she lied. 'She's my step-mother.'

'I'm her GP,' said brown-suit man. 'This was all arranged with Rose yesterday. She agreed to enter hospital voluntarily but now she won't come out.'

'Is that Suzanne?' Rose's voice from the bedroom window.

'Yes, Rose, it's me.'

The window opened and a key landed at her feet. 'Only Suzanne!' Rose warned from above. 'Anyone else and I'll slit my throat. I've got a straight razor here.'

'I think you should allow us to go in,' the doctor said.

'Has she been sectioned? You can't just cart people off to mental institutions against their will.' However, Suzanne knew that if Rose's behaviour was considered to be a danger to herself or to others, this doctor could easily have her sectioned as an emergency, thus depriving Rose of what little freedom of choice she had left.

'No, this was originally to be a voluntary admission,' the doctor said. 'But…' He glanced up at the white and anxious face peering out of the window above.

'I know all about the "but". So to save you all the hassle and the tedious paperwork, let me try to talk her down.'

'Leave the door open, miss,' the young policeman advised. 'And if you have any trouble, just shout and we'll be right in.'

'There won't be any problem.' This was her attempt to sound more confident than she felt as the thought of Rose lurking upstairs, all wild-eyed and wielding a razor struck her just as she stepped across the threshold.

Rose was sitting on the stairs, her eyes more teary than wild, with not a blade in sight. Suzanne sat beside her and put her arm around her shoulders. It had been less than two weeks since she had last seen Rose but the woman seemed to have shrunk into herself in that short time. In fact, Suzanne could feel Rose's shoulder blades protruding from beneath her pink cardigan.

'Have you not been eating?'

'They've been trying to poison me,' Rose said. 'But I fooled them. I only eat tinned stuff. You can't poison that.'

'Very clever,' Suzanne said, for want of a better response.

'Don taught me that.'

Oh great, one more up for Dad, eh? Well done, Don, you evil bastard.

'You're not well, Rose.' Suzanne hoped Rose wasn't about to deny it and take fright again, thinking Suzanne was on the side of the bad guys.

'Keep that house key.' Rose calmly got to her feet. 'I'll go with them now. But you must take the books and the money.' She leaned down to where Suzanne was still seated on the stair. 'And all his keys,' she whispered. 'Then it will be okay for me and Don to come back again. We'll be happy then.' She smiled broadly. 'We'll be safe.'

Suzanne watched Rose walk to the door and take the doctor's arm, just like a shy young girl with her sweetheart on their first date. Together they walked towards the ambulance. Rose meekly climbed aboard and beamed at the paramedics.

Suzanne followed her to the rear door of the ambulance. 'Where are you taking her?' she asked the doctor.

He handed her a card that read Redstone House, Borehamwood, Herts. Suzanne pictured the place, out in the countryside, just an hour's drive from London.

'I take it you are Suzanne Woods?' The doctor scrutinised some forms he had taken from the ambulance. 'She has you down here as her next of kin,' he said. 'She'll be sedated for a while though. They'll get in touch with you once she's ready to receive visitors.'

*

Suzanne placed the card with the address of Redstone House on the dining table and set about searching the house, although nothing she told herself could dispel the feeling that she was intruding as she rummaged through Rose's scrubbed and polished home. They were virtual strangers, yet Rose, poor vulnerable soul that she was, had given Suzanne permission to go though all her cupboards, wardrobes and drawers. And she was looking for what, exactly?

Well, Don's notebooks for one, as they had disappeared from the corner where she had neatly stacked them after she'd taken them out of the wooden chest in the hallway. The chest was as bare as she had left it. Downstairs, the cupboards contained the usual domestic paraphernalia such as cups, pans and the like, yielding nothing of interest. She went upstairs to the bedrooms. Wardrobe one drew a blank. It was empty, though she had expected to find Don's clothes in there. Rose's wardrobe, meanwhile, was filled to bursting with clothes, many of which seemed very dated, and Suzanne smiled to see a slightly worse-for-wear feather boa, which had the look of a half-plucked purple chicken about it. Even in its pomp it was not an item she could imagine that poor soul now being hauled off in the ambulance ever wearing. *There but for fortune*, she thought. Clearly, there was no room in that wardrobe for any notebooks. Nothing under the beds either. She had begun to despair when she glanced up, and there, on the top of the wardrobe, were three suitcases.

The first one was so heavy that it slipped from her grasp as she tried to haul it down and it hit the floor with such a thump that the bed did a little jig and one of the framed seascape prints on the bedroom wall came crashing down.

She clicked the case open and there were the notebooks. She closed it up again and wondered how in the hell she would be able to carry it to her car. But it was the contents of the second large case that was the revelation. For inside, neatly stacked and bound together with those red rubber bands that postmen like to discard on people's doorsteps, was money. More cash than she had ever seen in one place, in bundles of fifty-pound notes. She sat on the floor aghast. This must be the money that Don lived on. She had a vague recollection of Rose saying that someone paid Don in cash but at the time Rose's behaviour was so unhinged that Suzanne didn't really take it all in. Perhaps it was true that Don had been involved with some shady organisation.

She looked up at the smaller case remaining on top of the wardrobe and with a sense of trepidation she took it down. This contained a mobile phone and charger, a blank matt-black plastic swipe card and a large key. Also inside were Don's passport and a letter written in his hand, authorising Rose to collect money on his behalf. Tucked into the bottom of the case was another envelope; it was so small that she almost overlooked it. Inside was a note in what might have been Don's handwriting. It simply read AC371.

Suzanne went downstairs, took her mobile phone out of her handbag and rang Mark.

CHAPTER TWELVE

He watched the ambulance arrive, heard that crazy Rose hollering from the bedroom window and saw the slim, dark-haired woman turn up.

The last time this woman had visited Rose Anderson, she had taken a white folder with her. He had followed her to the tube station as instructed, but she vanished into the chaos that is Victoria Station at rush hour.

'I lost her in the crowds,' he had explained on the telephone but had not been let off the hook – not that he expected to be.

'Stay with Anderson,' she told him. 'And don't mislay this one.'

He hadn't, but tailing her closely had got him nowhere, apart from a circuitous trip around London. Since that day things had become more bizarre. Rose had stopped going to the shops and he wondered how she was managing to feed herself. Nobody called on her and there were no deliveries of groceries or anything else at all. A guy in a Royal Mail van turned up one morning and banged on her door, but she didn't open up. The one trip she did make was to her doctor's surgery and she appeared to be crying as she walked back home.

Then today happened, with all its screeching high drama, and afterwards he was at a loss as to what to do next. He decided to wait until dark and break into the house to search the place. Then he saw the slim brunette double park her car outside Rose's house and emerge with two suitcases. She had already sprung the boot when he ran across the street towards her.

'Let me help you with that, ma'am.' He flashed her what the lassies called his devastating smile.

'Thank you.' She barely looked at him. Although he had seen her only twice before, he wondered why she seemed so familiar. She was good-looking enough, with her shoulder-length brown hair and hazel eyes, and she looked just fine in her blue jeans and white shirt. She was certainly attractive but nothing special. So what was it?

'You could give me a hand with this,' she said, her voice warm, syrupy and very English. And she started to drag a huge and heavy battered suitcase out of the house. 'It might take two of us to lift this into the car.'

The case bumped over the doorstep and when the hinges sprang open, Don's notebooks spilled onto the street. One of the books fell open to reveal his semi-literate scrawl.

She gathered them up and haphazardly stuffed them back into the case. 'Old school books,' she said dismissively.

But just a glimpse and he knew. *This is it*, he thought, as he helped her load the overstuffed suitcase into her car. *This is what I've been sent here to find.*

*

She thanked him and drove off with her car boot full of what he wanted, so he sprinted to his own vehicle and set off behind her. At the corner of the street, which was less congested than usual, one motorist let her into the main flow of traffic but he had to wait for another two vehicles to go past before pulling out himself. He was sweating with the strain of tailing her, not having a clue where she was heading, while also coping with lunatic London drivers.

At one point, after crossing one of the bridges over the Thames and somewhere around Elephant and Castle, he found himself in the wrong lane with his quarry right next to him. He cautiously glanced across at her, praying she didn't do the same, but she appeared to be lost in thought. He indicated left and the motorist behind her red Alfa waved him into that lane. He raised his hand in thanks and breathed a sigh of relief.

Once out of the centre and into the suburbs, she was easier to keep track of, though she sailed through one set of traffic lights just as they changed on him. He'd have chanced it and accelerated through were it not for an enormous yellow truck, transporting flowers from Holland, which lurched across the lights in front of him. No point getting killed. He'd never hear the last of it.

Anxiety set in when he was finally free to speed off after her and there was no sign of her red car. Not really hard to miss, but he couldn't spot it. He drove along the main drag slowly, much to the annoyance of a white van man, who was gesticulating and roaring obscenities behind him. So he hit his hazard lights and the van chugged past, belching black exhaust fumes in a fart of disgust.

Eventually he saw her car parked by the side of the road in a tree-lined street opposite a railway station. Saved!

The house was one of those Edwardian two-storey buildings, with gables, sash windows and an open porch, though the front door had been painted a fashionable battleship-grey. In the driveway stood an old dark-blue Mercedes. *A husband or boyfriend would complicate matters*, he thought. *I'll have to be more careful.*

CHAPTER THIRTEEN

Mark sat on the floor in the living room. It was his day off and he was unshaven, wearing a grey T-shirt and jeans. He sat cross-legged, yoga-style – a position he claimed helped his posture and alleviated the back injury he had received playing rugby. Suzanne had a go at him about that, saying rugby was too risky at his age.

'Someone in your business should know better.'

Okay, so he was thirty-four now, and he knew all about injury cases, seeing the claims made each day. And he was ridiculously well covered, as there's nobody easier to sell insurance to than an insurance salesman. But he had stopped playing rugby anyway. Just to please Suze, he told himself.

Mark had one of the suitcases open and was systematically counting out the money onto the stripped-pine floorboards.

'Forty-two thousand, four hundred,' he declared, wrapping the last bundle with its red rubber band and glancing at his watch. 'Shall I ring Luke and tell him I can't play tennis with him today?'

'No,' she said. 'You don't see your brother often enough as it is.' Suzanne was very fond of Luke. After all, if it hadn't been for him she would never have met Mark. Luke had been devastated when his wife divorced him and took their son, little Marky, to live with her new 'daddy' in Ireland. Luke had started drinking then and it was only Mark's fraternal support – persuading him to go to AA meetings and urging him into playing tennis – that had saved his reputation, his job and his health. 'You should go,' she insisted, 'I'll carry on here.'

Mark stood up and collected his gym bag from the cupboard in the hallway. 'Maybe Luke can find out if your father had a criminal record,' he called through. 'You never know what might come up. Money laundering, maybe, or a payoff of some kind.'

'Via Western Union?'

'Stranger things have happened.' He came back, sports bag slung over his shoulder, and kissed her on the top of her head. 'But really, it's just to protect you, Suze,' Mark said. 'And if there is no evidence of any wrongdoing, then I reckon this little stash is yours.' He reached down and grabbed one wrapped bundle of notes, threw it in the air with one hand and caught it with the other. Then he tucked the bundle under his T-shirt, laughing. 'Ours,' he chuckled gleefully, wringing his hands, Fagin-style. 'Or mine, all mine.'

'It's perfectly legit to have cash, or have it sent to you,' she said, playfully wrestling the money off him. 'Though I don't fancy my chances of paying an amount like this into the local branch of my bank without a lot of questions being asked.'

'Maybe he just didn't trust banks,' Mark said. 'And who can blame him?'

'But I haven't found a will of any kind. He died without making one it seems, so I suppose I should go and see a solicitor or something.'

'What's the point? You're his next of kin as far as you know.'

'There's Raymond and, from what Vera told me, there's Jared in the States, maybe a wife.'

'Well, Raymond can't do much from a prison cell. Maybe you could use this money to get a private investigator to look into his case.'

Suzanne felt cheered by the suggestion. 'So then, are you coming around to the idea that he's innocent, too?'

Mark smiled at her. 'You believe it, and that's all that matters to me. And, ultimately, whatever you decide to do with this little windfall, I see it as being all down to you. Besides, you've got no information on this Jared character or his mother. As far as I understand it, you don't need letters of administration, because your dad's estate is what we see before us. No cars or houses, no business assets. *Nada*.'

'Forty-plus grand in cash, a mobile phone and this card thing and key – not much to show for sixty-odd years, is it?' Suzanne sat on the floor and looked down at the sum total of her father's life.

'There are the journals, of course. Might be a good read.' He nudged her with his elbow, all Monty Python. 'Eh, eh? Might be a bestseller. Eh, eh?'

'The ramblings of one sick fuck, more like.'

'Let's have another look at that card.' Mark picked up the blank plastic swipe card and examined it, then scrutinised the key and the envelope containing the code. 'You know, I think this lot is from one of those private safe-deposit places.' He smiled, pleased with himself. 'And I think I know which one…'

*

He was watching the house as a tall guy came out. Around six feet three, good-looking, with dark-blond hair and wearing jeans and a T-shirt, he looked like someone who worked out. The tall guy got into the Mercedes, backed it out of the driveway and was off down the street.

He decided to follow the Merc, hoping to find out who exactly the driver was, only to see it pull into the police station car park minutes later. He followed it in and cruised by the building, trying to look as though he had driven in by mistake. He watched the tall guy take the steps two at a time, greeting a cop in uniform, and they both laughed, then entered the building together.

He pulled into a free space and called her. *She'll know what to do*, he thought, *she always does*.

'How long has she been at home?'

'Thirty minutes max.'

'Not long enough to read everything.' He could hear her taking short breaths.

'Then why go to the cops?'

'I don't know, but it may be something unrelated.'

'Maybe he is a cop?'

'And maybe he's just paying a parking fine.' She sounded irritated. He kept quiet. It was always best not to antagonise her, or get her too overheated. 'But we can't take any chances,' she said finally. 'You have to get a hold of those notebooks.'

'And Tyler?'

'This woman might know where he is. Get the information. Do what you have to. Whatever it takes. Understand?'

He understood only too well: do as you're told and don't ask questions. That was the way it had always been.

He parked his car and walked purposefully down the high street. If there was one thing he had learned from being so long in this miserable country, it was that newsagent stores were the hub of the crap-selling universe. Their windows were always plastered with ads scribbled on white postcards and advertising everything from babysitting services to out-of-date stereo equipment. He found one shop, apparently run by a bored-looking woman wearing a sari, with a heavy woollen cardigan draped around her thin shoulders – the remnants of the British Empire writ large. He scanned the cards in the window: 'Swedish Massage', 'Baby Pram, Almost New', 'White Ford Transit For Sale: 2,000 pounds or nearest offer'. Bingo! He rang the number on the card and the voice at the other end of the line sounded just a little too eager. It was definitely a case of 'nearest offer'. From what he'd been told, Tyler wasn't the kind of guy he could confine in a saloon car. He'd need a vehicle he could transport him in securely on the journey. This might just be it.

He drove to the antsy vendor's home straight away. The guy was a hard-luck case whose wife had recently run off and whose light removals world domination plan had been curtailed by the dire need to pay a huge mortgage without a second income coming in. Mom had drummed it into him that a soft heart was indicative of a soft head, so he had beaten the guy down by waving a bunch of fifties at him and refusing to go any higher than fifteen hundred. The guy had caved.

Now lumbered with two vehicles, he decided to abandon his rental car in a side street. He still had three months left on the lease, so nobody would be looking for it until he failed to return it, by which time this entire mess could be over and done with. He wiped the steering wheel clean, took a package out of the glove box and placed it in his holdall, which he then slung over his shoulder.

The van owner, having handed over all the documentation, would be dismayed to learn later that the van's new owner hadn't re-registered it. By the time the owner's documentation had been processed, the van would have been disposed of. 'But I sold it, for cash,' he would tell police when the registered owner of the burned-out wreck was finally tracked down. Yeah, life can really be shit for some people.

He cruised around in the van until he found the right spot: Banstead Common, a vast swathe of parkland edged by large trees, but still close to the A217 road back to London and the motorway. And, very conveniently, just half a mile from where she lived. This was it. He drove the van off the road following the churned-up grass tracks of some farm vehicle that had recently passed that way – perfect for disguising tyre markings in all that mess. Once he reached the trees he left the tractor trail and slowly backed the van under the cover of the dense overhanging branches. Satisfied that the van could not be seen from the road, he set off on foot back across the grass.

CHAPTER FOURTEEN

'Sheila' Tommy Roe, 1962. Sheila, typical Liverpool girl, not so much as a feel-up until you say I Love You – my first and worst shag. Forgotten all about her until she turns up at the funfair and catches me shafting some slag. She goes mad, tells me she's up the stick and will run and tell my mam unless I marry her. I tell her to fuck off.

Mam calls her a tart and throws her out of the house then lays into me. 'There's one too many bastards in this house already!'

Sheila keeps coming to the fairground, saying she'll be showing soon and she'll have to tell her dad. And when she does he'll come round with her older brother and batter me. So I sneak off the fair on the Friday night when it's busy and nobody will notice me skive off for a bit. I go to her house with a bunch of flowers, the cheapest ones on the stall outside the railway station. Sheila's mum and dad are down the pub and she's on her own. I tell her that we should get married and she is really happy. She's walking me back to the fair clutching the freesias like they're made of gold. We're crossing the railway bridge. It's dark, and some of the streetlights aren't working. I get her to sit on the wall of the bridge above the track. She's laughing as I get down on one knee to propose. I can hear the express train in the distance. She's saying something like, 'Oh, Donny, this is so romantic.' I grab both her ankles and tip her over the edge, straight onto the railway track below. She doesn't fight or even scream. I chuck the flowers over after her and, seconds later, the express hits. I can hear the train braking in the distance as I leg it back to the fair.

Suzanne felt a pressure behind her eyes, her heart was thundering and her head buzzing. She stopped reading, she felt faint. This was the slim young lad smiling out of Vera's silver frame. This was Donald Albert Tyler. This was her father.

I cried when the police interviewed me. 'Poor kid.' I heard one of them saying. 'He must have been really fond of that girl.'

Suicide, they called it, but I had a permanent hard-on for weeks after and I took it out on any slapper who'd let me slip it to her.

No remorse, no claims of this being an accident, no excuses. Just the recollection of a sexual thrill. Suzanne looked at the photo of Sheila again, in her flared skirt, white stiletto heel stuck in the mud, and found it hard to dismiss the image that insinuated itself into her brain; the sudden tumble from the bridge that ended in a body mangled beneath the wheels of a train. It seemed so unreal. Was this fiction, the last act of self-aggrandisement, the final lie?

I kind of got a taste for it after that. The next one is a skanky thing, around fourteen, coming on to me as I'm spinning the ride. Just her and her friend in the car, the fat one – there's always a fat friend. The other one, the skinny little skank, has a stained yellow jumper on and she pulls it up over her tits, flashing them at me, twisting her nipple inside her grubby bra.

'Get rid of your mate,' I say to her above the poofy sound of Mark Wynter singing 'Venus in Blue Jeans'.

'Why?' All innocent.

'Because she'd put me off.'

The skank almost puts me off on her own, with the tidemark on her neck and funny musty smell to her. Says she'll only do a hand-job behind the caravan. 'But you can do me proper in the woods later on.'

And she's hanging around when we close down at two in the morning. They're packing up and moving the fair on to Northampton tomorrow, so everyone's running around like blue-arsed flies. And me and the skank are walking into the woods and she's gabbing away about a haunted pond, about some fair maiden in the Middle Ages preferring to drown rather than be ravished by the king's men. And she's laughing. 'That's why I like to get fucked here,' she says. 'One in the eye for prissy virgins.'

But there is something spooky about the place. The water is still, silent and dark. The wind rustles through the trees but she doesn't seem to feel whatever it is that's lurking there, watching us from the dense bushes. She lies down at the edge of the pool, takes off her knickers and pulls up her skirt.

'Drown her!' it whispers to me.

So I'm up her, fucking her hard and slowly pushing her closer to the edge, until with one more thrust her hair is in the water. That's when she takes notice and starts to fight me, so I pull out of her and sit on her chest, her arms trapped between my thighs. I've got my hands round her throat, holding her head under the water, and I come on her as she finally stops struggling. I shove her body into the pool and chuck her shoes in after her. And I walk back to the fair. But I'm not alone. Whatever was at the Silent Pool comes with me.

Suzanne felt like the stunned victim of a hit-and-run but did her best to try to reason it out. Maybe this was some kind of a masturbatory fantasy. If it was, then it was pretty sick. But if not, then when was this, where was this and who was the girl? Suzanne looked at the front of the notebook again to see what he'd written on the cover: 1962–63.

And what was all this stuff about something watching him? Vera had told her that their drunken mother used to see demons in dark corners. *Mark may very well be right*, she thought. *Maybe there is madness in the family.*

There were three more in all. Derbyshire, the New Forest and Carlisle. Woods and forests are good places, with lots of animals, foxes and the like, to devour the bodies. I came and they went.

She read that last sentence and a chill overcame her. She could visualise the grin on Don's face and hear his mirthless laugh. Her skin prickled with the gradual realisation that this was no fantasy – this was real. He did all of this. What she was reading was the last confession of a dying man. She took a deep breath and continued.

Some family out on Sunday walkies found the skank floating in the Silent Pool. The fat friend told the police that earlier that night Brenda had gone off with me so they came to Northampton to question me. I said, 'Sorry, don't know any Brenda.' And I didn't, I'd never asked her name. They showed me her photo, one of her in her school uniform. 'She wasn't dressed like that then,' I told them. 'But when I realised she was just a kid I sent her on her way.' The other lads told the police I was helping to pack up the fair later on. Then the cop let slip that he thought she'd been drinking and tripped into the water and drowned. Her dad used to knock her around, the cop said, so she'd go to the Silent Pool on her own to get away from him. Just another useless girl nobody gives a flying fuck about. Anyway, that was the last I heard of it.

Appalled and distraught, Suzanne tried to catch her breath. The words in her father's spidery scrawl were weaving into crazed patterns before her eyes. As an excuse not to resume reading, she began sorting them into date order, stopping to search for anything that included 2000, the year of Sophie's death, apprehensive about what she might discover.

The phone rang and she jumped with fright, then calmed herself with the thought that perhaps Mark was on his way back home.

'Mrs Woods?' The voice asked. 'I am the chaplain at HMP Isle of Wight. Your brother, Raymond Tyler, has been admitted to our hospital wing and has asked me to contact you.'

'Is he ill?'

'Raymond was involved in an incident with another prisoner. He was seriously injured but his life is no longer in immediate danger.'

'What happened? How badly hurt is he?'

'He was severely beaten. But he's being well cared for.'

'But Raymond is a model prisoner.' Suzanne was overcome with a sense of guilt that her visit may have disrupted Raymond's equilibrium. 'He's never been in trouble before, has he?'

'No, he hasn't. He wasn't responsible for the attack. But sometimes, when others learn the details of a prisoner's offence…'

'This kind of thing has happened before, hasn't it?' Raymond hadn't mentioned intimidation or aggression from other prisoners to her but, deep inside, she knew.

'There have been other such incidents over the years, yes.'

Suzanne told the chaplain that she would visit Raymond as soon as possible and finally put the phone down. It had never occurred to her before but now it seemed obvious: the assault on Betty had been so horrific that Raymond was an easy target for any violent psychotic scumbag to take out his grievances on. She imagined the jeers of 'Pervert' and 'Motherfucker'. And along with the taunting, there would have been the physical confrontations and the violence he'd had to endure over the years. Her heart went out to him. She now felt a sister's obligation to get him out of there. Hopefully these notebooks held the truth.

*

Half a mile from Banstead Common, in what he now knew to be the woman's tree-lined road, the old Merc was nowhere to be seen and her red Alfa had been moved from where she had parked it on the street. He searched the immediate vicinity, wondering if maybe she'd gone out too. But then he saw, hidden behind the tall hedge at the front of the house, her car in the driveway. How very obliging.

He walked up the drive and clicked the latch on the high wooden gate at the side of the house. It wasn't locked and he walked through, cautiously easing it closed behind him. He tried the kitchen door and found that too was unlocked. He opened his sports bag, took out the black cotton drawstring bag and stuffed it into a pocket of his jeans. He jammed the handgun into his waistband, dropped the bag outside the door and walked into the kitchen.

*

Suzanne hoped Mark would return home soon. She was sitting on the floor, searching through the notebooks piled up beside her, when she heard a sound behind her and felt relieved that he must be back at last. She desperately needed to share what she'd read with him and get him to understand how urgent it was to find the evidence needed for her brother's case to be reviewed that might lead to his subsequent release.

She heard movement behind her again. 'I'm in here, Mark!'

*

At the sound of her calling, he followed her voice into the bright sitting room, where the French windows were open and the breeze from the garden filtered through the room. She was sitting on the floor, surrounded by the notebooks. A couple of suitcases, with currency in neatly banded bundles, were piled on the seat of an easy chair. She didn't turn around, assuming he was this Mark character. Just time enough to whip out the cotton bag, shove it over her head and pull the drawstring tight around her neck.

She gasped and her hands went to her throat, but he pulled the gun and pressed the muzzle against her head.

'I will shoot you if you scream, or struggle, or do not do exactly as I say. Do you understand?' he said.

'What do you want?' Her voice sounded measured, as though she was weighing up the situation. She was a cool one.

'No questions. Just do as I tell you.'

'What *do* you want me to do?'

'When I remove the bag, you will put everything belonging to Donald Tyler back into the suitcases. Then we will carry them to your car and take a little drive.'

'Where to?'

'You are going to take me to Donald Tyler.'

CHAPTER FIFTEEN

Suzanne's mind was racing. *He doesn't know where Don is*, she realised. *If I tell him Don's dead and he believes me, he may just take all the stuff and leave me alone. Or, because I am no longer of use to him, he may kill me. But if I follow instructions then where do I take him?* She took a breath and the fabric of the bag caught in her mouth. She gagged.

'I'll do whatever you want,' she said. 'But please take this off me, I get claustrophobic.'

The bag was roughly pulled from her head. The good-looking young man from Rose's street, the one who had helped her with the suitcases, was standing in front of her. He pointed a small handgun directly at her chest. Suzanne didn't know anything about guns but this one looked real enough.

'Sit on the sofa and keep your hands together where I can see them.'

'Look,' she blurted out, 'I don't know who you are and I don't want to know. So, please, just take what you need and go.' A cliché straight out of a hammy old movie and she might have laughed, had her heart not been thundering in her chest. Seeing guns brandished on television is one thing but confronted by the genuine article, up close, was more threatening and menacing than she had ever imagined.

'I can't do that.' He had an American accent. She hadn't noticed that before.

'I hardly knew Donald Tyler.' She could hear her voice quivering. *Get a grip*, she reminded herself. 'But you won't find him.' She made one of those crossroads decisions that could seal her fate. 'Because he's dead.'

'What the fuck! Think I'm stupid, do you?'

'He died five months ago.' Suzanne pointed to the white folder on the dining table. 'You'll find his death certificate, driving licence and passport in there.'

He went over to the table and Suzanne considered trying to make a run for it but quickly decided against it. A bullet could travel faster than she could. *Mark, please come home*, she pleaded silently. But if he did come back suddenly and it all turned nasty, someone might get shot. Maybe it was better to try to handle this alone.

He opened the folder with one hand and took out the documents. 'Why have you got all of this, if you hardly knew him?'

'I'm his daughter.' She hoped that telling the truth was the best way out of this.

'Stay where you are,' he ordered. 'Sit on your hands and don't move.'

He crossed the room, stood behind the sofa and made a call from his mobile.

'It's over. He's dead.'

He listened for a moment as the person on the other end replied.

'I've got them here,' he said. 'I don't know, maybe the mad woman?'

Suzanne recollected Rose's warnings about people stalking her. She'd been driven to a nervous breakdown by her fears and Suzanne hadn't believed her. Here was positive proof that 'they' really did exist.

'She says she's his daughter.' He paused as the other person spoke and Suzanne wished she'd listened to her mother's advice about not getting involved.

'I don't think that's a good idea.' He sounded unsure. 'That wasn't the plan.'

*

He instructed Suzanne to write a note to her husband. It read:

Marky. I have to get away for a few days to get my head round all this stuff. I'll be in touch soon. Love you. Suze.

'He'll want to know where I'm going.'

'Nice try,' he said. 'Cell phone?' He was looking around. 'Tyler had a cell.'

Don's mobile phone, the key and blank swipe card were in the third case. She explained that she had put it in a cupboard in the hallway.

He frowned and made a sideways gesture with the gun. 'Then get it.'

Suzanne moved to the hallway, pulled out the case and opened it, then, with her left hand, she slid the key and card into her jeans pocket, and returned with the small case along with the mobile phone and set them down on the sofa.

He seemed uncertain but satisfied. 'Anything else in there?'

'No, nothing.' She tried to sound sincere. She'd never been a very convincing liar, but he appeared to believe her.

'Pack some overnight stuff in there and we'll be going.'

He followed her upstairs with the gun at her back. He watched her closely as she put underwear and a couple of tops in the case that she had placed on the bed.

'Hand me that, will you?' She pointed to a jacket that she had left on the back of a chair.

He turned to get it and she quickly slipped the card and key out of her pocket and secreted them under the pillow on Mark's side of the bed. She prayed he found them quickly.

Her car was in the driveway behind the hedge and hidden from view of the road. He helped her load the suitcases into the boot and told her to drive. He slid into the passenger seat beside her and she backed the car out into the road, trying to keep calm, willing Mark to appear – but there was no sign of him. Right now, all she could do was follow instructions. 'Make a left here, now a right.'

She had to stop the car at a pedestrian crossing and Mrs Jones from number 14 began to cross. She glanced at the car and gave a friendly little wave of recognition. Suzanne saw Mrs Jones eyes flick to the passenger side and the abductor lowered his head. He grunted as Suzanne waved back to her.

'She's a neighbour of ours,' she explained. He grunted once more. 'She would think it odd if I didn't acknowledge her. I don't think she noticed you, though.'

'Makes no difference,' he said darkly.

She considered putting her foot down hard on the accelerator, imagining herself driving full pelt at a brick wall then jumping free when the car crashed. *Who do I think I'm kidding?* she thought. *I'm not Bruce Willis.* And, anyway, the traffic in the road was too heavy to get up to even ten miles an hour. She contemplated putting her hand on the horn to draw attention to her plight, but feared he might shoot her if she tried a stunt like that. She decided to bide her time, maybe slide out of her seat belt, accelerate when she got a chance and jump out of the car at speed. But did she have the guts to do that? Her mind was doing somersaults as she tried to concentrate on driving and think out a plan at the same time. Her car was almost sideswiped by another car that she hadn't noticed coming out of a turning.

'Watch it,' he said.

'You try driving with a gun pointed at you,' she snapped back.

He gave a snorting laugh that reminded her of someone but she couldn't recall who.

'Just concentrate.'

Minutes later, in only slightly lighter traffic, they were passing Banstead Common. He instructed her to turn off the road and head across the grass towards the trees.

CHAPTER SIXTEEN

He held Suzanne at gunpoint and told her to sit at the back of the van. He produced some rope and ordered her to tie her feet together with it. After checking to see it was tight enough, he forced her to turn around, and bound her hands behind her back.

'Shout and I'll tape your mouth shut so you can hardly breathe. It's nothing to me whether you make it to the other end alive *or* dead. Try to escape or draw attention in any way, and I'll blow your head off.' He glared at her. 'Got that?'

'Yes,' she said as he pushed her down onto a couple of stinking duvets on the floor of the van. 'You are itching to blow my fucking head off.'

'Smart mouthing is another one.'

When he slammed the van's door, she was immediately engulfed by darkness, the only light seeping in through scratches on the blanked-out back windows.

She felt dazed, as though sleepwalking through some parallel reality. It was only when the doors closed out the outside world that she began to comprehend the danger she was facing.

She was sitting on the reeking duvets and the stench of mildew was overwhelming. When her eyesight adjusted to the darkness, she could see off-cuts from threadbare carpets, plus several tattered and stained bedsheets scattered about the floor, and a tarpaulin coated in dried mud. The van looked as though it belonged to someone who did light removals. Beside her was the suitcase filled with Don's notebooks while the other case held the few clothes she had been able to pack. Her abductor didn't appear interested in the case containing the money as that had been slung carelessly into the back of the van as though it was of no worth.

She took a deep breath and tried to reason this all out. If it wasn't the money this guy was after, then it must be the notebooks and whatever information Don had written in there. What he had wanted initially was for her to take him to Don. It seemed she had been brought along almost as an afterthought when she'd told him that her father was dead. And proof of that was in the white folder he had placed in the suitcase with Don's notebooks. So what did these people want *her* for?

The chilling description of the murders of those two girls flooded back into her mind. There was his pregnant girlfriend, thrown from a bridge into the path of an oncoming train and the poor sad young girl from the fairground, who'd been sexually abused and drowned. Could her kidnapper and his boss – for he was clearly following instructions – be cohorts in these deaths? Yet from the descriptions, both killings appeared random, stemming from a personal madness on Don's part combined with his deep-seated loathing of women.

Suzanne recalled what Rose Anderson had told her about her own relationship with Don. '*I don't think I ever really knew him.*' That vulnerable woman had been convinced that she was being followed. And she'd been right. Even though Rose had been emotionally damaged by her encounter with Don, she had survived it, which was more than any of the others appeared to have done. In Sheila's case, Don had confessed in the diaries to pushing her off the bridge. But what of the others, who were they? There was Betty, supposedly battered to death by her own son, Raymond, who was still insisting on his innocence even after all those years in prison. But then there were the women in the other photographs. The inference in the stories Don had told to Rose was that he was paid by some clandestine organisation. Just because he seemed to be a natural-born killer didn't mean that he hadn't been recruited by people who could exploit his particular talents to their own advantage. Sophie's parents had run an import–export business in Hong Kong that could have made them a target for someone. Suzanne had met the parents briefly at Sophie's funeral and they appeared to have come to terms with the fact that their daughter's death had been a terrible accident. But what if there was much more to it? Suzanne wished now that she had been braver and forced herself to read Don's journal from around the date of Sophie's abrupt demise.

Suzanne's father's face materialised in her mind, and the way he had behaved the last time she had seen him. It was her one and only adult memory of him and she thought of it with disgust. There was his peace offering of flowers, the cat and mouse games, the leering grin that had turned to charm personified the second Sophie had appeared on the scene, only to vanish when Suzanne had been alone with him. His joking about not being able to tell her what he did for a living or 'I would have to kill you'.

This was the stuff of movies – this wasn't real life – not *her* life. But the van was real enough. She could feel every bump, every lurch each time the driver hit the brakes. Then she noticed he had not been braking hard for a while, so it was probable that they were out of the London traffic, maybe on a motorway. She was losing track of time and not being able to see the world outside was making her feel travel sick.

The gun had been real too, at least genuine enough not to chance making a run for it. Although, from what she had read over the years in various newspaper and magazine articles, it was worthwhile risking injury attempting to escape before reaching the abductor's destination, where torture and death might await you in their lair. She decided at that point, come what may, she would make a bid for freedom.

CHAPTER SEVENTEEN

Mark Woods arrived home just after seven. He was steering his old Mercedes into the driveway when he noticed that Suzanne's car was not parked on the street, or in its usual place just behind the hedge. He assumed she'd popped to the shops, though he did find it annoying that she'd left the gate to the rear garden ajar. How many times had he told her not to do that? How embarrassing would it be for the house of a policeman's brother to be burgled? *Bloody women*, he groused, as he opened the front door. She hadn't even double-locked it.

He went to the kitchen to make a coffee. The outer door to the garden was also open. He banged it shut and locked it. *Sodding hell, woman*, he swore under his breath. *What are you thinking? All this Daddy crap has gone too far, you're way too involved. And leaving doors open with all that money in the house, do you think that Luke's badge makes us immune?* He was still seething when he carried his coffee to the sitting room.

As he made his way along the hallway, he glanced up at the painting Suzanne had recently completed. *The Garden*, she had titled it, but it didn't look anything like a garden to him, just a smattering of green splodges with a few red and blue spears sticking out of them. In his view, it resembled a psychedelic hedgehog.

When they had first started going out together, Suzanne had dragged him around all the art galleries, explaining this and that in detail until he was cross-eyed and muddle-headed. It had been quite a relief for him when she got the teaching job. To his practical mindset, it was far better for her to be working at the local high school, earning a good salary, with long holidays and a pension. The same went for his brother: policemen got early retirement and an index-linked pension, which made for valuable perks nowadays. What do artists get? Not a thing worth having as far as Mark could see, apart from a wall full of weird-looking wildlife. So he had never really encouraged Suzanne to take up the brush again and it pissed him off that she had. But, to be fair, he did work a lot in the evenings, seeing prospective clients in their own homes, and Luke's ex was a perfect example of what women get up to when left to their own devices – they find another man. So maybe he should be pleased that Suzanne had got back into all the arty-farty stuff. Better that than going out on the town with recently divorced friends. He gave the hedgehog the finger and walked into the room where he had last seen Suzanne sifting through the diaries of her deranged father.

Everything was as it had been when he had left but the notebooks were gone, along with the suitcases. And there was no sign of all the money he'd counted out so diligently. She must have tidied it away before she went out, he assumed. Yet that big suitcase was far too heavy for her to bother moving on her own. He looked in the hall cupboard where she had previously stashed the smaller suitcase that held the phone, the key and the unidentified swipe card. That was gone too. A feeling of unease settled on him. Then he saw the note on the coffee table and, with a sense of relief, he picked it up and started reading.

The name Marky jumped out at him. Never had she called him that. What the hell was this about? And where was she going? Her mother? To visit her long-lost aunt in Liverpool, perhaps? Then why not say so? Disturbed beyond his immediate comprehension, he ran upstairs to root out her passport. She always kept it in her top drawer and it was still there but her everyday handbag was missing, along with her purse and credit cards. It appeared that she had taken a few clothes with her but he couldn't be sure. Their luggage was still there, though.

This was wrong: it felt wrong, and it smelled wrong. He sat on their bed, not sure what to do next. He had carried her note upstairs with him and he read it again. *Marky*. That was the name everyone called Luke's kid, the son who had been taken away from Luke by the boy's mother. Mark wanted to laugh at himself for being so dramatic about what may well have been just a slip of the pen, but the feeling in his gut was churning. Joan? Maybe Suze had gone to see her mother? He picked up the phone.

'No,' Joan told him, 'Suzanne hasn't been here. I haven't spoken to her for days.' But she sounded worried. 'Is she still investigating her father's affairs?'

'Yes, she found his notebooks and money in the house he was staying at.'

'I always tried to shield Suzanne from the madness of Don's life,' Joan said. 'This seems as though he is reaching out to her from beyond the grave.'

From beyond the grave indeed. *The woman's demented*, Mark thought. But best not panic her. 'I'm sure she'll ring me.' He tried to sound calm. 'It's probably just a misunderstanding. I'll let you know when I hear from her.'

As he said goodbye to Joan, he remembered the mobile Suzanne always carried in her handbag, and tapped out the number. The phone rang three times then switched to voicemail. Suzanne's husky tones caressed him, something that usually gave him a warm feeling inside – but not today.

'Suze, where are you?' Mark said into the ether. 'I'm worried. Please ring me as soon as you get this message.'

He rang her friends and her colleagues but nobody had spoken to her recently. He finally telephoned Luke at the police station. He was off duty by then and Mark reached him at home, in what Luke laughingly called his 'bachelor pad': a one-bedroom sparsely furnished apartment in a modern block just a stone's throw from the police station.

'What do you mean, missing?' Luke demanded. 'She left you a note.'

'Addressed to Marky. When have you ever heard her call me that?'

'Have you two had a fight?'

'No, I'd have told you if we had. And all that stuff, the notebooks and money that I mentioned, that has gone too.'

'Maybe she needed to read them in private.'

'She left all the house doors open.'

'Oversight. You said yourself that she was distracted.'

'This doesn't feel right at all, Luke.' Fear replaced unease, like the darkness that was gathering outside as evening was overwhelmed by night. 'Isn't there some way you can help me?'

'Give me her car registration and we can report it stolen tomorrow, if you want to.' Luke offered. 'But if she's just gone off on her own to think for a while and is hauled in for stealing her own car, then I reckon yours will be the next divorce in the family.'

Luke's joke at his own expense did nothing to assuage Mark's anxiety. 'I really don't know what to do next. Suze doesn't behave like this.'

'Hold on, didn't she go off to Liverpool without telling you?'

Mark recalled carping to his brother about that. No dinner on the table and when she finally did get home, all the earache about this aunt she never knew and all the stuff about her mad dad.

'Yes, she did,' he admitted. 'But she rang me when she got there.' And he had blasted her, he remembered, made a big row out of it. He swore he would never do that again. Right now, he just wanted to know where she was and that she was okay.

'Then she might do the same when she gets wherever she's going.' Luke paused, the concerned brother switching roles with the sceptical copper. 'Try calling her again. Then you just have to sit it out. If you haven't heard from her by the morning, then you can decide about the car.'

'Can't I report her as missing?'

'Look, Mark,' Luke said calmly. 'There is a missing persons' process but it's far too early to go down that road. You can make a report before forty-eight hours are up but that is generally in exceptional circumstances. We're not talking about some vulnerable old person or a young kid here. This is Suzanne, a happily married teacher, sound of mind and body. And, let's not forget, she did leave you a note.'

'But that doesn't feel right either,' Mark persisted. People go missing every year, around two hundred thousand in the UK alone, he had read somewhere. That's probably the equivalent to the entire population of Newcastle. How many were found? Maybe he should report Suzanne as missing. But then, if his own brother wasn't taking him seriously, what would he get from other police? They'd probably give him the same advice that Luke was handing him.

'Do you really want my esteemed colleagues tramping all over your house?' Luke asked. 'Sifting through your bank account, monitoring your phone records and talking to your neighbours? I'll tell you straight, I wouldn't want that, not unless it was absolutely vital. So sit it out, Mark. And if you haven't heard from her by the morning, report her car stolen. That's the quickest way to get results. But you didn't hear that from me.'

CHAPTER EIGHTEEN

Suzanne had been in the back of the moving van for what seemed like three or four hours when she felt the urge to pee. She was unsure what to do. She considered sliding to the cab end of the van and kicking the panel behind the driver's seat. But he had warned her not to make a noise. *Mark, where are you?* she thought desperately. *Have you recognised the clue in the note? Have you found the key? Have you informed Luke? Have the police found my car? Are you looking for me? Pull yourself together*, she told herself. *Whatever Mark is doing, you're on your own right now and you'll have to do whatever it takes to survive.*

Her need to pee became too great. The duvets smelled horrible enough without wetting them. With her heart thundering, she decided to take a chance and began to shuffle on her bottom towards the front of the van. She hoped to find some chink in this guy's armour, to appeal to any humanity he may possess. She reached the front, her bladder aching, and banged the back of her head against the side.

'Shut the fuck up!' His voice was muted through the metal and the hum of the road beneath the van. 'Or I will kill you.'

'I need to pee,' she shouted back.

'Like I should care.'

'I won't make any trouble. Just let me get out to go to the toilet.' No response.

'You don't want me to soil your nice van now, do you?' The comment slipped out before she could stop herself. *Oh, you bloody fool,* she thought, *you sound like a schoolmarm talking to a six-year-old. Now he is going to come back here and shoot you.*

After a few moments he called back, 'I'll pull off the road and you can take a piss in the bushes.'

She felt the van taking what she imagined to be a slip road off the motorway. It lurched as it rounded a sweeping bend then it slowed down, driven cautiously, almost crawling along before pulling bumpily off the tarmac road. She heard the sinister noise of branches brushing against the top of the van, trailing their wooden fingers along the sides. This was not what she had in mind. She'd supposed he might pull off at a motorway services. She almost laughed at her own naïvety. *Idiot! You thought he'd allow you to waltz into the ladies' loo alone and maybe write messages in lipstick on the mirror, nip out the back way or scream for help.* Of course he'd get off the road, to stop in a secluded spot where she didn't know the territory and there was nowhere to run.

She didn't have much of a clue where they were. The van had been on what she calculated to be a motorway for far too long to be travelling south or east because they would have reached some kind of destination by now. She guessed they were heading north or west. Plus it was getting chilly in the van. She remembered a time when she'd gone to Birmingham, accompanying Mark on some boring insurance conference. The minute they'd stepped out of the car, the temperature had been several degrees cooler than it had been in Surrey, even though it had been the middle of a summer afternoon with the sun still high in the sky. She decided that they were probably heading north.

The van stopped and she heard him slide the driver's door across. Seconds later, he opened the back door. It was pitch-black out there. He had turned off the headlights but in the hazy moonlight she could see that they were parked in a small clearing surrounded by trees.

'Move forward,' he said evenly, pointing the gun straight at her. 'I'll untie your hands and you do your feet.'

She shuffled forward, her bladder bursting, feeling the wet beginning to leak into her jeans.

'Don't make me regret doing this,' he said, 'because I *will* shoot you.'

Once she was unbound and out of the van, he shoved her towards the encircling trees and she began to shake with a fear she had never experienced before. There was a distinct possibility she was about to die in this remote place.

Was this supposed kindness a mask for sinister intentions? He was going to rape and kill her, just as her father had done to those girls. *Three more*, Don had written, *there were three more after the young girl at the Silent Pool. Derbyshire, the New Forest and Carlisle. Forests are good places*, he had commented, with all the clarity of an unhinged mind, *with lots of animals – foxes and the like – to devour the bodies.*

Those words reverberated in her brain, carved into the gnarled wood of every tree surrounding her. Still she walked on, with the gun muzzle pressed hard against her spine, into the darkness.

CHAPTER NINETEEN

Suzanne stumbled towards the trees. The terror of being raped and killed was so palpable that she had been psyching herself up to make a run for it. Better a gunshot in the back than whatever horrors might lie in wait for her at the end of this journey.

'Here is fine,' he said. 'Get on with it.'

She unzipped her jeans and squatted. He held the muzzle of the gun to the back of her neck. The metal was cold against her skin. Was it some kind of sick game he was playing? Would he shoot her with her pants down and walk away laughing? Waves of fear coursed through her body, bile surged into her throat and she could hardly keep her balance because her legs were shaking so much. The emotions were so physically powerful that she felt sharp pains in her chest, so distressing that, had she not been at bursting point, she may well have not been able to pee at all. And yet she was fearful of evacuating her bowels at the same time. Fight or flight, one reaction to extreme anxiety is for the body to lose all its excess waste, so as to be lighter and able to run faster. But she was neither fighting nor fleeing; she was behaving like a compliant little victim and that idea rankled. As though she wasn't humiliated enough, she was crouching down in front of this stranger. She began to wish she had just pissed herself in the van and had done with it.

'Have you finished yet?'

It was such a relief to hear his voice, to not hear the click of the gun being cocked, that she felt tears welling up. *Keep control, you have to get yourself out of this. The cavalry is not going to come charging over the hillside, and helicopters will not swoop to the rescue. Your survival is all down to you.* With her heart thundering, she reached out sideways as though to steady herself, scooped up a handful of soil and slipped it into her pocket.

'Stand up,' he ordered. 'Pull your pants up and let's move.'

She obeyed him, zipped up and prepared to walk back to the van. She felt the gun barrel pressed against her lower back. *Do as you are told*, her practical mind said. *Screw that!* She reached into her pocket and purposely stumbled to her right, turned around fast and chucked the handful of earth into his face.

'What the fuck!' Caught off-guard, his hands jerked upwards to protect his eyes.

Suzanne bolted, charging through the trees and deeper into the woods. She expected to hear a gunshot but none came. She'd taken him by surprise but that was her only advantage. He was younger than she was and he looked fit enough to catch her in a straight chase. The dry leaves and twigs beneath her feet crackled and snapped with every step she took, giving her position away. Her one hope of escape was to find a place to hide. She hurled herself at a large holm oak, its wide trunk split by centuries of animal excavation, one lower branch jutting out at right angles. She managed a foothold and hauled herself into the safety of the evergreen leaves, praying the branches didn't give way under her weight.

She heard the van's engine start, saw the lights illuminating the trees and realised that he was using them in an attempt to track her. She saw him silhouetted against the headlight glare as he made his way through the trees. She tried not to breathe. He was coming straight towards where she was hiding. Was he looking up? She wanted to close her eyes, like a child who believes that if you can't see your pursuers, they can't see you. She resisted the temptation and watched as he searched the area below her.

Then he turned and walked deeper into the woods. Why didn't he shout to threaten or cajole her? And she couldn't understand why he hadn't fired a shot when she ran. She held tightly onto the branch directly in front of her, and twisted slightly to see where he had disappeared. She could hear movement but it was too dark to see much, apart from some lights in the distance. She strained to peer through the gloom. The warm glow was coming from a house at the other side of the woods, maybe just a few hundred yards away. That's why he was keeping quiet, so as not to draw the attention of the occupants. If she could just get to that house she could phone the police. Without warning there was a sound from beneath her tree. Suzanne froze, not daring to move, holding her breath, fearful that he might hear the pounding of her heart. But he was walking away, back towards the van. She took a breath and waited. She heard the driver's door slide open, the engine roar, saw the headlights dip, and she watched as he backed the van out of the clearing. This was her chance to get away. If she acted fast, made it to that nearby house and called the police, they'd be able to find the white van, and the journals. She climbed down carefully and cautiously made her way in the direction of the house.

She was walking through the remnants of what was once a proud forest, now possibly a preservation area on part of some farmer's land. The moon gave scant illumination but just enough for her to pick a pathway. She stopped, too scared to breathe as something scuttled away ahead of her. Startled, and with her pulse pounding, she held her resolve by attempting to reassure herself that it was probably just a fox or a badger. She could see the lights of the house through the trees. She was almost there. There was a dirt road just beyond the wood. A traditional thatched-roofed cottage stood at one end but, with no streetlights, it was too dark to see what lay in the other direction. She assumed it would be an unadopted country lane that led back to the motorway.

The lights of the cottage whispered to Suzanne of safety but with a wire fence dividing the edge of the wood from the garden of the house, she had to break cover to get there. She hoped that her abductor had given up on finding her and driven away. Just another hundred yards and she'd be at the cottage. Suzanne stepped out of the trees and onto the dirt track.

'You nearly blinded me, you bitch!' His fist came out of nowhere and she was felled.

*

Suzanne woke up with a jolt as the van took a wide bend at speed and rolled her over, face down. Her mouth had been taped shut and she found it hard to breathe. She lifted her head off the foul-smelling duvets. Her ankles had been bound together the same as before but he had secured her hands in front of her body this time. She instinctively looked at her left wrist, but her watch was no longer there. Her abductor had compelled her to remove it and leave it in the glove compartment of her car, along with her mobile phone. Surely they must have found the car by now, abandoned beneath the trees on Banstead Common. Perhaps they were searching the woods at this moment, believing her to be wandering around drunk or drugged. Maybe they were dragging the local ponds right now, whatever time this was. Though it was still night as far as she could make out; there was vague illumination from the headlights behind that she could just about discern through the two square blanked-out back windows. She felt that they must have been travelling for at least ten hours, which suggested they were heading very far north, to somewhere in Scotland perhaps.

*

The van was slowing down and she guessed they were no longer on the motorway. The drone of other traffic had gone now and all she could hear was the sound of the van's engine and the tyres on an uneven road. Images from horror movies of tortured bodies and screams for mercy unheeded in the wilderness filled her mind. *For fuck's sake*, she chided herself, *pull yourself together and think.* Her wrists were raw from her attempts to loosen the knots, because the more she struggled the tighter the rope became. This guy must have been in the fucking Sea Scouts. The van stopped, then rocked slightly when he got out and she listened to the clank of metal gates being opened. Moments later he was back behind the wheel and they were off once more, on a gravel road, she assumed, as stone chippings clattered against the sides. After what seemed like miles, the van pulled to a halt, the back doors opened and he was standing before her once more, gun in hand.

'Out!' he ordered with a jerk of his head.

She shuffled on her bottom along the floor. He tucked the gun into the top of his jeans and untied her ankles. When she looked up, she noticed they were parked in front of an imposing country house. A chink of dim light escaped through a heavily curtained downstairs room but the rest of the building appeared to be in total darkness. Suzanne shivered in the cold early-morning air and glanced over his shoulder. Dawn was breaking across a vast lawn and she could see tall pine trees in the distance. Scotland seemed likely, then – with nowhere to run and nowhere to hide.

He spotted her scanning the horizon. 'Keep your eyes on the ground,' he said.

The main entrance to the house was at the top of a short flight of white stone steps but there was a door to the side at ground level and he shoved her towards it. He opened it up and pushed her inside. When the light was switched on, she found herself in a small windowless room. It looked like some kind of servants' quarters, with a small wardrobe, a single bed and a chest of drawers. There were only two ways out: the door she had been steered through and another at the back of the room. He noticed her looking at it.

'Don't bother,' he said. 'That will take you down to the cellar and there's no way out of there. This house is thirty miles away from the nearest village.' He ripped the tape from her mouth and she winced. 'So you can shout until you're hoarse but nobody will hear you. You'll just annoy the person upstairs. She'll make me come back down here to shut you up.'

'And you'll blow my fucking head off!'

His response was to untie her hands.

'Please, just tell me what this is all about. Why have you brought me here?'

'You'll be sent for.'

He closed the door firmly behind him and she heard the key turn decisively in the lock.

*

Mark repeatedly phoned Suzanne's mobile until he fell asleep in his chair. By 11 p.m. he was wide awake again and ringing hospitals, his mind filled with scenarios of car accidents, with his unconscious wife unable to tell them who to contact. But every enquiry drew a blank.

At 4 a.m. he finally went to their bedroom. He slept on Suzanne's side of the bed, breathing in the fragrant scent of her hair from her pillow. He slept fitfully, alert to every night-time sound the house made: the wind through the trees in the garden, the clatter of a fox or cat raiding a nearby dustbin. He awoke at 6 a.m. to the sound of a phone ringing and sat bolt upright, wide awake in seconds, only to realise it was coming from the house next door. He sat in bed, staring at the telephone on the desk beneath the window, willing it to ring, but it remained silent. He lay back down and realised that his pillow was damp. He had been crying in his sleep. So he moved back to his own side and, as he plumped up the pillow, his hand touched a metal object. Throwing his pillow aside he found the key and the envelope containing the code number together with the black swipe card.

These items had been in the missing suitcase, so why would they be under his pillow? Now he felt certain that something was amiss, that Suze had been trying to tell him that she had left under duress. This was the evidence he needed.

Mark jumped out of bed, grabbed the telephone and called Luke. Maybe *now* his brother would believe him.

CHAPTER TWENTY

By nine that morning, Mark and Luke were sitting in Luke's car, parked in a busy road in South Kensington. The road was lined with small yet swish upmarket shops selling overpriced clothes, a few deceptively modest white-stucco houses with a price tag of at least five million quid each, pricey restaurants and an art gallery that Mark remembered Suzanne dragging him to way back when. It had been one of those art show openings where everyone stood around with a glass of champagne clamped in their hand pretending to understand what the hell the artist was on about. At least, that was his recollection of the evening, added to the fact that he couldn't wait to get out of there.

Luke had found a parking space almost directly opposite the safe-deposit-box building and Mark looked across at the barrier of its smoked-glass doors and discreetly barred windows.

'You sure this is the one?' Luke asked.

Mark turned the anonymous swipe card over in his hand. 'I'm positive. One of my clients stashes all his important papers in this place. I gave him a lift here about a year ago. I glimpsed his card then and it was identical to this one.'

Luke scanned the piece of paper with Don's scrawl across it: AC371. 'This looks like a box number to me. But you still have to get into the building with that.' He indicated the swipe card. 'There'll be a PIN. Any idea of what that might be?'

'His birthday?' Mark ventured.

'Bit obvious for such an otherwise over-cautious man.'

'Well,' Mark said, 'I could try it.'

'You've got to be sure. I don't know how many chances you get with these cards. A high street bank gives you three before the machine snatches it back.' Luke shook his head and instantly reminded Mark of their father with his grey eyes and hangdog expression. 'But these places may be even more security conscious. You might only get the one go, and after that have to show identity to prove the box belongs to you.'

'My client used his wife's birth date.' Mark said. 'Maybe Suzanne's father did the same.'

'Which wife, though?'

'Joan,' Mark decided. 'Suze once told me that when she last saw her father he had asked about Joan. He seemed obsessed with her. I'm going to try her birthday: November 1951, I'll bet money on it.'

'Well, I hope you're right the first time,' Luke said. 'I don't want to have to try to blag our way in using my warrant card. This isn't my manor and I'm sure anyone manning the door over there would clock that right away and get suspicious. If they insisted on seeing a search warrant, that could land us both in a whole world of shit.'

Typical, Mark thought. *Play it by the book, Luke – just like Dad.* To be fair, his brother had come along to provide moral support, although he hadn't allowed Mark to report Suzanne's car as stolen. He'd made dark warning noises about it being an offence to file a false police report.

'I could lose my job and my pension for going along with something like that,' Luke had said.

'Then why did you suggest it?'

'Moment of madness.' Luke told him that he'd put the idea forward to give Mark something to hang on to when he was beginning to sound desperate. 'Look, I've got time coming to me. I'll take a few days off and help you.' Luke's grey eyes showed genuine brotherly concern so Mark reckoned he was as solid as, well, those smoked-glass doors their gaze focused on.

The brothers got out of the car and crossed the road together. Tall, muscular Mark matched the image most people had of a police detective whereas his shorter mousey-haired brother had the look of a permanently worried accountant – or bank manager. So much for typecasting; this would never be the case in the movies or on telly. Mark would be the good-looking, all-business professional, not the guy bricking it as he was doing right at that moment. Luke would be the plain, hero-worshiping sidekick, following along and hanging on his guvnor's every word. That had always been how the brothers were perceived, even by their own father, but the reality was something very different.

The machine positioned by the doorway to the safe-deposit company glowered defiantly from the recess in the wall. Its screen was blank. There was no welcoming greeting, no customer-friendly promo or sales blurb, not even instructions for use. There was just a slot for the card and a numbered keypad.

The black card was swallowed greedily, almost snatched from Mark's fingers in its haste to unmask him. The screen remained blank until a fuzzed-out upper-crust voice from an unobtrusive speaker beside the forbidding glass door instructed, 'Please enter your code number now!'

Mark took a deep breath and tapped in 1151, then waited with sweat trickling down his neck. The screen leapt into life as four large stars appeared in the middle of it, twinkled briefly and then vanished almost immediately. The machine spat back the card in apparent disgust and much to Mark's relief the smoked-glass doors slid open silently, expelling a gust of cool air-conditioned superiority from the interior.

An elegant grey-haired man stood behind the desk in the small foyer and didn't even look up as the brothers entered. His eyes remained fixed to his own monitor as he busied himself with whatever it was he did all day.

Mark and Luke breezed past him, with Mark trying to appear as though he had been in there a million times. Luke was much more casual about it and Mark surmised that his brother's nonchalance came from his experience of walking into unfamiliar situations and taking control. Luke headed for the stairway and Mark followed him; it appeared to be the only exit and he assumed it would lead down to the vault.

'I've opened the door for you, gentlemen,' the man said in refined tones, as they reached the top of the stairs. 'Please close it firmly behind you and press the bell on the wall once you have finished. If you wish to have more privacy, please take your box to one of the cubicles provided.'

The stairs ended in another small, softly lit foyer containing a large antique-finish leather sofa and a coffee table with the latest issues of *Horse & Hound*, *Vanity Fair* and *Vogue* artfully fanned out on its polished walnut top. To the right, the heavy copper-coloured vault door stood open. They entered. Inquisitive CCTV cameras surveyed them from all sides as they walked along the narrow corridor between banks of locked and numbered metal boxes slotted into the walls.

Luke casually glanced once more at the code written on the paper in his hand, and ambled along the lines of boxes, checking the numbers. The smallest boxes were AA, while AB were medium sized, enough to contain papers or jewellery. However, the AC prefixed boxes were much larger, the size of a suitcase. Mark found number 371 and turned the key. The box was at knee height and he pulled it out fully. Sensing it was heavy, he and Luke carried it together into one of the small cubicles. Once inside, Luke drew the curtain across and they were concealed from the prying eyes of CCTV. Mark opened the steel lid.

The box was filled almost to capacity with money, in stacks of fifty-pound notes all carefully bound together. Mark whistled at the sight but Luke put his finger to his lips and breathed 'Shh!' There may have been no CCTV in there but he appeared concerned that they might be overheard. This box was not their property to be tampering with. Luke took some latex gloves out of his pocket and slipped them on. Mark raised an eyebrow but stood back in the confined space and let his cautious brother get on with it.

A large white envelope lay on top of the stacks of cash. Luke picked it out gingerly and, as it wasn't sealed, he lifted the flap and slid out the contents. There were fourteen six-by-four-inch colour photographs taken of various locations. He held them up one at a time to show Mark without allowing him to touch them. Mark looked puzzled, as there was nothing pertinent in these, it seemed. There were several photos of forests, a thatched-roof country cottage, and a smart apartment block. He studied them all. There was one of a woodland pond surrounded by trees and another was of a rather shabby council house with a broken-down front fence. Mark shrugged.

Luke turned to the next photograph and immediately felt a jolt of recognition, for it depicted the building from which he had seen the ambulance crew carry out the body bag containing Sophie Chen. He had been a young uniform at the time and until then it had been just another day's work to him. Later he had been sent to accompany Suzanne to identify her friend's body and had supported her in her horrified grief when she almost fainted. In his youthful innocence he had taken her for a coffee, had befriended her and subsequently introduced her to his older brother. And here in his hand was a photograph of the aftermath of what had been written off as an accidental fire – a full-colour representation of the smouldering and blackened wreckage of Suzanne's studio in Dalston.

At that moment, Luke began to appreciate the extent of what he might be dealing with.

CHAPTER TWENTY-ONE

Six hundred miles away from home, after spending a cold and virtually sleepless night in her windowless room, fully dressed and shivering beneath a blanket on the uncomfortable single bed, Suzanne was roused by her abductor. 'Come on,' he said, 'someone wants to see you.'

The door to the outside was standing open and a chill wind blew in as she put on her shoes. He indicated that she should follow him and she saw her surroundings in daylight for the first time. He had told her that this house was miles from the nearest village and she could well believe it. There was no sign of the van she had travelled in, only a long gravelled drive that disappeared into the distance behind tall pine trees. During her long night of worry, she had determined to find out exactly what this mysterious person upstairs wanted from her. So she followed and was led up the short flight of white stairs, through the entrance and into the main body of the house.

He stopped in the hallway and knocked on the first door on the left, turned the round brass handle and ushered Suzanne into a room that had clearly once been elegantly furnished with Persian rugs, large bookcases crammed with leather-bound volumes and fine oil paintings on the walls. However, in its current incarnation it more closely resembled an infirmary. In the far corner were a hospital-style bed and a medical hoist, designed to lift an incapacitated patient. A table crammed with bottles of pills, kidney dishes and other medical supplies stood beside it.

The place had a faint whiff of disinfectant about it, not entirely masked by the patchouli incense burning in the clasped hands of an ornate Buddha meditating on an Edwardian table at the other side of the room. On that same table Suzanne could see Don's tatty lined journals, neatly stacked. In front of the bay window, facing out between the partially drawn, heavy red velvet curtains, was a figure sitting motionless in a wheelchair. As Suzanne's eyes adapted to the dim light, the whir of the motorised chair drew her awareness and she turned towards it. Though apparently otherwise immobile, the occupant held one trembling hand hovering over the control situated on the arm of the chair and slowly guided it towards Suzanne.

The woman in the wheelchair looked pale, as though teetering at death's door, her dark hair lank against the sides of her face. But it was her eyes that caught Suzanne's attention – they were an extraordinary violet blue. This person had once been very beautiful though gauging her age was difficult. Whatever ailed her had taken its toll and she could be aged anywhere between her early fifties and late sixties. When she spoke, to instruct the young man to leave the room, her accent was that of a southern belle. '*Just like Scarlett O'Hara*,' Vera had said and Suzanne knew she was in the presence of Don's wife, Cynthia.

The woman introduced herself. 'Cynthia Beaulieu,' she said, 'I was once married to your father.'

'If I had been told who you were,' Suzanne said impatiently. 'I would have come here voluntarily. There was no need for all this drama.'

Cynthia emitted a sound that was a cross between a cough and a laugh. 'Would you, indeed?'

'Yes. And it would have saved me a lot of distress.'

The comment was ignored. Any distress caused was clearly of no concern to this woman. She got what she wanted and allowed nothing to stand in her way. She came directly to the point. 'How many of the journals have you read?'

There was an edge to her voice that made the question sound more like a threat and Suzanne considered telling Cynthia that she hadn't had the time, and that she was unaware of the contents. But then she suspected she wouldn't be believed for those intense violet eyes seemed to bore into her soul. 'Only part of the first one,' she replied truthfully.

'Enough then to know the kind of murdering, lying scumbag that sired you?'

'And your son, too, I gather.' Suzanne indicated in the direction of the door that her abductor had recently closed behind him. 'That, I imagine, is Jared?'

'Sit down, girl,' Cynthia said and the wheelchair whirred into action, moving towards some chairs on the far side of the room.

'What about the Anderson woman?' Cynthia asked, once Suzanne was seated. 'How much does she know?'

'Rose is unwell. She's been admitted to a mental hospital.'

Cynthia snorted. 'Typical of the man! He could pick out the weak ones at thirty paces. It was his one talent. Anything she said against him would be taken as the ravings of a lunatic.'

'She still loves him,' Suzanne said and then noticed a sudden twitch at the side of Cynthia's eye. Was this symptomatic of her illness or had Suzanne's words provoked a reaction? 'Don told her to burn everything, but she thought I should have his things.'

'Burn them?' Cynthia raised an eyebrow. 'That makes sense. No longer able to blackmail me once he's dead.'

Blackmail? Another of his lies unmasked. 'Were you sending him money?'

'Every week, on the nail, for fifteen years.'

'He told Rose he was working for the government, that he had been in the Special Forces and that they paid him in cash.'

Cynthia laughed. 'Jesus goddamn Christ! That man would say anything to anyone to get his own way. He was all smoke and mirrors, as phoney as they come. He'd lie to anybody about anything, sometimes just for the hell of it, to test how far he could take it, to see how much he could get away with.'

'Well, he certainly had Rose terrified.'

Cynthia hissed her obvious irritation. 'Look, sugar, at least she's still breathing. Which is more than can be said for most of them.'

A cold breeze drifted in even though the window was firmly closed against the elements and Suzanne shivered.

'You're sure he's dead?' There was a note of uncertainty in Cynthia's voice, a crack in her composure, perhaps?

'You've got the death certificate in that folder over there.'

'Then that makes two,' Cynthia said. 'My sources tracked him down in Thailand four years back. They almost had him nailed when he was reported drowned, alongside some young slip of a thing he'd been screwing.'

Nailed? The expression chilled Suzanne and she wondered if Cynthia had sent hired heavies to either scare Don off or even to kill him. Not that she was about to ask her a question like that.

'The girl's name was Annabelle.' Suzanne remembered the photo of the young blonde woman taken on the tropical beach, at sunset. 'There's a photograph of her. She was really beautiful.'

'Show me.'

Suzanne went to the Edwardian table and found the picture. 'Don must have been in his late fifties then. How could he attract the attention of someone like this?'

Cynthia let out a laugh heavily laced with cynicism. 'It's easy to rent the trappings of wealth – a hotel suite, a boat – though nothing too ostentatious. Throw in a few stories of a glamorous lifestyle elsewhere, drop a few famous names and it's a simple matter to impress the young or the vulnerable.' She glanced briefly at the photograph of Annabelle before appearing to lose interest.

'And this one was probably both. I told you, he could spot them a mile off. They have "victim" written all over them.'

Suzanne suppressed a shudder. So this was how the game was going to be played. 'You say there was a death certificate for Don, but there was no body, I suppose?'

'Her body was found, but not his. The two of them had been on some kind of boating trip, I was told. The vessel was found drifting. The Thai authorities surmised his body had been swept out to sea, then closed the case.' She laughed. 'But that's Thailand for you, sugar. Ever want to disappear? Just be seen walking off a beach into the sea, then get out of the country on a false passport and you'll be pronounced dead in no time at all.'

'But this time he died in England. And Rose said he'd been ill.'

The dark eyebrow arched. 'Did you see the body? Go to the funeral? Watch them lower his coffin into the ground?'

'He died in November. I didn't know he was dead until a couple of weeks ago. That was when Rose contacted me. So no, I didn't see his body with my own eyes. But I have no doubt that he's dead.'

'That's what I thought after Thailand. And then he popped up again just a few months later, with his hand out as usual.'

Cynthia recalled his voice on the phone. '*Guess who, Cyn?*' Gleeful as usual. '*Thought you'd got rid of me, eh?*' Sneering. '*Sent your guys to see to me, eh? Well, I fooled them, didn't I? I'm always one step ahead of you, baby. Always was, always will be. So don't try it again, Cyn, or you'll live to regret it.*' Laughing. '*We don't want our little boy to know what a fucking slag his momma is, now do we? So more of the usual, please, Cyn.*' Like he was ordering a coffee in Starbucks. '*And back pay too. For the three months you missed. Four in one week then back to weekly. There's a good girl.*'

She had told him that her business had just gone under. She'd been declared bankrupt and had to file for Chapter 7, while her accountants had been robbing her blind all along. '*Send me the money, Cyn. Let's not forget what's buried at the bottom of your garden, eh?* Silence. '*You don't want me coming to collect, now do you, Cynthia?*'

She had sent him the money.

'Why all the cloak and dagger stuff?' Suzanne asked.

'Something to do with the dead girl, I should think.' Cynthia said this as though it was of no consequence. 'His little peccadillo.'

'Why were you paying him? Was it some kind of divorce settlement?'

Cynthia ignored the question. 'If they found the dead girl in Thailand, then it was because he didn't have time to dispose of her properly.'

Suzanne was having trouble taking it all in. Don's journals were one thing, but to be told straight out that her father was a killer left her temporarily stunned.

Cynthia noticed her hesitation. 'Haven't you got it yet, sugar? Your father killed women. All of the women in those pretty pictures he left behind. All of them – apart from your mother – will be dead. He'll have murdered the lot of them.'

'One of them was my friend, Sophie Chen.' Suzanne felt sick and about to faint, but she took a breath, fought her way back and steadied herself. Instinctively she knew not to display any weakness in front of this woman. 'She died ten years ago in a fire at our shared studio. I was an artist back then.'

'An artist?' Cynthia said. 'Just like Don's mother. Then I guess you had a lucky escape there, sugar.'

'You think he was after me?'

'Who the hell knows? He does it because he enjoys it. To my own personal knowledge, he's killed eight. But there may have been more.'

'Don't the parents of those dead women deserve to know what happened to their daughters?'

The violet eyes darkened. 'That is never going to happen and when you've read those journals, you'll understand why.'

'How did you know he was writing them?'

'Because he told me.'

The sneering text message when one payment had been a day late.

Life story almost finished. Pay up or it gets published. Love ya! D

'You've gone to an awful lot of trouble to get them here. Why didn't Jared destroy them in London?'

'That was the original plan. But when he told me about you, I thought I might just indulge myself one more time.'

Suzanne's stomach knotted. What did this stone-cold woman want with her?

The chair buzzed, indicating that Cynthia was taking herself back to the window. 'Come over here and look at this view.'

Suzanne followed and saw the early spring sunshine strike the ornate sundial in the middle of the lawn. A vast swathe of grass stretched towards dense trees, divided only by the long driveway, with the entrance gate hidden beyond those dark, mournful sentinels. Grey clouds glowered but the sun still fought its way through.

'My one remaining pleasure,' Cynthia said. 'I have no sensation below my waist. Can't feel a thing in the places where I used to play. And my eyesight is fading too. Ironic, don't you think? Doubly so, if I acknowledge my other, more voyeuristic tendencies – which was where Don came in, if you'll pardon the vulgarity.'

'I'm not sure…' And she wasn't. Was this some kind of confessional?

'No, all I have left is the most powerful sex organ of all – my mind.' Cynthia turned her chair swiftly until she was facing Suzanne. 'And you are going to read his journals to me. Every dirty, filthy, twisted sentence and I intend to savour every word of them.'

CHAPTER TWENTY-TWO

Luke was silent and introspective on the drive back to his flat, even by his morose standards. The photos he had slipped back into the white envelope were now on the back seat of the car. It was the photograph he remembered a man taking on the street outside Suzanne's burned-out studio that had unnerved him. His thoughts dwelt on the face that had emerged from behind the camera. He vividly recalled standing in front of the man. 'You can't take pictures here, sir.'

But the man had just laughed. 'Finished now.' He put the camera back in the canvas bag he had slung over his shoulder. 'Press,' he said. 'Just doing my job, mate.'

'You move along now, sir,' Luke said. One of his colleagues noticed the exchange and made his way across the road towards them. The man tipped Luke a wink laced with mockery then made himself scarce, disappearing from sight down an alleyway.

'Who was that?' the other policeman asked.

'Just a scumbag snapper from some newspaper.'

'Bunch of fucking ghouls, if you ask me,' the officer said, losing interest and walking away.

Luke had been disturbed by the encounter, though he'd been unsure why. Doubly so, as no images of the fire-demolished building had ever been published in the press. But it was the photograph of the woods he had known all of his life that left him in a state of high anxiety. A squirm of fate that dredged up all the guilt he had felt for all these years. His mind was revving so hard it felt about to shut down. Mark, on the other hand, seemed to think they had hit a blank wall. If only.

'What a waste of time,' said Mark. 'No info in there about where Suze might be. I should have stayed by the phone.'

'There's a re-direct on that number. If Suzanne had been in contact, you'd have received it on your mobile.'

At that precise moment Mark's phone trilled 'Riders On The Storm'. 'No,' he told the caller, his voice deflating by the second. 'She's not around right now. I'm her husband.'

The social worker from Redstone House had phoned to say that Rose Anderson could now have visitors. And as Suzanne Tyler was listed as Miss Anderson's next of kin, and the only contact they had, could he please inform her and any other relatives of the fact. Mark assured her that he would pass the message on and ended the call.

'I should go and visit this Rose,' he said. 'See if she's got any idea about where Suze could have gone.'

What Luke said was, 'Might as well. I'll check out these pictures out, make some enquiries. They've got dates scribbled on the back of them that might ring some bells somewhere. I'll ask around.' What he thought was, *Get some breathing space, have some time to decide what to do.*

CHAPTER TWENTY-THREE

Cynthia Beaulieu had been a wild child, the only offspring of an American multi-millionaire, whose wife, Cynthia's mother, had committed suicide. Mr Moneybags could have had many wives and sired more heirs had he wished, but, in truth, he wasn't too keen on female sexual partners and preferred to indulge his taste for transvestism combined with onanism. Simultaneously ignored and thoughtlessly overindulged by her otherwise engaged father, Cynthia took off for Europe in her twenties. There she regularly got tanked, popped every pill in the known universe and screwed her way around several capital cities. Late one night, while bored, drunk and alone in Amsterdam, she stumbled into an SM club and discovered a new thrill: voyeurism. And one of the performers that night was Don Tyler.

Don was down and out in Amsterdam. He had been fired from one of his roadie jobs when he was found in the dressing room with a young groupie sucking his dick. 'That's band swag,' he was told by the irate lead singer as he shoved Don out of the way and unzipped. Don tucked his cock back in his pants, punched the singer in the mouth and marched out. With no money to get back to England, he had accepted a job as a bouncer at a sex club.

After a week, the English owner, Naomi Silver, took a liking to Don, so much of a liking that she had him whipping her arse that very night. His innate talent for 'breath-play' emerged a little later. And it seemed that ladies into such games would pay quite a lot of money to be brought to the brink of orgasm and then strangled to unconsciousness in a 'safe' environment. Not only that, but people would cough up even more to watch the action from behind discreetly concealed two-way mirrors. So Don Tyler was out on show at exactly the moment that Cynthia Beaulieu discovered the pleasures of voyeurism.

*

'A match made in heaven,' Suzanne commented.

'Just read what he writes about it,' Cynthia said impatiently. She recalled going to the club every night to see Don at work, eventually asking Naomi to introduce her to the star performer. Naomi was an entrepreneur who could smell money a mile off and so she made the introduction.

'When was this?'

'Oh, back in 1984.'

'Just after my mother divorced him.' Suzanne was shuffling through the notebooks, looking for the relevant dates written on the front covers. 'Here it is.'

N owned three clubs in Amsterdam. The first night I worked the door at the gay one. A bunch of Tom of Finland clones ponced about with their arses hanging out of leather chaps, with queer trannies done up like everyone from your Auntie Mabel to Carmen Miranda. All dancing to the music, hyped-up on amphetamines, pretending to be hardcore fetishistas. Some Madonna clone rubbed its hand up and down my crotch. Nothing stirred. But the geezer came very close to being lamped. N clocked the look on my face. 'I think you'd be better suited to my other club. There's no customer contact in that one.' She gave me a sly look. 'Unless you want it.'

Next night she took me to her club in the red-light district, hidden just behind the ground-floor apartments where women in brightly lit rooms sit by the windows waiting for punters. All shapes and sizes they were, every colour, every age. Jesus, their marks had to be desperate. I wouldn't have fucked one of them with someone else's dick!

N's 'specialty' club was a members-only joint, unless you happened to have a wedge of dosh in your back pocket. For that kind of client they made an exception. I was acting all cool. I thought I'd seen it all on the road with the bands. But the barely legal backstage skanks always up for giving a blowjob were Virgin fucking Marys by comparison.

There were rooms off the dimly lit corridor with closed doors; beside each door was a curtained alcove. N pulled a curtain back on the one-way window that gave a full view of the action. For a price. In the first room was a St Andrew's cross with a guy having seven colours of shite beaten out of him by a masked dominatrix. In another, some wizened old bloke was lying down in what looked like a kids' paddling pool. He was stark bollock-naked, sporting just a snorkel and a pathetic little hard-on. A group of women and men stood around him, pissing on him. I was laughing my tits off before N told me to shut it. 'He's paying good money for that,' she said. So I got over it and, after a bit, it all seemed dead ordinary. There were geezers with butt plugs shoved up their jacksies, crawling on hands and knees, licking the boots of tarts all dolled-up in rubber and six-inch heels. Whips, electrodes, fellas done up in nappies and baby clothes, punters in cages or being hoisted from the ceiling in black bags. It was all in a night's work.

'This was where you met Don?' Suzanne asked.

'Best and worst day of my life.' Cynthia sounded reflective.

N wanted to bring out my dark side, she said, like she had a clue what she was on about. But thrashing her and screwing her up the arse was a turn-on for a bit. The best, though, was knowing that some fat old cunt would pay money to be on the receiving end of my little specialty. I had to be careful not to take it too far and some of them

hated it if I came on their tits. Not that it happened too often 'cos
most of them were real old dogs.

'This is sordid stuff,' Suzanne said.

'Too much for you, honeybunch?' Cynthia scoffed. 'Jesus, you
must have lived a sheltered life!'

Suzanne felt her face colouring up at the remark. 'Each to their
own, I suppose. I don't care what people get up to. It's just the
language he uses, it's so ugly.'

'He was an ugly man,' Cynthia said. 'I don't mean physically
– he wasn't handsome, though he was good-looking enough, I
guess. No, he was ugly inside. He had a dark soul.'

'But you stayed with him.'

'He was exciting. For a time.' She shook her head. It took some
effort on her part. 'When does he get to me?'

Cyn by name and sin by nature. Now she was one spoilt cunt – too
much fucking money and an old man who preferred tossing off while
wearing women's clothes. Cyn had seen him do it. Turned her on,
she said. She got off watching me do my thing. She wanted to take it
further, wanted to see me strangle some bitch for real. N was jealous
at first but after Cyn did her with a strap-on while I choked her on
my cock, N was up for anything. Even after that old crone croaked at
the club and N had to get out of Amsterdam, she was still hot to trot.

'Someone died at the club?' Suzanne realised that she was
asking the question out of mere curiosity and felt disturbed by
her own lack of emotional response to all this. It was as though
she was becoming inured to what just a few weeks ago she would
have found horrifying.

'Don mis-timed it with one woman and she had a seizure. But if you can't take the heat…' Cynthia said dismissively. 'Get on with it.'

'I can understand why you didn't want Jared to read this to you.'

'My son is no concern of yours.' Cynthia's expression hardened but Suzanne knew that she was on the right track. *Jared doesn't know; Jared mustn't be allowed to know.*

She filed that piece of information away. Maybe that could be her trump card. If she could talk to Jared, get him on her side, then maybe she could find a way out of this.

CHAPTER TWENTY-FOUR

To Mark, Redstone House looked like the type of Victorian nursing home he'd seen in tub-thumping British war films. Establishments where jolly young English officer chaps were rehabilitated after a prang and steered about the lush grounds in wheelchairs by fresh-faced pretty nurses.

He parked and braced himself to walk towards the entrance. If he were frank, he'd have to admit that mad people scared him shitless. He'd seen them wandering the streets, all wild-eyed and blabbering, with their clothes transformed to rags overnight, and he'd always given them a wide berth. 'Care in the community,' they termed it. Yeah, right! Chuck 'em out on the street to get on with it, more like. But here it was different, he reassured himself, here they were restricted.

Rose Anderson was alone in her room, which was pleasant enough and contained a built-in wardrobe, a single bed, a couple of easy chairs and a small table positioned by the window that looked out onto the immaculately mown lawns. She smiled at him distractedly when he entered. Mark thought she looked zonked: her face was pale and drawn, her short brown hair still wet from a shower. She was wearing a plain T-shirt and baggy sweatpants that looked two sizes too large for her slim frame. Initially, it appeared, she assumed Mark was a social worker.

'Suzanne's husband,' he explained, but Rose didn't seem to take in the message at first so he had to repeat himself several times.

When the information finally sank in, Rose brightened momentarily. 'Such a lovely girl.' Her barely comprehending eyes searched Mark's face. 'Do you know my Don, too?'

'I never met him.' Mark wondered why the hospital had deemed Rose capable of receiving visitors when she barely knew what day it was.

'Don is a good man,' Rose slurred. 'He's the love of my life. Suzanne is lucky to have him as a father. So kind.' Her eyes glazed temporarily.

Talking about Suzanne's father as though he was in the next room made Mark increasingly uneasy in her company, but Rose swiftly changed tack.

'Suzanne should have the things he gave to me,' she said. 'It's only right. They all belonged to his mother, to Suzanne's granny. I've got them all in a jewellery box at home. There's rings, necklaces, lots of items. I don't wear much jewellery so Don tells me that Suzanne must have them.'

Rose turned away from Mark and rummaged inside her baggy pants. She turned back with a smile, took a tissue from the box on the table between them and wiped it across the object she was now holding in her hand.

'This is my front door key.' Her voice dropped to a whisper. 'I hide it from the snoopers in this place. They'd be in my house and loot it before you could say ninepence.' She leaned further towards him. 'I learned from Don where you hide keys. He's a very clever man, you know.' She polished the key once more before handing it to Mark. It was still warm. 'Of course, women have one more place to hide things than men do.'

He took the key from her, wrapped it in another tissue and put it in his pocket. Rose seemed to focus on his face and began to look nervous, sitting back in her chair with a suddenness that indicated she was backing away rather than getting comfortable. Her eyes narrowed. 'Why didn't Suzanne come with you?'

'She's gone away for a while.' This was his opportunity to question Rose, but he was apprehensive. Memories of his mother's drift into a twilight world sent shivers down his spine. Was Rose in any fit mental state to answer his questions? Would she scream or attack him? Bare her teeth and growl or burst into inconsolable tears?

But Rose appeared to be unfazed by his answer. 'Best way,' she said. 'They might be looking for her. Good idea to lay low.'

'Who are *they*?' He used his best soothing tone but Rose's smile was fading as swiftly as it had appeared. Did he dare question her further?

'Them,' she said conspiratorially. 'The people Don worked for. They'll be after Don's diaries. He wrote it all down, you know. Said it was his insurance.' Rose's whole demeanour changed in an instant. Fear leapt into her eyes, and a trembling hand flew to her mouth.

'I should have burned them like he told me to.' She wrapped her arms around her body defensively and began to rock, almost imperceptibly at first, but the movements building to become compulsive and almost childlike. 'All up in flames! Burn them. He warned me not to open the chest.' Her voice grew louder. 'Burn them, burn them!'

Rose wasn't looking at Mark now. She had withdrawn into her own world, detached from reality, her head filled with her own swirling, troubled thoughts. 'Burn, burn, burn!' Over and over she said the words, each time louder and more insistent. Mark shrank away from her, resisting the urge to get up and run, as images of his own mother's final plunge to mental oblivion crowded his brain.

An orderly in a white coat rushed into the room, followed by a young nurse. The nurse put her arms around Rose, making pacifying sounds, and the orderly firmly ushered Mark into the corridor and shut the door behind him. Mark could hear Rose sobbing and he shuddered.

*

It was dark by the time Mark got to Rose's house. The commuters were back home at this hour and every space in front of the terraced houses had been taken, so he had to park in the next street and walk. He passed a pub on the way and wondered whether this was where Rose had worked. He found the house and opened the door, willing himself not to think about just where on her person Rose had secreted the key.

The curtains were closed and he tripped on a wooden chest in the hallway before he was able to find a light switch. A jewellery box in her bedroom, she had said. He wasn't even sure why he was here, unclear about why he was prioritising this while Suze was still missing. He knew he was working on instinct, doing something, anything, until she came home to him, or at least rang him. Or until sufficient time had elapsed for him to file a missing persons' report.

No doubt 'they' were all in that mad woman's mind. Some kind of control device cooked up by Don Tyler to maintain his hold over her, to keep her scared and malleable. He'd never met the man but Suzanne's description of her father's visit to her studio had provided Mark with pointers to Don Tyler's behaviour.

Bullies, he knew all about them. He'd grown up with one. His dad, Matthew M. Woods, a loveable country bobby, worshipped by everyone from the vicar to the postmistress, always ready to do a good turn for anyone. He'd been all twinkling eyes and bicycle clips. Dixon of fucking Dock Green incarnate! Firm but affable to the outside world, he had ruled their home with an iron fist and a heart twice as cold.

Mum took a beating for nothing worse than buying the wrong brand of biscuits. Mum with her sad eyes and quiet stoicism, Mum who would turn her head away and pretend the ill treatment of her son wasn't happening. She'd even defend the bastard. Mark still hated confined spaces after he'd been locked in the cellar overnight so many times that he would have said or done anything not to displease his father.

Luke had been the only one Dad never harmed, or intimidated. In fact he had coddled and spoilt him. Taken him out on walks in the woods, laughed and played with him. Not that it ever made Luke any happier. He'd always been a miserable little sod. Even so, Dad's overt favouritism had driven a wedge between the brothers that, Mark later realised, had resulted in their lack of empathy towards each other as kids. Divide and rule. Set every family member against each other and they won't gang up on you – the classic tactics of a bully.

He packed his memories away and got on with the task. In one of Rose's bedrooms he picked up a framed seascape picture that had fallen off a wall and placed it on the single bed. But there was no sign of the jewellery box in there. It was in the other bedroom, on the dressing table, that he saw it. It was one of those wooden inlaid Moroccan jobs and it held several cheap rings, one rolled-gold wedding band, two pairs of plastic earrings, a silver ankh on a chain, a thistle-shaped brooch and a gold bracelet. Apart from the bracelet, nothing was of much value to his practised insurance-assessor's eye. But then nothing looked old enough to have belonged to Don Tyler's mother, either. Still, Rose had said it all should go to Suzanne so he scooped the lot into his pockets.

It was only while he was driving home that a notion began to nag him. He was sure he'd seen the ankh before. He parked the car in the first available space and fished out the tangle of jewellery from his pocket. He vividly recalled the photo of the black woman – one of the pictures Rose had found in the chest – that Suzanne had shown him. The woman in the snapshot had been wearing a silver ankh on a chain. The ankh had a star-shaped jewel in the middle and he remembered commenting on how unusual it was to have that combination. He had wondered at the time if it had been custom-made. He turned on the light in the car and stared at the necklace in his hand: an ankh with a star.

CHAPTER TWENTY-FIVE

Mark arrived home to find Mrs Jones standing on his doorstep. She had a cat basket at her feet and the old ginger tom inside was kicking up a racket, growling and clawing to escape. Mark disliked cats – they made him sneeze and itch. Mrs Jones, a tiny woman who had once been an art teacher, smiled up at him apologetically.

'I've been trying to reach Suzanne,' she said. 'She promised to take Sultan to the vet for me in the morning.'

'You've seen her today?' Hope surged through him.

'No, yesterday morning. She promised. It's all the way into Coulsdon to the vet and I can't manage this basket on the bus. And taxis! Do you know what they charge for taxis these days?'

'She's been called away. It was urgent. Family business.'

'Is her mother ill? Such a nice lady, her mother.'

'No, she's fine. It's something else.'

'Well, I must say Suzanne did look worried when I saw her yesterday afternoon.'

'Really, when was this?'

'She was driving along the high street in her car with that handsome young man. Is he a relative? I thought he might be, they do have a look of each other.'

'She was with a young man? Are you sure?'

'My legs might not work as well as they used to, but my eyesight's still sharp.' The schoolmarm came out fighting. 'Suzanne stopped to let me cross the road and I got a good look at her companion. He was a few years younger than Suzanne and, you know, I would have thought he might have been her brother. Except, of course, I know she's an only child.'

'Do you remember which way they were headed?'

'Is there something the matter, Mark?' Her eyes narrowed. All those years in front of classes of unruly kids had given her an insight into human behaviour that was second to none. 'Have I said the wrong thing?'

'No, Mrs Jones, not at all.' He made an attempt to sound calm. 'Suzanne left me a note, but she hasn't been in touch since. So perhaps you can tell me which way she was headed.'

'South,' she said, sensing there was more to this than met the eye. 'Towards Banstead Common.'

'And what time was this, do you think?'

'It was around five. I'd been to see my friend Lily and the bus dropped me by the station at five. I always get home by five because Sultan gets hungry and if I don't feed him on time he tears at the curtains and piddles on the carpet.'

Mark mentally filed away this information as two more reasons to hate cats. He thanked Mrs Jones for the update and gave her twenty quid for the cab fare to take the moggy to the vet herself in the morning. She asked him to inform her when he heard from Suzanne and toddled off with her cat basket.

Mark rushed indoors to ring Luke.

His brother sounded unimpressed, reasoning that if Suzanne had been driving her own car, her disappearance wouldn't qualify as abduction. *Sit it out*, was his advice. *It's not even been forty-eight hours yet.* Though, he added, he had been looking up the dates written on the back of the photographs they'd found in the safe deposit box and trying to match them to unsolved crimes around those times in those locations.

'There is one that might be a lead,' Luke said. 'In 1985, a woman named Naomi Silver was found hanged at her house in Hampshire. It was dismissed as auto-erotic asphyxiation gone wrong, but a local sergeant had his doubts. This Silver woman was pretty well off. She'd made her money from nightclubs in Amsterdam by all accounts, but had to sell up after some scandal. Apparently, a punter had a heart attack at one of her clubs and the Dutch police closed her down. The story goes that she sold the clubs and premises pretty sharpish and skipped back to England. She was a bit of a swinger, it seems, and she used to have big parties at her house. There were reports that a man and a woman had been staying with her on the weekend of her death, but there was no evidence to confirm that. Still, this sergeant – Morris, I think – was convinced there'd been foul play and kept banging on about it until he retired.'

Mark thought back to Suzanne telling him about the deaths of three of the other women in the photographs and his own cynical dismissal of her fears. But now Naomi Silver was one more.

With a growing sense of unease, he explained to Luke about the ankh and the other jewellery he had collected from Rose Anderson's home.

'Pity you haven't still got the snaps of all the women,' Luke said.

'Find Suzanne and we find the photos.'

'Stay put. I'm coming over.'

N invited us to her country house in Hampshire – cool place. We got coked up for the whole weekend, with me screwing N all ends up. The deal was that Cyn just watched, but she was a horny little slut and N caught us at it. N went mad and I mean mad *– screaming, yelling and throwing stuff.*

'I'll tear your fucking face off!' she screeched at me, her grey-streaked hair tatty and unkempt, her face a vile stew of fear and hate. She looked like a thing you'd keep locked in the attic. But N was minted, a rich middle-aged coke-fiend. The one who took me to bed and shagged me ragged, the woman who craved SM play, the one who begged to

have her arse beaten black, blue and bloody. The one who threw back cocktails of champagne, pills and cocaine until she became deranged. The one who made the big mistake of coming at me with a knife.

My demon can beat your demon any day of the week. Like some snot-nosed playground boasters, we circled each other in her Hampshire cottage on that gloomy Sunday afternoon.

Cyn was laughing. 'She's the one,' she said. 'Strangle this one.'

Women can't fight, they give up too soon. They never believe that you are actually going to kill them. I choked the life out of N, watched the light die in her eyes, with Cyn wanking in the background. It was fucking brutal, fucking amazing, never felt anything so good.

Suzanne stopped reading aloud and glanced at Cynthia. Her eyes were closed and she was smiling. And at that moment Suzanne realised that once Cynthia had done with her, she was not going to get out of this place alive.

CHAPTER TWENTY-SIX

Mark had laid out everything collected so far that related to Donald Tyler on the dining table. He'd placed the items on a folded white tablecloth. The key to the security box and the black swipe card were on the left and arranged beside them was the jewellery he had gathered up from Rose Anderson's house. The ankh on the chain took pride of place, as he was convinced he'd seen it in one of the photographs. Next to it was a plain gold wedding band that looked like something purchased from a mail-order catalogue at a fiver a week. The silver ring in the shape of a butterfly reminded Luke of one his ex-wife had bought when they'd been on holiday in Phuket. The brooch was a simple silver design, with an amber thistle in the centre – the distinctive emblem of Scotland. There was also an antique yellow-gold gatelink bracelet Luke weighed up, which was heavy and probably expensive. When Luke came to the red plastic earrings his gut churned and he felt like he'd been kicked in the balls.

No, he tried to reason with himself, *they'd been bought from some chain store, and thousands of young girls must have been wearing them back then.* But somewhere deep inside he had to admit that they had belonged to her. He remembered her wearing them on the day she disappeared – a cluster of little red plastic daisies dangling daintily at her ears – with her laughing and telling him that her mum would kill her if she was spotted wearing them.

'She'll say I look common in them,' she'd said. She pushed her mousy-coloured hair behind her ears to show him. 'What do you think? Dead smart, eh?'

Anita. It had been years since he had allowed himself to even think of her by name.

He'd put his arm around her shoulders and brushed against her breast with his hand. She'd playfully slapped it away. 'Oi, none of that hanky-panky!'

He'd laughed at her use of such a dated term and Anita had giggled. 'That's what my mum always says. "Now, don't you get up to no hanky-panky."' She twisted her hair into a knot. 'When I leave school I'm gonna go blonde.' She pouted at him, all Lolita-like. 'Bet you'd fancy me more as a blonde?'

'No hanky-panky, you said.'

'Well, maybe just a bit.'

He'd been sixteen and he and Anita had bunked off school for the afternoon to be together. But they'd had a fight when she refused to deliver on her flirty promises. Luke had marched off in a huff and gone back to school. He'd left Anita alone in the woods close to Cannock Chase.

The girl was never seen again.

*

'That Rose woman has totally lost it.' Mark's voice brought Luke back to the present. 'I mean, Suze's dad was sixty-odd. So *his* mother would now be eighty at least. None of this stuff could have belonged to her.' Mark picked up the thistle brooch. 'This maybe, at a push, but that gold bracelet looks far too expensive. It must be worth a couple of grand. Not something Tyler's mother could have afforded. And the rest of the stuff is just tat.'

'Like something a teenager would wear,' Luke said distract-edly.

She had been too young for him, he had known that even then. How his dad would have sneered if he'd found out his son was knocking about with a girl of thirteen. *'You need to man up, lad. You some kind of pervo, running after little girls like that?'*

But it had been Anita who'd done all the running. He'd see her hanging around on the street corner he passed every day. She'd find excuses to enter the sixth-form building on their communal school grounds. A third-year student running errands for the teachers just so she could bump into him in the corridors. And Luke had been flattered. He didn't have many mates. They were all reluctant to hang out with a copper's son; they thought he might grass them up to his dad. All the youngsters feared his dad, and with good reason. When Luke's friend Danny had been picked up for some minor misdemeanour, he was taken to the police station and had been on the receiving end of a couple of kidney punches. Danny reported his mistreatment to his parents but they hadn't believed his story. All the grown-ups thought the world of good old Sergeant Woods. He was an old-fashioned copper. He sang in the church choir. He found time to call in on the elderly who lived alone, stopped to chat to all and sundry, and was always ready to stand his round in the local pub. He was a good sort. Not a word was said against Sergeant Mathew M. Woods. But the village lads knew differently – and so did his family.

Mark put his hand on Luke's shoulder. 'You alright?'

'Fine. Just thinking.'

'Do you reckon the bracelet may have belonged to that Naomi what's-her-name?'

'Silver. Naomi Silver.'

Mark had the ankh in his hand. 'Well, this is definitely the one in that photograph of the black woman. I'm certain of it.'

'But you can't prove it without the picture.'

'Maybe she lives in one of those locations in those other photos. You've got access to all these things. Can't you find out?'

'I'm working on it.'

Of course, Luke already knew who she was: Gloria Davison, a suspected drug-dealer, high on her own stash, drowned in her bath. One of the candles in her sitting room had fallen over and set fire to the curtains. Neighbours had smelled the smoke and called the fire brigade. After they'd broken down the door and put out the flames, they discovered the body.

Luke was not about to share that knowledge with Mark. And he definitely didn't want investigations into the deaths or disappearances of certain women being re-opened.

*

She was naked, my chemical witch. A little bit of this, a little bit of that, and my dick in her hand. The lights were switched off. The corners of the room were smoothed out with the glow from a dozen candles, standing proud and tall in ornate gothic-black holders. My vision was blurred one minute and crystal clear the next, in and out of focus as the sound of trance music caressed my whole body and throbbed softly in my head. My feet were warm; everything I touched felt sensual, something other than it was. She smiled, stood and floated across the room, her dark skin glistening, curly pubic hair shaved into a heart-shape. My hard-on had subsided, but I didn't care. I tried to speak but my mind wouldn't formulate the words.

'Just getting some water.' Her voice echoed and the candles all flickered as her breath swept across the space between us like a warm Jamaican wind. 'Have to drink lots of water.'

My heart was pounding like a thousand mad drummers. I wanted to stand up, walk away, escape my heart, leave it behind on the sofa, but my legs felt boneless and I knew they wouldn't support my weight.

'Don't leave me,' I said, 'I don't feel good.'

Her laughter carried in from the kitchen. 'You'll be better once you've had some water.' That breeze again, filling the room with so much air that the candles guttered. One flickered so crazily that the corner shimmered with life. The panther in the painting on the wall shuddered and padded out of the frame, breaking loose from its confines. The candle died. I tried not to look, scared of what might be there, but my eyes were drawn to the blackness. I realised that I was staring into an empty space. There was nothing hidden there. I breathed a sigh of relief, laughed out loud and heard my own voice detached from myself.

'What're you looking at?' She was back, holding a tall glass of water. There was little sign of a troubled thought in her limpid brown eyes as she turned her head to follow my gaze into the dark corner. But once she twisted back towards me, it was here, it was there, it was everywhere. It was in her face. Her grin revealed newly formed fangs and I shrank away from her.

'Settle down,' she said with its rasping voice. 'It will be okay, trust me.'

The bath was full of water and her small breasts bobbed as she half-floated, eyes closed. I turned off the light and walked away, careful to scatter her pills and drug paraphernalia across the floor. I knocked over the candle in the sitting room, watched the curtains catch alight and then I left.

*

Cynthia's face was set. 'I knew it,' she said. 'He swore to me he had nothing to do with Gloria. But I always suspected there was something between them.'

'You knew this woman?' Suzanne asked.

'Sure. She was his contact, his dealer. Expensive, but she always had the best and purest stuff.'

'And according to this, he killed her.'

'Him and his freakin' demon.' She laughed. 'He was full of shit, your father.'

'Your husband, you mean. I was just his daughter. I had no choice in the matter. But you married the bastard.'

Cynthia remembered Don coming home to their apartment in Chelsea – wired, twitchy, grinding his teeth.

'Where's the coke?' she'd asked him.

'Gloria wasn't home.'

'You took your time.'

'I looked up some guy I know but he only had shit.'

'But you had a little taster of the product, I see.'

He'd crossed to the window and looked out at the rain. 'I'm sick of this fucking country, Cyn. Why don't we get married and go and live in the States for a bit? Start over.' He'd put his arms around her, held her close. 'You're the only woman for me, Cynthia Beaulieu. We understand each other's little ways. You're the love of my life. Let's get away and forget all the crap that's gone down. What do you say?'

She'd said yes.

'At least he couldn't blame you for Gloria's death,' Suzanne said.

Cynthia raised her eyebrows.

'Not like he appeared to blame you for Naomi.'

'I make no excuses for what happened to Naomi. Though fantasy is one thing – reality is something else again.'

'Are you saying you didn't realise that he might actually kill her?' A game gone wrong combined with a fatal misreading of a dangerous man.

'Who knows what I was thinking, because I sure as hell don't. It happened and we dealt with it. What does it matter now?'

'It does matter, Cynthia. Don had another son, Raymond, and he's serving a life sentence for murdering his mother.'

'The apple doesn't fall very far from the tree.'

'Raymond is adamant that he's innocent.'

'Liars and killers, both.'

'I don't agree. I think *Don* killed Betty Tyler. And somewhere in these notebooks is the proof that might get Raymond released.'

'Well, sugar, that ain't never gonna happen. Once you've read me my little bedtime stories, all these journals are going to be burned, just as Don wanted.' She gave a sour smile. 'His last wishes should be honoured.'

'And me?'

'What about you?'

'You're going to let me just walk away, are you?'

'Of course.' Cynthia smiled with her mouth but her eyes told a different story.

Suzanne wanted to probe deeper into the other woman's tarnished soul but she already knew what fate awaited her. Cynthia might not be making any long-term plans for herself but Suzanne guessed that Jared was not to learn about his precious momma's past. And, once the journals had been destroyed, Suzanne would be the only remaining witness. Would Cynthia take the chance that, once she was gone, her son may very well believe Suzanne? As Cynthia appeared to take Don's crimes so lightly, would she be inclined to be merciful? Suzanne was not about to gamble with her life like that; she knew that she had to get away somehow.

There was loud knock on the door. 'Come in, Raul,' Cynthia called out.

The door opened. A sallow-skinned man with a shaved head and wearing a white coat came into the room.

'My nurse is due soon,' Cynthia said without looking at Suzanne. 'Raul will take you back down to your room. You will have no further contact with Jared. Do you understand? You are not to speak to him. From now on you deal only with Raul.'

Since Cynthia had just voiced what Suzanne suspected, she decided to play the only card she had left. 'If you want me to cooperate, to play along with this sick little game, then you'll have to do something for me.'

Now she had Cynthia's attention. 'What did you have in mind?'

'Let me phone my husband. He'll be worried. I need to put his mind at rest.'

Cynthia seemed weary and her face showed signs of pain. She appeared in dire need of her medication. 'I'll think about it, maybe.'

Suzanne stood to follow Raul. 'You do that. Just one phone call or no more reading.'

'Maybe I don't want to know any more.'

'Oh yes you do. You didn't really know Donald Tyler and you've lived with the guilt of Naomi's death for all these years. You want to know alright.'

'You don't know what you're talking about, sugar. Bring me those photographs.'

Suzanne opened the white folder and took out the pictures, pointedly not even glancing at the one of Sophie Chen.

'Young girl, fair hair, freckles,' Cynthia said.

Suzanne found it and held up the picture of the girl with the bright smile and a thistle brooch attached to her jacket.

'Moira Campbell.' Cynthia gazed at the photograph, her expression unreadable. 'She was Jared's girlfriend. I stopped paying your father five years ago, so he came here. He strangled Moira in this house. When he threatened to frame Jared for her murder, I paid him off.'

Suzanne attempted to conceal her disbelief at Cynthia's matter-of-fact explanation but could not disguise her curiosity about this revelation. 'What did you do with Moira's body?'

'Don buried her in the garden, somewhere among those trees out there. So I could see them every time I looked out of the window. A constant reminder of the hold he had over me.'

CHAPTER TWENTY-SEVEN

Bridget Daly parked her car in one of the cramped spaces outside her block of flats. She hated this place – a flat on the tenth floor was no place to raise a baby – but she had no choice. On her nurse's salary she was lucky to have found anywhere she could afford. She turned to check on baby Emma, snoozing soundly in her pink seat at the back of the car. Emma had been the only good thing to come from her relationship with Frank. What a selfish, self-centred prick he was. Though at least he was a reasonably caring father, prepared to take Emma every other weekend to give Bridget a break. Not that he paid anything towards the extortionate cost of childcare, which had to come out of Bridget's pocket. But there was no way she was giving up her job at St Francis' hospital to be a stay-at-home mother living on benefits.

She was struggling with the straps on the car seat-cum-carrycot when she spotted Frank strolling around the corner, looking his usual sharp self. Pity he didn't spend any of his flashy clothes money to help out with the baby.

'You're early. I'll have to go and collect all Emma's stuff.'

'Don't bother, Mum'll have everything.'

'You back living with your mother again? What happened to the new girlfriend?'

He shrugged. 'Well, you know…'

Yeah, Bridget thought, *she threw you out when she found out what a lazy shitbag you are.* 'Emma's probably better off with your mum, anyway.'

'Sure she is. Mum dotes on her.' When he picked up the baby carrier, Emma stirred and he cooed at her. Without another word to Bridget, he disappeared back around the corner. *He's probably got a new motor and doesn't want me to see it*, Bridget thought. But she was in no mood for a fight with Frank. She didn't want him buggering off in a huff. She needed him to take the baby this weekend. She reached into her white car and gave a twirl to the green frog that dangled from the driving mirror. 'Wish me luck.' The frog jiggled its best wishes and she steeled herself for the confrontation to come. Men were the bane of her life and she seemed destined to repeatedly choose a total arsehole. Her next task was to get the old fella out of her flat.

*

Bridget stepped into the lift that would take her to the top floor. The smell of disinfectant thankfully disguised the usual stink of stale piss, and someone had made an attempt to remove the graffiti. *About time*, she thought. The doors were closing when she saw a small blonde woman rushing towards her. 'Wait for me!'

The woman dumped her two bags of shopping inside the lift and hit the button for the ninth floor. 'Phew!' she said. She lived in the flat directly beneath Bridget and was the archetypal nosy neighbour. Frank used to call her 'Mrs Rat', and with her small eyes, sharp features and protruding teeth the description was unkind, but accurate.

'How's that baby of yours?'

'She's fine. She's with her dad for the weekend.'

'Oh!' The nose twitched and the eyes narrowed. 'I thought your new friend might be looking after her for you.'

Oh shit! This woman would be on the phone to the council and child support agency in a flash if she knew Bridget was cohabiting. 'New friend?' Bridget feigned innocence.

Mrs Rat's nose twitched in annoyance. 'Older man, white beard.'

Bridget said the first thing that came into her head, a half-truth. 'Oh, him? That's my uncle. He's staying with me while he recovers from a triple heart bypass. He'll be going home soon.'

The woman let out a sigh of disappointment and nodded her head. 'I did wonder, like. I thought he looked a bit too old for you.'

Mrs Rat got off at the ninth floor. 'Tell him to keep the noise down, will you?' she said tartly. 'He has the telly on too loud.'

The doors closed behind her and Bridget added this to the list of reasons to get her lodger/lover out of her life.

*

He was watching morning TV as usual. He wasn't bad looking for his age. With his white hair and newly grown beard, he looked a bit like Kris Kristofferson. But he was still older than Bridget's father and she was finding it difficult to remember what had attracted her to him in the first place. The charm and stoical humour he had exuded when he was one of her patients on the hospital's heart ward had hooked her. She'd felt sympathetic when he told her about his wife. How she'd left him while he was working abroad, and how he'd come back to find that she'd emptied out their joint bank account and there was another family living in his rented flat. Bridget had always been a sucker for a sob story. She was also impressed that, despite all the personal grief he had in his life, he'd fought like mad to get well. He'd been an inspiration to all the other patients by getting out of bed and walking soon after his operation. He'd made them all laugh with his silly antics, and got them involved in a sing-song on the day he'd said was his birthday. He'd sung a comedy version of 'Anyone Who Had A Heart' that had ended with him miming looking for his own heart under the bed. The whole performance had the patients and staff in stitches. On the surface he was grateful to be alive and full of the joys of spring. Yet when Bridget was alone with him in the dayroom, he revealed a far more vulnerable side that appealed to her tender nature. One time he'd been holding back the tears while they talked until they burst from him like a dam breaking. She had held him close until his sobs subsided. Bridget was a sucker for a damaged hero too and compassion had overwhelmed logic.

As he'd had nowhere to live, she'd offered him a room in her flat while he recovered from surgery. 'It's just until I get on my feet again,' he'd assured her. That had been five months back and she told herself that she'd had enough of having another mouth to feed. He said he had money and that once his friend was back on leave from his job in the Middle East he'd contact him, collect the money and pay Bridget back for everything she had laid out on his behalf and then some. 'The money is all in cash,' he'd said gleefully. 'Untraceable, tax-free.'

Bridget didn't approve of that and she told him so. 'How is the NHS supposed to survive if people like you don't pay their taxes?'

He'd smiled and told her she was being naïve. 'If I was working in the UK, I'd be happy to pay. But it's a different world in Arab countries. Everything is *baksheesh*. Nobody would get anything done without giving someone a bung.' He held her gently in his arms. 'I never liked it either, sweetheart, but that's just the way it was.' Then he'd chuckled. 'You know, when in Rome, and all that.'

Early on she'd used her almost maxed-out credit card to obtain a copy of his birth certificate online and with that he'd applied for a new passport, as his old one had been stolen, along with his wallet and his suitcase full of clothes just before he'd been admitted to the hospital, he told her. She'd purchased clothes for him too, also online. And he'd been so grateful for all her help that Bridget's gentle Irish heart had swelled with pride and growing affection for this man who'd had such a hard time of it. Gradually, though, the holes in his stories began to grow ever larger and sympathy for his misfortunes gave way to doubts. Why, for example, hadn't he contacted his employers during all this time? Why was he planning to take another driving test, when surely his details would be on the DVLA computers and they could just reissue another licence? The questions were building in her mind but she felt reluctant, curiously anxious even, about challenging him.

At close quarters she had noticed a meanness about him, a dark soul that she glimpsed from time to time. It disturbed her. There was something about the way he looked at Emma when she cried that sent a shiver of apprehension down Bridget's spine, and so she had refused his offers to babysit when she was on nightshift. 'She's used to the childminder,' she told him.

After the few first times they had made love, he changed from the gently seducing lover to… she didn't want to think about it. Recently, the things he wanted to do in bed turned her stomach and also frightened her. They represented the dark recesses of the mind that she had no intention of exploring but that appeared to come so naturally to him. All this had fuelled Bridget's resolve to get him out of her life. Right now she didn't even want compensating for all the money she'd shelled out on him. The old fella had to go, and soon.

She was exhausted from her nightshift, but determined to have him out of the flat before Emma was back home again on Monday. She didn't know where he would go, but go he must.

'We have to talk.' Bridget picked up the remote control and switched the TV off.

'If it's about the money, babe, then don't you worry. I feel well enough to drive now. So if I can borrow your car, I'll go to my friend's house today to collect what's owed me. Then we'll be in clover.'

'It's not just the money.' She sat beside him on the sofa. 'My downstairs neighbour knows you're here.'

'Does she now?' His expression darkened. It was a look that made her nervous.

'So I'm afraid you're going to have to find another place to stay. I can't afford any trouble.'

'But, Bridget, you know how much I love you and baby Emma.' He turned to her, his hazel eyes full of affection. 'Tell me, sweetheart, what have I done to upset you?'

'It's not working for me, this… this… relationship.'

'Why not, Bridget? You're the love of my life. You know that.'

This was it. She was going to tell him straight. 'Your sex games, I don't like them. I can't take it any more.'

He smiled and reached out for her. 'Then we'll stop. I never want to do anything to hurt you. I keep forgetting how young you are. Maybe breath-play is a bit too sophisticated for my innocent Irish colleen.'

Even his strong arms holding her did not weaken her resolve. 'I want you to leave.' She tried to pull away but he tightened his grip.

He stroked her hair and caressed her face. 'You don't mean that. You're tired, baby.' His voice was gentle. 'Go to bed and we'll talk again when you're rested. We've got all weekend with just the two of us.'

Bridget made an attempt to move away from him, but he held her tightly, rocking her as he gradually moved his hands around her throat. 'There, there,' he soothed. 'I just want to hold you.'

*

Bridget was unconscious when he unlocked the door to the balcony of her tenth-floor flat. His knees almost buckled under her weight when he lifted her and the scar on his chest throbbed with the effort. *Fat cow*, he cursed. *I don't need you any more. Now I've got my new passport, I'll collect my money from Rose and deal with her at the same time, then I'll skip the country.* He'd have preferred to stay around until he got his new driving licence, but what the fuck, the chances of a man of his age being stopped by the cops were almost zero. The scars on his leg, from where the surgeons had taken the veins to replace the ones in his heart, itched like hell. They were playing up because he was hauling Bridget across the room. Hang on in there, boys, not long now.

Lonely women commit suicide, he mused as he carried Bridget out into the fresh morning air. *You read about it all the time. Probably won't even make the news. Try and throw me out, would you? Well, cop for this, you fucking bitch.* He raised her up, balanced her for a moment, then tipped her over the barrier. He chuckled as Bridget flew away. *Kersplatt!* Don almost laughed out loud. *Pick the bones out of that, Batman!*

CHAPTER TWENTY-EIGHT

Raul ushered Suzanne to her room. She tried to engage him in conversation but he didn't even acknowledge that she had spoken to him. He simply opened the door for her, flicked on the light switch and then locked the door behind him when he left. Someone – she presumed Jared – had placed a two-bar electric fire at the far end of the room and she was glad of it. It was a small kindness that she was grateful for, a sign that maybe Jared had a softer side she could appeal to, if given the chance. Maybe he'd respond to the fact that they were half-brother and sister, though he'd shown little outward sign of any empathy towards her so far.

Too far under Cynthia's thumb, she thought.

The room had been cold on her first night in there and she'd slept fully dressed under the blankets. A small portable television set had been placed on top of the chest of drawers. The remote control sat beside it. When she switched it on, the *Reporting Scotland* regional news appeared instantly. She'd been correct in her initial assessment; she was definitely north of the border.

She heard a vehicle approach the house and turned the sound down on the TV. If this was Cynthia's nurse, then maybe she could attract her attention by banging on the door and shouting for help. She put her ear to the door and was listening when suddenly the door was unlocked and opened by Raul, who stood there with a tray. It was the first time she had taken a close look at him. He was older than she had first thought, mixed-race, perhaps in his mid–late seventies and rather stooped. He had the obsequious manner of a lifelong servant about him. Vera's observation of Cynthia sounding like Scarlett O'Hara sprang to mind, raising images of a plantation in the American Deep South which was accentuated by Raul's reverence to his boss.

'Miss Cynthia says you'll be able to phone your husband later,' he said. 'But you gotta be quiet while the nurse is around.'

His accent was one Suzanne had heard before. The Hurricane Katrina disaster came instantly to mind with the vox pop TV interviews of survivors.

'Are you from New Orleans?' she asked Raul, but he didn't reply.

He kicked the door closed behind him and set the tray down beside the television set. 'Eat your lunch,' he said. 'Miss Cynthia will send for you.'

'Have you worked for the family for long?'

'Long time, miss. Long time. You be quiet now.'

Raul wasn't a big man and Suzanne considered pushing past him. She could run out to the nurse's car and drive away. She could find a police station and report her abduction. But by the time the police took her complaint seriously, she'd bet that all Don's journals would have been destroyed. And bang would go the chance of her finding any evidence to help free Raymond. She couldn't take that risk, so she decided to sit tight and wait to phone Mark.

'Don't worry, Raul. I'll be a compliant little prisoner.'

*

Jared stood outside his mother's room and waited for the nurse to finish.

'How is she?' he asked as she came out and closed the door behind her.

'As well as can be expected. Try not to tire her. I'll be back tomorrow.'

He opened the door for the hardy Scottish nurse and watched her leave.

When he entered the room, his mother was propped up in bed in her usual position but with her eyes closed. There was a serenity about her, as though she was aware that death was at hand. These days he often found it hard to remember that she had once been a Southern belle whose beauty could stop men dead in their tracks. The same men she could shake to the core with her hard-nosed business acumen. The very same men who had run the family business into the ground once Cynthia fell ill and was no longer around to keep a wary eye on them. One day, Jared vowed, he would find a way to take his revenge, but for now he would do everything his mother asked of him, just as he always had.

'Is that you, Jared?' Cynthia opened her eyes.

'Yes, Mom.'

'Give me an hour to rest and then have the woman brought back up here.'

'I don't like this.' He'd followed his mother's instructions, not wishing to upset her and sure that she knew what she was doing. But on the journey to Scotland, with Suzanne in the back of the van and him attempting to play the hard man, his doubts began to nag at him. *What the hell has she got me into?* The plan had been to simply track down Don Tyler but it had all spiralled out of control. Then, having done his duty as required, Jared had been rewarded for his diligence with a sleepless night.

'You don't have to like it. Just do as you're told.'

'And when you're done with her, then what? She goes home and has me arrested for kidnapping?'

'It won't come to that.' She smiled at him. 'Nobody will ever do anything to harm you.'

'You think you'll be able to pay her off, just like you did with him?'

'Something like that.'

'She doesn't seem that type to me.'

'You're too unworldly, boy,' she said sharply, then softened her tone. 'Maybe that's my fault, for giving you everything you ever wanted, for keeping you safe from all the bad things in life. So you don't understand these types of people as I do.'

And Jared knew this was true. Until his mother's illness he'd had the carefree life of a rich Florida kid, a top-of-the-line car at sixteen, parties and pretty girlfriends, ski holidays: the soft life, all due to his mother's acumen. And unlike many of his contemporaries, who disliked their emotionally semi-detached parents and who took their lives of privilege for granted, he had worshipped his always attentive mother and appreciated everything she had done for him. And now that *she* needed *him*, he would never, ever let her down.

'Don't you be fooled by anything she has to say,' Cynthia was saying. 'That woman is no kin of yours. She's *his* daughter; I can see him in her eyes, hear him in her voice. They are two of a kind – liars, both.'

Jared saw her face take on that look, the one of determination she used when she strode into a boardroom, her high heels clacking on the polished marble floors. The steel magnolia who'd had the grey-suited men quaking in their handmade shoes. And he recalled how he had admired her and realised just how much those misogynistic Southerners must have hated her.

'I don't want you anywhere near that woman, you hear? She'll fill your head with lies and confusion. Leave me to deal with her.'

He left the room with her words echoing in his ears. *Leave me to deal with her.* And he wondered just what she meant.

*

Rose was roused from a drugged sleep when she sensed a presence in her room. She struggled to open her eyes but her eyelids were stuck fast. Through the fuggy haze, she half-remembered that bastard Filipino nurse injecting her. She was a rough one and Rose's arm felt like a pincushion. 'Get away from me!' Rose had screamed at them but the orderly held her down as the nurse jabbed her arm. 'Be quiet now. You won't get better if you carry on like this.'

Rose tittered to herself as she recalled the last thing she had said before the sedative kicked in. 'Fuck off, you slant-eyed cow!' That had told her, all right. Bitch!

Finally overcome by the soporific effects of the drug, Rose had been cast back into the darkness. But even in this dream-like state she sensed she was no longer alone.

'What have you done with the money?' A baritone voice echoed around her room.

She managed to open one eye.

'Who's there?'

'I've been to your house, Rose. And everything's gone.'

All she could see was a faint illumination between the drawn curtains. It was still daylight outside while she was in this medicated twilight world. She slowly turned her head towards the shadowy figure that kept fading from view. The soft tread of footsteps brought it nearer. She felt a hand on her shoulder. Someone shook her lightly. She heard the voice penetrate the fog of her sedation but couldn't make out the words. Strong hands took her by the shoulders and rolled her from her foetal position onto her back.

'Where is it?'

The voice was so close now, like it was whispering in her ear. She could almost feel breath on her face. Though her vision was blurred, her other senses gradually heightened and she felt like a trapped animal. The people who had been after Don had found her. She wasn't safe, even here. Panicked, she tried to scream but her throat was constricted and no sound came.

'Where's my stuff?'

She felt a weight on one side of her bed as the man sat beside her. His bulk drastically reduced the light available to her but she instantly recognised the smell of him.

The voice softened. 'It's okay, my sweetheart. Don't be frightened. I'm here with you.'

She struggled to focus as the face came closer and the hazel eyes appeared gentle and loving.

'You've come for me,' Rose slurred.

'I'm going to take you home, Rose. It will be the two of us together – forever. Just like I promised.'

'I love you, Don,' she whispered.

Her eyes were fully open now, but it was as though she was in a swimming pool, trying to see through the constantly swirling water. He clambered onto the bed and straddled her. The pressure of his thighs was on both sides of her body, pulling the blankets tightly around her, holding her firmly in place.

'The chest is still in your hallway. You were told to burn it.' His tone switched to admonition. 'You opened it, didn't you?'

Rose felt her heart fluttering like a butterfly in a net. 'I'm sorry. Don't be mad at me.'

The voice softened. 'I'm not angry, my love. Just tell me what you did with everything.'

He wasn't furious, then. A feeling of blessed relief filled her soul. 'I gave it all to Suzanne.'

'The suitcases?'

'The notebooks and the money, I gave her everything. Please forgive me.'

He reached down and stroked her hair with one hand, raised her head slightly and pulled a pillow from beneath it.

'You're going home, Rose,' he assured her.

And she believed him. He was the love of her life and she was his. So she surrendered herself to the white cloud that descended over her head. She had no need to resist the pressure that took away her breath. He was taking her with him and that was all she had ever wanted.

*

Donald Tyler calmly made his way from Redstone House, leaving Rose Anderson to be discovered later by the staff he had sidled past with such ease. *Bunch of lazy bastards*, he scoffed, *standing around chatting when they were in charge of a loony bin.* If he could gain access so easily, then any of their barking mad patients could get out and wreak havoc in the outside world. It was disgraceful.

Rose hadn't even struggled. He'd replaced the pillow under her head. Her mouth had lolled open obscenely, so he'd closed it. It would take a while before anyone established exactly how she had met her end. And in a building crammed with crazies, who would suspect a dead man?

Fucking women, he fumed, *you can't trust any of them. They are so easy to manipulate, so easy to fool, so easy to steal from.* Liberal use of the L-word did it every time. Before long they'd be saying it back to him. And the minute 'I love you, too' came tripping off some bitch's tongue, that was when he'd stop responding. It always made them nervous and that was when he knew he had them hooked. After that, he could get away with anything.

He jiggled the car keys in his hand. The old magic had worked a treat on Bridget, the Irish nurse from the hospital – so plain and eager to please. He let out a mirthless laugh. *So fucking dead.*

He opened up the white Twingo that had been Bridget's prized possession, tore off the annoying green frog swinging from the mirror and threw it out of the window. He looked at the card he had found on the dining table in Rose's house and gave a snort of derision. The address of the nuthouse she'd been carted off to. It was a lucky break that, but then he always had been one lucky bastard. No more need for it now though, so he tore it into little pieces and tossed that out of the window as well. He pulled down the vanity mirror and winked at his reflection. His new look pleased him. He stroked his silver-white beard. *Should have grown one of these years ago*, he preened. *Makes me look distinguished. Born again.*

Best of all, it concealed the distinctive deep cleft in his chin that Joanie had always thought so cute.

Joanie... He recalled the last time he'd seen her. Two months into the new millennium. He'd been driving down King's Road, with the traffic at a virtual standstill and him watching all the girls go by. Joanie toted a large carrier bag as she stepped out of the Marks & Spencer store. The same red hair, though shorter now; the same face, though older now; the same smile as she waved to her husband across the road. He'd rushed across the road to meet her, straight out in front of Don's car. Don had watched them stroll off together, with Joanie talking in her lively, animated way and her man laughing at some amusing observation she had made.

Don's guts clenched at the memory and he slammed the mirror back into place. He reached for the notebook on the passenger seat. He'd retrieved it from under the mattress at Rose's house. He flicked through and found what he was looking for. It had been a couple of years since he'd scoped the place out and he wanted to double-check. Not a bad address, as he remembered it. Suzanne had done okay for herself during the ten years since he'd last seen her at her studio. He'd kept tabs on her all that time, of course, just in case. She was a teacher now and married to an insurance salesman. That was far better than pissing around with that crappy art of hers, he reasoned. No good would ever have come from that. Painting was for losers and lunatics. He'd done her a favour, if she only knew it. Sophie Chen had been his added bonus. He smiled at *that* memory – fire and pain.

His next step was to recover everything that dullard Rose had turned over to his daughter. He started the engine, drove out of the hospital car park and headed south, to Suzanne's home address.

*

When Suzanne was summoned again, she found Cynthia propped up in bed. The woman looked exhausted, like someone not long for this world. Jared was sitting in a chair beside her.

'I've had Jared charge up Don's cell phone,' Cynthia said. 'It's registered to his last address so any trace put on it will lead straight back to his home and not to us.'

Jared looked up at Suzanne. 'Tyler was getting sloppy. That's how we found him. He used to change his number every few months and then that stopped.'

'I suppose that was when he fell ill,' Suzanne suggested.

'Make the call,' Cynthia commanded.

Jared stood up and produced the phone. 'You tell him you're okay and you'll be seeing him soon. Nothing more. What's the number?'

He tapped it in, waited for an answer, handed it over and remained close beside her.

*

'Suzanne! Thank God. Where are you?'

'I'm fine. I just needed to get away.'

'I've been out of my mind with worry.'

'I'm sorry. I'll be home soon, Marky. And we'll go on a second honeymoon. Just like last time.'

The phone went dead. Mark rang the last number that came up. Nothing. The automated female voice advised him: 'This number is not available.'

He phoned Luke immediately. 'I know where Suzanne is,' he told his brother. 'She's in Scotland.'

CHAPTER TWENTY-NINE

Donald Tyler silently opened the high gate to the right-hand side of the front porch and crept around the side of Suzanne's house. Once in the garden, he spotted the French windows. With his back to the wall, for a quick getaway in case someone clocked him, he peered in. Inside the house was a tall young guy, fair-haired with a fit-looking physique. Suzanne's husband, presumably. He was pacing the room anxiously, obviously deep in his own thoughts, when he sprang into action and headed towards the hallway beyond. Don listened carefully for the sound of him running upstairs. He took this as his cue. Nobody locks their kitchen door when they're at home, he knew. Moments later, he was inside.

He entered the hallway, alert for the sound of footsteps on the floor above. There was no sign of his suitcases in the hall and the understairs cupboard yielded nothing. But he noticed a gym bag, tennis racquet and cricket bat. He grinned broadly – that bat might come in handy. He pulled it from behind the bag and weighed it in his hands. *Nice*, he thought as he carried it into the sitting room.

He immediately spotted some of his swag neatly arranged on the dining table. That stupid bitch Rose really had given everything up. He pocketed the swipe card and key to his safe deposit box, then glanced at the other stuff. Naomi's bracelet was worth a couple of grand, yet he might get just five hundred quid for it from one of those dodgy gold-buying businesses that had sprung up on every high street since the economy had turned to shit. He picked up the silver ankh. Gloria, she'd been one juicy slut. But you can't get much for silver nowadays, so he placed it back on the table dismissively. What he'd trousered would be enough for now. Though he could have done with that money in the suitcase and was narked that he couldn't find it. If he were able to comb the entire house he might uncover it but with Suzanne's husband about… He considered the cricket bat. A couple of whacks with that could crack a head wide open but this guy had the advantage of being many years younger and six inches taller than Don. So that money would have to wait. His journals didn't matter any more. Though since he'd learned that they hadn't been destroyed he'd come up with a fantasy of sitting on an exotic beach reading a book about the deceased multiple killer Donald Albert Tyler. He envisaged the title as *Never Brought To Justice*. It would be all wrapped up with the usual psychobabble, with horseshit theories about motivation, lousy childhood, blah, blah, blah. And there he'd be, lying in the sun with one hand on the curvy bum of some local slapper, laughing his tits off. 'What's so funny?' she'd ask him. And he'd reply, 'People are so fucking stupid.' Now that would be really cool. That would be his ultimate triumph. The downside being he didn't want anyone who read them to find a way of getting his idiot son out of prison. But he could always scrub any mention of Betty's murder. Yes, that's what he could do. Lying by omission, works every time.

The mobile phone on the coffee table in front of the TV trilled 'Riders On The Storm'. Don retreated back into the kitchen as the guy ran back down the stairs to answer it.

From his position by the door, Don believed he heard, 'Suzanne! Where are you?' Now that was interesting. It wasn't so much the words themselves but the tone of voice used that caught his attention. Suzanne hadn't simply gone shopping. She'd gone AWOL.

Don waited, intrigued by the dawning realisation that something was amiss here. But it was the second conversation that got his antennae buzzing. 'She's in Scotland,' Suzanne's husband explained.

And Donald Tyler suspected that he knew where in Scotland. But he had to be sure.

He sidled along the hallway until he was at the sitting room door. Suzanne's husband had ended his phone call and was standing by the dining table with his back to Don. He moved a dining chair out of the way and began searching for something, probably the items that Don had already pocketed. The guy had bent down to check if anything had fallen under the table when Don made his move. Gripping the handle of the bat with both hands, he approached stealthily and swung hard. There was a sickening crack as the heavy wood connected with the unprotected blond head and the man was floored.

Don prodded him in the ribs with his shoe to make sure he was unconscious, then he picked up the mobile from the table to search for the last incoming number. He recognised his own phone number immediately. Suzanne would naturally use her own mobile to call her husband but this kind of skulduggery could only be down to that twisted bitch Cynthia. Now he knew his daughter's whereabouts precisely.

Don bent down and saw blood seeping from the tall guy's ears and nose. He casually raised the cricket bat, turned it side-on for more heft and, putting all his weight behind the swing, he smashed it down on the head of the prone figure one more time. The sound it made reminded him of the cracking of an egg. Satisfied with his handiwork, he whistled tunelessly as he set about searching the house.

CHAPTER THIRTY

Despite her fragile state, Cynthia's expression exuded ill-disguised displeasure. 'I told you to say no more than instructed.'

Suzanne stood her ground. 'I was trying to reassure him.'

Cynthia eyed her suspiciously. 'Where did you go on honeymoon, sugar?'

'Corfu.' Suzanne hoped the lie wasn't apparent in her voice. Anyway, it was half-true. She had wanted to go to Corfu until Mark confessed that he had a phobia about flying. So she had suggested a driving tour of France but his fear of confined spaces put the kybosh on any journey involving the Channel Tunnel. Suzanne didn't fancy a ferry trip, so Mark had come up with the idea of Scotland. She had been decidedly underwhelmed, though reluctantly agreed. Big mistake. She'd been miserable for the entire two weeks. They had ended up in Elgin, the smallest city in that land of incessant rain that teetered on the edge of the North Sea. Inverness, *Mac*-bloody-*beth*, the Loch Ness sodding monster and the Battle of Culloden – they could stick it! The honeymoon had been a total disaster. There were only so many whisky distilleries, cashmere factories and ancient churches that Suzanne could bear being dragged around, though Mark had appeared fascinated. Had she been asked to nominate the very last place in the world that she would ever wish to visit again, Elgin would have won, hands down. However, a regional news item she had recently caught on the TV in her room had mentioned Elgin, so she'd taken a leap of faith that this house was not too far from there.

'Leave us, Jared,' Cynthia commanded. 'We need to get on.'

Cynthia wanted to hear about Thailand, around the date of Don's initial death certificate.

'When would that have been?' Suzanne asked as she stood by the Edwardian table on the opposite side of the room to the bed and where Don's journals were set out in orderly piles.

'Two thousand and six,' Cynthia wheezed. 'Come on, girl, get on with it.'

While sorting through Don's journals, Suzanne stood with her back to Cynthia and searched surreptitiously for one that covered the early nineties, the time of Betty Tyler's murder. When she spotted it, she set it to one side, out of Cynthia's sight.

'What's taking you so long?' Cynthia was becoming increasingly impatient.

Suzanne picked the one marked 2002–06. 'Got it.'

'And bring me the photograph of the girl on the beach.'

Suzanne found the shot of the beautiful young blonde and the relevant journal, then handed the photo to Cynthia. 'Annabelle,' Cynthia cooed the name written on the back.

Suzanne sat in the chair beside the bed and began reading aloud.

We walked along the moonlit beach together, drank a bottle of tequila and smoked a couple of joints. Her skin was soft, as white as the moonlight and oh so young. Annabelle, with the long, lustrous hair and tranquil eyes; the one who was drunk and as high as a kite; the girl who writhed beneath me.

My demon came out of the retreating tide, hissing, swearing and slithering its way across the warm tropical sand. She laughed when first she sensed it, then her expression changed to fear and she started to yell.

'Shhh,' I said. 'It's alright, I won't let it harm you.'

She stared right at me, her eyes full of fear. She screamed and tried to wriggle out from under me. I put my hand over her mouth and she bit down hard. The rock was within my reach and I grabbed it, felt its heft, sensed its gravity. I ejaculated deep inside her. There was so much blood. Her eyes remained open but her face was a disgusting, pulped mess. I hurled the rock into the sea and dragged her in after it.

'You said Annabelle had been reported as drowned,' Suzanne said, 'but Don says here that he beat her to death with a rock. Wouldn't the Thai police have noticed that?'

'Thai police are notoriously lax. And it depends on how long she'd been in the water,' Cynthia slurred. 'Fish eat the face and eyes first.'

Horrified by that revelation, Suzanne glanced up to see Cynthia's eyelids drooping. 'Do you want me to continue?'

Cynthia murmured something inaudible so Suzanne leaned closer to her.

'Fetch Raul.'

Suzanne jumped from her seat, crossed to the Edwardian table, snatched the journal she wanted, held it by her side in one hand and banged on the door with the other. 'Raul! She needs you.'

The door was flung open immediately and the servant rushed in, his face full of concern. He took one look at Cynthia and ushered Suzanne firmly into the hallway.

'You stay there, miss, and wait for Jared.' He closed the door firmly behind him.

Run for it, Suzanne's instinct screamed at her. *Take the evidence that could free Raymond and get the hell out of here.* She walked along the corridor towards the front door and opened it as softly as she could. The clouds glowered overhead, threatening a downpour. This house is thirty miles from the nearest village, Jared had told her. But perhaps he'd lied. Maybe if she could get to the trees, she could hide until nightfall and then make her way along the unlit roads to the nearest house, ask for shelter and call the police. There was no sign of Jared, so she dashed across the lawn towards the sundial. The trees were several hundred yards ahead of her. She glanced back over her shoulder towards the house, her pulse racing. All was quiet and so she began to run. It would take a couple of minutes at full pelt to get to the trees, while Jared would probably be searching the house for her. She clutched the precious journal in her hand and concentrated on the trees with the sound of thunder echoing in her ears. The heavens darkened, then opened and the rain thudded down, making the grass beneath her feet slippery.

'Suzanne!' Jared's voice rang out across the garden behind her.

She urged her body forward, towards the tall green sentinels, not daring to look back. The trees were close now and the soles of her shoes skidded on the wet grass yet she kept going. She was practically out of breath already, her thighs aching from the exertion.

She didn't feel the blow, just a jolt that flung her momentarily out of existence followed by the sensation of falling. She held out both arms to break her fall and to prevent ending up flat on her face. Shockwaves shuddered up from her wrists to her shoulders as she hit the ground. The journal dropped from her hand and was caught by a sudden gust of wind. It flew for a moment like a damaged bird before it came to rest at the base of a pine tree.

Jared left her where she was and picked up the notebook. 'What the hell is this?'

Suzanne turned onto her back and stared up at him. He'd caught up with her so effortlessly, yet he was hardly out of breath, while she was still completely winded. 'That's one of our father's journals. You should read it to get a handle on just what's going on here.'

'Not interested.' He rolled up the notebook and tucked it into his jacket pocket, then held out a hand to help her up.

'Well, you should be.' She clambered to her feet and tried to regain her composure. 'We have a brother. His name is Raymond and he's already served twenty years in prison for a murder he didn't commit.'

'Bullshit!' He gripped her tightly by the arm and steered her around towards the house.

She elbowed him in the ribs and turned to hit him with her free hand. He slapped her hard across the face, open-handed. She attempted to pull away from him but he twisted her arm behind her back.

'I don't want to hurt you. But you're going nowhere until Mom says so.' He pushed her forward across the lawn as the rain pelted down. 'You'd have died of exposure out there before you got anywhere.'

'Read the journals, Jared. Our father killed many women, including your girlfriend, Moira.'

He loosened his hold on her arm and spun her round to face him, his expression a mixture of apprehension and disbelief. He gripped her by the shoulders, his fingers digging into her flesh. 'Moira isn't dead. Moira went to Glasgow.'

'Have you seen her since? What about her relatives, have they seen her?'

'She never got on with her mother. She left to get away from her.'

'That's not what Cynthia told me. She said that Don strangled Moira and buried her body somewhere among those trees,' Suzanne indicated towards the wooded area they had just left behind.

Jared's eyes filled with mistrust. 'Mom warned me not to talk to you,' he retorted angrily. 'She said you were a born liar, just like him.' He grasped her arm again and urged her back towards the house.

'Isn't it time to start thinking for yourself, Jared?'

'I'm not listening.'

'You really need to before you get in any deeper. Before your mother orders you to shoot your own sister. Before you condemn your own brother to spending the rest of his life behind bars.'

He wrenched her arm further up her back until she felt her wrist might snap. 'Shut the fuck up!'

'That hurts.'

'It's meant to. And I'll break it if you say another word.'

They reached the house and he opened the door to her windowless room. He roughly pushed her in before locking the door behind her.

Suzanne beat on the door with her fists. 'Read the journals, Jared,' she yelled. 'Don't you want to know the truth? Then read the fucking journals.'

CHAPTER THIRTY-ONE

Once he'd done for the husband, Donald Tyler searched every room in his daughter's house and came up empty. He opened each and every door and cupboard but encountered only the objects of middle-class domesticity. By the time he reached the attic, his frustration at not finding what he'd been looking for was at fever pitch. He kicked at the attic door and it swung wide, revealing a bright room that was flooded with sunlight from the overhead dormer window. Several of Suzanne's paintings were propped up against the white walls and he felt an urge to kick each canvas all to pieces. One, half-completed, sat on an easel directly in front of him and instantly conjured images that he had always kept at bay. The red-headed mother leading a child over shifting sand, a metaphor for his own life. The kiss from those booze-laced lips, followed by the bite of the leather strap Julia Tyler kept hanging behind the kitchen door. But it was the portrait of Joanie that caused Don's chest to tighten, his breathing to shorten and his hands to tingle. For the first time he saw a likeness he had never previously admitted to. His mother's image flashed before his eyes, her red hair falling across her face as she sat sketching, her voice filled with hatred, the blows raining down on him, his childish pleas of, 'No, Mam, don't hit me again.' Julia Tyler's breath, rotten with whisky, as she lashed out at him. *'Don't say no to me, you little bastard!'*

Don snatched up the Stanley knife from a shelf and slashed all of Suzanne's paintings to ribbons. Then he ran back down the stairs to her bedroom, yanked open her wardrobe door and shredded her clothes.

Anger almost sated, he stood and stared into the full-length mirror that was mounted on the wall. He imagined Suzanne standing naked in front of it. He raised his hand and, as a shaft of sunlight glinted on the angled blade, Don slashed viciously at the empty air: left and right, left and right. Someone, he assured himself, was going to pay for this latest betrayal. Everyone he had ever loved was against him, and always had been. His mother hating him, Betty running away, Joanie divorcing him, Cynthia throwing him out at gunpoint; each wife choosing the child version of himself over the real thing. But he'd show them all.

Keeping his eyes on the mirror, he took a deep breath and made an attempt to reassemble his thoughts. He watched his reflected self begin to smile as a thought hit him. Perhaps the death of the guy downstairs could be blamed on Suzanne. The body found by… he didn't know who, but eventually the smell would hit the streets and someone would get curious. Don stared at the mess he'd made of his daughter's clothes and his grin widened. What with the ruined togs and the slashed paintings, how easy it would be for the cops to assume that Suzanne and her husband had had a blazing row. In a rage, the husband did the damage. Suzanne comes home and takes her revenge with the guy's own cricket bat. Then she disappears, never to be seen again. It was a sordid family saga guaranteed to make the Sunday papers.

Don Tyler laughed out loud and winked at his reflection. Thinking on his feet, that was his main talent. Whatever tight spot his demon got him in, his agile mind had never let him down. Don trotted down the stairs in high spirits, closed the door of the house behind him, walked calmly back to his car, placed the retrieved cricket bat in the boot and then headed back towards the high street to the gold-buying emporium he'd spotted earlier.

*

Luke repeatedly rang his brother's landline but got no reply. There was no response on his mobile either. *Scotland*, he wondered. *Where in bloody Scotland?* It must be something to do with Donald Tyler, but what? He had to get hold of Mark. He'd mentioned Elgin and a honeymoon, but Luke's mind was elsewhere at the time. He'd been on his way to interview some low-life picked up on an indecent assault charge when he'd taken Mark's call and had told his brother he'd ring him back as soon as he was done. The interview had taken over two hours yet all they'd got out of the suspect had been a list of excuses. And when he'd been vigorously challenged he'd suddenly clammed up, insisting on a solicitor. Right now he was back in his cell and Luke was expected to wait until the duty solicitor could be bothered to turn up.

*

Donald Tyler was chuffed. He'd squeezed six hundred quid out of that swindling git in the gold-buying shop for Naomi's bracelet. That would do him for now. He'd retrieve his own money from the safe deposit box when this unfortunate business was all over. Rose had been a big disappointment to him. Who'd have thought she had enough nous to find Suzanne and to hand all his stuff over? He'd had it all planned and she'd fucked it up for him. Still, a smart man knows to blow with the wind and now he had other things in mind. But first he'd complete what he had to do, tie up all the loose ends in his life, then he'd be a free man again. *Don't get ahead of yourself. Take it one step at a time.* He was sure he'd done for that stupid twat Suzanne had married. *Howzat!* Don chuckled to himself. The guy hadn't seen that one coming. But then, they never did.

Don reckoned he could get to Cynthia's gaff in eight or nine hours if he drove at a fair lick with just a couple of stop-offs for a piss, a sandwich and essential supplies. In the old days he'd have been starving by now, but after his triple heart bypass he'd cut down on all the fatty foods he used to eat and now he was back to the weight he'd been in his twenties. He might be getting on a bit, but he was fit again and raring to go. He felt like a new man.

Donald Tyler was reborn and life was good.

It was six hundred miles to Elgin and would probably cost a hundred quid in petrol, but it would be well worth it. Don revved the Twingo's engine with glee, then followed the signs for the M25 motorway and his journey north.

*

Luke rang both of Mark's numbers again. No reply on the landline, straight to voicemail on the mobile. Something was a bit off here. Mark had been sleeping with his phone under the pillow just in case Suzanne called him. The stupid sod had most likely gone out and forgotten to take it with him but best to check it out. Luke told his colleagues he was going out, picked up his personal radio and asked to be informed when the perv's brief deigned to arrive.

More intrigued than concerned at this point, he took the short walk from the police station to his brother's home. This stretch of the high street had undergone a lot of changes of late. The sweet shop where Luke used to take his son had gone bust, as had the coffee bar next door. A tatty pound shop had replaced one and the other was now a gold-buying emporium, run by a bloke the police kept a wary eye on. Luke rounded the corner past the bakery and entered Mark's road. He spotted the Merc in the driveway, skirted by it and rang the doorbell.

*

Don had been driving for two hours and felt the grumble of hunger. He'd stopped only once on the journey so far, at a Halfords store to buy four five-litre jerry cans. While he was there, he'd spotted a packet of non-releasable plastic cable ties and a pack of bin sacks and bought them too. You never knew when something like that could come in handy, he reasoned as he sauntered back to the car. He put his purchases in the boot, alongside Bridget's well-equipped first aid kit, plus the Stanley craft knife he'd pinched from Suzanne's attic studio, along with his holdall containing his clothes and the bloodied cricket bat. Sorted!

He passed the sign for the Northampton turn-off. He hadn't been there for forty-odd years, when he'd tracked Betty down after she'd fled Liverpool with baby Raymond. He'd discovered she was living in a rented house near her mother's place. He'd been to see her, but Betty wouldn't let him into the building. So he'd gone out that night, got tanked up and kicked her door down. He remembered trying to find his feet along a long narrow corridor and bouncing from wall to wall as the floor undulated beneath him like shifting sand. He emerged into a room dimly lit by the glow from the dying embers of the fire in the grate and Betty was standing at the window with the full moon nestling on the roof opposite. Her dark hair was swept up into a tight ponytail, her hands on her too-slim hips, a suitcase at her feet.

'Where's the baby?' he demanded.

She turned to face him. 'He's with my mother,' she said. 'I won't have you anywhere near him. He's not going to grow up to be like you.'

Don was across the room at her in seconds, lunging at her, grabbing her by the hair. He got her in a headlock, punched her three times in the face. *Bitch, cunt, whore!* She struggled loose from his grip, ran out of the house, barefoot and bleeding, and slammed the door behind her. He'd grabbed her suitcase and hauled it into the garden, tossed her clothes onto the grass, searched for lighter fuel and struck a match. The pile of shoddy garments flared, smouldered then burst into flames. The glare had almost blinded him. She'd escaped him that time. But he found her again, years later in Stoke-on-Trent, and exacted his revenge. Oh, hadn't he just! On both her and their moron of a son. He chortled at the memory.

Just before he reached Birmingham, he pulled off at a motorway services, took his holdall and one of the bin sacks out of the car. He locked it then strolled into the toilets to change his clothes. He had blood splatters on his trainers and jeans, so he placed them in a black plastic sack that he dumped in the large rubbish bin outside the men's toilets. He casually entered the shop, bought a pack of ham sandwiches, a Diet Coke and some water. After that, he drove to the petrol station by the exit, topped up the tank and one of the jerry cans with petrol. He didn't want to draw attention to himself by filling them all up at once. Then he was on his way again, singing along with the radio.

Half an hour later, he was passing Cannock. He hadn't been in this neck of the woods since 1995, a year after Cynthia had chucked him out and he'd returned to England. At that time he'd been travelling the country, living like a gypsy in a camper van, reliving his exploits on old stomping grounds and looking for new adventures. A sweet memory invaded his mind and stirred his groin. Oh, she'd been a tasty little piece, all done up in her short skirt and dangly red earrings. He remembered watching her and the lad through the trees. With the kid pinching her bum and laughing while she pretended she didn't want it. They'd stopped walking and the girl stood with her back against a tree. The lad was grinding his crotch against her, his hands all over her body. Spying on teenagers canoodling didn't get Don's mojo up and running so he was about to stroll away and leave them to it when he heard the girl shouting 'Stop!' She was attempting to get her tits back in her blouse and the lad was yelling at her that she was a prick-teaser. The girl pushed the kid away and he ran off through the woods, back towards the road. The girl started snivelling and it looked like she might follow her boyfriend.

Don had grinned. This was more like it. He looked around and found a heavy branch that had been torn off a tree by the recent storm. He picked it up and crept up behind her. He hit her hard on the back of her head and she pitched forward. He turned her over and straddled her. 'Shh!' he'd hushed her as he put his hands around her slim white throat, squeezed, and watched the light gradually fade from her terrified eyes. Afterwards he had pocketed her cheap red earrings and taken a photo of the spot where she died. Memories are made of this.

Don recalled that he then did what he had done so many times before. He loaded her body into his camper van and took it to a remote part of Cannock Chase. It was ideal, a place of natural beauty with its miles of open heathland, forests and the ruins of old coal mines. He'd dumped the girl where she would never be found. At least, they'd never found that skanky little hitchhiker, so why should they find this one? And after all these years, no one ever had.

The M6 for Manchester and beyond was coming up and Don looked for signs of a service station to top up the Twingo's tank and fill another jerry can.

'Down, boy,' he told his erection. 'Plenty of time for that once we reach our destination.' Time to collect what was his. Time for everyone in Donald Albert Tyler's past to be obliterated. Just like the man himself.

CHAPTER THIRTY-TWO

Luke had a thorough knowledge of the procedure but it was the first time he'd been on the receiving end of an investigation. He was also well aware of the police adage that the first person to discover the body was probably the one who committed the murder. Therefore he expected to be treated as a suspect. He'd given an initial statement to ill-at-ease colleagues, then voluntarily surrendered his clothes, shoes and mobile phone for forensic examination. He was sitting in Detective Chief Inspector Colin Etheridge's office wearing the tracksuit they'd handed him, waiting.

After he'd found Mark, his police training swiftly kicked in. Check for vital signs of life in the victim – although the head injury was extensive and it appeared that Mark had been dead for some time. Be careful not to step in the blood. Make a cursory search to ensure the perpetrators were no longer on the premises. Once he'd radioed in to the station, he'd stood across the room from his brother's body with his emotions in a state of paralysis. What was he supposed to feel? It surely wasn't to be dispassionately assessing the crime scene that now preoccupied his logical mind. No sign of a weapon. No visible signs of forced entry. The assailant or assailants had possibly gained access to the house in the same way he had, through the unlocked kitchen door. Yet nothing that any burglar worth his salt would have snaffled appeared to have been disturbed. The DVD player blinked away unmolested, and Mark's laptop sat open on the coffee table with his wallet beside it.

Luke stood in the room he knew so well and stared at his brother's lifeless body. He'd seen dead people before on the job – suicides, victims of motor accidents, a gang member stabbed in the street, a small child smothered in her bed by her junkie mother – they were the incidents that stuck in his mind. But no matter how horrific they'd been at the time, after a while he'd got over it and moved on to the next case. The first dead body he'd witnessed had been Sophie Chen and he recalled quelling his feeling of revulsion at the sight of her twisted remains, as he steadied the traumatised Suzanne at the morgue. That was the image he'd found impossible to erase from his memory. And now Mark. How would he ever again be able to visualise his brother in any other way but this? A sensation of dazed unreality settled around him while he waited for the scene of crime team to arrive.

Although DCI Etheridge's office was as familiar to Luke as his own flat, he was disturbed to find himself shivering. Delayed shock, he assumed. Any time soon the enormity of what had happened would hit home and he had to try to keep it together. If only he hadn't been caught up with that damn suspect, he'd have gone to see Mark the moment he'd phoned him. *If only…* he'd heard those words dozens of times over the years from friends, lovers, family – of victims, of criminals, of suicides. If only this, if only that. But his own 'if only' sense of regret had descended on him like a black cloud and he struggled to break free rather than break down – at least, not here. He took a deep breath and fought back the tears.

Etheridge was the senior officer in charge of the investigation and Luke could hear the sounds of frenetic movement outside as an incident room was set up just along the corridor. There was no chance he'd be allowed inside but he could imagine the board on the wall with photos being pinned up of Mark's body. He surmised that evidence had already been bagged and tagged as the SOCO team sifted its way through the house. Fingerprints, fibres and blood stains would be lifted from the scene and every available officer called in to canvass the neighbours, check bank statements, phone records and computer data. As the senior investigating officer, Etheridge would have all the information collected by the investigating and the interviewing teams. He was a good copper and he never missed a trick. They'd be putting a search out for Suzanne's car through the National Police Computer. If she was driving, they'd find her through Automated National Plate Registration. Every CCTV, police car and speed camera would have her registration number flagged up. A trace would already be on her mobile phone, and in the incident room a team would be contacting the Scottish force in Elgin, where Mark and Suzanne had spent their honeymoon. And since Suzanne had recently been in contact with her aunt, they'd also get the local force in Liverpool to interview Vera Tyler, once they established her address. The police would get in touch with Suzanne's friends, her work colleagues and her mother, Joan. It would be a hive of activity out there, but all Luke could do was wait and be compelled to take what the force laughingly called 'gardening leave'. Once, that is, they had eliminated him as a suspect.

*

Three hours and two hundred miles after Birmingham, Don made another stop. He was just short of Carlisle, the unofficial border with Scotland. He filled the last empty jerry can with petrol, went into the shop and bought several packs of sandwiches and some cans of soft drinks. Just outside the petrol station, he spied a flower stall and picked up a bunch of freesias as well. He smirked. Can't go visiting a lady without taking flowers. It was already getting dark and it would be another four hours to reach Cynthia's place. He didn't fancy arriving at night. He considered it best to get this done in the daytime. He remembered he had once stayed at a Travelodge just outside Dumfries, which was another hour's drive away. He decided to rest up there for the night and set out again early the next morning.

'Sorry, pal,' he told the chirpy young man behind the motel desk. 'I had my wallet stolen yesterday and I'm waiting for my new credit cards to arrive. I'm only here for the night, so I'll pay cash upfront, if that's okay?'

The guy nodded sympathetically, took Don's money and handed him the room key.

*

Detective Chief Inspector Colin Etheridge leaned across the desk and held Luke in his quizzical stare.

'You say that, to your knowledge, your brother and his wife were getting along fine before she went walkabout. Is that correct?'

'He'd have told me if they were having problems. But he said everything had been fine before she started investigating her father's background. That was why Mark was so concerned about her. He thought she was becoming a bit obsessive.'

Etheridge leaned back in his seat and idly scratched his forehead just below his receding hairline. 'It's just that when the SOCO team were searching the house they entered Suzanne's studio in the attic. She's an art teacher, isn't she?'

'She was an artist when she was younger but she gave up after a fire at her studio. Though lately she's started painting seriously again in oils and watercolours. In fact, there's one of her watercolours hanging in the hallway of the house.'

'And there were several more paintings in her attic studio.'

'I suppose there would be. That's where she worked on them.'

'The thing is, Luke, the canvases in the studio had all been slashed to ribbons. Someone had made a right mess of them, though there was no sign of the implement used.'

'I know Mark would never do anything like that.'

Etheridge placed his elbow on the desk and leaned his chin on his closed fist. 'Not in a fit of temper, maybe, slashed her paintings and shredded her clothes because his wife had walked out on him?'

'What? Her clothes too?'

Etheridge nodded.

'No,' Luke said. 'My brother isn't like that at all.'

'Hmm.' Etheridge's florid features were set as he looked Luke straight in the eye. 'Well, someone is.'

CHAPTER THIRTY-THREE

Raul knocked on the door briefly before he unlocked it, as if Suzanne had any say in whether or not he entered the room. As he wasn't wearing the white coat he wore when dealing with Cynthia – for sanitary reasons, she thought – she supposed that those duties were over for the night. His dark shirt clung to his stooped shoulders like a second skin.

'Still raining, I see,' Suzanne said, in an attempt to establish some kind of rapport.

He shrugged. 'I'm sorry about this,' he said as he unplugged the portable TV. 'But Miss Cynthia is withdrawing privileges.' He glanced across the room at the electric fire.

'Please don't take the fire,' Suzanne pleaded. 'It gets bloody cold in this room.'

He picked up the television set and held it in both arms. 'Well, I'm supposed to come back for that. But at my age I gets a bit forgetful, if you take my meaning.'

'Thank you.' Suzanne stood and opened the door for him. 'You couldn't also forget to lock the door, I suppose?'

'You'd catch your death venturing out there on a night like this,' he replied with a sympathetic half-smile. 'I wouldn't want that on my conscience.'

She advanced to the threshold and looked out. The wind howled and the rain was bucketing down. The light from her room reflected like glass on the downpour and Suzanne shivered. If she had made her escape successfully earlier that day, she might now be either safe in a nearby farmhouse or wandering about in the pitch-dark, hopelessly lost and soaked to the skin. She retreated back inside and heard Raul lock the door behind him.

Suzanne looked around the room for the umpteenth time. The overhead single bulb gave off a harsh light that emphasised the starkness of the whitewashed walls. She stood, crossed the room and turned on the small table lamp that sat on the empty chest of drawers, then switched off the main light. She was trapped in this twelve-feet-square cell. What had possibly once been a large broom cupboard now contained a toilet and a rudimentary cold-water shower that she had shivered beneath that morning. The door that Jared had told her led to the cellar was denied her. The doorknob had come off in her hand when she'd tried to turn it, and kicking it hadn't worked either, as the solid door hadn't budged. Even if she had been able to open it, she wondered what was down there in that cellar. Maybe there'd be nothing but rats. She shuddered at the thought.

She sat down on the bed and a web of loss and despair descended on her. If she died in this place – if Cynthia did order Jared to shoot her, Suzanne had no indication that he wouldn't obey his mother – what had she accomplished in her life? Her art had been her all-consuming passion until that fire at her studio. But afterwards... Mark had been there when she needed someone, a steady hand when she found herself adrift; someone so unlike her feckless father that she had been attracted to a more conventional life than she had ever imagined for herself. She now knew that she'd been virtually sleepwalking for the past ten years. She'd settled for far less than she wanted, taken a teaching job to help pay the huge mortgage on the house that Mark had insisted they buy. '*It's an investment for the future,*' he'd said. '*Big enough to live in when we have children.*' Suzanne realised that she would have gone along with that too, taking the path of least resistance – if Rose Anderson hadn't entered her life. But Rose had contacted her and, instead of Suzanne listening to her mother's advice to stay out of this mess, she'd taken it as a challenge. And she knew now exactly why. Because her own life was so mundane, so stultifying. That was all going to change. If she got out of this alive, then she was determined to start life anew. One of her friends from art school now played with a rock band. Not that Suzanne had ever been to one of their gigs, because Mark disliked that kind of music. She'd travel again, as she had in her student years. Mark would either have to get over his fear of flying, or stay at home. She'd jack in her teaching job and begin painting full-time, despite any protests. If they couldn't pay the mortgage without two salaries coming in, then they could buy a smaller place instead. And she would one day tell him that, no, she didn't want to be a mother, thank you very much. And if he loved her too, then he would understand.

But first she had to get out of here. She looked at the entrance to the cellar and decided to give it one more go. She stood directly across the room and hurled herself at the door. Her body hit it with a thud and the wood creaked under the pressure. Though she couldn't see the hinges on this old door, they would be the weakest point and might just give way. She backed off and kicked the door with all her might. It shifted slightly, so she put her shoulder to it and heard a distinct clang as the doorknob on the other side hit the deck and clattered down what sounded like a long flight of stone steps. She imagined the door suddenly giving way and breaking off its hinges. She could easily be sent tumbling down those steps only to land on an unforgiving stone floor. On the other hand, there could be something down there that she could use as a weapon. She kicked the door again and again close to the hinges. When she heard the lowest hinge break, she kicked harder but the top one remained defiantly intact. She needed something heavier. She looked around the room. She switched the main light on, put the table lamp on the floor and dragged the chest of drawers across the room. Its feet scraped loudly on the stone floor and she prayed the noise wouldn't echo up into the main building. If she were caught then her electric fire would most certainly be confiscated. *Fuck 'em all,* she cursed under her breath. 'Fuck 'em all!' she said out loud as she placed the heavy sideboard against the cellar door and put her whole weight behind it. 'Fuck 'em all!'

Her anger and vehemence seemed to afford her extra strength and the door gave way. The chest of drawers was launched through it like a battering ram then tipped on its axis and lurched forward. She gave it one more almighty shove and sent it hurtling into the pitch-dark chasm of the cellar.

*

Donald Tyler strolled nonchalantly back to his motel from a nearby Indian restaurant, having chosen his favourite chicken tandoori meal and quaffed a pint of beer. Sated and relishing fevered fantasies of what he would accomplish tomorrow, he entered the reception area and asked the night man for a wake-up call at 3 a.m. Then he went to his room, took a hot shower, climbed into bed and slept soundly.

*

Luke couldn't sleep at all. He was convinced that he remained the prime suspect for Mark's murder. With a colleague involved in a murder investigation, Etheridge's team would be crossing every 'T' just to cover their own arses as any missed clues might come across like some kind of cover-up to an outsider. Luke knew that the investigating team had checked his phone record and established that the timing between Mark's call to him and the estimated time of death tallied. According to the SOCO boys, it appeared that Mark had been dead for at least an hour before Luke had found him, but everyone on the force was aware that TODs were estimates and not an exact science. So a shadow still loomed over Luke. Even so they had allowed him to go home but he was to report his movements each day to the police station. The search for Suzanne was on. And if she was found, all her possessions, including the suitcase full of money and Tyler's journals, might be taken into evidence.

The photograph of the woods where Luke had last seen Anita had convinced him that Tyler had something to do with her disappearance. He tried to console himself. He'd been just a kid, only sixteen, and terrified to tell his policeman father that he had bunked off school to be with Anita. So he had lied about that day. Nobody noticed that he'd been absent from one class as he'd been back at school in time for the next. He had denied that he even knew the girl and his dad had backed him up. So when she disappeared, nobody had searched the woods until days later. By which time it had rained heavily and any traces that might have been discovered had been washed away.

He lay in bed, opened his eyes and a word appeared before him in the light from the street lamps that filtered through the closed venetian blinds. *Guilt.* The long-held shame of that lie and the remorse he felt about keeping silent as he watched Anita's mother's anguish over her missing daughter. He'd pushed the whole affair to the back of his mind, shelved for all these years. But he now understood that it still gnawed away at him, kept him aloof, and had not allowed him to be either a proper husband or a decent father.

He closed his eyes again, desperate for sleep, but the image of Mark lying face down with his head caved in gatecrashed his mind and he couldn't shake himself free from it. He climbed out of bed and stumbled into his tiny kitchen. He yanked open the door of the cupboard beside the cooker and stared at the bottle of vodka he kept in there to remind him of how many days he'd been clean and sober. A note in Mark's handwriting was pinned to the door: *624 days.* Though that didn't include yesterday.

'And it doesn't include today,' Luke said aloud. He unscrewed the cap, glanced around for a glass and, not finding one to hand, he raised the bottle to his lips and took a long slug.

*

The ceiling light didn't cast enough illumination to give much visibility of the steps that led down into the dark cellar. The steps were narrow and without a banister, falling away on to the left-hand side. If Suzanne were to venture down there she'd need to see where she was going. The electric fire was plugged into a wall socket beside the shattered door. She unplugged it and replaced it with the table lamp. The flex was only a couple of yards long, but as she stood at the top of the precarious stairs with the lamp held at head height, she could see the demolished sideboard at the bottom of the twenty-foot drop to the left. She strained to see as far as the walls but they remained obscured. She placed the lamp on the top step and then, keeping close to the wall, began gingerly to make her way down into the darkness.

'What the fuck are you up to?' Jared's voice came from behind her. 'You could have woken Mom.'

She turned to see him standing in the doorway. He shone a torch in her eyes momentarily. 'I told you there was no way out.' He flashed the torchlight around the cellar walls. 'See?'

She looked down at the expanse of blank brick walls in the dank space. Shit! What the hell had she been expecting – an exit sign, a secret passage, an arsenal of guns?

'Come back up,' he said. 'There's nothing down there.'

With a sense of fatigue and desolation, she trudged back up to her room.

Jared grasped her arm and pushed her towards her bed. 'I've tried to be nice to you and what thanks do I get?'

Suzanne got her fight back, anger taking over. She pulled away from him and lashed out. '*Nice*? You kidnap me at fucking gunpoint, lock me in this room and you call that "nice". What's wrong with you people? You're a bunch of crazies.'

He reacted as though she'd slapped him.

Gotcha, she thought. 'When are you going to open your eyes and see what's going on? I'm just a pawn in some sick game your mother is playing. And so are you. Can't you get that into your head?'

'She's my mother.' He backed off, his face betraying a deep sorrow, a fleeting moment of indecision and doubt.

Suzanne calmed her anger, realising that she could use this. She tried another tack. 'And I'm your sister. Doesn't that mean anything to you?'

'I do what I have to.'

'Read the journals, Jared. Don't be such a blinkered fool.'

He slumped onto one end of her bed and indicated that she should sit too.

'I *did* read that journal,' Jared said, quietly. 'What Don did to those women, to Betty, was inhuman. And the way he describes it…' He shook his head as though lost for words.

'Our brother, Raymond Tyler, was convicted of that murder,' Suzanne reminded him, capitalising on his uncertainty. 'And he's spent the last twenty years protesting his innocence. He's in hospital right now after being attacked by another prisoner. All for something that our father did.'

Jared winced. 'Was this the kind of stuff Mom had you reading to her?'

Suzanne considered her options. Tell the whole truth or sugar the pill? From her years teaching art to sometimes troubled teenagers, she knew which path to take, so she followed her instinct, softened her tone and played the 'big sister' card.

'It was only those entries that referred to your mother. But we didn't get very far.' Jared seemed so innocent that Suzanne didn't think it wise to tell him about the twisted sex games Cynthia and their father had played all those years ago. And Cynthia had the nerve to accuse Suzanne of living a 'sheltered life'! If Jared really wanted to know the whole truth then he could find out for himself because he wasn't going to hear it from her. Right at that moment she needed his cooperation and she knew she couldn't afford to alienate him by bad-mouthing his mother. 'I think she wanted to understand what kind of man she'd married.'

'I don't remember much about our father,' he said. 'Mom threw him out when I was seven. He's been putting the squeeze on her ever since.'

'Do you know why she ended the relationship?'

'I was just a kid, so I don't know for sure. But I think it was something to do with a Cuban maid. Mom never mentioned Don again, not until he turned up here six years back.'

'Did you meet him then?'

'Briefly. But Mom sent me to the States to make arrangements for the Florida house to be sold. I was only seventeen but I was the only person she could trust. So I took a notarised letter to a real estate agent and helped Raul pack the place up. He was looking after the house at the time and Mom would never fire him. Raul's own mom and pop had been with our family from way back so Mom's known Raul all of her life. He's a lot more than just an employee to her, so I brought him back here with me. When I returned, ten days later, Don had already left.'

'And Moira had gone to Glasgow?'

'That's what I was told at the time.'

'You've been lied to, Jared. But there is more at stake here. We can't do anything about Don's other victims. They're dead. But we can help the living. Raymond is your brother, too. He's spent twenty years in prison for a crime he didn't commit. Doesn't he deserve a chance to prove his innocence?'

'I don't know what to do.'

'Give me that one journal, Jared. Let me go and I promise I won't say anything about your mother or what has happened here.' She reached across and touched his arm in an effort to reassure him. 'I promise you. I just want to help Raymond.'

He stared at her, his expression unreadable.

Not sure if she had got through to him, Suzanne played her trump card. 'Isn't that what Moira would want you to do? To help save one of Donald Tyler's victims?'

Jared stood and walked silently towards the door, then turned back to Suzanne. 'I'll give you a ride to Elgin in the morning. You can catch a train back to London and show that journal to the authorities.'

'You mean that?'

'I'll take you to the train station, but only if you promise me that you won't involve Mom. I don't care what happens to me but she hasn't got much time left.' He gazed at Suzanne with a haunted look in his eyes. 'What you said about Moira – that Don murdered her – I still can't believe it.'

'That's what Cynthia told me but maybe the whole story is in one of Don's other journals.'

'I never want to read anything like that ever again,' Jared said. 'I'll come for you at seven, before Mom wakes up. I'll give you the journal then. Be ready.'

He stopped and surveyed the room. 'You've made a helluva mess in here.'

'It's the cat in me,' Suzanne said.

He gave her a quizzical look.

'One of my neighbours has a cat, Sultan. If she leaves him locked up in the house for any length of time, he wrecks the joint.'

Jared smiled wanly, showing even white teeth, before he left, locking the door behind him.

CHAPTER THIRTY-FOUR

At three in the morning Donald Tyler awoke, fully alert in seconds, then dressed, dropped off his key at reception and was on his way out of the car park by ten past. The roads ahead would be deserted at this unearthly hour and he reckoned he could make it to his destination within four hours. If Suzanne was with Cynthia, then they'd all be under the impression that he was dead. 'Surprise!' he declaimed out loud. The tune on his late son-in-law's phone, 'Riders On The Storm', resonated in his mind and he laughed as he followed the signs that pointed him towards Elgin.

By six-thirty, with the weak sun shrouded by clouds on what threatened to be a drizzly day, Don had made good time and was at the 24-hour service station at Keith, topping up the petrol tank. Ten minutes away, that's all it was now. He was fizzing with anticipation while struggling to stay calm and remain in control. Today would herald the end of his old life and, once he'd paid a final visit to Joanie, he'd be as free as that buzzard he'd seen circling overhead. He had a new name, a new life, with more adventures to be had – everything just for the taking.

As the houses on the outskirts of Keith gave way to flat fields, Don turned left, past a long row of electricity pylons, then a lone farmhouse on the left, where he took a right turn. This was how Cyn liked to live: far from the madding crowd. Her Florida house had been the same, isolated and so close to the Everglades you could almost smell the alligator shit. She'd never get back there now, though, not if Don had anything to do with it.

The lane narrowed and the tall trees on both sides of the road cast a gloomy shadow. He was tempted to put the headlights on but couldn't afford to announce his arrival. So he drove slowly, searching for the gate to the driveway. He remembered that it was half-hidden in the trees that guarded the house. Crawling along, he cursed, sure he'd missed it, then he spotted the treeline just before he drove past.

He stopped at the gate, opened up, and then slowly motored along the driveway, keeping his car's noise levels to a minimum. As he passed the towering pine trees, he glanced across at them. Ah, Moira… trusting little Moira with her tousled hair and cascade of freckles. He imagined her haunting that area, unable to escape from the confines of the trees where she was buried. He conjured the image of her lips trembling as they had when she knew she was about to breathe her last, that she had no expectation of a tomorrow. 'You stay put, girlie,' he murmured as the wind rustled the leaves. 'You're a long time dead.'

There was a light illuminating a window on the top floor, though the rest of the building was in darkness. At the fork in the driveway he paused. The left turn would take him to the front entrance, so he took the right that led to the garage. He recalled that the garage was a separate, more modern construction, situated behind the main building. It was large enough to hold three cars and he was surprised to see a white van parked beside it. That wasn't Cyn's style at all. He spotted a Land Rover and another car covered with a tarpaulin inside the garage. Then he spied movement. He stopped his car beside the wall of the house, clicked the boot open, sidled to the back and retrieved the cricket bat.

Careful not to make a sound on the gravel drive, he crept towards the open garage door. Someone inside was busy taking the cover off the second vehicle, lifting it up to reveal the distinctive Jaguar emblem. Don clocked it immediately as Cynthia's car. He also recognised the bent figure of Raul. *Faithful Raul, the wrinkled old retainer*, Don had often joked to Cynthia. Raul was looking frail. He was huffing and puffing with effort as he tugged at the waterproof cover. Don tiptoed up behind him and swung the bat, though not too hard. The impact would be just enough to knock him cold. Don wanted him alive if not actually kicking.

*

Suzanne gathered her clothes together and placed them in the small suitcase. She prayed that Jared hadn't changed his mind. She would have to borrow some money from him for the train fare, then ring Mark from the railway station to tell him she was on her way home. She planned to read Don's journal on the journey and, once she was back in London, to take it to a lawyer. For Raymond's case to be reviewed, it was essential for new evidence to be presented. Suzanne hoped that the journal would provide the necessary proof. Once her belongings had been packed, she sat impatiently and waited for Jared to arrive.

*

Don was searching the garage. Cynthia had always been a creature of habit and he was sure that what he was looking for would be in there. This was where she'd always kept her gun in the States, safely locked away. The metal box, hidden behind some cans of motor oil, opened easily with the aid of a chisel and he pulled out the Smith & Wesson revolver that Cynthia had always been so fond of. She'd taught Don how to shoot with this very gun. She'd also threatened him with it. '*Get out of my house, you evil motherfucker!*' she had screeched. He had backed off, with his hands raised. '*All this fuss about a greasy little Cuban! You've gone soft, Cyn.*' Had dark-eyed Elena been worth it? He doubted it. He could barely remember her face or recall her dying moments. He'd kept no mementos either so the whole exercise had been meaningless. He knew there were times when his demon goaded him to kill out of boredom rather than for the pure pleasure of it but he'd sometimes wondered if he'd strangled Elena simply to provoke Cynthia. To force her to chuck him out and give him an excuse to escape. After she'd had the kid, she'd changed; she no longer had the same appetites and Don had become weary of her and the mewling brat. Sons, he thought, were highly overrated. Both of his had been right duds. Suzanne, though, she was different, she was his link to Joanie – and he intended to use her as bait.

He checked the mechanism, loaded the gun and pushed it into the waistband of his pants.

He heard the sound of footsteps and swiftly crouched behind the parked cars.

'Raul! What's happened? Are you okay?'

Don peered around the side of the Land Rover and saw a slim dark-haired bloke bending over Raul.

Don fished the gun from his belt and crept up beside him. 'Hello, Jared, my son. Remember your old dad, do you?'

Jared straightened up and Don saw a reflection of his own eyes staring back at him with a startled look on the young face. It took a moment for recognition to register, and another before Jared noticed the gun in his father's hand.

'So tell me, boy. Where's Suzanne? What has the bitch queen done with my baby girl?'

*

The key turned in the lock and the door was pushed open. Suzanne saw Jared standing there. He was white-faced and anxious. For a split second she thought he had come to tell her that he'd changed his mind about releasing her. Moments later, a shot rang out, Jared's legs appeared to fold under him and he pitched forward onto the stone floor. Frozen to the spot, Suzanne stared down at the blood oozing through the hole in the back of Jared's plaid shirt. Stunned, she looked up at the white-haired, bearded figure in the doorway.

'To the rescue, Suzy-Q!' announced the instantly recognisable voice of her father.

Frozen to the spot with shock, she managed to blurt out, 'You're dead.'

Don winked and chuckled. 'So they tell me.' He blew into the barrel of the gun like some old-time movie cowboy and grinned at her. 'You stay here, baby. I've got some other business to take care of.'

He yanked the door shut and locked it once more.

CHAPTER THIRTY-FIVE

Bells clanged in Luke's head. He opened one eye and the room lurched sickeningly. He cautiously opened the other eye, feeling as though his brain had shrunk overnight and was rolling around inside his skull. He lifted his head from the pillow and the pain hit him like a wrecking ball. The ringing was incessant and he was convinced that someone, somewhere, was knocking a nail into a wall while a woman's voice shouted, 'Luke! Open up!'

He dragged himself out of bed and noticed blearily that he was still fully clothed. He attempted to stand up straight but failed dismally. The shrill doorbell sent shockwaves through his system and the banging continued while he stumbled to his front door. He was in no fit state to see anyone but he desperately wanted the racket to stop. He squinted through the spyhole and saw a pale-faced redhead thumping the door impatiently and about to press the doorbell again.

'I'm here,' he shouted and his voice sounded as though it was shrouded in cotton wool.

He opened the door and Suzanne's mother, Joan, was standing there with an expression on her face that combined concern and distaste. 'Bloody hell,' she said. 'You look terrible.'

He stood to one side as she marched into his flat and headed straight for the kitchen. 'Let's get something inside you,' she called to him. 'Have you got any eggs in this place?'

He slowly made his way to the sofa and lowered himself cautiously into the seat, convinced he was about to throw up. 'I can't eat.'

'Got any Tabasco? Oh, here it is. Worcester sauce? Check! I'll be with you in a minute.'

He leaned against the back of the sofa and closed his eyes while the room revolved around him and Joan rattled about in the kitchen.

When he opened his eyes she was standing in front of him. 'Here, drink this.'

He stared at the glutinous concoction lurking in the glass she held in her hand. 'You're joking.'

'Just drink it,' she said as she sat down next to him. 'Or I'll hold your nose and force it down your stupid throat.'

He grimaced as he gulped it down. 'What are you doing here?'

'You rang me. Don't you remember? No, I don't suppose you do. Five o'clock this morning, babbling on about Mark being dead, Suzanne missing and some girl called Anita.'

Luke didn't remember anything about the conversation. He turned his head warily and saw Joan's intelligent green eyes surveying him. What had he told her in his drunken state? Whatever it was must have been serious enough for her to immediately drive sixty miles, because her appearance wasn't up to her usual glamorous standard. In fact, he'd never seen her in a sweatshirt and jeans before.

'What time is it now?' Luke asked.

'Seven-fifteen,' Joan replied. 'When you fall off the wagon, you don't mess about, do you?'

'I'm sorry.' He didn't know what else to say.

Joan waved his apology away with unvarnished fingernails. 'So, now you're half-way sober, would you like to tell me in a civilised manner just what the hell is going on?'

*

'Like the new me?' Don asked Cynthia. 'You always said I'd look good with a beard.'

'I don't recall.' Her voice was shaky and her expression that of a wounded animal that had finally been hunted down.

'Oh, Cyn, that's too many drugs talking. Anyway, I think I look good.' Don grinned with satisfaction as he plonked himself down in the chair at her bedside. 'Whereas you… you really haven't aged well. You do realise that, I suppose.'

'You're dead,' she wheezed.

'That's what they tell me. So maybe I am and I've returned from Valhalla to haunt you. On the other hand, perhaps you've just overdone your medication and I'm a figment of your fevered imagination. What do you think?'

'Raul!' she attempted to shout.

Don reached across and placed his hand over her mouth. 'Don't bother, Cyn, because he can't hear you.' He chuckled and removed his hand from her face, then pointedly wiped his palm on his trouser leg. He grimaced in disgust and sat back down beside her bed.

'What have you done? What was that sound I heard?'

'Oh that? I've just had a little encounter with our baby boy, sweetheart. He's downstairs, keeping his sister company.'

She stared at him in disbelief.

He rattled the hoist by the bed. 'What's all this? Can't move any more? Now that is a real disappointment. I was looking forward to this moment. But you know what, Cyn? You are no fun any more. Not like the old days, eh? We had some times, didn't we? And you were so beautiful, so elegant and so wild. Shall I fetch a mirror, Cyn, so you can see just how far you have fallen? I bet good old Raul brushes your hair for you, so you don't have to see yourself. I mean, to be perfectly frank, you look like shit. And to think that once upon a time I was proud to be with you. Christ, you are one disgusting sight, lady.'

'I'm ill, Don. Why have you come to torture me? I've been standing by our deal. I've been paying you on the dot.' Cynthia was wheezing and gasping for breath.

Don ignored her distress. 'The bargain didn't include sending sonny boy to spy on me though, did it? That's the only way you'd have found my baby girl. What happened to all those shit private detectives you sent to track me down, Cyn? Can't afford them any more? Boo-hoo! Cynthia Beaulieu is in the poorhouse.'

'Take your daughter and go. Just leave me and Jared alone.'

Don stood and leaned over her, nose to nose, looking directly into her eyes and whispered, 'But I've come to say goodbye, Cyn. This is the end of days for you *and* the kid. Just desserts, Cynthia, just desserts.'

He straightened up, stretched theatrically, then walked towards the door. 'Where's the kitchen? I don't remember exactly. Is it to the left or the right? Don't bother getting up to show me.' He threw his head back and laughed mirthlessly. 'I'll find it myself.'

He left the room and ambled down the corridor to the kitchen. It was pristine. Good old Raul, the perfect housewife. Whereas when he and Cynthia had shared their Chelsea flat she'd always been a messy slut. He glanced about and opened a cupboard under the sink. He found a green garden-waste bag and a pedal-bin liner – they would do nicely. He sauntered back with his find and paused in the doorway.

'Six years, Cyn,' he said. 'Can you believe it's been six years since we last saw each other?' He stood across the room, taking in the frail figure in the bed and shaking his head in dismay. 'I can't get over just how much you've changed. My, how have the mighty fallen.'

Cynthia pressed the back of her head – the only part of her body she could now move unaided – into her pillow. It was a feeble attempt to shrink away from him as he steadily approached her with the white bin liner in his hand.

'Six years without me and just look at what you've become – a wrinkled lump of useless flesh.' He sidled up to the bed, shaking the liner so it made a swishing noise. 'Do you piss in a nappy,

Cyn? Do you? Do you crap yourself and have faithful old Raul wipe your saggy old arse for you? I bet you do.' He laughed. 'The high and mighty Cynthia Beaulieu reduced to this. How can you bear the humiliation? You were so fastidious, Cyn, and so sexy. Do you remember what a randy little tart you were back then? And now you're just an ugly, twisted, stinking crone. Fuck me, lady, I'll be doing you a favour.'

'Jared?' Cynthia gasped out helplessly. 'What have you done to my son?'

'That's it, Cyn.' Don was so close to her now that he could smell her fear. His tight grin was replaced by a twisted grimace, filled with loathing. 'Jared was always *your* son, wasn't he? He was never mine. From the minute he crawled out of your fetid womb, he attached himself to your nipple. And he's never let go, has he? He was always the snotty little mommy's boy.' He stood beside her as she raised her horrified eyes to look at him. 'Well, he's paved the way to hell for you, Cyn. Your precious son has died for your sin, *sugar*!' He spat out the last word. 'Bang, bang, he's dead.' He raised the plastic bag above her head, with contempt in his eyes. 'I regret that this is not up to madam's usual posh standards. Maybe I should have stopped off at Harrods and snaffled one of their carrier bags. I had imagined that we might get to play our little game, just one last time.' He yanked the bag over her head. 'But, you know, you are so revolting that I really can't be arsed.'

Cynthia didn't have the ability to reach up. Her hands merely fluttered and clenched as Don drew the closure strings around her neck and tied them in a neat, tight bow. She instinctively fought for breath and the plastic moulded to the contours of her face. Donald Tyler turned on his heel and walked away.

When he reached the Edwardian table, he shouted over his shoulder. 'Goodbye, Cyn – I can't even be bothered to watch you die. How sad is that? There's no pleasure to be had from you any more. No pleasure at all.'

He scooped up the white folder, his journals and the photographs of his victims, then placed them in the green garden-waste bag.

He left the main door to the house on the latch, ambled nonchalantly down the front steps, and headed back to Suzanne's room.

CHAPTER THIRTY-SIX

Suzanne made a desperate attempt to stem the bleeding. She folded her cotton bed sheet into a pad and applied pressure to the wound in Jared's back. His pulse was erratic and his breathing shallow, yet he remained unconscious. She methodically searched his pockets in the hope of finding a mobile phone but came up empty.

The door opened and Don stared in at her. 'You know, you are almost as beautiful as your mother. Almost, but not quite.' A puzzled look crossed his face. 'What are you doing?'

Suzanne remained on her knees beside Jared. 'He'll die if I don't reduce the blood loss.'

'Get up!' He held out his hand to her.

'I can't leave him like this. We have to phone for an ambulance.'

'Suzy, Suzy.' Don shook his head ruefully. 'He was coming in here to shoot *you*, baby. I wrestled the gun off him. I got here in the nick of time.' His hand was offered to her once more but she ignored it. 'You don't know these people, Suzy. They're evil. This little shit…' Don nudged Jared's leg with his shoe. 'He raped and strangled his girlfriend. Moira, her name was. Pretty blonde. She was going to leave him, go off to university in Glasgow. So he killed her. That's the sort of person he was. So you keep your sympathy for someone who deserves it. You've had a lucky escape, my girl.'

Don grabbed Suzanne's arm and hauled her to her feet; she felt the yellow plastic tie catch her wrist. 'Don't fight me, baby. Daddy knows what's best.' He gripped her other hand with his and secured the tie around both her wrists at the front. 'Now you are going to sit in the car, like a good girl, while I do what has to be done.'

'Jared is your *son*, Don.'

He gave her a pitying look and stroked her hair. 'And you're my baby girl. I can't let anything bad happen to you.' He dragged her away from Jared and without even glancing back at his son, Don pulled Suzanne towards the open door.

Outside the door she spotted a large green sack. Don shouldered it, marched her to the other side of the house and pushed her into the front passenger seat of a white car. She watched as he opened the boot. He threw the green sack in there. She couldn't see what he was taking out but the motion of the car indicated that the objects were heavy. It was the first view she'd had of the large garage at the back of the house, but she couldn't see into it because the door was closed.

Don suddenly appeared by the passenger door with a green jerry can in his hand. He leered at her triumphantly and shook the can. Liquid sloshed about inside. 'Back in just a tick,' he said. 'Then we can be on our way.' He flipped his jacket open to reveal the revolver tucked into the waistband of his pants. 'Now don't you do anything silly, baby, understand?' His tone was sing-song – as though speaking to a small child – but the threat was palpable. She understood only too well that there are three responses to danger: flight, fight or freeze. Suzanne froze.

*

Donald Tyler toted two jerry cans up the white steps, pushed the door open, then entered the hallway and climbed up the stairs to the second floor. Here, he strolled from bedroom to bedroom, spilling the contents of the cans onto beds and rugs. That would make a really nice *whoosh* when the fire reached that far. With the remaining quarter of the second can, he splashed a trail of petrol down the stair carpet to the floor below.

Whistling tunelessly, he went outside once again to retrieve two more cans. When he entered Cynthia's room, he noted with revulsion that, beneath the plastic that clung mask-like to her face, she was staring blankly directly at him while her mouth hung open like a slaughtered animal in an abattoir. He crossed the room and emptied one of the cans of petrol over her bed. 'Frying tonight, Cyn!' he sneered.

In the kitchen Don picked up a cotton tea towel, then turned on the gas. Hearing the satisfying hiss, he sniggered. *Boom!* Chuckling, he proceeded to slop half the contents of the last remaining can all along the hallway and onto the outside step. He closed the front door, rolled the tea towel to make a wick and stuffed it into the top of the jerry can, leaving just a few inches protruding from the top. He took out his lighter and lit the tea towel.

Then he ran down the front steps, around the side of the house and back to Suzanne.

*

Suzanne saw her father rounding the corner. He clambered into the driver's seat and she could smell petrol on his clothing. 'Best go!' He started the engine, reversed, then turned the car sharply and drove at speed down the driveway towards the trees.

'What the hell have you done?'

Just as the end of the drive was in sight, an explosion from the house answered her question and she sat in stunned silence. *Stay calm*, she advised herself, *someone who will do what I have just witnessed will do* anything *so try not to react.*

'You were playing a dangerous game there, Suzy-Q. Cynthia would have killed you and not turned a hair. I've just saved your life, baby. Doesn't your old dad even get a thank you?'

Suzanne looked down at the yellow plastic ties that bound her hands tightly together. 'So if you're my saviour, what's this all in aid of?'

'You have been subjected to the lies of a very clever and manipulative woman. I just want to make sure you don't do anything silly before you hear the truth. I love you, Suzy-Q. You're my baby. I would never do anything to harm you.'

They were driving past the high trees that shielded the grounds from prying eyes and Suzanne looked across to where Cynthia had told her that Don had buried Moira. She tried to calm her heartbeat, breathing slowly in through her nose and out through her mouth, in a desperate attempt to keep herself from falling to pieces. She glanced across at him as he stamped on the accelerator and the car jerked forward, sending a spray of gravel clattering against the car. Dead man driving. The shock of his sudden appearance hit Suzanne for the first time and her hands began to tremble. She held them tightly together in an effort to stay in command of her fears.

Once past the trees, Don hopped out of the car and opened the gate. Suzanne looked back towards the house to see smoke rising in the distance. Then a second, far louder, explosion rent the air.

Don sat beside the wheel and gunned the engine. 'We'd better be long gone before someone sees the smoke and calls the fire brigade.'

He opened the window on the driver's side and the smell of petrol began to dissipate.

'How did you find Cynthia, anyway?' His tone was relaxed, almost conversational.

'*She* found *me*.'

'See what I mean? She was a devious woman. Even if you'd been able to escape, she would have hunted you down. She'd been trying to get to me for years.'

'But you still took her money.'

'That bitch owed me – big time.' He grinned. 'But we're both safe now.'

'Cynthia was in no fit state to kill anyone.'

'But Jared would have. That little shit always jumped whenever his mama called. You know, Suzy-Q, all men want sons but what did I get? One shambling idiot and a mummy's boy.' He changed up a gear then reached over and patted her knee. 'Daughters are the best.'

Suzanne strived to repress a shudder of horror and loathing but knew instinctively that she had to keep him talking. 'How did you find me? How did you know where I was?'

'I know everything.'

'Come on, even I didn't know where I was being taken.'

'For instance,' he said, sidestepping her actual question. 'I know that you're a teacher and your husband sells insurance.'

A memory, from the last time she had encountered her father, came rushing into Suzanne's mind. Ten years ago, just before the fire in her studio, she'd been convinced that Don had stalked her. His seemingly casual remarks about her housemates had been far too accurate for comfort. Had he been doing it again? Maybe he'd been following her, checking up on her without her knowledge. She imagined him rummaging through her dustbin, maybe even gaining access to her home, and the thought of his invisible presence in her life made her feel sick. Then Suzanne recalled her mother's comment that she had thought she'd seen Don in the street from time to time, 'though I could have been mistaken,' Joan had said. But was it possible that she hadn't made a mistake?

'Don't look so worried,' Don said. 'It's nothing sinister. Joanie told me all about you.'

'You're in touch with my mother?'

'It sounds to me like you don't believe me, Suzy-Q.'

Not a bloody word, she thought, but what she said was, 'I'm just surprised that she never mentioned—'

'Never told you about all the postcards I sent her from around the world either, did she?' He chortled and slapped the steering wheel with glee. 'I'm part of the secret life that she keeps in a drawer. You know that Victorian mahogany Duchess table in her dressing room? She's got every one of my postcards secreted away in there. I'll bet she takes them out and sniffs them, remembers all the good times we had together, before…' He glanced across at Suzanne with an expression in his dark eyes that she found hard to decipher. Then he looked back at the road they were driving along. 'So why should my Joanie share any of this with you or anyone else? I bet you don't confess all your dark and intimate longings to, what was his name?'

'Mark.'

'Yeah, Mark. Bet there's stuff going on in your dirty little mind that tall, buff, blond Mark knew nothing about, eh?' He turned his head and grinned at her, and his eyes had an empty glint like those of a circling shark.

Suzanne's blood ran cold as she realised that Don *had* been stalking both her and her mother. She looked down at the ties that bound her hands, took a breath and made a vain attempt to control the rising fear that had her heart racing. She had to remain calm, to try to figure a way out of this.

At that moment, Don began singing cheerfully about a carousel ride.

Suzanne watched the Scottish countryside glide by and was filled with a looming sense of despair.

CHAPTER THIRTY-SEVEN

'That's been one hell of a load weighing on your conscience all these years.'

Luke glanced up at Joan, not knowing what to expect from her: dismay, loathing, fear? But what he saw in her facial expression was sympathy.

'You were how old?'

'Sixteen,' he said. 'I should have said something about leaving her alone in the woods, but the longer I left it—'

'Because you were scared to death of that brute of a father.' Joan looked him in the eye. 'Mark told Suzanne all about him. And you've never breathed a word of this to anyone, have you?'

He shook his head.

'And you now believe that Suzanne's father was involved in this Anita's disappearance? And also the fire at Suzanne's studio?'

'Not a hundred per cent, but those location photographs were found in the safe deposit box belonging to Donald Tyler.'

Joan covered her face with her hands. 'My God, Luke! What did I marry?' She looked up at him, her face drawn and full of anguish. 'He was crazy enough when I knew him, but look at what he became!'

'You divorced him years ago, Joan. What happened after that has nothing to do with you.'

Joan bit her lip, as though about to make her own confession. 'He kept in touch with me, you know. He sent me postcards from all over the world. Always with the same message, "Thinking of you, Joanie. Wish you were here".'

Joan recalled the wedding invitation that had arrived at her house almost a quarter of a century ago. *You are cordially invited to the wedding of Miss Cynthia Beaulieu and Mr Donald Albert Tyler.* The wedding had taken place three months previously and on the back of the invitation Don had scrawled: 'Ha-ha, Joanie. You missed my big day.' A belated invitation to his son's christening had also turned up some months after the event.

She composed herself and sat up straight with her hands folded in her lap. 'But none of this brings us any closer to finding my daughter.'

'Mark told me that Suzanne had phoned him to say she was in Scotland.'

'Don's last postcard came from Scotland.' Joan leapt to her feet. 'Who's the policeman in charge of the investigation?'

'Chief Inspector Etheridge.'

'You stay here. Get some food inside you and pack a bag. You're coming home with me. In the meantime, I'll go and see this Etheridge. Don may be dead but he has another son, by a Cynthia Beaulieu. And he must be in his twenties by now. Maybe Suzanne traced him, the way she did Raymond.'

Luke caught her arm as she passed by him.

Joan understood. 'What you choose to do is up to you, Luke. The past is behind us and I'll make no mention of what happened to Anita to anyone. I just want my daughter back, and to find Mark's murderer. Agreed?'

'Agreed.'

*

The Scottish countryside was flashing by and Don was in fine fettle. 'Rose gave you my notebooks, didn't she? Have you read them yet? What did you think?'

'What was I supposed to think?'

'I mean, I want your opinion of the story. I read this book by Bret Easton Ellis, *American Psycho*. Do you know it?' He glanced across at Suzanne. 'You should read it. It's bloody brilliant. A work of pure genius.' He grinned and turned his eyes back to the road. 'Anyway, I thought: I can do that. You know, write. So when I was living at Rose's place, before I got ill, I went to one of those creative writing classes. It was bit of a joke, with all these people who thought their lives had been so fucking interesting they needed the world to read their self-satisfied memoirs. Bunch of stuck-up wankers, or old biddies wanting to write kids' stories for their grandchildren. What a waste of time and money that was. I did learn one thing, though: write what you know.'

'So you wrote about yourself. Your experiences?'

'Bloody hell, Suzy-Q, you didn't believe all that stuff, did you?' He guffawed theatrically.

'You tell me.'

'Lots of things have happened in my life, baby. People die, you know. It was all very tragic. So I created a character who'd murdered them all.' He looked across once more, his expression scornful. 'It's fiction, Suzy-Q. I made it all up.'

'Then I don't understand why you wanted Rose to destroy all that work you'd done on them.'

'She told you that?' Darkness returned to his voice.

Be careful, Suzanne warned herself as she both sensed and heard a potential seismic shift in his mood. But she'd started now, might as well continue. 'Rose said you had left instructions for the notebooks to be burned.'

More fire.

'I was very ill. I didn't know what I was saying most of the time,' he said with seemingly forced nonchalance.

Suzanne suspected that Don had ordered the destruction of the notebooks to prevent anyone finding a way to free Raymond.

She glared at him. *You total bastard*, she thought. *You wanted to take that secret with you to the grave.*

'Anyway,' Don was saying. 'I wouldn't be the first writer to want that, would I now? Kafka, for example, he did that, didn't he? He asked for his unpublished writing to be destroyed after his death.'

'You've read Kafka?' The words slipped out before she had the chance to haul them back.

Don turned his head and glared at her. 'What? You think just cos I left school at sixteen that I'm stupid? I've read fucking Kafka. I know the meaning of *Metamorphosis*, Suzanne. I've lived with it all my life.'

'Sorry,' she said, drawing back from the abyss that lay behind her father's eyes. 'I didn't mean anything by it.' *Metamorphosis*: man turning into a giant insect. She thought back with horror to Don's description of the salivating demon crawling out of the sea on a moonlit Thai beach, urging him to kill the beautiful young Annabelle.

'Apology accepted,' he grinned and his facial expression relaxed.

'Then I'm very impressed by your fertile imagination,' Suzanne said. 'So what about Naomi? How do you explain her away in your fiction?'

'You read that?'

'That's why Cynthia wanted me there. To read your journals to her.'

'Cynthia was one twisted whore. The world's a better place without her kind. She got no better than she deserved. *She* strangled Naomi Silver, you know. And to my everlasting shame, I helped her cover it up.'

'But in your journals, you confessed.'

'Let me tell you a little story.' He cleared his throat as though about to impart something meaningful. 'There was a Cuban girl, an illegal that Cynthia employed when we lived in Florida. She treated the girl like shit, though I was nice to her.' He shook his head to imply sorrow. 'But Cyn was a very jealous woman, very possessive. She had the girl killed, chopped into little pieces and fed to the alligators in the Everglades. And do you know who performed that little chore for her? Raul. Now I'm sure you took him for a kindly old man, didn't you? But let me tell you, baby, Raul is a stone-cold killer.'

'I find that hard to believe.' Suzanne wasn't buying this act. Raul was no hard man, he was an old-fashioned Southern servant. This was just one more lie. Don was trying to confuse her, make her doubt herself. Well, it wasn't going to work.

Don's jaw clenched momentarily before he was back on track but his tone had hardened once more. 'Of course, in my novel the hero murders the girl. What do you call that? Artistic licence. Just like your paintings. That one with the woman and child walking across the sand… or were they both kids, I can't remember.'

Suzanne froze. The painting he was describing was one she had been working on the day that Rose Anderson contacted her. That painting was in her attic workshop, in her home.

'Where did you see that?' She tried to keep her voice level.

'In your studio, the day I visited you all those years back.' He turned his head towards her, taking his eyes off the road ahead, his expression daring her to challenge him. 'Don't you remember?' He hit the accelerator and the engine growled its response. 'I'm sure of it.'

Don's eyes remained firmly fixed on Suzanne's face as their car closed up fast on a truck ahead. Closer, closer, until they were almost bumper-to-bumper. Another few seconds and she was convinced they'd crash into the back of the larger vehicle. Don's message was crystal clear. Agree or die.

'Yes,' she blurted out. 'You're right. Now please slow down.'

He hit the brakes and let out a snorting laugh. 'In my novel, the hero kills them all. Nobody would believe that this guy who'd murdered all these other women would play second fiddle to some spoilt bitch like Cynthia. Just think about it for a minute. It just wouldn't ring true, now would it?'

'I don't suppose it would.'

She had to stay in the zone. Don *had* been in her house, had seen her painting. What had he been doing there and what else had he done? *Breathe in slowly and try not to panic*, she told herself. *There's only one way to test the water.*

'I'd like to ring Mark and tell him I'm on my way home.'

'Who's Mark?'

'He's my husband.'

'Yeah, right, I forgot.' There was something in his voice that sent a shiver through her. He turned his head towards her and gave a tight grin that showed his small uneven teeth. 'You got a mobile on you?'

'No.'

'Me neither. You can call him when we get where we're going.'

'Then I'll have to use a call box. But I thought you were taking me home?'

'Just one little stop-off on the way and then you can decide.'

'Stop-off where, exactly?'

'We're going to see your mother. I want to give my Joanie a little surprise. Got to say goodbye before we skip the county. We'll travel the world, baby. We'll go on lots of adventures together. Just you and me.'

'I'm not going anywhere. I have a husband, a job, a life.'

'You don't get it, do you? I'd have thought a smart girl like you would have figured it out by now. No? Well let *me* paint a picture for *you*.' His hazel eyes mocked her. 'Raul was in the garage when the blaze hit. He'll be safe in there. He's going to wake up with a terrible headache. But he *will* wake up. And he'll tell the nice policemen all about the young woman who was staying at the house. How she must have been the one who attacked him and set the place on fire. Now do you see?' He reached over and patted her knee once more. 'They'll be looking for *you*, Suzy-Q. Because Donald Albert Tyler is dead, isn't he? Couldn't possibly have been him, now could it?'

CHAPTER THIRTY-EIGHT

Don slipped a CD into the player. 'Let's have some music. Do you remember when you were a little girl and we'd go out on drives and have a good old sing?'

'No, I don't recall.'

'That's a shame. I had the boys, of course, but you were the only one I ever really cared about. The other two mothers were tarts but you are part of Joanie and me, so I could never stay far away from you for long.'

'You seemed to manage.'

'That was down to that tosser your mother married.'

'Harry?'

'Yeah, him. Told me to stay away, didn't he? To get out of your life. He threatened me. He wanted you and Joanie all to himself.'

You've overstepped the mark there, Don, she thought, *projecting your own insecurities onto someone of whose decency and humanity you have no concept.* Liar! She wanted to scream at him but what she said was, 'I see.'

He seemed cheered by her answer. 'Oh, we've missed so much, baby. We'll change all that when we go travelling.'

The CD was Kris Kristofferson and Don sang along for a while. 'He wrote this one for me, you know,' he said as a new song began. 'I met him on the road years ago. He was a good guy. We hung out together for a while. This is about him and me.' When he got to the line about only living until you die he stopped singing and laughed. 'And for a while thereafter, eh?'

'How did you manage it this time?' Suzanne asked.

'This time?' He sounded surprised.

'Thailand? Cynthia had a death certificate for you from Thailand.'

'Is that what she told you?'

'And you got back in touch with her three months later, hustling more money from her.'

'Oh, she was such a good liar, wasn't she? I bet she didn't show you this so-called death certificate, did she?'

'No, but—'

'Don't you see what she was up to, baby? She would lie to anyone about anything, just for the *craic*.'

Which were almost exactly the words Suzanne's mother had used to describe Don. *Play along*, she told herself.

'Okay, Cynthia lied. But how did you manage your Houdini act six months ago?'

'Cock-up at the hospital. I really did think I was a goner. I was convinced it was "Goodnight Vienna" for old Donny boy. So nobody was more surprised than me when I woke up in ICU to hear the nurses asking me my name. I was expecting to see Rose sitting by my bed, all cow-eyed and teary, but she wasn't there. I was woozy, so the nurses let me sleep. When Rose didn't appear the next day or the day after that, I twigged there was something odd going on. So when they asked me my name again, I took a flyer and told them I was Michael O'Connor. He was a kid I was at school with. He died of leukaemia when he was fifteen so I'm sure he wouldn't mind being resurrected. And they fell for it!' Don chortled with merriment. 'I thought they might check up on that, but no one did. That's me though, babe, I always was one lucky bastard.'

'But you'd need to have given your National Insurance number, wouldn't you?'

'I told them I'd been working abroad. Came back and my wife had left me, emptied the joint bank account and someone else was renting our house. I was flat broke, ended up in a hostel and got robbed by some drunk when I was in there. That little story certainly got me the sympathy vote.' The smug look that flitted across his face made Suzanne shudder. 'Especially with the nurses.'

'So who got cremated as Donald Tyler?'

'I have absolutely no idea. Some homeless person, maybe. Who knows and who cares? Friday night, mad busy A&E department, two patients with heart attacks brought in one after the other, paperwork gets mixed up, misplaced, lost even… Could easily happen. And it did. Plus that silly cow Rose not wanting to see my dead body was a right turn-up for the books.'

'What if she *had* suddenly turned up, though?'

'What? After I'd said I was Michael O'Connor?'

'Might have happened if the hospital suddenly discovered their mistake.'

'Yeah, well, I'd have thought of something.' He threw back his head and laughed mirthlessly, then turned to her, his eyes and tone as dark as his soul. 'I always do. Been in many a tight spot, me and this…' Don let go of the steering wheel with his left hand and tapped his index finger on his temple. 'This has always got me away, scot-free.'

Suzanne wondered what would have happened had Don Tyler not been declared dead. Would he have gone back to Rose and kept up the blackmail of Cynthia? Either way Suzanne would never have been dragged into this hellish mess. But then there was Raymond… 'Lucky break,' she said.

'Sure was.' Don agreed. 'And a top result for me because I was all nicely fixed up as Michael O'Connor, courtesy of the good old National Health Service. Triple heart bypass. Want to see the scar?'

'No, thanks.'

'That's a thought.' He deftly changed the subject. 'We'd better steer well clear of Nashville on our travels, I know too many people down there. Kris, Johnny Cash, Dylan.'

'Johnny Cash is dead.'

'Is he? That's a shame. I haven't been keeping up with the news of late.'

'Clearly.'

'Do I detect a note of sarcasm there, Suzy-Q? Don't you believe your old dad?'

'Of course I do. Why would anyone lie about a thing like that?' She hoped she sounded sincere, when what she really wanted to say was, *not unless you're a delusional nutcase, who'll shoot his own son and leave him to die in a fire.*

'Good girl.' Don appeared convinced and began to sing once more.

*

The overfed ginger cat glowered at the young police constable while Mrs Jones went to fetch him a cup of tea.

'Oh, don't mind Sultan,' she said as she carried a tray into the sitting room and placed it on the table. 'He doesn't approve of strangers.' She took a seat on the sofa opposite him. 'Suzanne is the only other person he has ever taken to.' She handed the constable a cup. 'He's a very good judge of character. For a cat.'

The cop glanced around at the framed line drawings that crowded the walls. 'You have an artist in the family?'

'Oh, those,' Mrs Jones smiled modestly. 'I have a minor talent for portraiture. That one—' She pointed to the picture of a family group, a man, woman and three children, 'is of my son and his family. They live in Australia. The children are much older now, of course.' She sighed. 'I keep meaning to go to see them but at my age the years roll by so quickly. No sooner are you taking down the Christmas decorations but you're putting them back up again… and travelling is so expensive.' She indicated the portrait of a dark-haired young woman, smiling happily down at them. 'That one is Suzanne. She is such a wonderful artist. I encouraged her to paint again. She'd put her artistic life on hold since that nasty business at her studio. But I told her, you should use your God-given talent to the full, my dear. A life suspended is a life unfulfilled.'

The constable nodded his head and sipped his tea. He wanted to get on with it. Humouring old ladies in order to extract information was one thing but it was now becoming tedious. 'You said you saw a man leaving the Woods' house yesterday.'

'About an hour before Mark's brother arrived. How is Luke, do you know? What a terrible thing to find your brother like that. Such a dreadful shock.'

'Can you describe the man you saw?'

'I can do better than that.' Mrs Jones reached for the art folder on the table. 'I drew a picture of him. Not immediately, of course. He'd parked his car right outside of my house so I did get a very good look at him. When I saw him with a cricket bat, I assumed he was one of Mark's team. But when I heard about Mark being attacked, I drew this sketch.' She handed over the A4 sheet. 'I do have an excellent memory for faces.'

The constable glanced at the image of a white-haired, bearded man and immediately radioed in to the police station.

*

They were approaching Carlisle when Suzanne brought up the subject of Rose Anderson.

'Rose was a troubled woman,' Don said. 'She's better off where she is now.'

'She's in a mental hospital.'

She studied his reaction side-on as his mouth turned up at one corner, half-smile, half-sneer. 'Yeah, dead right she is.'

'You do know how to pick them, don't you?'

'What do you mean by that?'

'What with homicidal Cynthia and crazy Rose, it's a bit unfortunate, isn't it? That you appear to attract women like them.'

'You know what it is, Suzy-Q? I'm drawn to the vulnerable. I have this urge to protect and some women abuse that. They see it as a weakness and exploit my generosity. It's a cross I have to bear. I'm just too kind-hearted. And that's a fact.'

The jaw-dropping sincerity with which he said those words, with a straight face, almost took her breath away. He either believed what he was saying or was the world's best actor; either way she was not about to challenge him. 'Then will you please untie my wrists? My hands are getting numb.'

He let out a deep sigh. 'See, even you do it. I let my guard down to you and you immediately seek to take advantage of me.'

'No, really. I can't feel my fingers.'

'Okay then, baby. I understand. There's a little parking spot not far from here. Nice and quiet. I've got sandwiches and drinks in the boot. We'll stop and have a picnic, shall we? Just like when you were a little girl. Do you remember?'

'Yes,' she said. But she didn't. This man wasn't the father she vaguely recalled from her childhood. That dad had been funny, always cracking jokes, arms filled with presents and a mouth full of promises that never came true. It had been a saccharine fiction for a little girl who didn't want her charming daddy to leave her again. The child in her mourned for that father – for the one who had never really existed – while she glanced across at the stranger driving the car, the stone-hearted killer whose blood ran through her veins.

He noticed her staring at him. 'It's just you and me from now on, baby,' he repeated. 'Once we've paid my Joanie a visit.'

Don took the next motorway junction and they were soon driving once more down country roads. Suzanne spotted a hotel on the left-hand side of the road but there were no houses nearby. Rain spattered onto the windscreen and Don groaned his displeasure. 'Looks like we'll have to eat in the car.'

There was only one other vehicle on the road and that was travelling swiftly in the opposite direction. There was little sign of life anywhere. *This is an island of sixty million people*, Suzanne fumed, *but where are they all when you need them?*

'Here we are.' Don braked and turned left through the open gates into a car park. It was deserted. 'Nobody comes here at this time of year,' Don said as he unbuckled his seatbelt. 'At least, not on a weekday.'

'You've been here before?'

He tossed her a wolfish grin. 'Years ago – when I worked the fairs.'

The words from the first journal she had read resonated with Suzanne. Boastful terms filled with venom and contempt for his victims – all the '*useless girls nobody gives a flying fuck about*'.

After the young girl he had raped and then drowned at the Silent Pool he had written: *There were three more in all. Derbyshire, the New Forest and Carlisle.*

This was Carlisle.

'I don't like this place,' Suzanne stated emphatically.

'Don't worry, baby girl. We'll just have a bite to eat and then we'll be on our way again.'

Don got out of the car and opened the boot. He returned moments later with a carrier bag containing packs of sandwiches and cans of warm Coke. He put them on his seat and brought out a Stanley knife from the bottom of the bag. 'See?' he said. 'I'm setting you free.'

Suzanne held out her hands while he sawed through the tough yellow plastic tie that bound her wrists. The blade had blue smears along its razor-sharp edge and a smudge of blue acrylic paint on the handle. Her heart lurched in her chest. This was her knife, the one she had used in her loft studio. She now knew for certain that he *had* been in her house.

'Hold still, Suzy-Q,' he ordered. 'One slip and I could cut an artery.' He reached out and tilted her chin upwards so she was forced to look him in the eye. 'We wouldn't want that now, would we?'

He was playing with her, daring her to confess her recognition of the knife in his hands, forcing her to comply with his warped version of reality. She had to get away from him, to warn her mother, to contact Mark. But how?

CHAPTER THIRTY-NINE

Luke locked the door to his flat, picked up his sports bag and walked down the two flights of stairs. Joan's grey Volvo was parked on a yellow line and he could see her red hair shining in the murky sunlight as she kept an eye out for predatory traffic wardens.

'You took your time,' she snapped, irritated by his tardiness. She started the engine and they headed for the high street. As they passed the railway station on the left, Luke couldn't help but glance across to Mark's road, where the police tape cordon flapped in the breeze around the house. What he wouldn't give to know what was going on in the incident room at that precise moment.

'What did you make of Etheridge?' he asked Joan.

'He doesn't give anything away, does he? I told him that Suzanne was searching for her siblings and that apart from the one in prison there was another son somewhere, and I gave them his and his mother's name. You'd already told him about Mark mentioning Scotland, and I said that Don had sent me a postcard from there. That's when his ears pricked up. Etheridge said they'd check out Cynthia Beaulieu and her son Jared to see if there was any connection to Scotland. He assured me that they were doing everything possible to contact Suzanne, and that was about it.'

'Taciturn,' Luke said. 'That's his style.'

They drove in silence for a while. 'I wonder what's going on there?' Joan said.

Luke leaned back to see two marked police cars heading across the grass towards the trees on Banstead Common.

*

Don handed Suzanne a sandwich and she shook her head.

'Not hungry?' He appeared dismayed. 'Go on, you must be. We've got another five or six hours before we get to your mother's place. Eat!' He cracked open a can of Coke. 'It's warm but it's drinkable.'

The sound of an engine caught her attention as a silver Ford Fiesta pulled in at the other side of the car park. She watched while a dark-haired man got out and walked up and down beside his vehicle, stretching his legs.

'Daddy needs a piss,' Don said. 'I'll go behind that tree over there. You stay put like a good girl.' He climbed out of the driver's seat, leaving the door open.

She watched the driver of the other car for a moment, then reached for the door handle.

Don leaned back into the car, his face alive with malevolent glee. 'Don't even think about it, Suzy-Q. Because if you involve that bloke over there, then you'll force me to do something you'll regret.' He indicated towards the Fiesta driver, who was standing by his car, smoking a cigarette. 'What do you think he is, eh? He's probably a rep for some company, travelling the country, selling shit that nobody wants. Now who do you think takes a crappy job like that? Some schmuck with a wife and kids and a mortgage, that's who. So you sit here and don't say a word to that nice man or I'll have to hurt him. Got that, baby?'

He emitted a hollow laugh and walked away towards the trees.

Suzanne looked back to the driver who had finished his cigarette and appeared to be preparing to leave. Even if she did manage to reach him without Don seeing her, what would she say to him? *Please help me, I'm with a psycho who kills people.* No doubt he'd gawp at her in disbelief, thinking this was some kind of sick joke. *There's a lunatic with a gun and he'll shoot us both if we don't get out of here now.* What would he say to that? *Get in*, he'd say. And he'd reverse out of the park pronto and drive her to the nearest police station. Suzanne looked towards the spot where Don had been heading. The trees shielded her view of him, and maybe his of her. She unbuckled her seat belt, took a deep breath and opened the car door.

'Hey, mate!' Don shouted out.

The dark-haired man looked around and Suzanne watched in horror as Don approached him. He must have doubled back behind her as she was deciding what to do. Don pointed towards the car Suzanne was sitting in and the man nodded his head, walked to the back of the Fiesta and opened the boot.

Don was smiling and chatting away to him as the man took out a set of jump leads and headed her way with Don trailing behind him.

Suzanne got out of the car. 'Run!' she yelled.

The look of surprise was etched on what remained of the man's face as Don shot him point-blank in the back of the head.

*

Detective Chief Inspector Colin Etheridge looked up from the notes on his desk as one of the team from the incident room entered his office. 'What have you got?'

'A house belonging to a Cynthia Beaulieu, just outside Keith, near Inverness, was the target of an arson attack early this morning. Two survivors. The son is in intensive care with a gunshot wound to the back and severe smoke inhalation. An older man, who works for the family, has concussion but identified a woman who was staying there as Suzanne Woods. One body found in the house – so far – is thought to be that of Cynthia Beaulieu.'

'Any news on our bearded gentleman?'

'Nothing reported yet, sir, but the local force has got the photofit now and will be circulating it in the event that the suspect was spotted in the vicinity.'

'Keep me updated.'

'Yes, sir.'

*

Suzanne was now driving the dead man's Ford Fiesta with Don sitting beside her, the revolver held in his lap.

'A full tank of petrol – result, eh, baby?'

'And when they find that man's body beside your car? What then?'

'Can't be traced back to me. It belonged to a friend of mine. She has no more use for it, if you get my drift.'

'Your fingerprints will be all over it.'

'It makes no difference if they are. I'm not anywhere in the system. Your daddy has never been arrested, Suzy-Q, never been fingerprinted. I'm Mister Invisible, me.'

He had instructed her to take everything out of the boot of the white Twingo and transfer it to the Fiesta. The dead man's briefcase, jacket and a folder full of paper samples had been placed inside the other car. 'Just to confuse matters for a while,' Don had said. 'Buy us a bit of time.'

He stood, calmly puffing on a cigarette he had retrieved from the dead man's jacket. 'Ah, that hits the spot. Nothing wrong with a little bit of self-indulgence from time to time, eh?'

He watched as Suzanne walked back and forth between the two vehicles.

'What if someone heard the shot?' she said, carefully skirting around the body, trying not to look.

'What, here?' Don threw the dog-end onto the grass. 'This is the arsehole of the country, baby girl. There's nobody for miles around. Our friend here might not be found for days.'

He then pushed her into the driver's seat. 'You drive. There's an automated tollbooth on the M6, so any photos will be of you driving your victim's motor.' He went around and sat in the passenger seat. 'You see, I'm already one step ahead of the game. So don't think you can get the better of me, because nobody ever has.' He handed her the ignition key. 'And no one ever will.'

*

They were merging with the M1 motorway as Don sifted through the CDs. 'That saddo rep must have got these free with petrol or something. U2! You-fucking-two! Bunch of Irish twats. I hate the fucking Irish. My mother was Irish, you know – a red-haired colleen with a voice like a banshee and a temper to match. Bitch!' He opened the window and tossed the CD out.

'That why you hate women, is it?'

He gave her an offended look. 'I don't hate women. I love them…' He laughed. '… in my own way. Though I love my Joanie the most. And you, of course.'

'You love me, so you're setting me up. Framing me for a murder, just like you did with Raymond.'

'You've been doing your homework, eh? And you think you know it all, don't you? Well, let me tell you, Raymond is an imbecile. He's better off locked up. Forget him. I saved you, my baby. I rescued you from Cynthia.' He leaned forward so he could see her face. 'Though, you see, if you hadn't been so curious, hadn't gone digging around in the dirt, then you wouldn't have been in Scotland, would you? I wouldn't have had to come to your aid and Cynthia might still be alive.' He sat back in his seat and folded his arms. 'Similarly, if you hadn't shouted to the man in the car park, I wouldn't have had to shoot him, now would I? His little wifey wouldn't now be his widow or his children fatherless.' He reached across and placed his hand on hers as she changed down to fourth gear to overtake an annoying middle-lane straddler. 'The responsibility for all this mayhem is yours, Suzy-Q. All yours.'

She slapped his hand away. 'Bullshit! You planned to kill him the minute he drove in there. You wanted this car.'

Don sat back, grinning. 'But you'll never know for sure, will you? You'll always wonder. You'll lie awake at night in your perfumed bed and think, *Did I do the right thing? If I'd kept my lip buttoned would Daddy have let the nice man go on his way? Is it my fault he had his stupid head blown off?*'

Sickened by him and angered beyond her comprehension, she decided to call his bluff. 'What if I try your trick, Don?' She hit the accelerator just as a truck pulled out into the fast lane to overtake a car that was straddling the middle lane. 'Drive this full pelt into the back of that truck in front. Kill us both. How about that?'

'Do it!' he hissed. 'Go on, I dare you. You think I give a fuck what happens to me?' He pressed his face close to hers, his voice rising to a shout. 'Do it!' He was bellowing in her ear, deafening her and splattering her cheek with venomous spittle. 'Let's go out in a blaze of glory, baby! Yeah, yeah, yeah!' He backed off for a moment, studied the traffic ahead and in the left-hand lane, while not missing a ranting beat. 'Come on. Go for it. Take some other bastard with us. Fucking do it!'

He made a sudden grab for the steering wheel and yanked it to the left. The Fiesta veered into the middle lane, cars hooted and tyres screeched. Don's face was filled with a childlike excitement. 'Yeah, baby!' he screamed. 'Yeah, fuckers!' Suzanne tried to regain control of the steering wheel but Don lurched sideways and head-butted her. Stunned, and with her head buzzing from the impact, she was forced to release the wheel. Don hauled it further to the left, directly into the slow lane just after a huge white pantechnicon roared by, its horn blaring like a manic steamboat.

Don steered one-handed onto the hard shoulder, just beyond a flyover, then pulled on the handbrake. He reached across to the driver's side, undid Suzanne's seatbelt, opened the door and shoved her out of the car. She tumbled out, banging her head on the tarmac. A twelve-wheel truck, hauling a trailer, thundered past mere feet away from where Suzanne lay. She felt the drag of diesel-fuelled air that rocked the car like a rowboat and tore the breath from her lungs.

Don was out of the car and kneeling by her side, making soothing noises while keeping an eye on the traffic in the slow lane, making it appear as though he was tending to her.

'You shouldn't upset me like that, baby girl,' he soothed. 'Why do you make me do things to hurt you?'

She looked into his eyes, which were brimming over with apparent concern and affection. He lowered his face to hers and kissed her gently on the nose. He smiled benignly, pulled away abruptly, took one quick look at any passing cars to see if anyone was taking notice, then he head-butted her again. Suzanne's world went black.

CHAPTER FORTY

Detective Chief Inspector Colin Etheridge addressed the team in the incident room. 'Apart from the usual nutters, what have we got on the phones so far?' The first TV broadcast of Mrs Jones' drawing of the suspect had had the phones ringing within minutes and the room was abuzz with talk and activity.

'A woman in Edmonton thinks she remembers seeing our suspect in a lift. She can't be certain but she believes he was living with a nurse in her block of flats. The nurse, Bridget Daly, worked at St Francis' hospital. The thing is, sir, Bridget Daly committed suicide on the day of the sighting.'

'Suicide?' Etheridge's radar was on full alert. 'How did she die?'

'It would appear that she threw herself off her tenth-storey balcony. Though this neighbour claims that Daly's car is missing.'

'Got the registration?'

'I'm on it.'

'Contact the hospital. See if anyone there recognises the photofit.'

'Will do, sir.'

'Anything else?'

'A man visiting his father at Redstone House psychiatric hospital claims to have seen our suspect in the car park, getting into a white car. He remembers because the man in question threw a green frog out of the car window before he drove away.'

'A frog? What kind of frog?'

'One of those dangly mascot things.'

'Email the photofit to Redstone House. Maybe our man was a visitor.'

'Or a patient.'

Etheridge turned to the drawing pinned to the incident-room board and looked Donald Tyler straight in the eyes. 'Who the fuck are you?'

A uniformed policeman knocked on the door and entered.

'We've found Suzanne Woods' car, sir. It was abandoned on Banstead Common.'

*

Suzanne opened her eyes, feeling as though her head was clamped in a vice.

'You're awake,' Don said, cheerily. 'That's good because it won't be long now. We're coming to the Basildon turn-off.'

Suzanne realised she'd been unconscious for some time because in twenty more minutes they'd be at her mother's house. Still groggy, she tried to raise her hands but they'd been bound together once more with another yellow plastic tie.

'I had to restrain you, baby. You went a bit crazy out there, you know. You're a danger to yourself and to others. Maybe you should spend some time at Redstone House, keep Rose company.' He chortled to himself and began to sing, 'They're Coming to Take Me Away, Ha-Haaa!'

'Fuck you, Don.'

'Now, now, that's not very nice. But I'll let it pass. You're not well, baby. There *is* mental illness in the family, you know. My mother was about your age when she lost it, went totally loco.'

'Your mother had a drink problem.'

'Who told you that?' His voice hardened. 'Because it's a lie.'

'It was Vera.' Suzanne braced herself for his reaction and noticed he was gripping the steering wheel tighter, his knuckles whitening.

'You've seen my sister? You had no right to go bothering Vera. She's a sick woman.'

'She seemed fine to me. She was very forthcoming, in fact. A nice lady, I thought, extremely loyal to her family.'

She noticed his jaw clench – she'd hit a nerve. 'Why haven't you visited Vera for over twenty years, Don? Does she know too much about you? Does that make you nervous?'

'Leave her out of this.'

'Mum didn't know you had a sister. She thought you were an orphan. Is that the tale you tell all your lady friends, Don? Does it get you the sympathy vote?'

'You had better be quiet now.'

Suzanne ignored the threat in his tone. 'So I've been wondering why you chose to tell Cynthia the truth? I mean, you even introduced her to Vera.'

'Shut up!'

She was getting to him and she knew she was playing a dangerous game but she couldn't stop. 'I know! You wanted your rich American wife to see how humble your original home was. Cynthia cared nothing for family so she wouldn't give a damn about your poor orphan-boy story. But show her what she would view as poverty, something she had no idea about, *that* would stoke the fires of her interest.'

'I don't think like that.' He sounded insulted, hurt even.

'Oh yes, you do.' She decided to push it. 'I'm beginning to get a handle on you.'

'You have no idea about me.' His voice was flat now, a toneless drone. 'None at all.'

There was a lay-by coming up on the left and Don swerved into it, stopped the car, turned in his seat and grabbed Suzanne by the hair. He pulled her close to him until they were nose-to-nose, his teeth bared like a cornered animal.

'I could kill you with my bare hands,' he growled. 'Or beat your brains out. Just like I did to your precious Mark. Smashed his skull with his own cricket bat.' He pushed her away contemptuously, started the car, revved the engine and drove out of the lay-by. 'Think you know me, do you? Well, think on that one, bitch!'

*

Luke gazed out of the window onto Joan's immaculate garden while she pointed out and named various shrubs and plants. 'This garden is Harry's pride and joy,' she said. 'Or it was until he got involved with a local charity. He does their accounts, among other chores, and that seems to take up most of his time these days.' She sighed. 'But if he's happy then I'm happy.'

'Where is Harry today?'

'He's involved in a fundraising event. He'll be home later tonight, probably a little the worse for wear. I left this morning before he got up so he has no idea what's been going on. But no matter, we can talk about all this with him tomorrow. He's the most grounded person I've ever met; he'll know what to do.' She patted Luke's arm. 'In the meantime, I'll cook us some dinner.' She picked up the remote control and flicked on the TV. 'You watch some early-evening telly. It'll rot your brain but it might take your mind off things.'

Luke watched Joan head for the kitchen. Suzanne had her mother's walk, easy grace and elegance. He now wished he'd taken Mark's initial fears for Suzanne's safety seriously. He wished he'd been a better brother. He wished he'd risked his father's wrath and told the truth about Anita. He wished… he wished. *If only*, he was back with *if only*. He needed a drink. The bottles of whisky, gin and vodka taunted him from the drinks cabinet across the room. What harm would one drink do? But the thought of the kitchen cupboard in his apartment and the note in Mark's handwriting – 624 days – kept him on track. The one way he could honour his brother's memory was to stay sober. So he sat down in front of the television. Two bright-faced people were rambling about something or other, so he switched to a news channel.

'Joan! Come and look at this,' he called. 'Now!'

Joan came in from the kitchen, wiping her hands on a tea towel, and stared at the image on the screen.

'Police want to interview this man in connection with a serious incident in Surrey…' the announcer was saying. 'Do not approach him… if you have any information, please contact the incident room on this number…'

Joan reached for the telephone.

CHAPTER FORTY-ONE

DCI Etheridge picked up the clear evidence bag containing a gold bracelet. 'Does the manager of the shop remember the precise time that he acquired this?'

'He stated that it was an hour or so before he heard all the sirens in the high street. So that would be just before Mark Woods' body was found.'

'So our bearded gentleman kills Woods and then walks around the corner to the high street to sell the bracelet. Cool customer. Does the manager recall anything about the man?'

'He said the suspect was laughing and joking with him but that he drove a hard bargain. We've got the shop's CCTV footage.'

'Let's take a look at it.'

'We've had a call from a nurse at St Francis' hospital, sir,' said another young cop. 'The caller says that the man in the photofit was a patient on Bridget Daly's ward a few months back. He's grown a beard since then but the caller was sure it's the same person. He'd had heart surgery and she remembers his name as Michael O'Connor. Apparently Daly was quite taken with him.'

'Get the hospital records people on the line.'

'Sir,' a young policewoman interrupted, handing Etheridge the phone. 'I think you might want to take this one. We've got Suzanne Woods' mother on the line. She claims to recognise our suspect.'

*

Suzanne's heart was thundering as Don drove into the crescent where Joan's house was situated. 'My mother doesn't live here any more.'

'Oh, she moved, did she? When was that, then?'

Suzanne winged it. 'It must be a year ago.' From her conversations with Rose, she knew that Don had been incapacitated for that long. 'Mum and Harry have a place in Brighton now.'

Don lashed out, hitting Suzanne in the face with the back of his fist. 'You're a liar. I always know where my Joanie is. Let me describe her house to you. Five bedrooms, gable-fronted detached with a heated swimming pool hidden behind a wall of shrubs in the garden. Ungated driveway with separate garage and Joanie drives a Volvo. I've been in there. I can get in anywhere. Just ask your husband.' He chuckled. 'Oh, you can't, can you? Boo-fucking-hoo!'

Mark was dead. Suzanne didn't want to believe it. She was desperately hanging onto to the hope that this was another of Don's lies. But he had been in her house, he'd described a painting that he could never have otherwise seen and he had her Stanley knife in his possession. Of course, that didn't prove that he'd killed Mark. Maybe he'd just broken into the house. She clung to that thought. But his callous murders of Cynthia and Jared, the house fire and then the shooting of that man in the car park had unnerved her and would haunt her for many years to come. It was also clear that Don had been stalking her mother. He might have seen Joan's house on Google Earth but that wouldn't necessarily have shown the Volvo. It had been his accurate description of the antique dressing table in Joan's bedroom that confirmed her suspicions. That piece of furniture had been a surprise gift from Harry for Joan's fiftieth birthday and Suzanne couldn't imagine her mother giving Don a guided tour of her home. So the only way he could have seen it was if he had somehow gained access to the house. Suzanne's mind raced while her head ached from his blows.

'Joanie's house backs on to some snotty country club and that wanker she's married to is a member there. Stuck-up bastard!'

He reached across and poked Suzanne with his finger. 'I know everything about them. So don't you lie to me, you stupid bitch. Don't you ever lie to me.'

Suzanne was filled with a sense of dread and helplessness as they drew nearer to her mother's home but she gave it one more try. 'She *has* moved, Don. It must have been when you were ill. What a fool you'll feel when a complete stranger opens the door. What are you going to do then? Shoot them?'

'Fuck you, liar! I know my Joanie. She's a settler, she'd never move from here. Never! The only reason she moved house when you were a teenager was because she thought I'd never find her. Thought she could get way from me. But she never has and she never will.' A smile of satisfaction spread across Don's face. 'There it is,' he said. 'That's Joanie's place alright.'

He turned the car into the driveway and parked outside the front door.

*

Joan put the phone down, and turned back to Luke. 'Please tell me that this is a nightmare. Tell me I'm going to wake up.'

'Did Etheridge say who'd identified Tyler?' Luke asked.

Joan walked unsteadily towards the sofa and sat down. 'They said the suspect was seen leaving the house just after Mark was attacked. I can't believe this.'

'Neither can I. Mark told me he'd seen a death certificate for Tyler.'

'I'm truly sorry, Luke, but all I can think is, thank God Suzanne wasn't there at the time.'

'I understand.' Luke moved beside Joan and put his arms around her. Joan began to sob and Luke made an attempt to comfort her as they held on to each other.

*

The pinboard in the incident room was filling up. The sketch provided by Mrs Jones now had two names written beneath it: Donald Tyler and Michael O'Connor.

'Okay,' Etheridge said to nobody in particular. 'Hospital records have confirmed that Tylor got all fixed up at St Francis' under the name Michael O'Connor. Subsequently he shacks up with Bridget Daly.' He pointed to the photograph of the woman smiling in the nurse's uniform. 'She very conveniently commits suicide.' He threw out another question, 'Anything from the post-mortem to suggest she didn't go over that balcony voluntarily?'

'I'll find out.'

'Tyler takes Bridget Daly's car and is next sighted at Redstone House.' He looked at the thin-faced DC seated across the room. 'Anyone recognise him from there?'

'I'll speak to them again.'

'Do it now!' Etheridge moved further along the board to the pictures of the dead body of Mark Woods that had been taken by the SOC photographer. 'Tyler goes to his daughter's house, maybe looking for her. She's not there. So he kills her husband and then calmly walks to the high street to sell that gold bracelet. This bastard's got balls of brass.'

'Sir!' The gaunt DC put down the phone. 'The chief medical officer at Redstone House has reported the suspicious death of one of their patients, a Rose Anderson.'

'And?'

'Rose Anderson's next of kin was recorded as being Suzanne Woods.'

*

Suzanne stood at her mother's front door, sensing the pressure from the muzzle of the gun pressed against her spine. She raised her tethered hands and rang the doorbell.

'Please don't do this, Dad. Let's just drive away. I'll do whatever you want. Go wherever you want.'

'Oh, it's Dad now, is it?' he snarled in her ear. 'Too little, Suzy-Q, and far too late.'

'Please leave my mother out of this.'

'I'm not going to hurt my Joanie. But you…' He prodded her with the gun. 'You blew it, lady.'

Luke opened the door and his face betrayed dismay at the sight of Suzanne's bruised face. 'Suzanne!'

She raised her hands to show her bindings. Don pushed her forward and Luke's expression changed to one of horrified recognition.

'Well, well,' Don said. 'I never forget a face but I'm having trouble placing you, son.'

'Luke's my brother-in-law,' Suzanne explained.

Don laughed. 'I've got it! A copper. You're a copper, aren't you?'

'Yes, we met outside Suzanne's studio after the fire.'

Suzanne's heart lurched. Sophie. She had introduced Sophie to death.

'Small world, eh? Well, copper brother-in-law, you be a good boy and take me to my Joanie, okay?'

Joan walked slowly into the hallway. 'Hello, Don,' she greeted him. Her manner was composed and detached although Suzanne spotted that she had been crying. 'It's been a long time. Why don't we all come into the sitting room and talk this thing through?'

Don threw his car keys to her. 'You're as beautiful as ever. Do you know that?'

The keys landed at her feet and she picked them up. 'Why, thank you, Don, that's very nice of you to say so. What do you want me to do with these keys?'

'In the boot of that Fiesta out there, you'll find a bag of ties. You bring them in here, babe. Okay? And we'll go in there and wait for you.'

'Of course, Don. Whatever you want. I'm sure we can work everything out.'

'Don't do anything silly out there now, will you?'

'You know me, Don. I'm the soul of discretion.'

'And you, mister copper.' Don sneered at Luke. 'Speak only when you're spoken to and don't try and be some kind of hero. Because I'm the man with the plan. Oh yes, and the gun.'

Don was ushering Luke and Suzanne into the sitting room when Joan caught her eye. Joan raised her finger to her lips momentarily as if to say, keep quiet and do as you are told. She left the front door open and went swiftly to the car.

Joan opened the boot, picked up the bag of yellow ties and spotted the Stanley knife. She shut the boot, pocketed the knife, went back into the house and closed the door behind her.

*

Etheridge ran his hand over his receding hairline. 'Okay, how does this one fly? Tyler chucks Bridget Daly off the balcony, takes her car, goes to Redstone House and kills his other girlfriend, Rose Anderson, then heads off in search of his daughter. But she's in Scotland, so he murders Mark Woods instead. Was he looking for something else there? He was careful not to make the house look as though it had been tossed… but when he gets to the attic he slashes his daughter's paintings to ribbons. Looks like our man suffers bursts of uncontrollable rage.' Etheridge stared at the image of Donald Albert Tyler for a moment then turned back to his assembled squad. 'And how the hell did Suzanne Woods get all the way to Inverness, when her car was abandoned on Banstead Common with her handbag, purse and credit cards inside?'

'A van found at the Beaulieu house in Scotland was registered to a man from this area. He reckons that he sold it to an American on the day that Suzanne Woods disappeared.'

Etheridge shook his head. 'Who are these fucking people?'

'I've been checking with the immigration people, sir. Cynthia Beaulieu had been living in that house in Scotland with her son. She suffered from MS. Been ill for the past few years.'

'Isn't she an American? How come she was allowed to stay in the UK?'

'Her son, Jared Tyler, claimed British citizenship through his father.'

'Anyone spoken to this Jared yet?'

'He's still alive, sir, but only just. The local force is waiting to question him.'

'And the other survivor?'

'He's an old family employee but he didn't see his attacker. The only person he identified was Suzanne Woods.'

'So, Tyler drives six hundred miles to find his daughter. Any news on Bridget Daly's car?'

'It's been impounded in Carlisle, sir. There was a shooting in a park there, with one man dead. The local force took the car, believing it belonged to the victim.'

'When did this happen? What was he driving?'

'Six hours ago. The victim's car was a silver Ford Fiesta. It's the standard-issue rep's model. I've flagged it up on the ANPR.'

'Keep on it.' He looked back to the image of Donald Tyler. 'He sets fire to the Beaulieu house, drives back through Carlisle and jacks a car. It looks to me as though he's picking off his ex-lovers, one by one.' He turned to the scrawny DC. 'Frost, get Suzanne Woods' mother on the phone… Mrs Joan Lester. And warn the local station that they need to get an armed-response unit round there. I think Tyler may be on his way to see his ex-wife.'

*

'Well, isn't this nice.' Donald Tyler remarked contemptuously as he surveyed his captives sitting together on the three-seater sofa. Luke's arms had been bound behind his back and his ankles strapped together by Joan while Don held the gun to Suzanne's head. 'One big happy family.'

Joan remained unbound and was bathing Suzanne's face with damp tissues to reduce the swelling that was coming up over her left eye. She hadn't asked what had happened to her daughter's face, but was just dealing with it in her usual pragmatic manner. Don stalked the room, muttering under his breath, agitated, picking up ornaments, only to set them down again. He finally came to a family photograph that had been taken in the garden on Joan and Harry's recent wedding anniversary. He gave a hollow laugh and pointed to the white-haired man. 'Who's the ancient gentleman?'

'That's Harry,' Joan said.

'Bit of a crumbly for you, isn't he, Joanie? Still get it up, can he? Still give my Joanie a good seeing-to?'

'What do you want, Don?' Joan's voice was so quietly controlled and neutral that Suzanne marvelled at her mother's ability to maintain such composure.

'Just wanted to see you again, babe. Who's the tall blond chappie?' He thumbed at the image of the happily smiling Mark.

Hope surged through Suzanne. How could Don not recognise the man he claimed to have killed? 'He's my husband,' she said. 'Luke's brother.'

Don coughed out a laugh, then looked pointedly at Luke, who had kept silent so far. 'He got the looks in the family, didn't he, son?'

'I asked you what you wanted,' Joan repeated evenly.

Don ignored her. 'Mind you, he didn't look this good when I last saw him.' He winked at Suzanne. 'Ugh, what a mess. Blood and brains all over the floor.'

Luke was sitting beside Suzanne. His body tensed suddenly and she glanced up at him. His face showed no sign of emotion but she knew then that it was true. Her father, the man who now stood before them wielding a gun and gloating, had murdered

Mark. Suzanne stiffened, stifling a mournful moan, fingernails digging into her own palms.

'Shh…' Joan breathed a warning and squeezed her daughter's hand to remind her that she shouldn't react, then turned to Don. 'Would you like a drink, Don? I can make some coffee maybe. Are you hungry? How about a sandwich?'

He stroked his face thoughtfully with the gun barrel. 'I could do with a shag, Joanie. You up for that? It's been a long time, babe.'

'You let Suzanne and Luke walk out of here and we can do whatever you want,' Joan spoke in a matter-of-fact tone.

'Hmm,' Don mused. 'Tempting offer, Joanie, but this is what I think of it.' He threw the anniversary picture onto the carpet and slammed his foot down on it, smashing the glass. 'Oops!' He sneered at her. 'Tell you what, babe. How about we do it right here, on the carpet, right now? Show our little girl how we used to go at it like rabbits before she came along to spoil our fun, wailing in the night, sucking on your tits. How's about it, Joanie, my love?'

Joan released Suzanne's hand, stood up and walked slowly towards her ex-husband. 'I tell you what, Don. I'll make something to drink and we can discuss this.' Her voice was soft and seductive. 'I'm sure we can sort something out between us, just you and me.'

Don moved fast and grabbed Joan by the hair, pressing the gun to her temple. 'Joanie, don't you try anything stupid now.' He let go of her hair, wrapped one arm around her body, held her close with her back to him and nuzzled her neck. 'Oh, you smell so good, babe. I always felt like I could drown in your long red hair.' He ground his crotch into her backside. 'Ooh, baby!'

Suzanne was sickened; she wanted to rescue her mother, to rush at this monstrous man and tear his face off. What she was feeling must have shown in her expression because her mother's mask of indifference was raised momentarily as she mouthed, '*Don't move.*'

Don, lost in some kind of reverie, appeared not to notice the silent exchange. 'You made me love you, Joanie. You're in my head.

You're in my balls. Every woman I fuck is you.' He squeezed her breasts as he dry-humped her passive body. 'You've still got it, babe. You still give me a hard-on.'

Suzanne stared at the scene unfolding in front of her in horrified silence, recalling Vera's comment about how much Joan reminded her of their mother. Had that likeness been a part of Don's obsession with Joan? Was there some kind of Oedipus complex involved here – Don wishing to sexually control his own mother's likeness? She shuddered at the thought as a previous conversation with Joan crept into her consciousness. '*After you were born he became increasingly jealous and violent,*' Joan had told her. '*There were times when it seemed as though he was lashing out at someone else entirely, trying to punish them and not me.*'

The phone rang.

CHAPTER FORTY-TWO

'Mrs Lester, this is Detective Constable Frost from—'

'Harry, when will you be home?' Joan kept her tone light and conversational, aided and abetted by a broad smile. 'Suzanne's here, darling, isn't that wonderful? Luke's here too.'

DC Frost hit the record button. 'Is Donald Tyler in your house, Mrs Lester?'

'Yes, yes, yes, darling. I understand. Well, you get here as soon as you can, okay? Must go. See you later, Harry.'

Joan put the phone down and her smile faded as she turned back towards Don. He was standing behind the sofa with the gun muzzle pointed downwards onto the top of Suzanne's head.

'He's still caught up with this charity do. He won't be home until later tonight.' Joan returned Luke's enquiring look with an almost imperceptible nod, although her expression remained neutral.

'We'll wait.' Don's face was twisted with malevolence. He cradled the gun in both hands. 'I've got this plan, Joanie. I'm going to take everything from you that you hold dear: your *darling* Harry, your perfect house, your daughter... You just watch me.'

Suzanne realised that this sudden change in Don's tempo had been triggered by things he could not control. The phone call had clearly thrown him. The outside world was intruding into his stage-managed scenario. Joan's calm was also spooking him and her reference to Harry as 'darling' had pushed Don over the edge. Angry and unnerved, like a cornered rat, hissing and threatening to bite, Don was upping the ante. The question was, would he carry through with this latest threat?

'Why are you doing this, Don?' Joan asked. 'None of us have done anything to harm you. It makes no sense at all.'

'It does to me. I've done all this before.' He slapped Suzanne on the back of her head. 'Haven't I, bitch? And I've always walked away unscathed. So don't think I won't do it this time.'

Joan ventured closer, palms held upwards as though in offering. 'Why don't you just get in your car and drive away? I assure you that we'll say nothing about what has happened here today.'

Suzanne followed her mother's lead. 'Yes, Dad, just think about it. You've got a new identity. You can go anywhere in the world. Start afresh. Isn't that what you wanted?'

'You don't know what I want.' His eyes swept the room. 'Fucking poncey place you've got here, Joanie. You've done well for yourself, girl. On the board of directors, eh? It's long way from your bohemian little pad on King's Road and our little semi in Mitcham.' He stood back and aimed the gun directly at her. 'And I can destroy it all.' He closed one eye as though lining her up, taking aim and about to shoot. 'Just like that.'

Joan stood motionless, unflinching, head held high. 'If you're expecting me to beg for my life, Don, then you don't remember me at all.'

'What about her, though – your precious daughter?' Don waved the gun in Suzanne's direction. 'Beg for her, Joanie, beg for her.'

'Suzanne is your daughter too, Don. Remember seeing her born? You loved her so much. We had some good times, didn't we? Let's see if we can find a way to sort things out. Can we just sit and talk this through, logically?'

He gestured to a chair and Joan sat down.

'Let's work this out, Don. You shoot Suzanne and me, and then what? Turn the gun on yourself? Is that what you're going to do, Don? Bang, and it's all over?'

He paced up and down behind the sofa, agitated and wound tight. 'I might do. I can do anything I want.'

'But then you won't find out how all this turns out, will you?' Joan soothed. 'The Don Tyler that I knew would want more from all this than just a bullet in the brain.' She leaned forward, elbows on her knees, chin on her folded hands. 'So what *do* you want?'

Suzanne saw a look of confusion flit across her father's face, and that was when she finally realised. *This man hasn't a clue what he wants. There is no master plan here.* All those girls he'd confessed to killing, it was all just happenstance. The wrong place at the wrong time, victims of spontaneous aggression just as Mark had been. Her heart wrenched at the thought of her husband but she battened down her distress. She couldn't allow her emotions to sweep her away. She had to keep thinking clearly, because if Don had not thought any further beyond being in this room, if he had no exit strategy, then he may well suddenly fall foul of the overwhelming impulse to kill them all.

The phone rang.

Don grasped Joan by the arm and pulled her to her feet. 'If that's Harry, you tell him to get here right now. Tell him it's an emergency. Tell him what you want but you get him here.' He pushed her roughly in the direction of the phone. 'Now!'

She stumbled across the room and picked up the phone.

'Mrs Lester? This is the police. Let me talk to Donald Tyler.'

Joan tried to control the trembling in her hand as she turned to Don. 'The police want to talk to you.'

Don blanched. With the gun trained directly at Suzanne, he took the phone from Joan's hand. 'Go and sit with them and don't you move,' he told her before addressing the caller. 'Who do you want to speak to?' he asked brusquely.

'Hello, Don, my name is Chris and I'm with the police.'

'My name's O'Connor, Michael O'Connor.'

Bond, James Bond, Suzanne thought, as she watched her father's face. She could almost see the cogs working, the signs of desperation in his demeanour.

'Well, you see, Don, we don't think so. We believe you to be Donald Albert Tyler. But if this is just some big mistake, then all you need do is to come out and talk to us and we can clear everything up.'

'What do you want with him, anyway?'

'Let's drop the charade, shall we? We know who you are, Don, you've been positively identified. So, tell me, is there a problem in there?'

'No problem at all, just having a nice family visit.' He sneered at Suzanne and she braced herself for the impact of the bullet.

'Then if there's no problem, you won't mind allowing the people with you in there to come and talk to us. Just to reassure us that everything's tickety-boo, eh?'

'Nobody's going anywhere.'

'So there is a problem, then? Talk to me, Don. Tell me what the trouble is and we'll see what we can do.'

'Fuck off!' Don slammed the phone down on the table.

'You won't get away this time,' Luke said evenly. 'They'll have cordoned off this area by now, and the house will be surrounded...'

'It doesn't have to be like this, Don.' Joan's voice was gentle.

The phone rang again.

'Talk to them, Don,' Joan advised.

He stared at the phone for a moment and then picked it up. 'What?'

'We know what you've done, so you have to realise there is no way out of this, Don. You *will* be going to prison. But I can make life easier for you, get you a good lawyer, whatever it is you need.'

'And what if I shoot them all? Eh? What can you do to me? Hang me?' He clicked the call off once more.

'Immediately after a shot is fired, they'll break in here,' Luke said. 'They'll take you down. No questions asked. That's how this works.'

'In a hail of bullets?' Don grinned manically. 'Not a bad way to go. What do you say, Brother-in-law?' He pointed the gun at Luke.

'What about your journals, Dad?' Suzanne cut in, in an attempt to plant the seed of an idea in his mind. 'That was *really* why you wrote them, wasn't it? So the world would know how you got away with murder for all these years? How you killed all those women and made fools of the police?'

Joan turned to Suzanne, her face a mask of serenity but with uncomprehending alarm in her eyes.

'Before you met him,' Suzanne told her mother. She looked up at Don, who was pacing in front of them. 'How many was it, Dad? Four?'

'Five maybe, or more.' Don sat on the arm of the sofa next to Joan, the gun held in his right hand. He reached out to stroke her hair with his left. 'But I was a different man with you, Joanie. If you'd stayed with me then, nothing else would have happened. All those others would still be alive.'

Joan didn't respond, didn't brush his hand away; she sat still with her hands folded in her lap. Suzanne was fighting her own inner battle. This man was a narcissist, an unpredictable sadist, shifting the blame for his own actions onto others. But what was clear was that nothing he did had been planned, his behaviour was dictated by outside forces over which he had no control. So, while her instinct was to confront him she realised that might send him into a tailspin of violence that could end in self-annihilation. She must remain calm.

Suzanne felt her mother's tranquillity wash over her. She had to keep her father talking. 'What about Betty? You did a good job of framing Raymond for that one, Dad. And Naomi, then the girl in Florida. As well as Moira, we mustn't forget Moira.'

'And counting.' Don released his grip on Joan's hair, slid his left hand into her trouser pocket and extracted the Stanley knife. He waved it under her nose. 'Were you about to cut me with this, Joanie?'

Joan stiffened.

'Tell Mum about the others,' Suzanne interrupted fast. She had to distract him. 'For instance, Gloria, the one you drowned in the bath.'

'Yeah,' Don pocketed the knife. 'I wrote it all down, Joanie, everything. They'll write books about me, make films perhaps. I'll be infamous.'

'But you'll never know, will you, Dad? You can't bask in the spotlight. Not if you're dead.'

The phone began to ring once more and Don banged his hand on the back of the sofa in frustration.

'And they'll never know the truth about Mark.' Suzanne held back the catch in her voice as she said his name. She felt the tears welling inside her but knew she had to keep it together. 'Or Cynthia and Jared, or that man in the car park. Some journalist will make it all up. They won't know your side of the story, will they? Not unless you're able to write about that, too.'

'There's more than that,' Don said. 'You don't know about them all.'

'Then you have to complete the book, Dad. And you can't do that if you allow the police to kill you.'

'Listen to her, Don,' Joan urged.

'Be quiet. I need to think.' He looked around the room anxiously. The phone rang incessantly.

'Talk to them,' Luke said. 'Before it's too bloody late.'

Don leapt to his feet and strode purposefully around the back of the sofa. The memory of the man in the car park, shot point-blank from behind, sent an apprehensive tremor through Suzanne. Don could swiftly execute them all before the police broke in.

Joan turned slowly to face her ex-husband. 'Think before you do anything rash, Don.'

He met her gaze and slapped Luke on the back of the head. 'You're the expert, copper. I want chapter and verse about what's going on out there.'

Luke's training kicked in. Although he had never actually been in a hostage situation before, he knew that the truth was the best policy and hoped that his colleagues would be in situ. 'All calls to and from this number will be redirected through the command centre and the negotiator will keep on ringing until you answer the phone. The nearest armed-response unit will be deployed. Right now, police officers will have evacuated the neighbouring houses and blocked off the crescent. And there will be armed officers and marksmen at the back of the house. There's no way out.'

'Close the curtains, Joanie,' Don ordered. 'No sniper's going to get me.' He was panicking, Suzanne could see it in his face, hear it in his voice. She had to keep him focused and help him to plan a viable exit strategy.

'Of course, Don.' Joan stood and walked to the window. She could see into her garden and, although she couldn't spot any movement, she could almost feel gun sights trained on her from behind the hedge.

'I can't see anyone out there, Don.'

'They'll be there,' Luke said.

'Shut the fuck up.' He pressed the gun against Luke's temple. 'Or maybe I'll kill you now. One more won't make any difference, will it?'

'The minute you fire even one shot, those armed police will be in here and you won't be walking anywhere, ever again,' Suzanne warned. 'But, if you let us go, surrender to the police and let them read all of your journals, you'll be a big celebrity. Just think about it, Dad: books, TV, a film, maybe. You could drag it out for years; take them to where you buried all the bodies. You'd never be out of the newspapers.'

'And we'll have to endure all that notoriety.' Joan stood beside him and caressed his arm. 'You will be a part of our lives forever, Don. Everywhere we go we'll be reminded of you. For as long as we live.'

Don gripped her around the waist and held her close to him. 'That is the reason I've always loved you, my Joanie. We think along exactly the same lines. Because we are one, you and me, always have been and always will be.'

He released her and crossed the room to the phone. 'I'll tell you my demands,' he said to the caller. 'I want a journalist here.'

'Plenty of them at the end of the road, Don. It's a media circus out here.'

'Oh no, you don't. I want one I can recognise, not some copper in disguise. Get me Terry Vincent from the BBC. He writes books, doesn't he? As I recall he did one about the Yorkshire Ripper. Yes, I want Terry Vincent.'

'Well, Don, that may take some time. But I'll see what I can do. I'll have to call the BBC and get him over here. These guys aren't just waiting by the phone, you know. And in the meantime, you can do something for me in return.'

'You know as well as I do, Chris, that I don't have to do a thing.'

'Of course you don't, Don, but as an act of good faith on your part, you let your daughter come outside and talk to us.'

'I'll think about it.'

'You let her out and I'll make the call for you. I'll try to get Terry Vincent here. Do we have a deal, Don?'

Don turned to Joan. 'Cut the copper loose. Get some scissors from the kitchen.'

Joan stood, and headed for the kitchen while Don talked to the caller.

'You'll get your colleague. How's that, Chris?'

'It's a start, Don. The minute he's out of there, I'll make the call. This line will remain open. All you have to do is pick up the phone and I'll be here.'

Joan came back with kitchen scissors.

'Just his legs, so he can walk out of here.'

'I'll stay,' Luke said. 'Let Suzanne go.'

'That is not an option. We do this my way.'

'Go, Luke. Please go,' Suzanne begged. 'Tell them we'll be okay if Dad gets to talk to Terry Vincent. This will be a big exclusive story for him. I'm sure you can persuade him to come here.'

'And my sister,' Don was telling the negotiator, 'I want my sister here.'

*

Vera Tyler was on the train from Liverpool Lime Street to London's Euston station. Two hours and seven minutes, the man in the ticket office had told her. Such a short time to get to a city she had never visited in all of her seventy years. The Big Smoke, they used to call it, with its soot-blackened buildings. All cleaned up now, of course, but still alien territory to her. She pictured Buckingham Palace and the Houses of Parliament, St Paul's Cathedral, the Tower of London: all of the sights she would have liked to visit. Places that she and Donny had talked about when they were kids.

'I'll make loads of money and take you there, Vee,' he'd promised, his squishy little face alive with excitement. That had been their shared ambition back then.

She looked out at the countryside whizzing by and recalled the images on the TV that had forced her to make this journey. *It can't be true*, she thought. She didn't believe it. Donny would never hurt anyone, let alone hold them hostage. She refused to believe it any more than she'd swallowed Suzanne's story about Donny being dead. Despite all the paperwork, the death certificate she'd been shown, Vera had held fast to the conviction that her brother was still alive. And the photofit that the police had shown her when they visited earlier had proved her right. Not that she told them that she recognised him. She wouldn't give them the satisfaction.

'I haven't seen my brother for twenty years,' she told them. 'Could be him, I suppose, but then it could be any man in his sixties.'

Donny had always got the blame for everything bad that happened. It had been the case ever since he was a little boy. The canary that flew away when he left the cage door open: how was a child of five supposed to know that the window wasn't closed? Mam had given him a right leathering for that, despite Vera's protests. Vera recalled the kerfuffle when the tiny puppy belonging to the girl next door had died. *'Donny Tyler did it!'* the girl had screamed. Vera knew that was rubbish too. Donny loved that puppy. He was always cuddling the pup and begging Mam to get one for him. Not that she ever did. Then there was the little lass who got pushed over on Bonfire Night and fell into the flames. It was tragic that the poor child ended up blind and badly scarred like that, but there were lots of kids larking about around her, so Vera could never understand why the girl's mother put the blame on Donny. What had he been then, eight or nine, maybe? Boys of that age didn't understand the danger.

Even when that baby disappeared from its pram in the next street, the police had come knocking. Vera remembered returning home from her job at the biscuit factory to find the local bobby in the house. Donny was holding on to Mam and sobbing his little heart out. He could have been no more than ten years old. Mam's face was stricken but, to give her her due, she had stood up for him.

'Where do you get off, accusing my son of doing something terrible like that?'

'Donny was seen near the baby's pram,' the policeman had said. 'Then, when the mother came out of the shop, the baby was gone.'

Once the policeman left the house, Mam rounded on Donny. 'Did you touch that baby?'

'No, Mam, honest! I was just looking at her.' He held onto his mother but she pushed him away.

'How did you know it was a girl?'

'The policeman said.'

'No, he didn't. He just said a baby.'

Donny had wiped his snotty nose on his sleeve. 'Well, it had a pink bonnet on, so it must have been a girl.'

The baby was never found.

Vera knew that these days there'd be DNA tests and CCTV cameras to prove Donny was innocent, but not back in the fifties. So people gossiped behind the family's back and it was a long time before the incident was laid to rest – if it truly ever was. Folk in her neighbourhood had constantly wagging tongues and long memories.

After that episode, Mam had taken Donny to the doctor, who referred him to a specialist at Alder Hey children's hospital. Vera recalled asking Donny about it.

'They showed me ink blots that looked like demons but I told them they were butterflies.' He grinned. 'And they got me to do drawings of my dreams.'

'What did you draw?' Vera asked him.

'I drew a witch with bright red hair, carrying a big stick.'

Mam never took him back there again. There was nothing wrong with Donny that a bit of love couldn't cure but, Vera was compelled to admit this, their mother had no love to give the boy.

It was no wonder Donny had taken the job with the travelling fair. It was to get away from Mam's constant abuse. She had even blamed Donny for Sheila's suicide.

'He should have been a man and taken responsibility for that baby,' Mam had slurred. 'That poor girl was at her wits' end. I told her she should have the baby adopted and she agreed it was the right thing to do. So there was no excuse for her to go jumping in front of that train. I bet Donny goaded her into it.'

Betty had been another of Donny's girls. Mam had been on the wagon after Donny left home and she'd even got herself a job. Then Donny turned up with Betty and Mam had taken her in and been kind to her. Baby Raymond was a lovely little chap and Vera had hoped that Donny would settle down in the neighbourhood and they could be one happy extended family. She'd fantasised about babysitting Raymond, being called Auntie Vee, taking Raymond to the zoo and the pictures – all the things that normal families do. But Mam started drinking again and telling all sorts of lies about Donny, until Betty packed her bags and left. Donny had never forgiven Mam for that. And neither had Vera, deep down, although she'd looked after her mother until she died. *Poor Donny*, Vera thought, *nothing ever seemed to go right for him.*

She watched the scenery changing constantly, the vibrant greens of the English countryside, the railway stations flashing by – places she had heard of but never been to. Under different circumstances she might have enjoyed this journey, as it was all so new to her. An attendant with a trolley clattered by selling drinks and sandwiches, but Vera couldn't eat a thing because she was too tensed up. She felt much like she had when she'd heard that Raymond had killed poor Betty. Newspaper reporters had tracked Vera down, and pushed notes through her letterbox when she'd refused to speak to them. They'd even talked to all her neighbours. She had been devastated and couldn't imagine why or how Raymond could have done such a thing. Still, she consoled herself with the thought that at least nobody could pin Betty's murder on Donny. He was safely in America with his new wife, Cynthia, and their son, Jared. At least, that was what Vera had believed until Suzanne turned up on her doorstep and raised so many doubts. Even so, she had brushed such qualms away like so many pesky flies. Suzanne seemed like a nice girl, Vera thought, but she was muddle-headed about her father. Donny was a good man, just misunderstood. She had always felt that – until now.

Just two hours ago the hostage story had been all over the telly, with Donny's picture being flashed up on every news report. That's when Vera had decided she must travel to London. She'd tell them that her brother would never do anything like that. If he was in that house, then this was the fault of someone else. She'd show them that she was on his side. The way she always had been.

*

Luke walked out of the front door of Joan's house. He spotted two armed officers crouched behind the silver Ford Fiesta in the driveway but didn't acknowledge them. They were waiting for the command to take Tyler down the moment he showed his face at the window. Just out of sight of the house was a substantial police presence. The crescent had been cordoned off and beyond the tape he spotted a mobile command unit vehicle and several vans from TV and radio stations. Cameras flashed as uniformed officers accompanied Luke to the command centre. There he expected he would have to provide details of the layout of the house and be questioned as to Tyler's state of mind and how well Joan and Suzanne were coping.

Just behind the police cordon he spotted Harry, who looked like he'd aged ten years since Luke had last seen him at the wedding anniversary party, just a few months ago.

Harry rushed towards him. 'I've just got here,' he said. He eyed Luke suspiciously. 'Why did he let *you* go? You should have stayed to protect them.'

Luke's police escort cut loose the binding around his wrists, then ushered him and the distraught Harry into the command centre.

'What is that evil bastard doing to Joan?' Harry asked desperately.

Luke had no answer to give him.

CHAPTER FORTY-THREE

Vera trudged up the ramp from the train platform into the bright modernity of London's Euston station. It was strikingly different from the faded Victorian grandeur of Liverpool Lime Street. A confusion of kiosks, an array of departure boards, signs pointing to the underground tube stations, cafes and a mass of humanity all confronted her. She had no idea where she should be heading or who she should speak to. Everyone else appeared to know where they were going and her ears were assaulted by well-spoken voices making announcements over the PA system.

Vera's first flustered response was to get back on the train and retreat to the safety of home. But Donny needed her, so she braced herself and wandered into the mêlée. Signs blinked on the arrivals boards – Birmingham, Manchester, Wolverhampton – nowhere that she needed to be. Not that she knew exactly where she should be going. Vera caught sight of her reflection in a shop window: an elderly woman with a tight white perm, wearing a shapeless grey coat, carrying a once-fashionable red handbag and looking lost.

'Can I assist you, madam?'

Vera turned to see an Asian man standing beside her. The reflective high-visibility jacket he wore over his dark-navy uniform bore a blue flash that read Transport Police. He was smiling at her.

'My name is Vera Tyler,' she said. 'I've come to help my brother.'

'Is he supposed to be meeting you here?' he asked kindly.

'He's in trouble,' she said. 'They said on the television that he's holding some people hostage.'

PC Patel guided Vera across the busy concourse to the waiting room while he spoke to someone on his personal radio.

'Let me get you a cup of tea,' he suggested, 'then I'll wait with you until someone arrives from the local police station. They'll be able to help you.'

*

Donald Tyler sat by the table next to the phone and gazed down at the gun in his hand. *Kill them*, it whispered to him. *Kill them and kill yourself. Put an end to this. You'll never survive banged up in prison for the rest of your natural life. Imagine the sound of the cell door clanging shut, confining you within those four walls, the crap food, the stink of other men's sweat and piss and shit. Every day the same routine, every night, for years and years on end, surrounded by perverts, rapists, murderers, thieves and child molesters – all the dregs of humanity. You'd never be a free man again. You'd go insane.*

'Talk to me, Don,' Joan said encouragingly. 'Tell me about all your travels. About all the places you sent those postcards from.'

He glanced up at her. From across the room, she looked the same as she had when he'd first set eyes on her, thirty-odd years ago, with her long auburn hair glistening in the sunlight, her green eyes alight with humour and glorious youth. Glastonbury, with the music throbbing in his ears, his heart thundering and Joanie's luscious body beneath him. He had loved her then and he loved her now. How could he put an end to her?

She'll get old, the gun murmured. *Her hair will turn white, her face wizened, she'll die one day, maybe drugged up to the eyeballs to ease her pain. Release her now, and allow her to die beautiful. Make her open her mouth wide – like she used to when she sucked your cock – and pull the trigger.*

'I kept all your postcards, you know,' Joan was saying. 'They're in my desk upstairs. Shall I go and get them so we can look at them together?'

He knew her room. He had gained access to the house four summers previously when the new kitchen was being installed. He had driven by on the off-chance of catching a glimpse of her. A van was in the driveway and he had walked straight in behind the two kitchen fitters, dodged straight upstairs and they hadn't noticed a thing. He'd gone through all the cupboards and drawers in the master bedroom, caught the scent of her from her underwear, touched all her clothes in her walk-in wardrobe, and found his postcards, hidden away at the back of her dressing table drawer.

Follow her up there, the gun taunted. *Fuck her on the bed she shares with Harry. Fuck her and strangle her. Nobody would hear that. That's what you came here for. Admit it. To stick your dick in her one more time before you left the country for good. You can still do that. She's just a few feet away, waiting to be had. I bet she's still got a wet snatch, all slippery and hot. Just like the first time at Glastonbury, the sweetest shag you'd ever had. Why let it go to waste? Don't allow her to go back to that old codger, with his cold hands and saggy arse. Look at her and imagine how it would feel with her writhing on your cock.*

'Or would you like something to eat – an omelette and chips, maybe? That was always your favourite.'

Don shifted in his seat, the weight of the gun wearing him down, its voice reverberating in his brain.

'The phone's ringing,' Suzanne reminded him, as he seemed to ignore it.

Don thought she looked nervous, as well she might. Stuck-up little bitch. He should have pushed her out of the car at speed and left her to die by the roadside. She'd been nothing but trouble since the moment she was born. She'd been an accident. He hadn't ever planned for her. She took his Joanie away from him. Before her, it had been just Joanie and him. They had been the ideal match, so good together.

'Isn't she perfect?' Joanie had gushed when the nurse laid Suzanne in her arms for the first time. She looked like a female version of himself. It had been history repeating itself: the red-haired mother and the dark, malevolent child. Maybe if Suzanne had looked like Joanie, he'd have felt differently, he mused. Even so he'd pretended to love the brat because that's what you're supposed to do. You grin like a lunatic and go around handing out cigars as though the result of one thoughtless ejaculation turns you into some kind of superhero. No wonder guys love to see porno cum-shots. *Splat!* All over the tits or in the chops, there's no fall-out from that: no screaming, shitting speck of humanity squelching out of a permanently stretched cunt to ruin your life forever.

All Suzanne did was get in his way. He remembered when she was just a few days old, how he had stood over her cot and watched her sleep, quiet at last, with an exhausted Joanie crashed out in their bed. How easy it would have been to smother the baby. *You've done it before*, the demon in the dark corner urged. *It was a piece of piss*. Cot deaths are common enough with nobody to blame but Mother Nature and then you'll have Joanie all to yourself again. At that moment the baby had stirred, opened her eyes and yelled blue murder. Instantly, Joanie was beside him, her hair tousled and her green eyes full of freshly minted motherly concern.

'Go back to bed, Don,' she'd said. 'You're back on the road tomorrow and you need your rest.' He returned home three months later, after the tour with some bunch of drug-addled arseholes that called themselves musicians, to find that Suzanne had taken over completely. He had been shut out of Joanie's affections. It was Suzanne this, and Suzanne that, no time for him. Hurried sex, the putrid smell of baby shit and vomit – the beginning of the end.

Don glared at his daughter. It was her fault that Joanie divorced him. 'You play too rough with her,' she'd told him, over and over again. 'Look at that bruise on her arm. How did she fall like that? Why is she crying?'

'Daddy pushed me,' four-year-old Suzanne had told her mother after she tumbled down the stairs. And then it was all over. He received the divorce papers in the post when he was on a tour in Paris.

The little bitch!

He could have walked away; he should have walked away like he had from his sons, but something kept pulling him back to see Suzanne. He'd told himself she was his excuse to see Joanie again and again, to keep reminding her of the old days. But each time the child had always been so happy to see him that he had warmed to her. Even fantasised of travelling the world with her. Until the Dalston visit when he was pulled up short, when he saw what she had become. The sight of her paintings had maddened him, sickened him. It was as though his bitch of a mother had imbued the only child he had ever cared for with her evil female spirit by passing on to her what she laughingly called her 'talent'.

It should have been her that night at the studio in Dalston – Suzanne, instead of Sophie Chen. Though Sophie had been a pleasant enough diversion. So trusting, as she'd let him into the building, preening after his praise for her work, smiling as he took her photo, standing beside that piece of junk she called sculpture. Just moments later, he had floored her. She'd fought him and she'd been far stronger than she looked, though that had intensified the buzz. He'd straddled her, taking his time, choking her into unconsciousness, allowing her to revive over and over until all the fight drained out of her.

Yeah, exotic little Sophie.

He stared at Suzanne now, with the bruises coming up on her face, her hands still tied. He could bind and gag Joanie, force her to watch while he killed Suzanne. Then Joanie would be scared of him. Then she'd take him seriously instead of coming on with this bullshit cool-and-collected act. How sweet it would be to screw her beside her daughter's lifeless body. Joanie would fight him then, tear at him while he fucked her senseless. He'd fantasised about it so many times, alone at night with his hand wrapped around his rearing cock. Savouring it, holding back, pushing it further until the final expulsion of the little death. All those girls, all those women, yet none could ever replace Joanie. She was a drug that had him hooked and compelled him to come here. The ringing telephone intruded on his thoughts and it finally hit him. His obsession with Joanie, with the one that got away, had led him straight into this trap.

'Don't you want to answer the phone, Dad? The police may have Terry Vincent on the line for you.'

Keep them at bay until you decide what to do, the voice in his head counselled. Don reached for the phone.

'Everything okay in there, Don? Your sister is on her way. She turned up at Euston and is in a car coming over right now.'

'What about Terry Vincent?'

'We're trying to get in touch with him. Is there anything else I can do for you in the meantime? Get you some food? You must all be hungry.'

Yeah, the voice scoffed. *You order some Kentucky Fried Chicken and the snipers shoot you when you open the front door. Or they drug the food. They must think you're a moron.*

'We're fine. Let me know when Vincent gets here.' He ended the call.

He had made his decision.

*

'Why won't you let me talk to my brother?' Vera was distraught. She looked around the command centre. All these strangers behaving as though Donny was a dangerous criminal, it just wasn't right. If she could only speak to him, let him explain to them why he was in that house, everything would be all right. There had to be some good reason for him to hold Suzanne and her mother against their will – if that really was happening. It might be just a misunderstanding, a lack of communication. She could get to the bottom of it. But the police were adamant that only their negotiator was allowed to talk to Donny. The reporters outside had pushed microphones in her face, asked her questions that she didn't fully comprehend. She overheard snatches of conversations about shootings and fires and was disconcerted by the sight of police with guns. It was all so confusing, so distressing… so unreal.

'Would you like to talk to *me* about your brother, Miss Tyler?'

The voice was softly spoken and Vera looked into the blue eyes of the casually dressed young blonde woman sitting beside her. She seemed friendly, more like a nurse or a doctor than a policewoman. Perhaps Vera would be able to confide in her, tell her all about the misfortunes that had befallen Donny over the years. Then they'd understand.

*

'They're going to kill me, Joanie.' Don paced the room. 'The minute I set foot outside, they'll shoot me.'

'Not if you let Suzanne go and talk to them, Don. She'll tell them you want to give yourself up peacefully and that you haven't harmed us.'

He turned to her, his expression petulant. 'You don't care what happens to me.'

'Yes, I do, Don. Let Suzanne go and I'll stay with you. The police won't shoot you if I'm here.'

He sighed and placed the gun muzzle under his chin. 'There's no life for me now, no future, just a prison cell for the rest of my life.' He held Joan in his stare. 'I'll end it all now, Joanie. What do you say to that?'

'Don, please, no.' Joan leapt to her feet and started towards him.

'I've got nothing to live for.' He cocked the gun and held his other arm out like a cop halting traffic, to indicate that Joan should keep her distance. She stopped in her tracks just a few feet away from him.

'What about all the women, Dad?' Suzanne coaxed. 'All those murder groupies who will write to you in jail. I bet there'll be lots of lonely vulnerable women who'll want to contact you.' Don glanced at her and she spotted a sly glint in his eyes. *This is all an act*, she thought, *another one of his sick games. Even now, with the police outside, he's playing to the gallery. He wants Mum to beg him not to pull the trigger. He wants to blame her for his cowardice.* 'And you need to talk to Terry Vincent, don't you?' she continued. 'If you cooperate with him, then you'll get your book written just the way you want it to be.'

Don indicated that Joan should return to her seat. He put the gun on the table and picked up the phone. 'You there, Chris? My daughter is coming out, so call off your dogs.'

*

Suzanne stepped out into the cold, grey light. Just out of range of the house, she was snatched by uniformed police and taken to a safe area beyond the cordon. Harry rushed over to her, Luke took her in his arms and, from the corner of her eye, she saw Vera, looking defeated and ashamed. Suzanne held out her bound hands to Vera to show her the proof, the stark reality of her brother. A policeman cut them free. Suzanne untangled herself from Luke and approached Vera.

'It's not true, is it?' Vera said, her voice breaking. 'Did our Donny do all those terrible things?'

*

Don was on his knees in front of Joan, his face buried in the crotch of her jeans, his arms wrapped around her waist, the gun in his right hand.

'Oh, you smell so good, my Joanie.' He looked up at her, his eyes tearful, fear and anguish etched on his features. 'Save me, baby. Save me.'

She stroked his hair. 'You can only help yourself, Don.'

He smiled. 'Tell me you love me.' He grasped her hand and pressed the gun into it. 'Tell me you love me, or shoot me. I can live again if you say it. Just one more time.'

He gripped the barrel of the gun in her hand and moved the muzzle to the centre of his forehead. 'You are the love of my life, my Joanie. I fell apart when you left me. I went crazy. Without you, I was nothing, I was an animal.' Tears were streaming down his face. 'I lost my soulmate and I lost my soul. Only you can save me, Joanie. So say it, say you still love me. Or kill me. Kill me now!'

CHAPTER FORTY-FOUR

'It's over,' Joan told the negotiator over the phone.

She glanced at the gun she had placed on the table beside the phone.

'Where's the gun, Joan?'

'I have it. It's not loaded.' She looked across the room towards Don. He was sitting on the floor in the corner, his knees pulled up to his chin, his forehead resting on them. 'It was never loaded.'

'Are you sure?'

'He showed me.'

'Where is Don at this moment?'

'He's crouched in the corner. He's ready to give himself up.'

'Are there any other weapons in the house?'

'No,' she said. 'I'm going to open the front door now. I'll bring the gun with me.'

She put the phone down, picked up the gun tentatively and walked slowly out of the room.

*

Don raised his head to watch his ex-wife leave the room. She still loved him, she had told him so. Her hand had trembled when she held the gun, as he offered himself up for sacrifice. She could easily have pulled the trigger but he had sensed that she wouldn't – not that you could ever be one hundred per cent sure of anything people might do. He jiggled the bullets in his pocket. He had unloaded the gun surreptitiously before he entered the house.

Suzanne had been too terrified to notice. She'd witnessed him shooting Jared and that dipstick in the car park. What more proof did she need that he was prepared to kill her and Joanie? But it was so much sweeter to elicit what he wanted with threats rather than bullets. It had been a good game, well played. Not that Joanie knew that when she held the gun to his head. She'd believed she had the power to kill him. But she hadn't even considered it, not for one second. Instead, she had given him the only thing he had ever craved; she had confessed to him what he had known for all these years. '*Yes, Don. I still love you.*'

It was thirteen paces for her to get to the front door. He'd counted them out when he first entered the house. She wouldn't run there, not his Joanie. She'd move with dignity, head held high and hips gently swaying before she reached out her hand and unlocked the door to let in the outside world. Armed cops, hyped-up and bristling with testosterone, would have weapons trained on the doorway just in case he was with her. Once they established that she was alone, they'd take the gun from her hand and whisk her away. Then they would come for him.

He couldn't hear her footsteps in the carpeted hallway but he counted them off in his mind: seven, eight, nine, ten. Three more steps and she'd be at the front door.

'Hold on tight, Joanie,' he called out to her. 'It's going to be one hell of a ride.'

Donald Tyler unbuttoned the left cuff of his shirt, pushed the sleeve up to his elbow and flexed his hand repeatedly. He drew the Stanley knife from his pocket, slid out the razor-sharp blade and placed it midway between his wrist and forearm. He gritted his teeth, held his breath and slashed along an artery.

CHAPTER FORTY-FIVE

The police cordon opened for the ambulance to pass through. The eager media crowd surged forward, cameras flashing, microphones thrusting out from a sea of hands. Harry held on to Joan as though scared to let her out of his sight and Suzanne stood with Vera. Luke was in the command vehicle, talking to the officer in charge.

'Quite a dramatic exit,' Suzanne said under her breath.

Vera was enraged. 'What have those bastards done to my brother?'

Luke came out and spoke to them both. 'Apparently Tyler tried to commit suicide. He used that knife he took from Joan.'

'I don't believe you.' Vera pointed an accusatory finger at all the uniformed cops. 'They did it.'

'Typical. He used *my* Stanley knife as one final up-yours. I bet he didn't cut his throat with it, though,' Suzanne commented tartly.

'The paramedics reported that he'd opened an artery in his arm,' Luke said.

'Another move in his diabolical game.'

Vera shrank back from Suzanne. 'How can you say something as cold as that?'

'Cold?' Suzanne took Vera by the shoulders and shook her. '*Cold!* I've seen cold, Vera. Stone-cold murder, right in front of me.'

Luke pulled Suzanne away and placed a protective arm around her.

'Cold! That's your brother,' Suzanne insisted vehemently. 'That's my father. This kind of melodramatic gesture is all about him. Everything he does is calculated to do maximum damage to everyone else, but as little possible harm to Don Tyler.'

Vera hugged her big red handbag to her chest. 'You'll be sorry if he dies.'

'I think his imminent death is highly unlikely.'

*

Don lay back while the ambulance and its police escort sped through the traffic, the sound of sirens exploding in his ears. He was barely aware of the pain in his arm as the medics worked to stop the bleeding. Not for him the disgrace of being dragged from Joanie's house in handcuffs. No, this was the way to do it. Everything was to be on his terms. He smiled. Joanie's expensive carpet was soaked in his blood. Even after she replaced it, the memory of his sitting on the floor in the corner of that room would haunt her. He'd remain in her head forever. And that knowledge would sustain him.

He'd allow some credulous psychiatrist to gradually extract the truth. Don planned to reluctantly tell him all about his demon, the voices in his head and any other bullshit the daft shrink wanted to hear. Mention demonic possession straight off and it would sound like an excuse but let them drag it out of him and, hey presto, he's a looney tune. He'd put in a plea of diminished responsibility. It hadn't worked for the Yorkshire Ripper but Don was smarter than that one; he was smarter than any of those amateur so-called serial killers. They'd all been caught after just a few of years at most, whereas Donald Albert Tyler had been taking lives for over fifty years.

He speculated as to what name he might be dubbed by the press: 'The Fairground Strangler', maybe? 'Hell's Granddad', perhaps? He chuckled. Suzanne had been right on the money – he could keep this little contest going for decades. He'd get time out of prison to take the cops on wild goose chases to uncover the remains of his victims. The stupid bastards would be digging up half the countryside before he'd finished with them. And bugger the idea of getting that smart-arse BBC journalist Terry Vincent to write his life story. He'd do it himself. He envisaged the title, *In My Own Write*, and he would donate the royalties to a missing persons' charity – anonymously, of course. He laughed out loud, much to the consternation of the paramedics, but Don didn't give a shit what they thought. He was a man with a plan.

There were all the twisted whores that would contact him in prison, wanting to save him, to marry him even. What a bloody good diversion that was going to be, playing them along with the prolific use of the L-word in tear-stained letters.

The downside was that Raymond would finally be released when they read Don's description of Betty's murder. He would get out after – how long had it been – twenty years? Released into a world that had changed so much that the mumbling, stumbling oaf would have no chance of making a new life for himself. *Serves him bloody well right*, Don sneered. He remembered observing Raymond from a distance, ashamed that shambling creature was his own flesh and blood. He'd watched the house for days, seeing Betty return home from working some shitty factory job just two hours before Raymond turned up. He recalled the look of horror on her scrawny face when she opened the door and recognised him. After he'd taken his rightful revenge on the bitch, he'd hung around to see Raymond carted away by the cops. Months later, he'd read all the reports of Raymond's trial and laughed his arse off.

All this would be in his book. He was going to be the most feared and despised man in Britain. Monster, they'd call him. So be it. He might milk the tired old cliché of his miserable childhood to the max, if he could be bothered. Some gullible fools swallow that kind of bollocks whole because they always want to believe that monsters are created, not born that way, thrust into the world with venom and bile escaping from every orifice. His mother had realised the truth very early on but there had been fuck-all she could do about it apart from beating even more loathing into him. He swept the bitter memory of her from his mind and moved on with his strategy. No, he spontaneously decided, they'd get no poor-wee-lad excuses from him. Why did he kill? Because he could, that's why. And would he have done it had there been a death penalty looming in the background? Damn right, he would have.

He relished the idea of a trial, of all the attention and seething hatred heading his way. Bring it on, fuckers! If the press lost interest a few years down the line, he could get back in the headlines by converting to some religion or other. Islam, perhaps. He had the beard for it. And what a great big joke that was going to be.

He'd write to Joanie every week. She wouldn't reply but she'd be certain to read all his letters because she still loved him. Stupid cunt. She should have pulled the trigger. He'd have respected her then. But when push came to shove, she was just like all the others, all too easy to convince that she was the love of his life. Maybe she had been once, but not now. Not any more. That old git Harry was welcome to the bitch.

Only Suzanne had the balls to stand up to him, to try to beat him at his own game. She'd have pulled that trigger all right, and not blinked an eye. She'd scared him shitless in the car. He'd been convinced that she was about to kill them both by driving into the back of that truck. What a buzz that had been, a real challenge to have a worthy opponent for once. He'd misjudged her. She had the makings of something special, that one. He'd done her a favour getting rid of that tosser she was married to. He'd contact her when the dust settled and tell her so. And she'd understand because she was just like him. Suzy-Q was his baby girl. Though he doubted that he would ever set eyes on her again after the trial. But he'd find a way to keep tabs on her, no matter where she went.

Though the blunt truth was that, apart from lawyers, journalists, goggle-eyed shrinks and idiotic groupies, nobody who really knew him would visit him while he was behind bars. Except for one person.

He'd write to her. 'Come and see me, Vee. I'm the same boy I used to be.'

CHAPTER FORTY-SIX

April 2012

Suzanne stood in the room where Mark had been murdered, in an empty house filled with empty space. All the furniture had been sold or donated to charity while what remained of her paintings had been boxed up in preparation for shipping. The 'Sold' sign beside the front gate underlined the finality of this day. For a while she had tried to continue living in the house but found it impossible to deal with the memories. Ghoulish types turned up from time to time to take photographs of the exterior. She had even found one nerd in her garden trying to get a look into the room where the notorious Donald Tyler had smashed his son-in-law's head to a pulp. Suzanne escorted him off the premises. 'You're his daughter, aren't you?' the greasy-haired youth had asked. 'You should open this place as a museum to Donald Tyler. You'd make a bleedin' fortune.' She had a stout lock fitted to the gate after that freaky encounter. All the adverse publicity hadn't helped the estate agent's sales negotiations one little bit. Suzanne finally sold the house – but only for a knockdown price – to a dodgy developer prepared to ignore the fact that a murder had recently been committed there.

It was almost two years to the day since Suzanne had received that first phone call from Rose Anderson and twenty desolate months since Mark's funeral. She'd been sickened by the publicity that surrounded what should have been a private affair, with reporters and rubber neckers turning the funeral into a three-ring circus. She found the barrage of offers of money for her 'exclusive story' loathsome. But most of the time she felt she was walking through life in a daze. Reality finally set in the day she filled in a form that required her to declare her marital status. She had stared at the blank space for ages before tearfully writing one word: widow.

She'd decided that she needed to get away before the trial began and that opportunity had presented itself when she bought the tickets for Mrs Jones to fly to Sydney to visit her son and grand-children in Australia for three months. Mrs Jones had been taken aback by the generous offer but, as Suzanne told her, 'Without your accurate drawing of him, my father might never have been brought to justice and more people may have died. Including my mother and me.' Joan took the grouchy cat, Sultan, home with her. 'He'll have a big garden to roam about in,' she said. Mrs Jones cried as she watched her beloved cat carried away in his basket but Sultan didn't appear to care either way.

Suzanne accompanied Mrs Jones on the trip to Australia. The old lady's family was overjoyed to see her and her son begged his mother to stay on. Mrs Jones agreed and then authorised Joan to handle the sale of her house back in the UK. Suzanne loved the bustling modernity of Sydney, with its landmark opera house, Harbour Bridge, chilling out in Luna Park and sunbathing on Manly and Bondi beaches. She met plenty of fascinating people whose openhearted friendship filled her with a new can-do optimism. She soon involved herself in the lively arts scene and, through a new acquaintance, was offered a teaching job at an art college that was prepared to sponsor her immigration.

'You should go back there,' her mother told her after the trip. 'We can come and visit you every winter, can't we, Harry? I'm sick of cruises anyway and it will be summertime in Australia.'

Harry agreed. It would be a new start in a new country, he said. But first they all had to face the trial.

*

The sombre grandeur of the Old Bailey was intimidating and, combined with the intrusive media frenzy, groups of angry demonstrators plus the crowds of morbid onlookers, had all of the witnesses in a state of high anxiety.

Joan had been subdued after the hostage episode with Don and her relationship with Harry appeared strained, Suzanne thought. They were no longer the carefree, happy couple they had once been. Joan refused to talk about how she managed to get Don to hand over the gun and even on the witness stand at his trial she said only that he had given it to her. Don had shaken his head and called out to her across the courtroom: 'Oh, Joanie, Joanie…' The judge reprimanded him and warned him to remain silent.

The trial had been just that, a trial for everyone involved, though not for Don himself. He appeared to view the entire proceedings with an air of amused detachment.

His plea of 'not guilty to murder' though 'guilty to manslaughter on the grounds of diminished responsibility' had been dismissed.

Suzanne's own evidence against her father resulted in him smiling broadly at her from the dock. But she had steeled herself to look him straight in the eye. 'That's my Suzy-Q. That's my baby girl,' Don announced proudly to the mass of people squeezed into the courtroom, as though Suzanne were a child performing on stage for his entertainment.

Among the crowds outside the court, Suzanne spotted people carrying placards displaying photographs of their long-dead or missing daughters. Irate relatives were vociferously demanding that Don's now-notorious journals be released by the police. Details of their contents had not been disclosed though there had been leaks to the press that had caused a furore. 'Justice For Stephanie' was the plea from one handwritten sign and the woman carrying it had grasped Suzanne by the arm. 'You read your father's diaries, didn't you? Did he mention my daughter?' Stephanie, Lucy, Jean, Margaret; the names racked up while the requests for full disclosure about Don's victims were limitless and heart-rending.

Jared, now confined to a wheelchair for life, broke down in tears in the witness box as Don made his disdain only too obvious. The trial lasted for twelve long and arduous weeks and would have dragged on far longer had not Don finally admitted his guilt to the charges brought.

The judge was not impressed. 'I have no doubt that your guilty pleas are cynically timed to suit your own purposes, and do not reflect any remorse for what you have done.' He instructed the jury to determine Don's mental state. They declared him sane. Donald Albert Tyler was convicted of five murders, including those of Bridget Daly, Rose Anderson, Mark Woods, Cynthia Beaulieu and the rep in the car park, plus the attempted murder of his son, Jared. Other investigations into the deaths mentioned in Don's journals were pending though he strenuously claimed they were works of fiction. Don received five life sentences and was to serve a minimum of thirty years. He was imprisoned at Wakefield high-security prison, commonly known as 'Monster Mansion'.

*

The post-trial fall-out had been highly embarrassing for St Francis' hospital, with demands for an enquiry into how a death certificate had been issued for Donald Albert Tyler, and to establish the identity of the body that had been cremated in his place. The security at Redstone House came under scrutiny too; how had Tyler been able to enter the building with such ease to murder Rose Anderson?

The police force also got it in the neck. How was it possible for Tyler to have been rampaging around the country for almost half a century, killing predominantly young women and yet never appearing on the radar of the law-enforcement agencies? The agitated authorities made numerous attempts to soothe the nerves of the horrified public. Investigations into the contents of the journals were ongoing, they said. They were methodically matching the locations and dates mentioned in Tyler's journals to missing persons' reports. Further charges might well be brought against Tyler at a later date. Society had been very different when Donald Albert Tyler started out on his murderous path, a spokesperson declared. These days we have CCTV, DNA, sophisticated forensic analysis and, most importantly, a fully integrated police computer network nationwide. This situation could never arise now, he stated categorically.

However, questions continued to mount as each murder Don had confessed to in the journals was picked over in minute detail, particularly those that had involved a police investigation. Why had Naomi Silver's death been written off as a case of auto-asphyxiation? How could Gloria Davison's drowning have been ruled as caused by a drugs overdose? Sophie Chen's parents were in the process of suing the authorities for incompetence by not thoroughly investigating the cause of their daughter's demise, even though Tyler was denying his involvement in her death.

The Scottish police searched the grounds that had once belonged to Cynthia Beaulieu for the remains of Moira Campbell, which led to the unanswerable question: why hadn't any of the other bodies of missing girls Tyler had written about been found? And, all the while, Don lurked in the middle of the media storm like a giant, malevolent spider suspended within a gory web.

*

The first book off the blocks was published shortly after the trial, written by Terry Vincent, but evidently without Don's cooperation. Suzanne had been phoned by a journalist asking for her opinion of Vincent's account of her father's crimes. The woman seemed puzzled to hear that Suzanne hadn't read the book nor had any intention of doing so, nor any others that would inevitably follow.

Raymond Tyler's case was under judicial review. They were very hopeful that he would soon be a free man as Jared had stumped up the money for a top lawyer to appeal on behalf of his half-brother.

Jared, though wheelchair-bound and in constant pain, now devoted his time and resources to helping Raymond. He had also set up a charity to aid the families of his father's other victims. He'd called it The Moira Foundation. Jared's courage and determination impressed Suzanne. It was as though he had finally found his purpose in life.

Suzanne took Vera to visit Raymond and his gratitude had been overwhelming.

'For all these years I'd been hoping that, one day, my cell door would open and I'd be told it was all a terrible mistake.' He held back the tears. 'And, thanks to you and Jared, that wish may finally come true.'

Though elated by the thought of possible freedom, Raymond was understandably anxious about his future. What would he do if he got out? He was unlikely to be awarded compensation for an unsafe conviction and wrongful imprisonment, even if his appeal was successful. After all this time behind bars how would he cope alone? And where would he live? Vera promptly offered to share her home with him. 'It's the least I can do,' she told Suzanne. 'He's so like our Donny to look at. But not… well, you know… mad.' Vera had received a letter from Don but had burned it unopened. 'Fight fire with fire,' she declared.

*

After months of anguish, Suzanne was saying a final goodbye to her house. The art shippers turned up right on time and took the crates away just as her mobile sounded off. It was Luke. He'd resigned from the police force before giving evidence at the trial regarding the day of the hostage situation. As the death of Sophie Chen and Anita's disappearance were still under investigation they were not mentioned in court. Luke had not been able to assuage his guilt in front of a courtroom of people. He had started drinking again.

'I just wanted to say goodbye.' He sounded sober for once.

'Are you back at AA?'

'Yeah. But, once the police investigations are over, I'm thinking that I'll go to Ireland. My ex has split up with her husband and I'd like to be closer to my son.'

'Good luck, Luke.'

'And to you, too.'

Suzanne closed the door on her previous home, picked up her luggage and walked towards the taxi waiting at the kerb.

'Where to?'

'Heathrow, terminal five.'

Suzanne was embarking on a journey to a new life in a country where her name and face would not be immediately associated with Britain's most reviled multiple killer. She was free.

CHAPTER FORTY-SEVEN

Are you sitting comfortably? Well, you won't be for long.

I've been convicted of five murders. But they are just the killings I was willing to admit to at the time. I am going to tell you of all the others that no one else has a clue about. The bodies not discovered, the runaways that never ran, the girls who walked home alone at night and never reached their destination. I'll let you know about all the beautiful places in this green and pleasant land of ours where, just beneath the feet of the Sunday walkers, lie the bones of the missing.

So let's start at the very beginning – a very good place to start, as some screechy tart used to sing.

I killed my first victim when I was ten years old. Some stupid bitch left her baby girl in a pram outside of a shop in...

Donald Albert Tyler stopped writing and stared at the blank wall of his cell in Monster Mansion. Nobody bothered him much these days, though when he first arrived, he'd been threatened by one mad bastard and had ended up banged up alone for a while, for his own safety. But the pressure was off once they brought in that child-killer. Even in this nick, crammed to the rafters with Britain's most dangerous psychos and deviants, there was a hierarchy within which kiddie-fiddlers were pond-life. They always got the worst of it. Since then Don had been left in peace. But it just wasn't good enough. This was no way to live.

He tore the paper he'd been writing on into tiny pieces. That could all wait. Right now he had to concentrate on his new plan. He thought about the journalist he'd been talking to. There was a chance that this new publicity might set off one or two of the loony tunes. Although Don reckoned he'd timed it just right. Rumour had it that some African bloke was due in next week. This guy had been convicted of the ritual killings of young boys to be dismembered as sacrifices for some voodoo shit or other. Might have eaten them, for all Don knew. Not that he cared too much, just so long as it gave the nut jobs a new playmate to terrorise.

Don's confession to the Sophie Chen killing had been his way of apologising to Suzanne. One day he'd be able to tell her to her face but this would suffice for now.

*

In the taxi on the way to the airport, Suzanne's doubts surfaced once more. Was she running away? Nothing was truly sorted. Everyone was attempting to live with the fallout in their different ways. She thought about the last time she had seen her mother. It was supposed to have been a goodbye dinner but the atmosphere in the house had been icy. Harry greeted Suzanne at the door. He looked older, his face strained. 'Your mother is upstairs,' he said.

Suzanne stepped into the house where Don had held them hostage. The whole place had been redecorated with Joan's immaculate good taste but somehow Don's dark presence lingered.

'I want to sell up.' Harry handed her a glass of wine. 'But you know your mother, she says she won't be driven out of her home.'

Don's words came back to Suzanne. '*I know my Joanie, she's a settler, she'd never move from here. Never.*'

'Will she still not talk about what happened?'

Harry poured himself a large gin and tonic. 'It's the first time in all these years that we have been unable to discuss things.' He smiled sadly. 'But I'm sure we'll get over it, given time.' Strong, solid Harry was suffering. He'd been a wonderful step-dad, always playing it right, never overstepping the boundaries, yet always there when Suzanne had needed him.

'Do you want me to talk to her?'

'You've been through enough, Suzanne. I'm sure your mother and I can work this out for ourselves.'

But she was already heading for the stairs.

Joan was in her dressing room, brushing her hair in front of the mirror, deep in thought. Suzanne watched her for a moment.

How lovely she is.

Joan put on her bright smile when she saw her daughter. 'I'll be down in a minute, darling. Dinner is almost ready.'

'Have you and Harry had a row?'

'What has he been saying to you?'

'That he'd like to move house but you won't go. That you won't talk to him about what happened here.'

'He has no right to involve you in our problems.'

'Why won't you talk to him, Mum? After all these years together… Doesn't he deserve some consideration?'

Joan put down her hairbrush and turned to face her daughter. 'I can't tell him how I feel because I don't know.'

'Then at least tell him that.' She turned to go but stopped when she heard her mother's deep intake of breath.

'If you had been in my position on that day, with Don on his knees in front of you and the gun in your hand. What would you have done? Would you have pulled the trigger?'

'Is that what happened?'

This was a break-through. Joan had never spoken of this before. She hadn't even mentioned it when she gave evidence at the trial. Suzanne recalled Don chiding her from the dock, '*Oh, Joanie, Joanie!*' At the time Suzanne thought he had sought to humiliate her mother. Joan *had* appeared unduly ruffled, though she remained dignified until the judge had stepped in to silence the accused. But with this new revelation, she now realised there had been more to that particular exchange than met the eye.

'He gave me the gun and begged me to shoot him,' Joan said.

'But the gun wasn't loaded.'

'I didn't know that, did I? None of us knew. I thought I had the power to take his life. But I didn't. He was staring up at me at me with his eyes full of fear and I couldn't do it.' She turned back to scrutinise her face in the mirror. 'He asked me to shoot him or say that I loved him.'

'But you didn't shoot him.'

Joan sighed. 'What does that mean?'

'Don't you see what Don was doing? He was playing one of his twisted mind games. He knew you wouldn't shoot him. You are a far better person than that. And you would do or say *anything* to avoid having to kill anyone. Even him.'

'That's what it means for him, but what about me?'

'You loved him once. I'm the proof of that. And he played on the residue, on your memory of that love in order to leave you with doubt about your motives for not pulling the trigger.' As the words formed on her lips, Suzanne's understanding of her father's warped rationale deepened and her loathing for him increased tenfold. 'Don't let him do that to you, Mum. Don't let him win.'

Joan stood, crossed the room and hugged her daughter. 'Thank you so much for that, sweetheart.' Then she whispered in her ear. 'Now go down and keep Harry company. I'll be with you in a minute.'

'But you must talk to Harry about this. I'm sure he'll view it as I do.'

Joan pulled away and, with her hands still on Suzanne's shoulders, looked her daughter in the eye. 'But tell me. What would *you* have done?'

'I don't know, Mum. I really don't.'

Though what Suzanne had wanted to say was: I'd have blown the evil bastard to kingdom come and happily taken the consequences. And she was left with the fleeting question of whether there was more of Donald Albert Tyler in her DNA than she cared to admit.

*

As the taxi negotiated the roads, Suzanne glanced at the pavements, packed with everyday people going about their everyday lives. She spotted a man who reminded her of Raymond and pictured him walking about, a free man again after twenty years behind bars. His judicial review was due and she had to admit that she felt a little ashamed that she wouldn't be there to support him. But then, she reminded herself, Raymond had Vera and she was made of strong stuff. All her loyalty to her brother had been transferred to his son. If and when Raymond was a free man, Suzanne felt confident that he'd be safe with Vera. And there was also Jared to help out if Vera needed anything.

*

On what Suzanne came to think of as her goodbye tour, she had visited Jared in his new apartment in London's Knightsbridge, Cynthia's hefty life insurances having paid for most of that. The flat had been specially adapted for his needs and Raul was there to look after him. Raul answered the door to her. 'How are you, miss?'

'Fine, and you?' Although Raul had recovered well from Don's attack on him, the old man now got the occasional debilitating migraine – although he never made a fuss. 'Are you still getting those headaches?'

'No much, miss, not much. Mr Jared's in his office.'

In Jared's specially designed home office, three desks lined the walls, a computer screen on each with a large clear area in the middle for the wheelchair so that he could move about easily from one desk to the other. Suzanne was aware that her half-brother needed a focus. Raul had let slip that Jared was seeing a psychiatrist to help him come to terms with both his injuries and the fact that his own father had tried to kill him. 'He never mentions Miss Cynthia though,' Raul had confided. 'Not to me, anyways.'

Jared glanced away from a computer monitor as Suzanne entered.

'It looks like NASA in here,' she said.

'One screen for Raymond, one for the charity and the other for the US case.' He was busy suing the American accountancy firm that had brought his family business to its knees. 'I find it easier to compartmentalise these things,' he said. 'To keep my mind clear.'

'I really admire you, you know. For everything you are doing for Raymond. And with the charity you've set up.'

'It was something you said to me that day at the house. You said that Moira would have wanted me to help the other victims. So this is all because of you. *And* it keeps me sane.'

*

Ten minutes to Heathrow and a police car went roaring by at full pelt. 'Sirens, ahoy!' the taxi driver called out over his shoulder to Suzanne. 'Pizza must be getting cold at the cop shop.' It was a joke that Luke would have appreciated once upon a time. She reassured herself that he had sounded sober on the phone and with the prospect of being reunited with his son, she was hopeful for him.

The painful truth was that everyone else involved had other people to lean on, whereas she was alone. 'You're so brave,' people kept telling her. But they didn't have a clue about the emptiness she had to endure and they never would. Grief was enough in itself, without being expected to parade it before all and sundry. Suzanne pictured Mark once more, laughing as he had the last time she had seen him, and she was overcome by a deep sense of loss. Even though she had to admit that their marriage had not been perfect, that so much had been unresolved, she knew that she had loved him, and that you often don't appreciate what you've had until it's gone. But there was no way to go back, to undo what had been done, and she just had to learn to live with it. No, she decided, she was doing the right thing for herself in making an attempt to start over.

Her mobile sounded off once more. She didn't recognise the number.

'Suzanne Woods? This is Frank Boyd from the *Daily*—'

'I don't talk to reporters.'

'We'd just like your comments about the article in today's *Record*.'

'I'm not interested.'

'Have you seen it?'

'No, and I don't want to.'

'But Tyler has just confessed to murdering your friend, Sophie Chen.'

Suzanne ended the call. She'd thought she was about to start over and now that sick fuck was attempting to pull her back in.

'You alright, love?' the taxi driver asked. 'You look like you've seen a ghost.'

CHAPTER FORTY-EIGHT

Suzanne walked into the vast newsagents at Heathrow airport and picked up a copy of *The Record*. Don's face glared out at her from the front page. 'Tyler Confesses to Artist Murder', the headline screamed. 'Exclusive story on pages four, five and six.'

Suzanne turned the pages and there was Sophie, smiling in front of her sculpture, just minutes before she was murdered. The smaller photo of Suzanne had obviously been taken outside the court during her father's trial. In it she looked distraught and anxious. Behind her image there were placards held aloft by grieving and irate parents, demanding more information about missing girls.

'Suzanne Woods,' the caption read. 'Tyler's daughter and intended victim.'

This was something she had always suspected, but to see it in black and white was a kick in the guts. She steadied herself and went to pay for the newspaper. The woman behind the counter gave her a pitying look that Suzanne had come to recognise and always tried to ignore. She took the paper to the seating area and began to read.

The details of the arson attack were all there. The newspaper had also obtained the photo of the gutted studio taken by Don himself. The report said that the full dossier containing Tyler's confession had been handed over to the police. However, there was certain information they were able to reveal to their readers at this time: the revelation that Tyler had visited the studio that evening with the express intention of killing his daughter. As she hadn't been there, he had taken out his anger and frustration on Sophie Chen. Though Tyler had told the journalist that he was now filled with remorse for his violent feelings towards his own flesh and blood. When asked if that regret extended to the death of an innocent girl, he was unresponsive but had intimated that further revelations might be forthcoming.

'For now, I just want my baby girl to know that I'm sorry,' Don had told the reporter. 'I've come to realise that she has always been the best thing in my life. I hope that one day she will be able to forgive me. I love you, Suzy-Q. You are the real love of my life.'

Suzanne dumped the newspaper in the rubbish bin. *Hope away, you repulsive bag of shit.* She picked up her carry-on bag and headed for the departure gate. *My life belongs to me*, she thought. *I hope you rot in that hellhole.*

EPILOGUE

Don had come to the conclusion that being caged up with degenerates and sociopaths was no way to spend the final years of his life. He pictured his bolthole in Wales – a stone-built detached barn conversion, five miles from the nearest village. Not a soul knew about it, or that he owned it outright. He'd dreamed about it the night before. It was beckoning to him, and now he was beginning to regret his previous impulsive behaviour. Of late, he'd been brooding on the fact that his obsession with Joanie had fucked everything up for him. *The bitch! I should have headed to Wales when I acquired my new identity as Michael O'Connor*, he mused. *I could have lived a nice quiet life half-way up a mountain in Snowdonia. Though*, he contemplated, *it's a wise man that can admit to his own nature.* He was aware that his demon awaited him, no matter where he went.

He looked around his cell, heard the sound of some crazy bastard kicking off a few doors along on his landing and felt a new sense of purpose. There had to be a way out of here. And if escape were possible, then he'd be just the man to do it. What he'd need was someone on the outside, but far more important would be someone on the inside. Don had his eye on one of the screws. Not the sharing-caring-I-feel-your-pain arseholes, they were far too grounded. The bullyboys also knew exactly why they had chosen a career patrolling these life-draining corridors: a secure job, a pension, an 'I'm-The-Man-And-Don't-You-Forget-It' uniform, or because they were too brain dead even for the police force. But Don had spotted one he liked the look of: a man he could possibly use if he played it right. Mister Scruggs – proper Dickensian moniker that – you couldn't make it up! Six feet-odd, with a face like the end result of a thousand years of sheep-shagging, and a fuck-you manner that masked an inner squirming stew of seething longing.

'*It takes one to know one!*' His mother's Irish brogue entered Don's head and he swiped her away. But the drunken old bitch was dead right. Don had encountered the Scruggs type before. El-Macho to the outside world, to his colleagues and even in the eyes of the wife he beat on when he got drunk-angry. But he sensed that, in Naomi's club in Amsterdam all those years back, old Scruggsie would have been stark bollock-naked with a shit-coated dildo rammed up his arse and electrodes charging up his dangly scrote.

The glint in Scruggs' eye when manhandling sex offenders was all Don had to go by, but the bell attached to his perv-o-meter was chiming 'Oh Cum All Ye Faithful'. Don grinned. He'd do whatever it took to get Scruggs to play ball; he'd even fuck the bastard if he had to. Even so, he'd have to be careful, reel him in slowly. It would be a nicely dicey game to pass the time of day if nothing else.

I have nothing to lose, he thought, *but my chains*. He looked up at the small slice of sky he could see from his cell window and let out a bellowing laugh.

Donald Albert Tyler wasn't done yet. Not by a long chalk.

LETTER FROM LESLEY

Dear reader,

First of all, I'd like to say a big thank-you for reading *The Serial Killer's Daughter* and may I add that I hope none of you have the misfortune to encounter anyone even remotely like Don Tyler in real life – ever.

After my Bookouture editor had read *The Serial Killer's Daughter* for the first time, she turned to me and said, 'I do sometimes worry that Don Tyler came out of *your* head.' Yeah, I thought, me too.

So if getting inside the mind of Don scared you as much as it did me, then I do hope you'd be kind enough to write a review to give other readers your honest opinion of the overall story, plus the journey that Suzanne and the other characters make throughout the book.

www.lesleywelsh.com

ACKNOWLEDGEMENTS

First, I'd like to thank those wonderful folk who aided me with their expertise on police procedure, prisons and hostage situations, plus the legal and medical information that did so much to add authenticity to the tale of *The Serial Killer's Daughter*. So, cheers to Chris Duffin, Janet Read, as well as Liz and John Yardley. You were all fantastic and any mistakes made in those areas are purely down to me.

Next, there's a big thank-you to my fabulous agent, Caroline Montgomery, for getting me this gig with the Bookouture team – what a great bunch they are. And ta muchly to my editor, Abigail Fenton, who not only caught any clangers like an expert goalie but helped shape the book you see before you.

Big thanks too to my former mentor, Mr Les Edgerton, who read *The Serial Killer's Daughter* in its raw form way back when. Plus, as always, to my partner, Ian Jackson, for his patience and support along the way.

Besos.

Lightning Source UK Ltd.
Milton Keynes UK
UKOW01f2107140717
305333UK00003B/395/P